Sigrid Estrada

ANDRÉ ACIMAN is the author of *Call Me by Your Name* (now
a major motion picture), *Eight White Nights, Harvard Square,
Enigma Variations, Out of Egypt, False Papers,* and *Alibis,* and
the editor of *The Proust Project.* He teaches comparative litera-
ture at the Graduate Center of the City University of New
York and lives with his wife in Manhattan.

ALSO BY ANDRÉ ACIMAN

FICTION

Call Me by Your Name
Harvard Square
Enigma Variations

NONFICTION

Out of Egypt: A Memoir
False Papers: Essays on Exile and Memory
Entrez: Signs of France (with Steven Rothfeld)
The Light of New York (with Jean-Michel Berts)
Alibis: Essays on Elsewhere

AS EDITOR

*Letters of Transit: Reflections on Exile, Identity,
Language, and Loss*
The Proust Project

ADDITIONAL PRAISE FOR
EIGHT WHITE NIGHTS

"Sentences of Proustian complexity. Imagined scenes, conversations and intimacies . . . of an erotic obsession . . . Vivid and refreshing."
—*Los Angeles Times*

"If this spell works on you as it did on me, [this] will be one of the most pleasurable stretches of prose that you have read in a long time."
—*Open Letters Review*

"There is much in this snow globe of a book to commend it to readers . . . [*Eight White Nights*] envelops one in a blizzard of sensations, thoughts and images, recovering emotions that one had forgotten one even possessed."
—*Jewish Daily Forward*

"[A] luxurious, emotionally charged story of a love gone wrong . . . Aciman is a poet of the sensitive bystander—not arch like Salinger, combative like Cheever or fraught like Updike, but occasionally stepping into their territories . . . Smart, carefully written and always fluent."
—*Kirkus Reviews*

EIGHT WHITE NIGHTS

André Aciman

PICADOR

FARRAR, STRAUS AND GIROUX   NEW YORK

I wish to thank Paul LeClerc, who gave me courage when I needed it most; the New York Public Library's Dorothy and Lewis B. Cullman Center for Scholars and Writers, for giving me a study for a whole year; Yaddo, for housing me during two glorious Junes; Jonathan Galassi, my editor; Lynn Nesbit, my agent; Cynthia Zarin, my friend—all of whom gave so much to this book. And finally, my wife, Susan, who gave me roots, a home, a life, and all the love and blessings of family.

•

EIGHT WHITE NIGHTS. Copyright © 2010 by André Aciman. All rights reserved. For information, address Picador, 175 Fifth Avenue, New York, N.Y. 10010.

picadorusa.com • instagram.com/picador
twitter.com/picadorusa • facebook.com/picadorusa

Picador® is a U.S. registered trademark and is used by Macmillan Publishing Group, LLC, under license from Pan Books Limited.

For book club information, please visit facebook.com/picadorbookclub or email marketing@picadorusa.com.

Designed by Jonathan D. Lippincott

The Library of Congress has cataloged the Farrar, Straus and Giroux hardcover edition as follows:
Aciman, André.
Eight white nights / André Aciman.— 1st ed.
p. cm.
ISBN 978-0-374-22842-2 (hardcover) | ISBN 978-1-4299-3480-0 (ebook)
I. Title.
PS3601.C525 E54 2010
813'.6—dc22   2009025415

Picador Paperback ISBN 978-0-312-68056-5

Our books may be purchased in bulk for promotional, educational, or business use. Please contact your local bookseller or the Macmillan Corporate and Premium Sales Department at 1-800-221-7945, extension 5442, or by email at MacmillanSpecialMarkets@macmillan.com.

First published by Farrar, Straus and Giroux

First Picador Edition: February 2011

10 9 8 7 6 5 4 3 2 1

For Philip,
luz y dulzura.

FIRST NIGHT

THE FIRST NIGHT

Halfway through dinner, I knew I'd replay the whole evening in reverse—the bus, the snow, the walk up the tiny incline, the cathedral looming straight before me, the stranger in the elevator, the crowded large living room where candlelit faces beamed with laughter and premonition, the piano music, the singer with the throaty voice, the scent of pinewood everywhere as I wandered from room to room, thinking that perhaps I should have arrived much earlier tonight, or a bit later, or that I shouldn't have come at all, the classic sepia etchings on the wall by the bathroom where a swinging door opened to a long corridor to private areas not intended for guests but took another turn toward the hallway and then, by miracle, led back into the same living room, where more people had gathered, and where, turning to me by the window where I thought I'd found a quiet spot behind the large Christmas tree, someone suddenly put out a hand and said, "I am Clara."

I am Clara, delivered in a flash, as the most obvious fact in the world, as though I'd known it all along, or should have known it, and, seeing I hadn't acknowledged her, or perhaps was trying not to, she'd help me stop the pretense and put a face to a name everyone had surely mentioned many times before.

In someone else, *I am Clara* would have sprung like a tentative conversation opener—meek, seemingly assertive, overly casual, distant, aired as an afterthought, the verbal equivalent of a handshake that has learned to convey firmness and vigor by overexerting an otherwise limp and lifeless grip. In a shy person, *I am Clara* would require so much effort that it might leave her drained and almost grateful when you failed to pick up the cue.

Here, *I am Clara* was neither bold nor intrusive, but spoken with the practiced, wry smile of someone who had said it too many times to care how it broke the silence with strangers. Strained, indifferent, weary, and amused—at herself, at me, at life for making introductions the tense, self-conscious things they are—it slipped between us like a meaningless formality that had to be gotten over with, and now was as good a time as any, seeing that the two of us were standing away from those who had gathered in the middle of the room and who were about to start singing. Her words sprung on me like one of those gusts that clear through obstacles and throw open all doors and windows, trailing April blossom in the heart of a winter month, stirring everything along their path with the hasty familiarity of people who, when it comes to other people, couldn't care less and haven't a thing to lose. She wasn't bustling in nor was she skipping over tedious steps, but there was a touch of crisis and commotion in her three words that wasn't unwelcome or totally unintended. It suited her figure, the darting arrogance of her chin, of the voile-thin crimson shirt which she wore unbuttoned to her breastbone, the swell of skin as smooth and forbidding as the diamond stud on her thin platinum necklace.

I am Clara. It barged in unannounced, like a spectator squeezing into a packed auditorium seconds before curtain time, disturbing everyone, and yet so clearly amused by the stir she causes that, no sooner she's found the seat that will be hers for the rest of the season than she'll remove her coat, slip it around her shoulders, turn to her new neighbor, and, meaning to apologize for the disruption without making too much of it, whisper a conspiring "I am Clara." It meant, I'm the Clara you'll be seeing all year long here, so let's just make the best of it. I am the Clara you never thought would be sitting right next to you, and yet here I am. I'm the Clara you'll wish to find here every one day of every month for the remainder of this and every other year of your life—and I know it, and let's face it, much as you're trying not to show it, you knew it the moment you set eyes on me. *I am Clara.*

It was a cross between a ribbing "How couldn't you know?" and "What's with the face?" "Here," she seemed to say, like a magician about to teach a child a simple trick, "take this name and hold it tight in your palm, and when you're home alone, open your hand and think, *Today I met Clara.*" It was like offering an elderly gentleman a chocolate-hazelnut square just when he was about to lose his temper. "Don't say anything until you've bitten into it." She jostled you, but instantly made up for it before you'd even felt it, so that it wasn't clear which had come first, the apology or the little jab, or whether both weren't braided in the same gesture, spiraling around her three words like frisky death threats masquerading as meaningless pranks. *I am Clara.*

Life before. Life after.

Everything before Clara seemed so lifeless, hollow, stopgap. The after-Clara thrilled and scared me, a mirage of water beyond a valley of rattlesnakes.

I am Clara. It was the one thing I knew best and could always come back to each time I'd want to think of her—alert, warm, caustic, and dangerous. Everything about her radiated from these three words, as though they were a pressing bulletin mysteriously scribbled on the back of a matchbook that you slip into a wallet because it will always summon an evening when a dream, a would-be life, suddenly blossomed before you. It could be just that, a dream and nothing more, but it stirred so fierce a desire to be happy that I was almost ready to believe I was indeed happy on the evening when someone blustered in, trailing April blossom in the heart of a winter month.

Would I still feel this way on leaving the party tonight? Or would I find cunning ways to latch on to minor defects so that they'd start to bother me and allow me to snuff the dream till it tapered off and lost its luster and, with its luster gone, remind me once again, as ever again, that happiness is the one thing in our lives others cannot bring.

I am Clara. It conjured her voice, her smile, her face when she vanished into the crowd that night and made me fear I'd already lost her, imagined her. "I am Clara," I'd say to myself, and she was Clara all over again, standing near me by the Christmas tree, alert, warm, caustic, and dangerous.

I was—and I knew it within minutes of meeting her—already rehearsing never seeing her again, already wondering how to take *I am Clara* with me tonight and stow it in a drawer along with my cuff links, collar stays, my watch and money clip.

I was learning to disbelieve that this could last another five minutes, because this had all the makings of an unreal, spellbound interlude, when things open up far too easily and seem willing to let us into the otherwise closed circle that is none other than our very own life, our life as we've always craved to live it but cheat it at each turn, our life finally transposed in the right key, retold in the right tense, in a language that speaks to us and is right for us and us alone, our life finally made real and luminous because it's revealed, not in ours, but in someone else's voice, grasped from another's hand, caught on the face of someone who couldn't possibly be a stranger, but, because she is nothing but a stranger, holds our eyes with a gaze that says, *Tonight I'm the face you put on your life and how you live it. Tonight, I am your eyes to the world looking back at you. I am Clara.*

It meant: *Take my name and whisper it to yourself, and in a week's time come back to it and see if crystals haven't sprouted around it.*

I am Clara—she had smiled, as though she'd been laughing at something someone had just said to her and, borrowing the mirth started in another context, had turned to me behind the Christmas tree and told me her name, given me her hand, and made me want to laugh at punch lines I hadn't heard but whose drift corresponded to a sense of humor that was exactly like mine.

This is what *I am Clara* meant to me. It created the illusion of intimacy, of a friendship briefly interrupted and urgently resumed, as though we'd met before, or had crossed each other's path but kept missing each other and were being reintroduced at all costs now, so that in extending her hand to me, she was doing something we should have done much sooner, seeing we had grown up together and lost touch, or been through so much, perhaps been lovers a lifetime ago, until something as trivial and shameful as death had come between us and which, this time, she wasn't about to let happen.

I am Clara meant I already know you—this is no ordinary business—and if you think fate doesn't have a hand in this, think twice. We could, if you wish, stick to ordinary cocktail pleasantries and pretend this is all in your head, or we can drop everything, pay attention to no one, and, like children building a tiny tent in the middle of a crowded living room on Christmas Eve, enter a world beaming with laughter and premonition, where everything is without peril, where there's no place for shame, doubt, or fear, and where all is said in jest and in whimsy, because the things that are most solemn often come under the guise of mischief and merrymaking.

·

I held her hand a touch longer than is usual, to say I had gotten the message, but let it go sooner than warranted, fearing I'd invented the message.

That was my contribution, my signature to the evening, my twisted reading of a plain handshake. If she knew how to read me, she'd see through this affectation of nonchalance and catch the other, deeper nonchalance, which I am reluctant to dispel especially in the presence of someone who, with three words and barely a glance, could easily hold the key to all my hideaways.

It did not occur to me that people who bolt into your life could as easily bolt out of it when they're done, that someone who breaks into a concert hall seconds before the music starts may all of a sudden stand up and disturb everyone all over again on realizing she is sitting in the wrong row and doesn't care to wait until the intermission.

I looked at her. I looked at her face. I knew that face. "You look familiar," I was going to say.

"You look lost," she said.

"Does it show?" I answered. "Don't most people look lost at parties?"

"Some more than others. Not him." She pointed at a middle-aged gentleman talking with a woman. He was leaning against what must have been a false, chamfered pillar with a Corinthian-style topstone, holding a clear drink in his hand, almost slouching against the pillar as though he had all the time in the world. "Doesn't look lost at all. Neither does she."

I am Clara. I see through people.

Mr. and Mrs. Shukoff, she baptized them; Mr. and Mrs. Shukoff couldn't wait to rip their clothes off, he said with a wink as he gulped down his drink, give me a second and I'm ready for blastoff.

Shukoff: people you couldn't shake off but wished you could, she explained. We laughed.

Then, in a manner that couldn't have been less discreet, Clara indicated a sixty-something woman who was wearing a long red dress with black patent-leather pumps. "Santa Claus's grandmother. Just look at that," she said, pointing to a wide, gold-buckled, patent-leather belt strapping Grandma's tummy. She wore what must have been a sparkling blond wig whose sides, matted and hardened like two baby boar horns, curled around her ears. From her earlobes dangled two sliced large pearls mounted on tiny gold plates—miniature UFOs without the little green men, she said. Clara instantly baptized her Muffy Mitford. Then proceeded to demolish Muffy Mitford, enlisting me in the process, as though she never doubted I would join in the character assassination.

Muffy spoke with a warble in her voice. Muffy wore light blue shaggy froufrou slippers at home, I said. Muffy wore a housedress underneath, always a housedress underneath, she said. Muffy had an unshorn poodle named Suleiman. And a husband nicknamed Chip. And her son—what else—Pip. And her daughter, Mimi. No, Buffy, rhymes with Muffy. Muffy Beaumont. Née Montebello. No, Belmont. Let's face it, Schoenberg, said Clara. Muffy had an English housemaid. From Shropshire. No, Nottingham. No, East Anglia. East Coker. Little Gidding, I said. Burnt Norton, she corrected, and, on second thought, from the Islands. Majorca, she said. With a name like Monserrat, I said. "No, no. Dolores Luz Berta Fatima Consuelo Jacinta Fabiola Inez Esmeralda"—one of those names that never end, because their magic lies in their lilt and cadence as they soar and surge and finally come cascading on a surname as common as the sand on the beaches of Far Rockaway: Rodriguez—which sent us roaring as we saw Muffy laugh and agitate her hips to the rhythm of the singer with the throaty voice, jiggling the limp end of her belt like a fertility symbol dangling from her midriff, her martini glass all empty—and she said with a wink as she gulped down her drink, pour me another and watch me turn pink.

"You're a friend of Hans's, aren't you?" she asked.

"Why—how can you tell?"

"You're not singing. I'm not singing." Then, seeing I hadn't quite seized her explanation, she added, "Friends of Hans don't sing. Only Gretchen's friends sing." She wiped her lips with a napkin, as though to stifle the last flutters of a private joke she wasn't about to share but whose ripples you weren't meant to miss. "Simple," she said, pointing not so discreetly to those gathered around the piano, where a crowd was singing away exuberantly around the man with the throaty voice.

"Gretchen must be the more musical of the two, then," I added noncommittally, just to say something, anything, even if it limped its way to unavoidable silence. Clara's reply took the wind out of my words.

"Gretchen, musical? Gretchen wouldn't know music if it farted in her ears. Just look at her, nailed to the back of the door, greeting all her guests because she doesn't know what else to do with herself." I suddenly remembered the lame handshake, the perfunctory greeting, the kiss on the cheek that grazes your ear so as not to smear her makeup.

The words startled me, but I let them pass, not knowing how to answer or counter them. "Just look at their faces, though," she threw in, pointing at the singers. I looked at their faces. "Would you sing simply because it's a Christmas party and everyone's yuling about like overgrown goldfish sucking on eggnog?"

I said nothing.

"Seriously," she added—so this wasn't a rhetorical question. "Just look at all these Euro Shukoffs. Don't they all look like people who always sing at Christmas parties?"

I am Clara. I get nasty.

"But *I* sing—sometimes," I threw in disingenuously, trying to sound no less bland or naive than those who thought it was the most natural thing in the world to sing at parties. Perhaps I wanted to see how she'd take back her hostility, now that she had inadvertently caught me in its fire. Or perhaps I was just teasing her and didn't want her to know how much her cynical assessment of sing-along fellowship echoed my own.

"But *I sing*," she said, arching an eyebrow as though I'd said something complex and difficult. She nodded somewhat as she pondered the deeper meaning of my words, and still seemed to be weighing them, when it suddenly hit me: she wasn't talking about herself; she was mimicking what I had just said to her—*But I sing*—and was throwing it back at me with the taunting lilt of derision, like a crumpled gift being returned in its now dented box.

"So you sing," she said, still considering the matter. Or was she already backpedaling after her poisoned dart?

"Yes. I sing, sometimes—" I replied, trying not to sound too smug or too earnest. I pretended I hadn't picked up on the goading irony in her voice and was about to add "in the shower"—but immediately sensed that, in Clara's universe, singing in the shower was precisely what everyone confessed to when they cagily admitted that they liked to sing *sometimes*. It would have been such a predictable thing to say. I could already hear her unstitching every cliché in my sentence.

"So you sing," she started. "Let's hear you, then."

I was caught off guard. I shook my head.

"Why? Doesn't sing well with others?" she asked.

"—something like that." *Could do better* was a lame repartee to her report-card banter, which is why I suppressed it. But now I had nothing else to say.

Another moment of hesitation. Then, looking over my shoulder, she broke the silence: "Want to hear me sing?"

Her words sounded almost like a dare. I imagined she was joking and that, after showing such an aversion to Gretchen's friends and their sing-along *yuling*, the last thing she'd do now was to start singing. But before I had finally put the right spin to my words and answered her, she had already joined the chorus, but with a voice I would never have matched to her face and couldn't believe was hers, because it bordered total effusion, as though, in singing at that moment right next to me, she was revealing another, deeper side to remind me that everything I'd thought about her so far—from bustling wind to poisoned dart to quips and derision—might be mistaken, that "caustic" had a meeker side, that "dangerous" could turn apprehensive and tenderhearted, that she was so full of other, more surprising turns that it was pointless to keep up with any or try to second-guess them, or put up a struggle against someone whose curt, offhanded *I am Clara* reminded me that there were people in the world who, for all their gruff arrogance, can, with scarcely a few notes, easily persuade you they are inherently kind, candid, and vulnerable—with unsettling reminders, though, that their ability to flip from one to the other is what ultimately makes them deadly.

I was transfixed—transfixed by the voice, by the person, by my total failure to master the situation, by the pleasure I felt in being so easily swept over, helpless, clueless. Her singing didn't just come out of her body. It seemed to tear things out of mine, like an ancient admission I was still incapable of and which reached back to childhood, like the echo of forgotten tales finally breaking into song. What was this feeling, and where was it coming from? Why did hearing her sing or staring at her unbuttoned crimson shirt with her overexposed, gleaming neckline make me want to live under its spell, close to her heart, below her heart, next to my heart, a peek at your heart; that small pendant, I wanted it in my mouth.

Like a Ulysses grown wise to the Sirens' trick, part of me still groped for reasons not to be taken in, not to believe. A voice so perfect could make her too perfect.

It didn't take long to realize that what I was feeling was not just admiration; nor was it awe, or envy. The word *worship*—as in "I could worship people like her"—hadn't crossed my mind yet, though later that evening, when I stood with her watching a glowing moonlit barge moored across the white Hudson, I did turn to *worship*. Because placid winterscapes lift up the soul and bring down our guard. Because part of me was already venturing into an amorphous terrain in which a word here, a word there—any word, really—is all we have to hold on to before surrendering to a will far mightier than our own. Because in the busy, crowded room, as I listened to her sing, I found myself toying with a word so overused and hackneyed, so safe, that I was tempted to ignore it, which is also why I chose it: *interesting*.

She was *interesting*. Not for what she knew, or for what she said, or for who she was, even, but for how she saw and twisted things, for the implied, complicit jeer in her voice, for how she seemed to both admire and put you down, so that you didn't know whether she had the sensibility of gleaming velvet or of sandpaper. She is interesting. I want to know more, hear more, get closer to.

But *interesting* was not the word I wanted. One more drink and the word struggling to be heard, when it finally came to me, would have spilled out so naturally, so effortlessly, and in a manner so uninhibited that, staring at her skin as I stood speaking to her by the fireplace, I felt no less bashful or hampered than a dreamer who enters a crowded subway car, greets his fellow passengers, and doesn't feel the slightest shame on looking down at his feet and realizing he is not wearing shoes, no socks either, no trousers, and that he is totally naked from the waist down.

I made conversation to avoid saying what I wanted to say, the way only the tongue-tied say too much when they lack the courage to say just what's enough and not a word more. To stop myself, I shut my mouth. I tried to let her do the talking. Then, not to interrupt or say the word, I bit my tongue and held it in place. I bit, not its tip, but its midsection, a large, domineering bite that might even have hurt had I paid it any mind but which held my tongue without altering the outward shape of my mouth. And yet I so wanted to interrupt her, to interrupt her the way one does when one knows one is about to intrude and shock someone with a word that is at once exquisite, reckless, and obscene.

The word sprang so many times to my mouth. I loved the room, loved the snow on Riverside Drive, loved the George Washington Bridge speckling the distance like a drooping necklace on a bare neck, loved her necklace too, and the neck that wore it, I would have said.

I wanted to tell her how much I had loved her voice, perhaps with no reason other than to begin saying other things as well, shy, tentative things that I hoped might grow bold and lead elsewhere once I got started. But no sooner had I mentioned her singing than she cut me short.

"I was a music major," she said, clearly snuffing my compliment, yet underscoring it by the very impatience with which she seemed to ignore it. It meant, *Don't feel obligated to say anything. I know. I've trained for this.*

"I'm moving into another room. Too noisy, too stuffy here."

A pensive okay was all I could offer. Was this it, then?

"Let's go into the library. It's quieter there."

She wants me to follow her. I remember being amused by the thought: *So she wants me to follow.*

The library, which turned out to be equally crowded, had huge, rare, leatherbound volumes neatly stacked around its walls, interrupted by windows and what looked like a balcony facing the river. During the day this particular French window must have let in the most tranquil sweeps of light. "I could spend the rest of my life in this room."

"Many people could. See that desk over there?"

"Yes."

The desk was covered with hors d'oeuvres.

"I wrote my master's thesis there."

"With all that food around?"

She threw me a hasty nod, instantly dismissing the attempted joke. "I have good memories of this room. I was in this room for a whole year, from nine to five. They even let me come here on weekends. I can remember summer and fall here. I can remember looking out and seeing snow. Then it was April. It went so fast."

For a moment I pictured Clara arriving dutifully every winter morning to sit and write all day. Did she wear glasses? Was she totally focused on her project, or did she look bored when she was alone all day? Did her mind drift, did Clara dream of love in the heart of midwinter afternoons? Was there sorrow in her life?

"Do you really miss your thesis days? Most people hate even thinking of them."

"I don't miss them. But I don't hate them."

My question didn't seem to interest her. I had set her up to tell me she wished to go back to those days. Or wished she'd never lived through them at all. Instead, what came was the most levelheaded response. I thought of saying, What a lovely, straightforward outlook you have, but held back in case I seemed condescending or, worse yet, sarcastic. In her place I'd probably have said I hated those days but missed each one. I would have tossed the idea for effect, perhaps to tease something out of her, or out of myself, or to test whether she had a feel for paradox and see how far we could grope about together in the murky terrain of guarded ambiguities uttered in attempted small talk.

But I felt that this sort of thing wouldn't pass muster in her world either—saying you missed things you hated, hated those you loved, wanted what you'd turn down in no time—all these were affected torsions and spray-painted screens that would stir a withering nod goodbye from her.

I am Clara. Tell me another.

"And what was it on?"

"The thesis?"

"Yes."

"On the table, of course, what else?"

So she was returning the favor. Thank you.

"No, seriously," I said.

"You mean was it a dialogical treatment of marginalized women living in a hegemonic, monolingual world colonized by phalocratic institutions?"

Very funny.

"Well, it wasn't," she added.

Momentary silence.

"Am I supposed to keep asking?"

"No one asked you to ask anything. But, yes, you're supposed to keep asking."

For a moment I thought I'd lost her. I smiled back. "What was the thesis on, then?"

"You really want to know?"

"No, I'm only asking because I'm supposed to ask, remember?"

"On Folías. A musical genre. Totally without interest."

"Folías? Would someone like me know this music?"

"*Someone like you—*" She repeated my phrase as though it were a strange fruit whose unusual taste she was still mulling before passing judgment, which is why she said, "We're so sharp, so clever. Why, am I already supposed to guess who someone like you is?"

Right through me. She'd caught my trick question even before I had—my attempt to bring us closer, get her to say something about me.

I am Clara. Nice try.

"I'm sure you've heard Folías before, though you may not know it."

And suddenly there it was again, her voice rising above the din in the crowded library, singing the somber opening bars of Handel's famous sarabande. I, who had never understood why men love women to sing for them, saw the cobwebs clear before me.

"Recognize it?"

I did, but I didn't answer. Instead: "I love your voice," I blurted, hesitating whether to say anything else or, if still possible, to take it back. I was, once again, walking naked from my shirttails down, thrilled by my own daring.

"It's a standard melody set to a standard chord progression, very similar to a passacaglia. Want some fruit punch?" she broke in, as though nipping both my compliment and the rising intimacy hesitating in the wings. She had uttered these words so abruptly that, once again, I felt she did indeed want me to notice she was changing topics, but that she wanted me to notice it only if I'd picked up her poorly disguised aversion to compliments.

I smiled at the maneuver. She caught my smile. And, having caught it, smiled back almost in self-mockery, sensing that if she gave any sign of guessing I had seen through her feigned abruptness she'd be admitting that my reading of her feint was closer to the truth than she might have wished. So she smiled both to own that she'd been caught and to show that our game was really so much fun: *We're so sharp, so clever, the two of us, aren't we?*

Or perhaps her smile was her way of countering my reading tit for tat, and that, much as she'd been caught, she too had found something to smile about in me—namely, the guilty pleasure I derived from the ebb and flow of what wasn't being said. There may have been nothing there, and perhaps both of us knew it and were simply going through the motions of making contact by tossing empty signals. But I was—and I didn't care to hide it—wearing a big smile that bordered on laughter.

Had she seen through this as well? And could she tell I wanted her to know it?

Nervous hesitation hovered between us, like the quiver of a jibe she considered for a moment but then immediately suppressed. Was she really going to call me on my smile and make me spell out what could have been my totally twisted reading of hers? Who are you, Clara?

For a moment, and perhaps to play with worst outcomes as a way to avert them, I began to consider the woman in the wide-open crimson shirt from the distance of the years to come, as though I were waving at her from the wrong end of a spyglass. As someone lost. As someone I'd met at a faraway party once and never saw again and soon forgot. Someone I could have changed my life for. Or who'd have thrown it so thoroughly off course that it would take years and a lifetime, generations, to recover. Just by looking at her from the distance of time, I could already foresee hollow January weekday evenings and all-day Sundays without her. Part of me had run ahead of me and was already coming back with news of what had happened long after I'd lost her: the walk to and from her house, whose whereabouts I knew nothing of, the view from her window, which I'd give everything to see again but that overlooked places I'd probably never seen, the sound of her coffee grinder in the morning, the smell around her cat's litter box, the squeak of the service door when you put out the garbage late every night and heard the clatter of the neighbor's triple lock, the smell of her sheets and of her towels, an entire world drifting away before I touched it.

I suddenly stopped myself, knowing, by an inverse logic familiar to superstitious people, that the very foretaste of sorrows to come presumed a degree of joy beforehand and would no doubt stand in the way of the very joy I was reluctant to consider for fear of forfeiting it. I felt no different than a castaway who, on glimpsing a sailboat from a high perch on his deserted island, omits to light a pyre because he's spied too many such

ships before and doesn't want his hopes dashed again. But then, on urging himself to light a fire just the same, he begins to have second
thoughts about the strangers on board who could prove more dangerous
than the pythons and Komodo dragons he's learned to live among.
Weekday evenings alone weren't so terrible. Hollow Sundays weren't bad
either. Nothing would come of this, I kept saying. Besides, thinking that
I'd already lost her might ease the tension between us and allow me to
regain my footing and act a bit more confidently.

What I didn't want to feel was hope and, behind the hope, a craving
so fierce that anyone watching me would instantly guess I was utterly and
undeniably smitten.

I didn't mind her knowing. I wanted her to know. Women like Clara
know you're smitten, expect you to be, can spot every one of your feck-
less attempts to disguise it. What I didn't want to show was my struggle
to keep my composure.

To parry her gaze, I tried to look elsewhere and seem distracted. I
wanted her to ask why I'd suddenly drifted from her, wanted her to worry
that she could lose me as easily as I knew I could lose her. But I also
wanted her to laugh at me for doing precisely what I was doing. I wanted
her to see through my pretended indifference and expose every one of my
little maneuvers and, by so doing, show she was plenty familiar with this
game, because she'd played it herself many times, was playing it right
now, maybe. I bit my tongue again as brash thoughts welled up within me
and clamored to speak. Here I was, a shy man pretending to be shy.

"Punch?" she repeated like someone who snaps a finger in front of you
and brings you back among the living by saying *Boo!* "Them who sing
fetches," she added, all set to go and fetch me some punch.

I told her she didn't have to bring me anything; I'd get some myself. I
knew I was being unnecessarily fussy and that I could easily have
accepted her offer. But I was unable to extricate myself once I had started
down that slope. I seemed determined to show I was more uncomfortable
having someone bring me a drink than flattered that she'd offered to.

"I just want to," she replied. "I'll even throw in some goodies on
a plate . . . if you let me go now before these singing yahoos come and
gobble everything up," she added, as though this were her closing
inducement.

"You don't have to, really."

Perhaps what I wanted was not so much to spare her the errand as to prevent her from moving; the faintest step might throw us off—anything could come between us—we might lose our spot in the library and never recover our giddy pace.

She asked again. I caught myself insisting that I'd get the punch myself. I was beginning to sound coy and fatuous.

Then it happened, exactly as I feared.

"Oh well," she shrugged, meaning, *Suit yourself.* Or worse: *Hang it.* Her voice was still buoyed by the mirth that had sprung up between us moments earlier; but there was a metallic chime somewhere, less like the lilt of irony and good cheer than like the downscale click of a file cabinet being slammed shut.

I instantly regretted her change of heart.

"And where would these goodies be?" I fumbled by way of resurrecting her original offer, thinking there was food elsewhere in the apartment.

"Oh, just stay put and I'll get you some"—feigned exasperation bubbling in her voice. I caught sight of her neckline as she slipped on her levity again like a reversible coat, the flip side of *hang it*, sandpaper turned to velour. I wondered if rubbing people the wrong way was not her way of sidling up to them, her way of defusing tension by discharging so much of her own that if she got any closer it would be to dismiss you, but that in going through motions of dismissal she was actually sneaking up on you like a feral cat who doesn't want you to know it doesn't mind being petted.

I am Clara. She affected to snap. I affected to obey. In the packed, dark room where everyone's shadow merged with everyone else's, we couldn't have chosen roles that came more naturally.

With this air of chronic turmoil, she got you to mean exactly what she had in mind for you, not because she liked to have her way, but because everything about her seemed so unusually charged, craggy, and barbed that not to give in to her jostling was like snubbing everything she was. Which is how she cornered you. To question her manner was to slight not just the manner but the person behind the manner. Even her way of arching her eyebrows, which warned you she required instant submission, could, if questioned, be likened to the rough plumage with which tiny birds puff themselves up to three times their size, the better to conceal their fear of not getting things simply by asking for them.

All this may have been wishful thinking on my part. She might be concealing nothing at all. She held nothing back, puffed up nothing, feared no one. It was just I who needed to think this way.

Perhaps Clara was exactly who she appeared to be: light and swift, alert, caustic and dangerous. Just Clara—no roles, no catch-me-if-you-can, no waggish sidling up to strangers or stealthy angling for friendship and chitchat. One of the drawbacks that came from being just who she was and saying just what she felt was to let those who were not used to such candor think it was a pose, that she had learned to hide her shyness better than most, but that she was no less tentative or apprehensive *underneath*, and that all this fretful behavior, starting from the way she let her elbow rest on my shoulder to mean *just stop arguing* when I quibbled over punch to the hand that came out of nowhere, was a sham, the way certain diamonds sparkle for a moment and are quite conveniently deemed glass, until we take a second look and slap our foreheads and ask whatever made us think they were fakes. The sham was in us, not them.

There are people who come on to you with friction. Chafing starts intimacy; and strife, like spite, is the shortest distance to the heart.

Before you finish your sentence, they nip it from your mouth and give it an entirely different spin, making it seem you had been secretly hinting at things you never knew you wanted and would easily have lived without but that you now crave, the way I craved that cup of punch—and with goodies thrown in, exactly as she'd promised, as though the whole evening and much, much more hung on that cup of punch.

Would she forgive my wishy-washiness? Or had she read it as a triumph of her will? Or was she thinking in altogether different terms? And what were these terms, and why couldn't I begin to think in them?

She was gone in a second. I had lost her.

I should have known.

•

"Did you really want punch?" she asked when she returned, carrying a plate on which she'd arrayed a selection of Japanese appetizers in a scatter of tiny squares that only Paul Klee would have imagined. The crowd, she explained, had made ladling the punch too difficult. "Ergo, no punch." Sounded like *Ergo, lump it.*

I was tempted to hold this against her, not just because I was suddenly disappointed, or because the word *ergo* itself seemed a tad chilling despite the lighthearted way she'd said it, but as though the whole exchange about getting, not getting, and then going to get the punch had one purpose: to trifle with me, to bait me, to raise my hopes only to dash them. Now, to absolve herself for not keeping her promise, or for not caring to, she was trying to make it seem I'd never cared for punch—which was the truth.

I noticed that she had sorted the appetizers in pairs and placed them in neat little rows around the plate, as though she'd carefully lined them up for Noah's ark—her way of making up for neglecting the punch, I thought. The tuna-avocado miniature rolls—male and female—the kiwi-tile fish—male and female—the seared scallop with a sprig of mache on a bed of slithered turnips with tamarind jelly and a dab of lemon rind on top—male and female made He them. No sooner had I told her why the extravagant miscellany had made me smile than I realized there was something daring in my remark about the paired appetizers that were about to propagate and fill the earth—except that before I had time to backpedal, I caught something else neighboring this idea that moved me in my stomach as if I'd been buoyed up and let down on a high wave: not male and female, not male and female shifting on the cold banks of the Black Sea, filing up to book passage on Noah's Circle Line, but male and female as in you and me, you and me, just you and me, Clara, waiting our turn, which turn, whose turn, say something now, Clara, or I'll speak out of turn and I haven't had enough to drink to find the courage to say it. I wanted to touch her shoulder, wanted to rub the length of her neck with my lips, kiss her under her right ear and under the left ear and along her breastbone, and thank her for arranging this plate, for knowing what I'd think, for thinking it with me, even if none of it had crossed her mind.

"On second thought—" I began, uncertain whether to add anything, and yet hesitating, because I knew that hesitating would catch her attention.

"What?"—mock vexation crackling in her voice.

"Actually, I hate punch," I said.

It was her turn to laugh.

"In that case," also spoken haltingly—she too knew how to play the waiting game and make me hold my breath for her next word—"I detest—as in de-test—punch, sangria, ladely-lady drinks, daiquiri, harakiri, *vache qui rit*. They make me *womit*." It was her way of pulling the rug from under your feet just when you thought you had one-upped the last of her comebacks. *I am Clara*. I can do you one better.

What neither asked—because each already suspected the other's answer—was why we'd fussed so much over punch if neither cared for it.

Once again, not asking could only betray we'd both thought of asking and decided not to. We smiled at our implied truce, smiled for smiling, smiled because we knew, and wanted the other to know, we'd right away own up to why we'd tussled over punch if the other so much as hinted at the question.

"I'm not even sure I've ever liked people who like punch," I added.

"Oh, if that's where you're going," she said, clearly not about to be outdone, "I might as well come clean: I've never been crazy about parties that have a bowl of punch sitting right in the middle of them."

I liked her like this.

"And the people who attend parties where a bowl of punch sits right in the middle, do you like them?"

"Do I like *otherpeoples*?" She paused. "Is this what you're asking?"

I guessed this was what I was asking.

"Seldom," she said. "Most people are Shukoffs. Except those I like. And before I get to like them, they're Shukoffs too."

I craved to know where I ranked on the Scale of Shukoff, but didn't dare ask.

"What makes you want to know Shukoffs?"

I liked using her lingo.

"You really want to know?"

Couldn't wait to know.

"Boredom."

"Boredom behind a Christmas tree?"

With my innocent zap, I wanted nothing more than to show I enjoyed recalling how we'd met and that this moment was very much with me, that I didn't want to let it go yet.

"Maybe." She hesitated. Perhaps she did not like to agree with people so easily and preferred putting forth a *maybe* before a *yes*. I was already hearing the faint rumblings of a drumroll coming to a rise. "But then just think how boring this party would be without me."

I loved this.

"I'd probably have already left," I said.

"I'm not keeping you, am I?"

And there it was again, the message that wasn't the real message but might just as easily have been the real message all along.

Something comforting, almost heartwarming in this undertow of bristles and snags aroused me and made me feel she was a kindred spirit who'd alighted with me in the same afterlife, taken the words from my mouth, and, by saying them back to me, given them a life and a spin they'd never have had I kept them to myself. Under guise of spitfire minitantrums, her words suggested something at once kind and welcoming, like the rough folds of a trusted and forgiving blanket that takes us as we are and knows how we sleep, what we've been through, what things we dream of and so desperately crave and are ashamed to own up to when we're alone and naked with ourselves. Did she know me that well?

"Most people remain Shukoffs," I said, not knowing whether I meant it. "But I could be wrong."

"Are you always this amphibalent?" she taunted.

"Aren't you?"

"I invented the word."

I am Clara. I invent riddles and their cheats.

I looked away, perhaps to avoid looking at her. I scanned the faces in the library. The large room was filled with just the sort of people who go to parties where a bowl of punch sits in the middle of their shiftless chatter. I remembered her scornful just-look-at-these-faces and tried to cast a withering glance in their direction. The gesture gave me a pretext to keep looking elsewhere.

"*Otherpeoples*," I said, to fill the silence, repeating the word we'd tacitly agreed to give them, as though this one word summed up everything we'd felt about everyone else and would nail the coffin on our indictment of mankind whole. We were fellow aliens conspiring to renew our reluctant courtship with Earthlings.

"*Otherpeoples*," she echoed, still holding the plate, whose contents neither of us had touched yet. She hadn't offered it to me, and I didn't dare.

What threw me off was the way she'd said *otherpeoples*. It didn't seem as disenchanted as I had hoped, but had paled into something soulful, verging on sorrow and mercy.

"Are *otherpeoples* as terrible as all that?" she asked, looking up to me for an answer, as though I was the expert who had led her through a landscape that wasn't really hers and for which she had little affinity or much patience, but that she'd strayed in simply because our conversation had drifted that way. Was she disagreeing with me politely? Or worse yet: rebuking me?

"Terrible? No," I replied. "Necessary? I don't know."

She gave it some thought. "Some are. Necessary, that is. At least to me they are. Sometimes I wish they weren't—though we're always alone in the end."

Again she spoke these words with such mournful candor and humility that she seemed to own up to a weakness in herself, which she had tried but failed to overcome. Her words stung me to the quick, because they reminded me that we were not two intergalactic wayfarers who had landed in the same afterlife but that I was the alien and she the first native who'd run into me and extended a friendly hand and was about to take me into town and introduce me to her friends and parents. She, I gathered, liked others and knew how to put up with Shukoffs till they stopped being Shukoffs.

"So much for *otherpeoples*," she added, with a pensive, faraway gaze, as though still nursing unresolved feelings about them. "Sometimes they're all that stands between us and the ditch to remind us we're not always alone, even when there are trenches between us. So, yes, they are important."

"I know," I said. Perhaps I had gone too far in my wholesale indictment of mankind and this was the time to backpedal. "I too hate being alone."

"Oh, I don't mind being alone at all," she corrected. "I like being alone."

Had she snubbed yet another one of my efforts to align my outlook to hers? Or, in my attempt to understand her in terms of myself, had I simply failed to hear what she was saying? Was I desperately trying to think she was like me so that she might be less of a stranger? Or was I trying to be like her to show we were closer than we seemed?

"With or without them, it's always pandangst."

"Pandangst?"

"Pandemic anxiety—last seen stalking the Upper West Side on Sunday evening. But there were two unreported sightings this afternoon. I hate afternoons. This is the winter of pandangst."

Suddenly I saw it, should have seen it all along. She didn't mind being alone, didn't mind it the way only those who're never alone long to be alone. Solitude was totally foreign to her. I envied her. Probably, her friends and, I assumed, her lovers or would-be lovers didn't make it easy for her to be alone—a condition she didn't quite mind but enjoyed complaining about, as only those who've been everywhere in the world readily admit they've never seen Luxor or Cádiz.

"I've learned to take the best others have to offer." This was the person who goes over to perfect strangers and just greets them with a handshake. No arrogance in her words—rather the muted dejection over an implied long list of setbacks and disappointments. "I take what they have to give wherever I find it."

Pause.

"And the rest?"

This may not have been her drift, but I thought I'd picked up the suggestion of an undisclosed *but* rattling at the tail end of her sentence like a warning and a lure.

"The rest gets tossed?" I offered, trying to show that I was sufficiently experienced in the ways of love to have caught her meaning and that I too was guilty of taking what I needed from people and dumping the rest.

"Tossed? Perhaps," she responded, still unconvinced by what I was offering for her consideration.

Perhaps I was being harsh and unfair, for this may not have been what she'd meant to add. She had absentmindedly gone along with my suggestion when all she'd meant to say, perhaps, was "I take people just as they are."

Or was this a more pointed warning yet—I take what I need where I find it, so watch yourself—a warning I had momentarily failed to heed because it didn't agree with her distressed look of a few seconds earlier?

I was on the point of changing tack and suggesting that perhaps we never toss away or let go of anything in life, much less unlove those we never loved at all.

"Perhaps you are right," she interrupted. "We keep people for when we'll need them, to tide us over, not because we want them. I don't think I'm always good for people."

She reminded me of birds of prey who keep their quarry alive but paralyzed, to feed their young on.

What happened to those who had only the best taken from them and the rest junked?

What happened to a man after Clara was done with him?

I am Clara. Not always good for people.

Was this her way of drawing me out, or was it a warning asking to be disbelieved?

Was her life a flea-ridden trench dressed up as a high-end boutique?

Maybe, she said. Some of us have spent our entire lives in the trenches. Some of us tussle, and hope, and love so near the trenches that we stink of them.

This was her contribution to my image of trenches. Coming as it did from a woman like her, it struck me as too dark, too bleak, not quite believable. Did she, with the unbuttoned shirt, single pendant, and gleaming tanned body just back from the Caribbean really nurse so tragic a view of life? Or was this her spin on the demonic image I'd concocted to keep the conversation going between us?

What did she mean by love in the trenches? Life with someone? Life without love? Life trying to invent someone and finding the wrong one each time? Life with too many? Life with very few, or none that mattered? Or was it the life of single people—its highs and lows, as we bivouac from place to place in large cities in search of something we're no longer sure we'd call love if it sprang on us from a nearby trench and screamed its name was Clara?

Trenches. With or without people. Trenches just the same. Dating, especially. She hated dating. Torment and torture, the pit of pandangst. *De-tested* dating. Would rather *womit* than date.

Trenches on Sunday afternoons. This, we agreed, was truly the pits, the mother of all gutters and foxholes. *Les tranchées du dimanche.* Which suddenly gave them the luster of a twilit France. Ville d'Avray. Corot. Eric Rohmer.

Saturdays weren't too great either, I said. Saturday breakfast, in or out, always a sense that others are happier—being others. Then the unavoidable two-hour Laundromat where you feel you could just as easily shed your skin and throw it in with your socks, and, like a crustacean hiding in a rock while a new identity is being spun for you, hope to reinvent yourself from what comes out of the dryer.

She laughed.

Her turn: The trenches, the slough of amphibalence, the quag of awkward, the bog of boredom: hurting, being hurt, the cold, lame handshake

of estranged lovers who come out to inspect the damage, smoke a cigarette together, play friends, then head back to life without love.

Mine: Those who hurt us most are sometimes those we've loved the
least. Come Sundays in the quag, we miss them too.

Hers: The quag when sleep doesn't come soon enough and you wish
you were with someone, anyone. Or with someone else. Or when someone is better than no one, but no one better yet.

Mine: The quag when you walk by someone's home and remember
how miserable you were but how truly miserable you are now that you no
longer live there. Days that go down into some high-speed funnel but
which you'd trade back to have all over again, this time slower, though
you'd probably give anything never to have lived them at all.

"High amphibalence."

"The days I haven't spent in the quag recently I can count on one
hand," I said. "The days in the rose garden on one finger."

"Are you in the quag now?"

She didn't mince words.

"Not in the quag," I replied. "Just—on hold. On ice. Maybe in over-
haul, possibly recall."

The phrase amused her. She got my drift well enough, even if our
meanings and metaphors were growing ever more tangled.

"So when were you in the rose garden last?"

How I loved the way the question cut to the chase and brought out
what we'd been hinting at all along.

Should I tell her? Had I even understood her question? Or should
I assume we were speaking the same language? I could say: This right
now is the rose garden. Or: I'd never expected to see the rose garden so
soon.

"Not since mid-May," I heard myself say. How easy to let this out
In the open. It made my fear of speaking about myself seem so trivial,
so cagey, every word I'd speak now seemed charged with thrill and
denudedness.

"And you?" I asked.

"Oh, I don't know. Lying low, just lying low these days—like you, I
suppose. Call it in hibernation, in quarantine, in time-out—for my sins,
for my whatevers. In *Rekonvaleszenz*," she said, imitating the fastidiously
halting lisp of Viennese analysts determined to use a polysyllabic Teuto-

latinate for *on the rebound*. "I'm being reconditioned too. Not a party person, really."

It took me totally by surprise. In my eyes, she personified party people. What was I getting wrong? Fearing our messages were getting all coiled and twisted, I asked, "We are speaking about the same thing, aren't we?"

Amused, and without missing a beat: "We know we are."

This didn't clarify matters, but I loved the disclosure of conspiracy, by far the most stirring and exhilarating thing between us.

I looked at her as she began to head toward the other end of the library, where two bookcases of visibly untouched Pléiades volumes stood. She didn't look like someone in *torment and torture* at all.

"What do you think?"

"Of these books?"

"No, of her."

I looked at the blond woman she was indicating. Her name was Beryl, she said.

"I don't know. Nice, I suppose," I said. I could tell Clara would have preferred a devastating bashing on the spot. But I also wanted her to know that I was merely pretending to be naive and was just holding out before delivering my own demolition job. She didn't give me time.

"Skin's as white as aspirin, cankles the size of papayas, and her knees have knocked each other senseless—don't you notice anything?" she said. "She's walking on her hindquarters. Look."

Clara mimicked the woman's gait, holding both her arms with the plate limply in midair as though they belonged to a dog straining to act human.

I am Clara. I invented the hatchet.

"Everyone says she waddles."

"I didn't notice."

"Look at her legs the next time."

"What next time?" I said, trying to show I'd already dismissed and filed her away.

"Oh, knowing her, there'll be a next time soon enough—she's been eyeing you for a while."

"Me?"

"Like you didn't know."

Then, without warning: "Let's go downstairs. It's quieter," she said, indicating a spiral staircase I had totally failed to notice but had not stopped staring at all the time I'd been speaking to her in the library. I liked spiral staircases. How couldn't I have registered its existence? *I am Clara. I blind people.*

·

This was not an apartment; it was a palace pretending to be an apartment. The stairway was crowded with people. Leaning against the railing was a young man dressed in a tight black suit whom she obviously knew and who, after exclaiming a loud, almost histrionic "Clariushka!" put both arms around her while she struggled to hold the plate away from him with a mock-expression that said, "Don't even think of it, they're not for you."

"Seen Orla anywhere?"

"All you have to do is look for Tito," she snickered.

"Nasty, nasty, nasty. Rollo was asking about you."

She shrugged her shoulders. "Love to Pavel."

That was Pablito, she said. Did she know everyone here? Not a party person? Seriously? And did everyone have a nickname?

As we proceeded downstairs, she gave me her hand. I felt our palms caress, sensing all along that there was as much good fellowship as unkindled passion in this tireless rubbing of fingers. Neither really acknowledged it or wanted it stopped. This was no more than a play of hands, which is why neither bothered to stop or hide the tenuous, guilty pleasure of prolonged touching.

Downstairs, she navigated the crowd and led me to a quieter spot by one of the bay windows, where three tiny cushions seemed waiting for us in an alcove. She was about to place the dish between us, but then sat right next to me, holding the plate on her lap. It was meant to be noticed, I thought, and therefore open to interpretation.

"Well?"

I didn't know what she meant.

All I could think of was her collarbone and its gleaming suntan. The lady with the collarbone. The shirt and the collarbone. *To a collarbone.* This collarbone in two hundred years would, if it was cold in the icy silence of the tomb, so haunt my days and chill my dreaming nights that

I would wish my own heart dry of blood. To touch and run a finger the length of her collarbone. Who was this collarbone, what person, what strange will came out to stop me when I wished my mouth on this collarbone? Collarbone, collarbone, are you not weary, will I be grieving over collarbones unyielding? I stared at her eyes and was suddenly speechless, my mind in disarray. The words weren't coming. My thoughts were all tousled and scattered. I couldn't even put two thoughts together and felt like a parent trying to teach an unsteady toddler how to walk by holding both his hands and asking him to put one foot before the other, one word before the other, but the child wasn't moving. I stumbled from one thing to the other, then stood frozen and speechless, couldn't think of anything.

Let her know all this. For I also loved this. One more minute and I won't even want to hide how thoroughly her stare had thrown me off and worn me down and made me want to spill everything. One more minute and I'll break down and want to kiss her and ask to kiss her, and if she says no, absolutely not, then I don't know, but knowing me, I'll ask again. And I know she knows.

"So," she interrupted, "tell me about the six-and-a-half-month babe in the rosebush."

She'd taken the trouble to calculate the months. And wanted me to know it. Or was this a red herring purposely thrown in to muddy things further and give her—or me—an easy out of the silence we'd gotten ourselves in?

I didn't want to talk about the babe in the rosebush.

"Why not? Sulky-pouty?"

I shook my head, as in: You're way off base. I was trying to come up with something clever.

"Do you find love often?" I blurted out, turning the tables, thrilled by what I'd suddenly dared to ask. There was no turning back now.

"Often enough. Or some version of it. Often enough to keep looking for it," she replied instantly, as though the question hadn't surprised her or taken her aback. But then: "Do you?" she asked, suddenly tearing the veil I thought I had deftly placed between us. Her switch from questioned to questioner was too abrupt and, as I scrambled to fashion a good answer, I caught her smiling again, as if my hasty reference to last May's rose garden had come to haunt me and stood between me and the shroud I was wrestling to put on. The more I groped for an answer, the more I heard her mimic the ticking sounds of a quiz show clock. If she hadn't before, she made it clear she'd already intuited my answer but wasn't letting me off so fast. I wanted to explain how I didn't know whether it was harder to find love in others or in oneself, that love in the dale of pandangst wasn't exactly love, shouldn't be confused with, mistaken for, but she snapped—

"Time's up!"

I watched her hold an imaginary stopwatch in her hand, with her thumb pressing down on the rest button.

"But I thought I had a few seconds left."

"The sponsors of the show regret to inform their esteemed guest that he has been disqualified on grounds of—"

She was giving me one last chance to bow out with dignity.

Again I fumbled for something sparkling and clever to wriggle out of this corner, realizing all the while that my lack of wit stood as much against me now as did my inability to tell the truth and break the leaden silence between us.

"—on grounds of?" she continued, still holding the imaginary stopwatch in her hand.

"On grounds of amphibalence?"

"On grounds of amphibalence it is, precisely. As a consolation prize the house is pleased to have arranged this medley of appetizers on this here plate, which we urge our honorable guest to try tasting before this here show hostess gobbles everything up."

I put out two timid fingers to the plate.

"These are the best, they have no *garlique*. Hate *garlique*."

"We do?"

"Very much."

There was no point in saying that I, like those who liked singing in the shower, liked garlic.

"We hate *garlique* too, then."

Then she indicated a tiny piece of glazed meat over which a thin serrated leaf stood up like the mane of a groomed seahorse. "Eat it . . . elaborately!"

"Meaning?"

"Meaning, as if you were eating something that requires stupor and veneration."

Why did I feel that everything she was saying to me was a veiled, not-so-veiled reference to her, to us?

"What are they?" I asked, pointing at a square fragment of the Paul Klee arrangement.

"We do not ask, we put our hand out, and we reach for."

Her mouth was full and she was chewing slowly, implying she relished every bite. What a strange person. Was she going to be yet another one of these women who need to remind everyone they are sensual tornadoes held in check by mild civilities at the cocktail hour?

"Mankiewicz," she whispered a minute later.

"Mankiewicz," I echoed back, as if the word had a deeper meaning I couldn't fathom but which I took to be synonymous with *exquisite*. For a moment I thought she was referring to someone in the room. Or was it the appetizer itself, whose name I hadn't heard correctly? Or was this a mantra spoken only in moments of delectation? Mankiewicz.

"Qui est Mankiewicz?"

"Mankiewicz made these."

"Doesn't sound *japonais*."

"Isn't *japonais*."

Then it was the turn of a tiny meatball, which she cautioned was to be dipped ever so delicately in the tiny dab of very spicy Senegalese sauce on the plate. "Just a graze, not more."

"Love spices."

"Loves spices."

I was about to drop the meatball into my mouth when she asked me to wait.

Was she going to impose one of those intricate rituals that people who've just come back from the exotic spots adopt and try to foist on their baffled dinner guests?

"I must warn you, it's very, very spicy."

"How do you know?"

"Trust me."

I loved the way we echoed each other's words—and not just our words but the tone of our words, as if in exchanging these curt tit for tats we were being drawn into a magnetic field that required only that we yield to it. Our exchange made me think of a hand rubbing the soft down on someone's velvet sleeve, back and forth, with the nap, against the nap, with the nap, against the nap, as though the meaningless words we volleyed between us were nothing more than stray objects picked up without notice and swapped from one hand to the other, from one person to the next, and all that mattered was the traffic and the gesture, the give and take, not the words, not the things, just the back and forth.

"Mankiewicz," I said, as if toasting his health with his meatball and uttering an obscure spell meant to ward off evil. It reminded me of deep-sea divers who sit on the edge of a rowboat and mutter a one-word mantra before raising both thumbs and jumping head down, fins up.

.   "Mankiewicz," she whispered in mock sullenness.

It would take me a while to realize that I should have heeded her warning, because a scalding sensation began to take hold of me, rising all over my scalp, then rippling down my nape. Tears welled in my eyes, and even before I knew what to do with them—hold them back, strike an attitude, spit out the food—they overflowed, streaming down my cheeks, while the fire in my mouth intensified each time I bit the food or tried to send it down. I fumbled for my handkerchief, feeling helpless and mortified, and then terribly frightened, because no matter how long I waited for the fire to subside, none of it was going away—because even after I'd swallowed the whole meatball, it kept getting worse, as though the first burst hadn't even been a fire, and had nothing to do with the meatball itself, but was a preamble to a conflagration yet to come. Could it get any worse than this? Would I get sick? Would there be permanent damage to my body? I wanted to regain my composure and tell her what was happening to me, but my silence, my tears, my agony must have already told her enough. I threw my head back and found it resting on the windowpane, a chilly sensation which felt so welcome at that moment that, in my befuddled state, I understood why people loved huskies and why huskies thrived in cold weather and why, if I had my wish, I'd want nothing more than to become a husky too, roaming freely on the ice-cold banks of the Hudson immediately outside our window. Ask me again, Clara, whether I'm naked in the trenches now and I'll tell you how deep and deadly is this dun-colored ditch I've fallen into and how desperately I'm struggling to come out; all I want is snow, ice, more ice.

Clara was staring at me uneasily, as if I had fainted and was just coming to. She offered me a piece of bread, which, I realized, she had purposely placed on the plate, to follow the peppered meatball. I suddenly wished her mouth was on fire as well. I wanted her to feel as flustered, shaken, and naked as I felt just now, so that I wouldn't be alone in this, and with fire in both our mouths and tears streaming on our faces we might find one more thing to draw us closer—no words, no quips, no speeches—just our mouths burning as one mouth together, making love before we even knew we were.

Yet there she sat, leaning toward me, tranquil and collected, smiling probably, like a nurse bending down to wipe the sweat off a wounded soldier's face with a damp sponge. I thought of how the soldier might reach out to hold her hand and, because he's lost so much blood, opens up his heart to someone who, in other circumstances, would never have given him the time of day. Was she worried? Or would she wait for me to get better before jeering at me, *I warned you, didn't I, but did he listen—did he listen?* Just touch my face with these lips, Clara, touch me with your lips, your jeering, taunting lips, touch me with your thumb, Clara, dig into my mouth and pull out the fire, with your thumb and your tongue.

What made things worse was the shame of it. Was there anything I could do to dispel the indignity of being just a writhing human body? I tried to comfort myself by spinning feel-good platitudes—that our body is who we are, that our body knows us better than we do, that showing all was far better than my smokescreen of words, that this went to the heart of things. But I couldn't bring myself to believe it.

Or perhaps things were more complicated than I thought. For part of me liked nothing better than to show her how I was put together and where things easily came apart—the thrill of laying myself as bare and open as an anatomy book where you lift one transparency after the other to show the color of fire in my gullet and of the quiet hysteria coiled around the telltale organs of shame, the pleasure of my shame, of my petty, paltry, startled shame—a shame one puts on and tries hard to believe exists and even struggles to overcome, when, all along, as in nudist colonies, it was left in a locker with our watch and our wallet.

I tried to mumble something to cover up my agitation. But, like the stag in Ovid, had no voice left, or, sensing that something between a husky squawk and a puny squeal would come out and embarrass me further, I feigned having lost all speech. I wanted to moan. I wanted us to moan together, to moan and moan and moan, as if we'd become doe and hart, doe and hart, moaning together in a winter-blown forest where lovers never part.

So here was her piece of bread. And here I was, trying to show it was totally unnecessary, that I'd been through this before and would come out whole, just give me a moment, I'll be done in a sec, just let me save face, stop staring—the wounded soldier stanching and stitching the wound himself—there!

But she sat like a watchful nurse who is paid by the hour and won't leave until the patient swallows every last pill the doctor prescribed.

"Here, take this piece of bread," she said, "and hold it in your mouth, it might help." *I am Clara, the merciful.*

And I took it the way one might take a handkerchief, without struggle, without pride, because I knew—and this was the part I concealed behind a forced smile—that I had, against my will, against all odds, and against all explanations, come so close to it that my one concern now was to make sure that the seizure which seemed about to erupt in my throat wouldn't be a sob.

I finally swallowed the bread. She watched me gulp it in silence.

She turned around and looked out the window. She reminded me of someone taking my pulse while looking away, counting the seconds with a faraway gaze. I didn't know what to do, so I turned around as well and stared out at the Hudson, our shoulders touching—we knew better than to make too much of this, part of me now eager to show that silence is perfectly acceptable between strangers who meet at a party and need a moment to catch their breath. We didn't say anything about the view, or about the people she knew or didn't know in the room, or about the lights speckling the New Jersey shoreline, or about the mournful slabs of ice working their way downstream like a flock of scattered ewes shepherded by a large stationary barge that followed them with its vigilant floodlights.

Outside, on Riverside Drive, solitary lampposts stood out in pools of light, glistening on the snow, like the lost chorus of a Greek play, each a stranded magus with his head ablaze. We're too far, they seemed to say, and we cannot hear, but we know, we've always known about you.

•

She liked fresh air, she said. She opened the French windows a crack, letting a cold draft steal into the room. Then she stepped out onto what turned out to be a very large terrace and proceeded to light a cigarette. I followed. Did I smoke? I made a motion to accept, but then remembered

I'd decided to quit smoking just around the time of the six-and-a-half-month babe. I gave a hasty explanation. She apologized, she'd never offer again, she said. I tried not to interpret whether the word *again* boded well, but decided not to extort hidden meanings in everything she said.

"I call them secret agents."

"Why?"

"Secret agents always smoke in movies."

"Does this mean you have many secrets?"

"You're fishing."

Stupid, stupid me!

She mimicked the motions of a postwar agent lighting up as he scurries through the dark, cobbled lanes of old Vienna.

Outside, a pale silver hue hovered over the city. It hadn't stopped snowing all evening. She stood by the balustrade, moved her foot, and dreamily brushed aside some of the snow with her maroon suede pump, then gently swept it off the ledge. I watched the snow scatter in the wind.

I liked the gesture: shoe, suede, snow, ledge, the whole thing done distractedly, with a cigarette between her fingers.

I had never realized that there was a kind of beauty in stepping on fresh snow and leaving tracks. I always try to avoid the snow, am good to my shoes.

From our high perch, the silver-purple city looked aerial and distant and superterrestrial, a beguiling kingdom whose beaming spires rose silently through the twilit winter mist to parley with the stars. I watched the fresh furrowed tracks on Riverside Drive, the scattered lampposts with their heads ablaze, and a bus crawling through the snow, tilting its way past the knoll off 112th and Riverside before shuffling off, snow padding its lank shoulders, an empty, Stygian vessel headed toward destinations and sights unseen. I am like Clara, it said, I'll take you places you never knew.

A waiter opened the sliding door to the terrace and asked if we wanted anything to drink. Spotting a Bloody Mary on his tray, Clara, without hesitating, said she'd take that one. Before he had time to protest, she had already lifted it from his tray. *I am Clara. I take things.* The drink matched the color of her shirt. Then she stood the wide-rimmed glass on the balustrade, digging its base and part of its slim neck into the snow either to keep it cold or to prevent it from tipping over with the first wind. When she was done smoking, she stubbed out her cigarette with her shoe, and then, just as she'd done with the snow, gently swept it off the ledge. I knew I'd never forget this moment. The shoes, the glass, the terrace, the ice floes plying down the Hudson, the bus shuffling up the Drive. Sweet Hudson, I thought, run softly, till I end my song.

·

Earlier that evening I had taken a similar bus and, because of the blizzard, had totally missed my stop and gotten off six blocks past 106th Street. I remembered wondering where I was, and why I had erred, feeling ridiculous as I lugged my boutiquey plastic bag where two bottles of Champagne kept clinking despite the piece of cardboard the man at the liquor store had inserted between them. In the blizzard, off 112th Street, I sighted the statue of Samuel J. Tilden with its impassive, solemn gaze frozen westward, as I clambered up the steps and looked around, trying to avoid a drooling St. Bernard who suddenly appeared on the mound and didn't seem about to ignore me. Should I run away or just stay calm, pretend I hadn't seen it? Then I heard the voice of two boys calling it off. They were sledding down the mound. The dog, who had strayed somewhat, began to follow them into the park. And then the quiet, peaceful, blissful walk down those six deserted blocks on the service road off Riverside, by turns convex and concave, the sound of ice crunching underneath the snow. It made me think of Capra's Bedford Falls and Van Gogh's Saint-Rémy, and of Leipzig and Bach choirs and how the slightest accidents sometimes open up new worlds, new buildings, new people, unveiling sudden faces we know we'll never·want to lose. Saint-Rémy, the town where Nostradamus and Van Gogh walked the same sidewalk, the seer and the madman crossing paths, centuries apart, just a nod hello.

From the sidewalk, as I looked at the windows upstairs, I had pictured quiet, contented families where children start homework on time, and where guests, ever reluctant to leave, liven up dinner parties where spouses seldom speak. From the terrace where we stood now, the incident with the scary St. Bernard seemed a lifetime away. I remembered thinking of medieval Weihnachten towns along the Rhine and the Elbe,

especially with the cathedral looming down 112th Street and the river
so close by. To arrive more than fashionably late, I had walked around
the block and reached Straus Park on Broadway, glad to see that I still
had time to reconsider going to this party, especially now that I had
almost no desire to attend, and caught myself coming up with good
excuses to do a double turn and head back home, all the while holding
on to the invitation card with the address printed in gold filigree. The
script was so thin that I couldn't read it and was almost tempted to ask
directions of one of the lampposts, it too, like me, lost and stranded in
the storm, though ever so willing to shed the scant light it had to help
me read what began to look like ghost quatrains in the cursive hand of
Nostradamus himself. To kill time, I found a small coffee shop and
ordered tea.

Now I was here and I was with Clara.

After downing one Mankiewicz and almost bawling on a piece of peppercorn, I was standing on a terrace overlooking Manhattan, already
thinking of revisiting 106th Street tomorrow night to replay this evening
all over again—at my leisure, in my own time, the cathedral, the park,
the snow, the golden filigree, and the lampposts with their heads ablaze.
I looked down and, if I could, would have signaled to the *I* approaching
the building a few hours earlier and warned him to keep putting off
coming here—take a half step first, then half of that half step, and half
of the half of that half step, as superstitious people do when they half
reach out and push away the very thing they crave but fear they'll never
have unless they've pushed it far enough first—to walk and want
asymptotically.

Should I put my arm around her? Asymptotically?

I tried to look away from her. And perhaps she too was looking away,
both of us now staring out at the evening sky, where a faint unsteady
bluish search beam, emanating from an unknown corner of the Upper
West Side, orbited the sky, picking its way through the blotchy night as
if in search of something it couldn't tell and didn't really mean to find
each time it looped above us like a slim and trellised Roman *corvus* missing its landing each time it tried to come down on a Carthaginian ghost
ship.

Tonight the Magi are truly lost, I wanted to say.

But I kept it to myself, wondering how long we were going to stand like this and stare out into the dark, tracing the silent course of the light beam overhead as if it were a riveting spectacle justifying our silence. Perhaps, by dint of scouring the sky, the beam might finally alight on something for us to talk about—except that there was nothing for the beam to land on—in which case, perhaps, we'd turn the beam itself into a subject of conversation. I wonder where it's being aimed at. Or: Where is it coming from? Or: Why does it dip each time it seems to touch the northernmost spire? Or: looks like we're suddenly in London and this is the Blitz. Or Montevideo. Or Bellagio. Or there was the other, ineffable question I kept spinning to myself as though it were a mini-beam searching within me as well, a question I couldn't even ask, much less answer, but needed to ask, of myself, of her, and back to myself—because, if I knew I had stepped into a tiny miracle the moment we'd walked onto the terrace to look over this unreal city, I also needed to know that she thought so too before believing it myself.

"Bellagio," I said.

"What about Bellagio?"

"Bellagio's a tiny village at the tip of a land mass in Lake Como."

"I know Bellagio. I've been to Bellagio."

Zapped again.

"On special evenings, Bellagio is almost a fingertip away, an illuminated paradise, just a couple of oar strokes from the western shore of Lake Como. On other nights it seems not a furlong but leagues and a lifetime away, unattainable. This right now is a Bellagio moment."

"What is a Bellagio moment?"

Are we speaking in code, you and I, Clara? I was treading on eggshells. If part of me didn't know where I was going with this, another felt that I was intentionally seeking dangerous terrain.

"Really want to know?"

"Maybe I don't want to know."

"Then you've already guessed. Life on the other bank. Life as it's meant to be, not as we end up living it. Bellagio, not New Jersey. Byzantium."

"You were right the first time."

"When?"

"When you said I'd already guessed. I didn't need the explanation."

Snubbed and zapped again.

Silence fell upon us.

"Mean and nasty," she finally said.

"Mean and nasty?" I asked, though I knew exactly what she meant. Suddenly, and without knowing it, I didn't want us to get too close, too personal, didn't want us to start talking about the tension between us. She reminded me of a man and woman who meet on a train and begin talking of meeting strangers on a train. Was she the type who discusses what she feels in the very company of the stranger who makes her feel it?

"Mean and nasty, Clara. It's what you're thinking, isn't it?"

I shook my head. I preferred silence. Until it became intolerable again. Was I by any chance pouting without knowing it? I was pouting.

"What?" she asked.

"I am looking for my star." Change the subject, move on, let it go, put smoke between us, say anything.

"So we have stars now?"

"If there's fate, there's a star."

What kind of talk was this?

"So this is fate?"

I did not answer. Was this yet another derisive way of slamming the door on me? Or of ramming it open? Was she challenging me to say something? Or to keep my mouth shut? Was I going to be evasive again?

All I wanted was to ask, Clara, what is happening to us?

She'd not answer, of course or, if she did, she'd come back with a snub and a spur, carrot and stick.

Do I really have to tell you? she'd ask.

Then tell me what is happening to me. Should be obvious enough by now.

Maybe I'm not going there either.

As ever, silence and arousal. Don't speak if you don't know, don't speak if you do know.

"And by the way," she said, "I do believe in fate. I think."

Was this now the equivalent of a nightclub floozy talking Kabbalah?

"Maybe fate has an on and an off button," I said, "except that no one knows when it's on or off."

"Totally wrong. The button is on and off at the same time. That's why it's called fate." She smiled and gave me a got-you-didn't-I? stare.

How I wished that the staring between us might rouse my courage to

pass a finger on her lips, let it rest on her bottom lip, and then, having
left it there, begin to touch her teeth, her front teeth, her bottom teeth,
then slip that finger ever so slowly into her mouth and touch her tongue,
her moist and restless, feral tongue, which spoke such twisted, barbed-
wire things, and feel it quiver, like quicksilver and lava brewing in the
underground, thrashing the mean and nasty thoughts it was forever coming up with in that cauldron called Clara. I wanted my thumb in her
mouth, let my thumb take the venom when she bites, let my thumb tame
the tongue, let the tongue be wildfire, and in our death brawl let that
tongue seek my tongue now that I'd stirred its wrath.

•

To justify the silence, I tried to seem thoroughly rapt by the beam, as
though this blurry shaft of light traveling through the bruise gray night
did indeed mirror something bruised and gray in me as well, as if it were
half prying through a nightworld all my own, searching not just for something for me to say to her, or for the shadow meaning of what was happening to us, but for some dark, blind, quiet spot within me that the ray,
as in all prisoner-of-war films, seemed to probe but to miss each time it
circled the sky. I couldn't speak, because I couldn't see, because the ray
itself, like a cross between a one-handed clock that cannot tell time and
a compass magnetized to no poles, reminded me of me: it didn't really
know where it was going, couldn't grope its way around, and wouldn't
find anything out there to bring back to this terrace for us to talk about.
Instead, it kept pointing to the bluffs across the Hudson, as though something far more real lay across the bridge, on the other side, as though life
stood out there, and this here was merely lifelike.

How distant she suddenly seemed, so many locked doors and hatches
away, so many life-tales, so many people who had stood between us over
the years like the quags and quarries each one was and remained so still,
as she and I stood on this terrace. Was I a trench in someone else's life?
Was she in mine?

To persuade us that my silence was not the result of an inability to
come up with anything to say but that I was truly distracted by brooding,
somber thoughts that I wasn't about to share, I let my mind conjure my
father's face, when I'd gone to see him late at night after a party last year,
his ordering me to sit at the edge of his bed to tell him everything I'd

seen and eaten that night—*And start from the very top, not midway as you always do,* and then finding a way to say it: *I see you so seldom now,* or *I never see you with anyone,* or *When I see you with someone she never lasts long enough for me to remember her name,* and just when I thought I had deftly dodged the larger question about the weeks and days remaining to him, to hear him add that old bromide about children, *I've waited so long, but more I cannot. At least tell me there's someone.* Then, with distemper in his voice, *There's no one, is there?* There's no one, I'd say. *Their names, again, Alice, Jean, Beatrice, and that ballbuster heiress from Maine with the big feet who helped us stack the wines on the balcony and couldn't even wrap a napkin around the silverware because she smoked so much?*

Livia, I said.

Why so disaffected, so disengaged? His words. *MTH,* he'd say. *Marry the heiress, then.* And all I could think of saying was: Everything she has I never wanted. Everything I wanted she doesn't have. Or what was even crueler: Everything she has I already have.

From the scumble of grays and silvers on the horizon, I forced myself to conjure his face, but he kept wanting to drift back into the night—I need you now, I kept saying, tugging and pulling at an imaginary cord to my father, until, for a split second, the lank, sick face I'd summoned flashed through my mind again and, in its wake, a vision of many tubes hooked to a respirator in a cancer ward at Mount Sinai Hospital. I wanted to be stirred by this image so that something like the shadow of suppressed sorrow might settle on my face and justify my inability to say anything to the one person who had me completely tongue-tied.

I looked at Clara's Bloody Mary sitting on the balustrade and thought of the grisly inhabitants of Homer's underworld when they shuffle and drag their aching bunions toward a trough of fresh blood, meant to draw them out of their grottoes: "There are more of us where I come from, and some you wouldn't care to see—so let me be, son, let me be. The dead are good to one another, that's all you need to know."

Poor old man, I thought, as I watched him wither away into the pallid silver night, loved by few and hardly thought of since.

"Look downstairs, don't they look mammoth-sized?" said Clara.

From high above, a seemingly endless procession of larger-than-life stretch limousines was stopping at the curb of the building, unloading skittish passengers in high heels, and then inching on along the snow to

allow the car directly behind to unload more passengers, only to move on
to let the car after do the same. Something in me buoyed at the sight of
the extravagant display of black cars glistening in the white night. I felt
I'd stepped into a strange, high-tech version of Nevsky Prospekt.

The cars did not go away but were double-parked the length of 106th
Street. By the statue of Franz Sigel, a group of drivers had come out to
chat and smoke. In Russian, most likely. Two were wearing long, dark
overcoats, wraiths lifted from Gogol's underworld about to hum Russian
songs together.

Where were all these people going? The sight of the cars lined up
ever so regally made me wish I'd gone to their party instead. All these
posh jet-set types arriving in twos and threes. What wonderful lives these
people must live, what splendor, I kept thinking, almost neglecting
Clara, who was leaning on the balustrade next to me, equally mesmerized
by the spectacle. I felt something verging on pleasure in seeing how easily I'd been distracted and made to think about other things instead of
her. This was Hollywood grandeur, and I wished to see it from up close.
Then, realizing I had neglected my father, I felt ashamed of myself, especially after I'd summoned him up, only to be caught thinking of stretch
limousines.

•

Clara and I did eventually speak about the beam, and about the guests
downstairs, and about other things, and I did ask about this or that to
keep the conversation afloat, until I mentioned, in passing, that standing
on this terrace with her reminded me of my parents' balcony and how on
New Year's each year my father would stack and chill wine bottles, how
we'd blind-test the year's vintage that very night with friends and partners, as we all waited to see which wine was voted best, the wine tasting
always getting out of hand, Mother rushing back and forth, making sure
the vote was in before her husband delivered the same annual speech in
rhyming couplets minutes before midnight—until Mount Sinai. "Why
the balcony?" she interrupted. Obviously what interested her was why I'd
confused both balconies and put her in the picture. Perfect place to chill
white wine and soda when it's not quite freezing outside. Someone would
always help me set the bottles, cover up the labels, hand out improvised
score sheets. "The babe in the rosebush?" she asked. I shrugged compla-

cently to mean yes, maybe, why ask, not always a teasing matter, I didn't care for the joke. She had lost both parents in a car accident four years earlier. That was her snarky comeback to my miffed response to her irony.

I am Clara. Don't tread on me.

She told me about her last year in college, the icy road in Switzerland, the lawyers, the nights she couldn't sleep; she needed someone to sleep with, anyone, no one, so many. Mid-guilty-giggle just as I was growing solemn for her.

It was wan and hapless talk, without brio, certainly without the heady banter that had wrapped us like incense in a moonlit shrine. These were probably the trenches we'd made light of before, and during renewed pauses that thumped like heavy footballs portending the end, I found myself already struggling to take mental notes of the evening, as if a curtain were gradually being dropped on us and I had to salvage whatever I could and think of ways to live down our moments together without being too hard on myself. I'd have to sort through what to rescue and let go of, and to coddle what promised to keep radiating in the morning, like party glow-sticks beaming with last night's laughter and premonition.

I wanted to cull must-remember moments—the shoe, the glass, the terrace, the ice floes plying down the Hudson—all of which I'd want to take along, doggie-bag style, the way, after a dinner party, you remember to ask for a slice of cake for someone who is working on deadline, or for the driver downstairs, or for a sick brother or housebound relative who couldn't make it tonight, or for that part of us that ultimately enjoys care packages more than dinners and seldom goes anywhere but prefers to send shadow versions of itself out into the world like unmanned drones scoping questionable terrain, keeping the best part of ourselves home, as some do when they wear false jewels in public but leave the genuine article in a vault, or as others do when they start "reliving" moments even as they're living them in real time, in the real world, as I was doing right now. The body goes out into the world, but the heart's not always in it.

And I thought of my father again, asking me to sit at the edge of his bed last year and tell him everything I'd seen, whom had I danced with—*Names, names,* he'd say, *I want names, I want faces, your presence is like a gift to me, better to hear you than watch a thousand shows on television.* He didn't care how late I dropped by. *So what if I can't sleep now, we both know I'll make up for it soon enough.* Had he been alive tonight I'd have started with three words and taken the whole evening from the top. *I am Clara. Sounds very real-world,* he'd have said.

Was she real-world?

Was she others?

Did she worry I could be?

Or do Claras never worry about such things?

Because they know. Because they are the world, in the world, of the world. Because they're here and now. Whereas I'm all over the place, whereas I'm nowhere, whereas I'm lifelike. Whereas I this, whereas I that.

Whereas I wanted to think of this as an encounter that had yet to gel, or hadn't quite happened yet and was still being fleshed out by some celestial artificer who wasn't getting his act together and hadn't thought things through and would let us improvise our lines until a better crafts-man took the matter in hand and let us have a second go at things.

I wanted to go back and imagine her as someone who hadn't told me her name yet, or who'd already appeared to me, but the way people appear in dawn dreams before turning up for real the next day. Who knows, I might be given a second chance at all this. But on two condi-tions: that I end up at an entirely different party and that I forget I'd ever been to this one. Like someone coming back from a hypnotist or from a previous life, I'd meet new people, people I didn't know I hadn't met yet and couldn't wait to meet, and almost wished I'd met instead, and would promise never ever to forget or live without until someone came out of nowhere and said something awkward by way of an introduction and reminded me of a woman I'd met once before, or crossed paths with but kept missing and was being reintroduced to at all costs now, because we had grown up together and lost touch, or been through so much, perhaps been lovers a lifetime ago, until something as trivial and stupid as death had come between us and which, this time, neither of us was about to let happen. Tell me your name is Clara. Are you Clara? Is your name Clara? *Clara,* she'd say, *no, I'm not Clara.*

"I love snow," she finally said.

I stared at her without saying anything.

I was going to ask her why.

Then I thought of saying I envied people who could say they loved snow without feeling awkward or self-conscious, like writing poetry that rhymes. But that seemed unnecessarily fussy. I decided to look for something else to say.

And while I scrambled yet once more to fill the silence with something—anything—it hit me that if she could say she loved snow, it was probably because she too might have found the silence between us unbearable and decided it was more hackneyed to suppress a simple thought than to come right out with it.

"And I love it too," I said, glad that she had paved the way for simplicity. "Though I don't know why."

"Though I don't know why."

Was she telling me, yet once more, that our minds ran along parallel lines? Or was she absentmindedly echoing or deriding a meaningless phrase I had thrown in to complicate what couldn't have been simpler?

And yet I loved the way she had almost sighed, *Though I don't know why*. I would have leaned toward her and put my arm around her waist. Did one lean toward Clara and put an arm around her waist and kiss her?

A few years ago I would have brought my lips to hers without hesitating.

Now, at twenty-eight, I wasn't sure.

•

Someone pushed open the French window and entered the terrace.

"Found you," he said. Then, as though having second thoughts: "Interrupting?" he asked, with what I suspected was a flicker of mischief in his eyes. "So this is where you've been hiding," said the heavyset man as he leaned over and kissed Clara. "They said you weren't here yet."

"No, Rollo, just having me a smoke," she said, altering her voice and affecting a swankier mode of speech, which I didn't recognize. She motioned for him to shut the glass door. "Otherwise she kvetches."

"Like you care," he cracked.

"All I need now is to listen to Gretchen kvetching."

"Why would Gretchen kvetch?" I inquired, less out of curiosity than to wedge into her lingo and keep the intimate halo of a while earlier.

"She hates it when I smoke and her baby is about. Tetchy Gretchy, born to kvetchy . . ."

"Where is the wench's baby?" I asked, trying to sound roguish, espe-

cially since I hadn't seen any children about. Gretchen-bashing was the
party line in Clara's world, and I wanted to show I was perfectly capable
of dishing out some of my own, if this is what it took to join.

"Her baby was the asthmatic teenager who probably was kind enough
to greet you when you arrived," said the portly man, putting me squarely
in place.

"The little ferret," Clara added for my benefit.

"The little *what?*" he asked.

"Nuh-thing."

The portly man put his arm around her shoulder as a sign he forgave
her.

"Are you not freezing, Clariushka?"

"No."

She turned to me. "Why, you be freezing?"

Was she forcibly inducting me into their world, or was this her way of
establishing the pretense of a pre-existing friendship between us?

She wasn't really waiting for an answer. I didn't volunteer one. Instead, and as if by common agreement, all three of us rested our hands
against the balustrade and looked over the limitless southern expanse of
Manhattan's white-purple skyline. "Just imagine," Clara finally said, "if
all the electric streetlamps on Riverside Drive reverted to their original
gaslight jets, we might be able to turn off this century and pick another,
any other. The Drive would look so mesmerizing on gaslit nights you'd
think we were in another age."

Spoken by the here-and-now party person who wasn't a party person
but was a party person, but wasn't here-and-now and longed to be elsewhere in another age.

"Or any other city," I threw in.

"Any city but this one, Clara, anywhere but. I'm so fed up with New
York " started Rollo.

"At the rate you're going, you should be. Perhaps you should try slowing down and lying low for a while. Shouldn't he lie low?" She suddenly
turned to me. "It might do wonders for you. Look at *us*," she said, as if we
were an *us*, "we're both lying very *très* low, and we're the picture of bliss,
aren't we?"

"Clara lying low? Tell us another. Are you always faking, Clara?"

"Not tonight. This is exactly who I want to be tonight. And maybe, after all, this is exactly where I want to be—on this terrace, on the Upper West Side, on this side of the Atlantic. From up here you can see the entire universe with its infinitely small and petty humanoids striving to mingle body parts. From where I'm standing now, Rollo, you can see everything, including New Jersey."

The fat man sniggered under his breath.

"That, for your nymphormation," he said, turning his bulging eyes on me, "was an unwarranted jab at Gretchen—née Teaneck."

"And right across starboard, letties and gentimen," Clara went on, holding an imaginary mike in her hand in the manner of tour guides, "stands the pride of Teaneck's skyline, Temple B'nai B'ris, and next to it Our Mother of Tuballigation."

"All barbs tonight, aren't we?"

"Oh, get a grip, Rollo—you're starting to sound like a Shukoff."

"Nasty is not lying low."

"I said lying low, not comatose. Lying low as in rethinking things, and holding back, and dipping your toes in for a change instead of hurtling head-on into every hunk *we* fancy."

There was an instant of silence.

"Touché, Clara, touché. I strayed into a valley of scorpions and stepped on the erectile tail of the meanest queen mother of them all."

"I didn't mean it like that, Rollo. You know exactly what I meant. I'm all bite, no venom—Winter," she broke in, taking her last puff. "Don't you just love winter and snow?"

It was not clear whether she was addressing me or him, or both, or neither, because there was something so dreamy and distant in the way she suddenly interrupted, and wanted us to know she was interrupting, that she might as well have been speaking to Manhattan or to winter or to night itself or to the half-emptied glass of Bloody Mary standing on the ledge before her, which my father's ghost had barely sipped from before withdrawing from the terrace. I wanted to think that she was speaking only to me, or to that part of me that remained as ductile as the snow crested on the balustrade and into which she had let her fingers sink.

Looking out and following the beam again, I couldn't help myself. "I saw eternity the other night," I finally said.

"I saw eternity the other night?"

Silence.

"Henry Vaughan," I said, almost cringing with apology.

She seemed to search her mind awhile.

"Never heard of him."

"Very few have," I said.

And then I heard her say words that seemed to come back to me from at least a decade earlier:

> I saw Eternity the other night,
> Like a great ring of pure and endless light,
> All calm, as it was bright . . .

"Very few have?" She echoed my words with a look of mock-jubilation.

"Apparently more people than I thought," I replied, trying to show that I took the lesson well, because I couldn't have been happier.

"Courtesy of a Swiss lycée run by Madame Dalmedigo." The putdown and the caress. And before I had time to say anything: "Oh, look!" And she pointed at the full moon. "Emfordimoon, stretfordamoon, good night moon, what you be doing there moon, here today, gaunt tomorrow, my moon, my everybody's moon, good night moon, good night ladies, good night mooney-mooney."

"El gibberish," commented Rollo.

"El gibberish, yourselfish. Emfordimoon, misosoupoisalad, moogoo-gaipan, merrichrima, merrichrima, I swoon, I swoon, by delightofda-moon."

"And Merry Christmas to you too, New York," I threw in.

"Actually," she broke in, almost as though wanting to change the subject once again, "if anything, tonight reminds me of St. Petersburg."

What had happened to the *This is exactly where I want to be tonight* party girl?

Had our minds been crisscrossing while traveling on parallel lanes all evening long? Or would anyone looking out of our terrace instantly think of St. Petersburg?

"And this is a white night—or almost?" I asked.

We spoke about the longest night of the year, and about the shortest, and how so many things, even when they're turned inside out and

retwined like a Möbius strip, always come out the same. We spoke about
the man in Dostoevsky who meets a woman by an embankment and who
for four white nights falls madly in love with her.

"A white night overlooking New Jersey? I don't think so!" said Clara.

"A white night in winter? I don't think so either!" retorted Rollo.

It made me laugh.

"Why are you laughing?" he asked, obviously annoyed by me.

"Dostoevsky in Fort Lee!" I replied, as though the matter needed no
explanation.

"Why, is Dostoevsky on West 106th Street any better?" retorted Rollo.

"Can't take a joke, can you, Rollo? But here's the million-dollar question," Clara continued. "Is it better to step out onto a terrace on Riverside Drive and look out onto New Jersey, or to be in New Jersey and
make out the enchanted world of Upper West Side Jews celebrating
Christmas?"

"Fungible Jews."

"Runcible Jews."

"Decibel Jews," added Rollo.

"Amphibalent Jews," she said.

I thought about her question, and all I could think of was a gaping
New Jersey staring out at the Manhattan skyline asking the same question in reverse. Then I thought of Dostoevsky's stranded lovers straining
ever so wistfully to catch a glimpse of both Clara and me as we longed to
alight on their gaslit Nevsky Prospekt. I didn't know the answer to her
question, would never know. All I said was that if those in Manhattan
didn't get to see Riverside Drive, those across the Hudson who did see
the Drive wouldn't get to be on it. The flip side of the flip side is no
longer the flip side. Or is it? Haven't we been speaking the same tongue,
you and I? "It's the same with love," I threw in, not sure where exactly
the parallel was headed, except that I felt emboldened to draw it. "One
could dream of a relationship and one could be in one, but one can't be
the dreamer and the lover at the same time. Or can one, Clara?" She
mused a moment as if she had grasped, if not the meaning of the analogy,
at least its nudging, crafty drift.

"That's a Door number three question, and I'm not doing those tonight."

"Figures," Rollo jabbed.

"Phooey," she snapped back.

"You must be Rollo," I finally interjected, trying to adopt the man-to-man camaraderie of a Stanley high-fiving Livingstone.

She remembered she hadn't introduced us. He produced the beefy palm of a successful financier and, as he added, part-time cellist whose private life is an open closet.

"Phooey." She sputtered one last whimpered salvo.

"Gorgon!" he shot back.

Not a Gorgon, I thought, but the witch Circe, who turned men into the domesticated pets they unavoidably become.

"Gorg," he retorted under his breath, making an imitation dog bite, both of them enjoying these cat-and-mouse volleys.

Introductions were clearly not Clara's forte. Rather, she skirted them by making it seem it was your fault you hadn't shaken hands earlier. We should at least have had the courtesy to guess who the other was.

"A friend of Hans's," she explained. "Which reminds me: have you seen Hans?"

He shrugged his shoulders.

"Where's Orla?"

"I've hardly seen anyone. I saw Beryl, she was with Inky in the blue room."

"Inky is here?" interrupted Clara.

"I was just talking with him."

"Well, I'm not."

He looked at her as though he hadn't understood. "What are you saying?"

Clara's face assumed a look of impish sorrow designed to look purposely forged.

"Inky's gone." She turned away, studied the new cigarette she was about to light, and seemed to want to resume speaking of Dostoevsky's "White Nights," now that the news about Inky was settled. But Rollo was not to be easily distracted.

"I tell you he's gone. Gone. As in gone, *finito*. As in out of the picture."

The fat man looked totally flummoxed.

"Inky's left me. *Tu* get it?"

"*Je* get it."

"I'm just surprised he's even here tonight, that's all," she said.

Rollo made an exasperated gesture with his arms.

"You two are just too much—too much," he added.

"Actually, we were never much of anything. It was limbo and twilight from the get-go. Except that Rollo here, and everyone else we know, didn't want to see it." Again, unclear whether she was talking to me, New York, or herself.

"Did *he* know you were—in limbo and twilight, as you call it?"

There were bristles in his last words. I could also tell she was mulling something sharp.

"*I* was never—in limbo, Rollo." It had now become a source of humor to mimic a dramatic pause before saying in *limbo*. "*He* was—in limbo. He was—in limbo. He was the great tundra of my life, if you care to know. It's finished."

"Poor, poor Inky. He should never have. First of all—"

"Furstible!"

"First of all you get him to throw everything he's ever—"

"Furstible!"

"Clara, you're worse than a Gorgon! First and foremost—"

"Furstible, runcible, fungible!"

Clara lifted both hands in a gesture signifying, *I surrender and will say no more.*

"It's the cruelest thing I've heard all year."

"What do you care. It frees him up for you. Isn't that what you've always wanted?"

I didn't know how long this was going to go on, but it was getting uglier by the second.

"Will someone please tell me who's Inky?" I finally barged in, like a child trying to break up a fight between his parents.

I didn't mean to interrupt only. This was also a lame attempt to find out more about this beguiling world of theirs, where you come out on a terrace with a stranger and then, like a magician pulling an endless kerchief from someone's else's pocket, turn out to have a garland of numberless friends called Hans and Gretchen and Inky and Tito and Rollo and Beryl and Pablo and Mankiewicz and Orla and, on everyone's lips, Clariushka, Clariushka, while you stood there and thought of Bellagio and Byzantium, of white nights, and of the cold waterways of St. Petersburg, which made the limitless black-and-white skyline of the Upper West

Side look like a child's fairy-tale book, where all you have to do is say the word and you're in.

"Inky is from the trenches," she explained, using our lingo, which flattered me and made me think I suddenly ranked higher than Rollo. Then she turned to him. "He did the right thing, you know. I can't say I blame him. Though I did warn him."

"Damn your warnings. The poor kid is in pieces. I know him. This is so hurtful."

"Oh, sulky-pouty you, and sulky-pouty him—and it's all so very *hurtful*."

She did something that looked like a shrug, to make fun of his clumsy use of the word. "Clara, Clara—" he began, as though uncertain whether to plead and reason with her or curse her out, "you're going to need to rethink . . ."

"*Need*, as we're going to *need* to take our temperature this evening, and maybe *need* to watch our step or *need* to watch our diet, amigo? Don't say anything. Say nothing, Rollo." There was something suddenly indignant in her voice. What she meant, I could sense, was *Say nothing you'll regret*. It was neither a rebuke nor a warning. It came like a slap in his face.

"Clara, if you don't stop joking this minute, I promise I'll never speak to you again."

"Start now."

I didn't know what to say. Part of me wished to excuse myself and leave the two to wrangle by themselves. But I didn't want to disappear from this world, which, only moments ago, had opened its doors to me.

"It's gorgons like you make men like me queer."

With that he didn't wait for her to say another word and yanked open the glass door and let it slam shut behind him.

"I'm sorry, truly sorry." I didn't know whether I was apologizing for her or for having witnessed their row.

"Nothing to be sorry about," she said blandly, as she stubbed the cigarette against the stone balustrade and looked down onto the Drive. "Another day in the trenches. Actually it was good you were here. We would have argued, and I would have said things I'd regret saying. I already regret things as it is."

Was she sorry for him, for Inky, for herself?

No answer.

"It's getting cold."

I opened the French window, softly, so as not to interrupt the caroling in the downstairs living room. I heard her mutter, "Inky shouldn't have come. He just shouldn't have come tonight." I extended a half-doleful, friendly smile meant to suggest something as flat-footed as You watch, things will work themselves out.

She turned abruptly: "Are you with someone tonight?"

"No. I came alone."

I didn't ask the same of her. I didn't want to know. Or perhaps I didn't want to seem eager to know.

"And you?" I found myself asking.

"No one—someone, but really no one." She burst out laughing. At herself, at the question, at the double and triple entendres, at all sorts of intended and unintended ambiguities. She pointed to someone chatting with someone who looked like Beryl.

"Yes?" I asked.

"That's Tito, the Tito we were talking about."

"And?"

"Where there's a Tito there's bound to be an Orla."

I didn't see an Orla nearby.

"See the guy next to him?"

I nodded.

"He's the one I was—in limbo with," she said.

Another moment of silence. I was going to ask if all the men in her life ended up in limbo. *Why do you ask?* But she'd ask because she would already know why I was asking.

"Some of us may end up going to the Midnight Mass at St. John's for a short while. Want to come?" I made a slight face. "We'll light candles together, it'll be fun."

·

She did not wait for an answer and, as abruptly as she'd tossed out the idea—which was how she did everything, it seemed—said she'd be right back and had already stepped inside. "Wait for me, okay?" She never doubted that I wouldn't.

But this time I was sure I had lost her. She would run into Inky and

Tito and Orla and Hans and, in a second, slip right back into their little world, from which she had emerged like an apparition from behind a Christmas tree.

Alone on the terrace, I was revisited by the thoughts that had crossed my mind earlier in the evening, when I'd wandered from room to room upstairs, debating whether to stay, not stay, leave, or stay awhile longer, trying to recapture now what exactly I'd felt and what I'd been doing just seconds before she'd turned to me and told me her name. I'd been thinking of the framed Athanasius Kircher prints lining the long corridor outside one of the studies. These were not imitation prints but must have been removed from priceless bound volumes. It was then, as I was brooding over the crime of framing these pictures and then letting them hang outside the bathroom of a rich man's home, that out had come the hand.

Through the glass doorway now, I saw a clutter of Christmas presents heaped majestically next to a huge tree. A group of older teenagers, dressed for another party that hadn't even started and wouldn't start for many hours yet, had gathered around the tree and were shaking some of the packages close to their ears in a guessing contest of what was inside each. I was seized by panic. I should have handed my Champagne bottles to someone who'd know what to do with them. I remembered finding no one to relieve me of them and was forced to set the bottles down as furtively and as timorously, next to the swinging kitchen doors, as if they were twin orphans being deposited outside a rich man's doorstep before the guilty mother skulks away into the anonymous night. I had, of course, omitted to include a card. What had become of my bottles purchased on the fly before boarding the M5 bus? One of the waiters had surely found the bottles by the door and put them in the refrigerator, where they'd make friends with other orphans of their kind.

I felt like one of those awkward guests at my parents' house during Christmas week, when we had our annual wine fest. MGH was my father's code word for *Make guests happy*. My mother's was ROP, *Rave over presents*. And MTH was his reminder to me: *Marry the heiress, MTFH*.

To clear my thoughts, I paced about the terrace, trying to imagine how the place might look in the summer, picturing lightly dressed people flocking about with Champagne glasses, all dying to catch what they already knew would be one of the most spectacular sunsets in the world, watching the skyline change from shimmering light blue to shades of

summer pink and tangerine-gray. I wondered what shoes Clara wore in
the summer when she came out onto the veranda and stood there with
the others, smoking secret agents, arguing with Pablo, Rollo, and Hans,
tweaking each to his face or behind his back, it didn't matter which, so
long as she got to spit out something mean and nasty, which she'd take
back in no time. Had she said anything kind about anyone tonight? Or
was it all venom and abrasion on the outside, and a fierce, serrated, scalding brand of something so hardened and heartless that it could tear its
way through every clump of human emotion and skewer the needy, helpless child in every grown-up man because its name, spelled backward and
twisted inside out, might still be love—angry, arid, coarse, chafing love
that it was.

I tried to think of this very apartment on New Year's Eve. Only the
happy few. At midnight they'd come out on the terrace, watch the fire-
works, pop Champagne bottles before retreating inside by the fireplace,
and chat about love in the manner of old banquets. My father would
have liked Clara. She'd have helped with the bottles on the balcony,
helped with the party, added life to his tired couplets, snickered when
the old classicist threw in his yearly hint about Xanthippe pussy-
whipping her husband, Socrates, into drinking the poisoned brew, which
he gladly downed, because one more day, one more year like this without
love and none to give . . . With Clara, his yearly sermon to me on the
balcony as we tended to the wine wouldn't have been laced with so
much distemper. *I want children, not projects.* Seeing Clara, he would
have asked me to hurry. She'd walk in, say, *I am Clara,* and pronto, rav-
ished. The girl from Bellagio, he'd have called her. Together, one night,
he and I had stood before the chilled bottles staring into a neighbor's
crowded windows across the tower. "Theirs is the real party, ours is make-
believe," he said. "They probably think theirs is makeshift and ours real,"
I said, trying to cheer him up. "Then it's worse than I thought," he said.
"We are never in the moment, life is always elsewhere, and there is
always something that steals eternity away. Whatever we seal in one
chamber seeps into another, like an old heart with leaky valves."

A waiter opened the glass door and came onto the terrace and made
to remove Clara's half-empty glass. I told him to leave it. Noticing that
my glass was empty, he asked if I cared for more wine. I would love a cold
beer, I said. "In a glass?" he asked, suddenly reminding me that there

were other ways to drink beer than in a glass. "Actually, in a bottle." I liked the whim of it. I was going to have a beer and I was going to drink it from the bottle and I was going to enjoy it by myself, and if I didn't think of her image floating before my eyes, well, so be it. He nodded and, taking a moment from what must have been a very busy evening, looked to where I was staring: "What an amazing view, isn't it?"

"Yes, wonderful."

"Anything with the beer?"

I shook my head. I remembered the Mankiewiczes and decided to stay clear of anything resembling appetizers. But the thought and his kindness touched me. "Some nuts maybe."

"I'll get those and the beer right away."

Then, when he'd almost reached the French doors again, he turned toward me, holding his salver with other empty glasses on it: "Everything all right?"

I must look positively distressed for a waiter to inquire how I'm doing. Or was he making sure I wasn't planning to jump—boss's orders: Keep an eye out and make sure no one gets funny ideas.

A couple at the other end of the terrace facing the southern tip of Manhattan was giggling. The man held his arm on her shoulder and with his other hand had managed to rest his refilled glass on the balustrade. The same hand, I saw, was also holding a cigar.

"Miles, are you hitting on me?" the woman asked.

"To be honest—I don't know" came the man's debonair answer.

"If you don't know, then you are."

"I suppose I am, then."

"I never know with you."

"Honestly, I never know with me either."

I smiled. The waiter looked around for stray glasses and ashtrays, and then stood there almost as if debating whether to take a cigarette break. I looked at his clothes—the Prussian-blue necktie and loud yellow button-down shirt with sleeves rolled up all the way to his biceps—what a strange outfit.

"Beer!" he exclaimed self-mockingly, as if he'd neglected an important mission, and proceeded to pick up more empty glasses.

But I didn't really want a beer. This party wasn't for me. I should just leave.

What else was there to look forward to tonight? Bus, snow, walk all the way back to 112th Street, peer one last time at the cathedral and, through the snow, watch it fill for the Midnight Mass, then close the book on the evening. She had said something about heading out there tonight. I imagined the quick dash to the cathedral, the music, the coats, the huge crowd within, Clara and friends, Clara and Company, all of us huddled together. Let's go back to the party, she'd say. Even Rollo would agree, Yes, let's go back.

Better leave now before anyone cornered me for dinner, I thought, leave the terrace, go back upstairs, sneak into the coatroom, hand in my coat stub, and slink away as furtively as I had arrived.

But before I'd taken a step to go, the glass door opened again and out came the waiter with more wine and my bottle of beer. He put the wine on a table, then placed the beer between his thighs and instantly pulled the cap off. He had also brought Miles and girlfriend two martinis.

Then, for the last time, I spotted the beam circling over Manhattan. Half an hour ago I was standing here with Clara thinking of Bellagio, Byzantium, St. Petersburg. The elbow resting on my shoulder, the burgundy suede shoes gently brushing off the snow, the Bloody Mary on the balustrade—it was all still there! What had happened to Clara?

I had forgotten whether I had tacitly agreed to wait for her on the terrace. It *was* getting colder, and, who knows, perhaps asking me to stay put on the terrace may have been Clara's cocktail-party way either of drifting away without seeming to or of casting me in the role of the one who's left behind, who waits, who lingers, who hopes.

Perhaps I finally decided to leave the terrace to spite her. To prove that this wasn't going anywhere, that I had never staked the flimsiest hope.

When I finally emerged from the congested staircase upstairs, the size of the crowd had more than tripled. All these people, and all that hubbub, the music and glitz, and all these rich-and-famous Euro snobs looking as though they'd just stepped off private helicopters that had landed on an unknown strip on Riverside and 106th Street. Suddenly I realized that these imposing, double-parked limousines lining the curb all the way to Broadway and back and around the block were carrying people who were headed to no other party but ours, and that, therefore, I had all along been at the very party to which I wanted to be invited instead. The tanned women who wore loud jewelry and clicked about the parquet floor on spiked heels, the dashing young men who hurried about the huge room wearing swanky black suits with dark taupe open-collar shirts, the older men who tried to look like them by putting on clothes their bedecked new wives claimed they'd look much younger in. Bankers, bimbos, Barbies—who were these people?

The waiters and waitresses, it finally dawned on me, were all blond model types wearing what was in fact a uniform: bright yellow shirt with sleeves rolled all the way up, wide floating blue neckties, and very tight, very low-cut khakis with a rakish suggestion of a slightly unzipped fly. The cross between deca- and tacky-chic made me want to turn and say something to someone. But I didn't know a soul here. Meanwhile, the waiters were urging the sea of guests to work their way to either end of the large hall, where caterers had begun serving dinner behind large buffet tables.

In a tiny corner three elderly women sat cooped up around a tea table, like three Graeae sharing one eye and a tooth among them. A waiter had brought three plates filled with food for them and was about to serve them wine. One of the ladies held what looked like a needle to her neighbor. Checking blood-sugar levels before mealtime.

I saw Clara again. She was leaning against one of the bookcases in the same crowded library where she'd pointed out her old desk and where, at the risk of drawing too close to what I thought was the real, private Clara, I'd pictured her writing her thesis and, from time to time, removing her glasses and casting a wistful, faraway glance at the dying autumnal light shimmering over the Hudson. Facing her now, a young man her age had placed both palms to her hips and was pressing her whole body against his, kissing her deep in the mouth, his eyes shut in a stubborn, willful, violent embrace. To interfere if only by staring seemed an infraction. No one was looking, everyone seemed quite oblivious. But I couldn't keep my eyes off them, especially once I noticed that his hands were not just holding her but were clasping her hips from under the shirt, touching her skin, as if the two had been slow-dancing and had stopped to kiss, until I spotted something more disturbing and more riveting yet: that it was she who was kissing him, not the other way around. He was merely responding to her tongue, swooning under its fierce, invasive fire, like a baby bird lapping its feed from its mother's bill. When they finally relaxed their embrace, I saw her stare into his eyes and caress him ever so languorously on the face, a slow, lingering, worshipping palm rubbing his forehead first, then sliding down on his cheek in an expression of tenderness so heartrending, so damp to the touch, that it could draw love from a block of granite. If ever this suggested how she made love when she took off her crimson shirt and removed her suede shoes and was lost to her senses, then, until this very precise moment in my entire life, I had probably never understood what lovemaking was, nor what it was for, nor how to go about it, had never made love to anyone, much less been made love to. I envied them. I loved them. And I hated myself for envying and loving them. Before I had time to wish them to stop doing more of what they were doing, or to go on doing it for a while longer, I watched him press his pelvis against hers, as they began kissing all over again. His hand had now disappeared under her shirt. If only his hand were mine. If only I could be there, be there, be there.

So much for lying low. What a lame excuse. With all her talk of limbo and love in times of twilight and pandangst, the party girl had just caved in. And I thought she harbored a tragic sentiment of life shrouded in cocktail chitchat. All she was was a Euro chick mouthing empty vocables picked up *chez* Madame Dalmedigo's finishing school for wayward girls.

"Meet Clara and Inky," crooned a woman who was standing next to me and who must have watched me stare at them. "They do it all the time. It's their shtick." I was about to shrug my shoulders, meaning I'd seen such things before and certainly wasn't about to be shocked at the sight of lovers making out at parties, when I realized that it was none other than Muffy Mitford. We began speaking.

Maybe because I had drunk a bit too much already, I turned to her and, out of the blue, asked if her name wasn't Muffy. *It was! How did I know?* I proceeded to lie and said we'd met at a dinner party last year. The lie came far too easily to me, but with one thing leading to the next, I discovered that in fact we did know people in common and, to my complete surprise, had in fact met at a dinner party. Didn't she know the Shukoffs? No, she'd never heard of them. I couldn't wait to tell Clara.

Then, from a distance, I saw her waving at me. She wasn't just waving, but was actually headed toward me. I knew, as I watched her come closer, that I had, against all resolutions to the contrary, already forgiven her. I couldn't identify what this feeling was, because it was a mix of panic, anger, and a flush of hope and expectation so extravagant that, once again, without needing a mirror, I knew from the strain on my face that I was smiling way too broadly. I tried to tame the smile by thinking of something else, sad, sobering things, but no sooner had I started to think of Muffy and her jiggling fertility belt than I felt on the verge of laughter.

It didn't matter that Clara had disappeared or that I had let her down by not waiting on the terrace. We were like two persons who bump into each other two hours after standing each other up and pick up as if nothing remotely wrong had happened. I wanted to believe that I didn't care about their kissing, because as long as I wasn't hoping for anything and didn't have to worry how to draw her into my life, I would be able to enjoy her company, laugh with her, put an arm around her.

I was, and I knew it even then, like a drug addict who is determined to overcome his addiction in order to enjoy an occasional fix without worrying about addiction. I had quit smoking for the same reason: to enjoy an occasional cigarette.

Clara came right behind me first and was about to whisper something in my ear. I could feel her breath hovering on my neck and was almost ready to lean gently toward her lips. She was making fun of Muffy, then squeezed my shoulder in what I sensed was a motion of sneering collusion meant to induce giggling.

"Your twin daughters are the loveliest girls in the world," said Clara. I could tell Clara was leading her on.

"They are, aren't they," agreed Muffy, "they're great."

"*They're great,*" mimicked Clara, brushing her lips against my ear this time, once, twice, three times, "really fucking great." I could feel every part of my body react to her breath. People who made love to her had her breath all night long.

"We call them *le gemelline,*" said Muffy, saying the Italian words with a thick American accent.

"You don't fucking say?" Clara continued to whisper in my ear.

Meanwhile, guests were starting to push us on their way to the buffet tables. Muffy was about to be swallowed by the crowd.

"I think we should get out of the way, or they'll run us over. I know a shortcut."

"A shortcut?" I asked.

"Through the kitchen."

Meanwhile, Pablo, who had spotted Clara, was signaling from among another cluster of people. She told him we were headed to the kitchen from the opposite direction. They'd done this before, it seemed. We'd all meet up in the greenhouse.

I thought of Inky and imagined that Clara wanted to get back to him. But he was nowhere in sight. She wasn't even making a show of looking for him.

"Where's the man from the trenches?" I finally asked Clara, giving every indication by my gestures that I was not going to join her for dinner.

I received a blank stare. Would she fail to get the limp joke, or would she cast an indignant look once she'd remembered our lingo? It was taking her a very long while to respond, and I was already tempted to simper apologetically and spell out the shallow thing I'd hinted at, which would sound shallower yet with an explanation.

"I meant Inky," I said.

"I know what you meant." Silence. "Home."

It was my turn to show I did not know what she meant. "Inky went home."

Was she putting me on? Or shutting me up? None of your business—lay off—you've crossed a line? Or was she still trying to find a shortcut to the food and was focusing all her attention on how to get us from here to there before the others? I could sense, though, that she was not just thinking about the passage to the tables. Should I perhaps ask whether something was wrong? "We'll have to go upstairs by way of the greenhouse and down through another staircase into the back door to the kitchen." I watched her as she was saying this. I wanted to hold her hand on the spiral staircase as we'd done before and wrap my hand behind her neck and under her hair and tell her everything bursting in me.

"What?"

I shook my head, to mean *nothing*, meaning *everything*.

"Don't!" she said.

There it was, the word I'd been dreading all evening long. I had picked up wisps of it when hinting about Bellagio. Now it had finally come out, undoing Bellagio, dispelling the beam, trouncing the illusion of rose gardens and of Sunday lovers lost in snowbound lands. *Don't.* With or without an exclamation mark? Most likely with. Or without. She'd probably said it too many times in her life for it to need one.

On our way through the narrow stairway, she finally blurted the answer to the question I hadn't dared ask. "Tonight was our valediction forbidding mourning." She looked behind me.

A crowd of teenagers burst from behind and dashed past us on the way upstairs.

"So, you were saying about Inky?"

"Gone. Left for good."

I felt sorry for Inky. Here was a man to whom she'd just given all the proof of love a man needs, and a minute later she couldn't have spoken more disparagingly of a rat. Wasn't she trying a bit too hard for someone who was just indifferent? Or are there people who no sooner they're done with you than their love addles into something so unforgiving that what causes intense suffering is not the loss of love, or the ease with which you're spurned after being given the keys to their home, but the spectacle of being thrown overboard and asked to drown without fussing and spoiling everyone's fun. Was this what had happened to him? Spurned, kissed, sent packing? Or was she like a strange wildcat that licks your face to hold you down as she devours your insides?

I'd seen his face, tilted slightly sideways as she prepared to kiss him more savagely the second time, every part of his body transformed into one taut sinew. Minutes later she was walking up to me and asking me to sneak upstairs with her.

"He's probably on his way to his parents' on a peak in Darien. I told him not to drive in the snow. He said he didn't care. And frankly—"

We ascended a few more steps.

"I am so tired of him. He's the healthiest man in the world, and I'm the worst thing for him. There are days when, I swear, all I want is to seize the pumice stone in my bathroom and bash my face in with it, because it reminds me of the face he looks at each day and has no clue what's inside it, no clue, no clue. He made me stop being who I am; worse yet, I stopped knowing who I was."

I must have given her a startled and incredulous stare.

"Mean and nasty?"

I shook my head. "I even blame him for failing to make me love him—as if it's his fault, not mine. Because I tried so hard to love him. And all this time all I wanted was love, not someone else, not another person, not even another person's love. Maybe I don't know what others are for either. Maybe all I want is romance. Served chilled. Maybe that'll do just fine."

She caught herself.

"Take that into the pit of pandangst." The party girl smiled uneasily.

I stood behind her on the staircase. It frightened me how similar we were. Just the illusion of having so much in common was enough both to scare me and to give me hope.

"Tell me more."

"There's nothing more to tell. There was a time when the lights had gone out of my life and I thought he was the light. Then I realized he wasn't the light but the hand that turned the darkness off. Then one day I saw there was no light left—not in him, not in me. Then I blamed him. Then me. Now I just like the dark."

"Hence the lying low."

"Hence the lying low."

She stopped looking at me.

"This is my hell," she added. "It's not me Inky wants. He wants someone like me. But not me. I'm totally wrong for him, for me too, if you have to know. It's never really me men want, just someone like me." A tiny pause. "And I'm wise to it." It sounded no different than A word to the wise, my friend.

This is my hell. What words for a party girl. Someone like me but not me—where did one learn to say such things or come up with such insights? Experience? Long, long hours alone? Could experience and solitude go together? Was the party girl a recluse posturing as a party girl who was really a recluse—forever rectus and inversus like a fugue from hell?

I am Clara. Same difference.

She opened the door. The balcony overlooked the same view of the Hudson as the terrace two floors below it, except from much higher up. She indicated a narrow passage past the greenhouse. The view was indeed breathtaking, spectral.

"No one knows this, but he'd die for me, if I asked him to."

What a thing to say.

"And have you asked him?"

"No, but he offers to every day."

"Would you die for him?"

"Would I die for him?" She was repeating my question, probably to give herself time to think and come up with a plausible answer.

"I don't even know what the question means—so I suppose not. I used to love the taste of toothpaste and beer on his breath. It turns my stomach now. I used to love the torn elbows on his cashmere sweater. Now I wouldn't touch it. I don't like myself very much either."

I listened, waited for more, but she had stopped speaking.

"Just look at the Hudson," I said as we stood on the spot staring silently at the blocks of ice.

She had spoken with unusual gravity. I vowed to remember her like this. The greenhouse was totally unlit, and for a spellbound moment as I stood on what seemed the top of the world I wanted to tell her to stand with me and watch our silver-gray universe inch its way through space. I was even tempted to say, "Just stay with me awhile here." I wanted her to help me search for the beam and, having found it, tell me whether she thought it was like an arm transcending time, reaching out into the future to fade into the moonlit clouds, or whether it was one of those rare instances when heaven touches earth and comes down to us to assume our image and speak our language and give us this ration of joy that stands between us and the dark. She too must have been struck by the sight of the skyline, for she stopped of her own accord, looked out toward the southern half of Manhattan, and what finally made me want to hold her with both my hands under her shirt and kiss her on the mouth was the haste with which she grabbed my hand to lead me away, uttering an intentionally perfunctory "Yes, we know, we know, 'I saw Eternity the other night.' "

•

In the kitchen a man wearing a dark burgundy velvet jacket was speaking on his cell phone and looking very concerned. When he saw Clara, he grimaced a silent greeting, and seconds later clicked off the phone without saying goodbye, cursing his lawyer for our benefit. He slipped the phone back into the inside pocket of his blazer and turned to the chef. "Georges, trois verres de vin, s'il vous plaît."

"Some party!" he said, moving to the breakfast table. "No, sit with me, I need to catch my breath. Parties like this are so out of another era!"

He liked parties. But so gaudy, and all these Germans and Frenchmen, he added, you'd think this was the Tower of Babel. "Thank God we have us. And the music."

I gathered that music was what bound this inner circle of friends.

All three of us sat down, while several cooks and numberless waiters fretted behind us. In the corner, what could only have been two blond, burly, retired policemen types turned personal drivers and/or bodyguards were eating a last-ditch, *haute cuisine* rendition of baked lasagna.

Hans looked at us, then pointed a discrete forefinger at Clara, then to me, then back to Clara, as if to ask, "Are you two together?"

She smiled the limpid, self-possessed smile of a very young lawyer who is about to enter a boardroom and is suddenly told by her secretary that her mother is on the phone. That smile—it took me a few seconds—was the equivalent of a blush. She bit her lip as if to say, "I'll get even with you for this, just you give me a chance." And then I saw her do it. "Are you okay, Hans?"

"I'm okay," he muttered, then on second thought, "No, I'm really not okay."

"The Kvetch?"

"No, not the Kvetch. Just business, business. Sometimes I tell myself I should have remained an accountant in the music business, a simple, stupid accountant. There are people out there who want me ruined. And the way things are going, they may just succeed."

Then, as though to shake off a languorous cloud of self-pity—"I am Hans," he said, extending his hand to me. He spoke slowly, as if every word was followed by a period.

It suddenly must have hit Clara that I did not know Hans, or Hans me. This time she'd make the official introductions, though not without saying that she felt like a perfect idiot, thinking I was Hans's friend when all along I'd been Gretchen's.

"But I don't know Gretchen," I said, trying to show that it had never been my intention to deceive anyone, which is why this was as good a time as any to come clean.

"But then who—?" Clara did not know how to phrase the question, so she turned to Hans for help.

I imagined that within seconds the two beefy ex-policemen eating lasagna would pounce on me, twist my arms, pin me to the ground, handcuff me to the kitchen table, and hold me there till their bejowled pals from the Twenty-fourth Precinct came round.

"I'm here because Fred Pasternak had the invitation messengered to me and told me to come. I suspect he's stood me up. I didn't even know of this party until late this afternoon." In my efforts to exonerate myself and leave no doubt about my credentials, I began to spill more details than necessary, precisely the way liars do when a simple lie would have done well enough. I was also going to add that I hadn't even wanted to go to a party tonight—and besides, I wasn't even hungry, and as for their gimp-legged, flat-footed, flossy Eurotartsie fly-by-night crowd gathered round two hosts ignominiously named Hansel and Gretel, they did nothing for me either—so there!

"*You* are a friend of Pooh Pasternak's?" So they knew his old nickname as well. "Friends of Pooh's are always welcome here." Handshake, arm around my shoulder, the whole chummy locker-room routine. "He was a good friend of my father's," I corrected. "Sort of looks after things."

"The Swiss connection," joked Hans, making it all sound like a pact sworn in gymnasium English by abandoned boys in a postwar spy novel.

A waiter finally came round with a bottle of white wine and proceeded to uncork it. As he was just about to pour Clara her wine, he turned to me and asked softly, "Beer for you?" I recognized the waiter immediately. No, I'd have wine this time.

When he was gone, I told Hans that his waiter was convinced he had saved my life. How so? he asked. Must have thought I was planning to jump from the nth floor.

I'd made the whole thing up. A good story, I thought, though I couldn't explain why I'd made it up. Everyone laughed. "You're not serious, are you?" asked Clara.

I sniggered. Obviously more than one man had threatened to die for her.

"To Pooh," said Hans. "To Pooh and to all the feisty shysters on this planet, may their tribe increase." We clinked glasses. "Once more, and once again," he toasted. "And many more times again," echoed Clara—obviously, a familiar toast in their world.

To Pooh, who, but for a whim, I thought, might never have forwarded this invitation to me and never made possible an evening that had cast such a spell on my life.

I am Clara, I'll make you new. *I am Clara,* I'll show you things. *I am Clara,* I can take you places.

I watched one of the cooks behind Hans open what looked like large cans of caviar. He seemed impatient, with the cans, with the opener, with caviar, with kitchens as he scooped out dollop after dollop. His attitude made me think of Clara. She'll scoop you out of yourself, give you a new look, a new heart, new everything. But to do this, she'll need to cut into you with one of those can openers that date back to before the rotary model was invented—first a sharp incision, after which comes the tricky, patient, and persistent bloodletting work of prying and maneuvering the pointed shark-finned steel blade up, down, up, down, till it's worked its way around you and taken you out of yourself.

Will this hurt?

Not at all. That part everyone loves. What hurts is when you're out and have lost the hand that sprung you from yourself. Then the sardine key, with the can lid all curled around it like a molted old skin, sticks to your heart like a dagger in a murder victim.

I knew that it took more than a party to alter the course of a lifetime. Yet, without being too sure, and perhaps without wanting to be too sure for fear of being proven wrong, without even taking meticulous mental notes for later consumption, I knew I'd forget none of it, from the bus ride, the shoes, the rush past the greenhouse into the kitchen, where Hans pointed first at her, then at me, and then at her again, my made-up story of the suicide attempt, the threat of spending an evening in jail, down to Clara's rushing to the police station to bounce me out on the very night of Christmas, and the walk into the freezing cold outside the precinct station as she'd ask, *Did the handcuffs hurt, did they? Here, let me rub your wrists, let me kiss your wrists, your wrists, your poor, sweet, wretched, God-given hurting wrists.*

These I would take with me as I would take the moment when Hans, who wished to get away from his own party, asked Georges if he could be *bien gentil* to put together three platters and bring them upstairs *dans la serre.* For then I knew we were going to retreat to the greenhouse and I'd be closer yet than I'd ever been to Clara, the beam, the stars.

"And yet," said Hans, standing up, waiting to let us out of the kitchen first, "I could have sworn you two've known each other a long time."

"Hardly," said Clara.

It took me a moment to realize that neither she nor I believed we'd just met a few hours earlier.

•

Hans turned on the lights in the greenhouse. Awaiting us in what looked like an enclosed half veranda, half greenhouse was a small round table with three dishes whose food was arranged in intricate arabesques. Nearby was a bucket filled with ice in which someone had deposited a bottle with a white cloth strapped around its neck. It gave me no small thrill to think it must be one of the bottles I had brought and that someone had obviously held off serving it until now. Things happened magically here. Inside the napkin that I unrolled was a silver fork, a silver knife, and a spoon bearing initials carved in an outdated florid style. Whose? I whispered to Clara. His grandparents'. Escaped the Nazis. "Escaped Jews, like mine," she said. Like mine too, I was going to add, especially after unrolling the napkin and thinking back to my parents' own parties this time of year when everyone had tasted too much wine and Mother said it was time to have supper. The unremembered souls whose florid initials were inscribed on our silverware had never even crossed the Atlantic, much less heard of 106th Street or Straus Park, or of those generations down who'd inherit their spoons one day.

Around us were three small tables that were already laid out but on which nothing had been served yet. What a wonderful spot to have breakfast in every morning. The herbarium stood to my left: spices, lavender, rosemary, shades of Provence all around.

I stared at the white cloth, which had a starched sheen and which seemed to have been washed, fluffed, pressed, and folded by devoted hands.

"So how did you two meet, again?"

"In the living room."

"No," she said, before placing her elbow once again on my shoulder, "in the elevator."

"In the elevator?"

And then I remembered. Of course. I had indeed noticed *someone* in the elevator. I remembered the doorman who showed me to the elevator and, sticking his large uniformed arm behind the sliding door, had pressed the button for me, making me feel at once honored and inept

before a woman wearing a dark blue raincoat who was busily stamping
the snow off her boots. I'd caught myself hoping she'd be one of the
guests, but then stopped wishing it when she'd stepped out floors before.
I was so thoroughly persuaded I would never see her again that I failed to
comprehend how the woman sitting before me now in the greenhouse
was the exact same one whose eyes, now that it was all coming back to
me, had stared me down in the elevator with a gaze that hissed something between "Don't even think of it!" and "So, we're not doing
chitchat either, right?" Did Clara introduce herself at the party because
she felt we'd already broken the ice in the elevator? Or did good things
happen to me precisely because I'd given up on them? Or is there design
in our stars provided we're blind to it, or, as in the case of oracles, provided it speaks with a coiled tongue?

Had we spoken in the elevator? I asked.

Yes, we had.

What had we said?

"You said something about how strange it was to find a building in
Manhattan with a thirteenth floor."

What had she said in reply?

Did so stupid a pickup line merit a reply?

What if I hadn't asked about the thirteenth floor?

That's a Door number 3 question. And, I already told you, tonight I'm
not doing those.

Had she gone to another party in the same building, then?

She lived in the same building.

•

I live here. At first it sounded like *I live here, dummy.* But then I immediately realized that it came like an admission of something very private, as
though my question had backed her into a corner, and this corner was
none other than the four walls within which she lived her life, with Inky,
and her clothes, her cigarettes, her pumice stone, her music, her shoes.
She lives in this building, I thought. This is where Clara lives. Even her
walls, from which she has no secrets and which hear everything when
she is alone with all four of them, and speaks to them because they're not
half as deaf as people make them out to be, know who Clara is, and I,
and Inky, and all those who've caused her *torment and torture*, haven't a
clue.

I live here. As if she'd finally confided something I would never have known unless she was forced to admit it—whence the slightly peeved and bruised whine with which she'd said it, meaning: *But it was never a secret, why didn't you ask before?*

Then I had a sudden change of heart. Could Inky have gone home there now instead of heading out to Darien? Was he pouting for her downstairs? Where were you all this time? Upstairs. I waited, and waited, and waited. You shouldn't have left the party, then. You knew I'd wait. What happened to Connecticut? Too much snow. So you're staying tonight? Yep.

"Wait a minute," said Hans. "You mean you were having drinks together and didn't know you had already met in the elevator?"

I nodded, a helpless, ineffectual nod.

"I don't believe it."

I could feel the blood coursing to the very tips of my ears.

"He's—blushing," Clara whispered audibly.

"Blushing doesn't always mean one's hiding anything," I said.

"*Blushing doesn't always mean one's hiding anything,*" Hans repeated in his usual deliberate manner, lacing my words with humor. "If I were Clara, I'd take all this as a compliment."

"Just look at him, he's blushing again," she said.

I knew that denying a blush would right away set off an avalanche of mini-blushes.

"Blushing, flushing, flustered. All you men."

I was about to counter when it happened again. In the midst of our bantering, I mistook a raised biscuit for a cube of sushi sitting on a bed of rice and ended up dunking it in some sauce and gulping down yet another slice of peppered hell. This time it came without any warning whatsoever from Clara. No sooner had I bit into it than I immediately sensed this was no wafer or raw fish or pickled cabbage but something else, something surly and ill-tempered that had only started a process that could last for a very long time, forever even. And in the midst of it, I hated myself, because after biting into it, I knew I should have spat it out instantly, even if there was nowhere to spit in the greenhouse but into my napkin. Without knowing why, I decided to swallow it instead.

This was worse than fire. It scorched everything in its wake. Suddenly, I saw my life and where it was headed. I felt like a man who wakes up in the middle of the night and, under cover of darkness, finds that most of the defenses normally in place by daylight have deserted him like the poor, underpaid, straggling porters they are. The monsters he tames by day are untethered, belching dragons, and before him, as he sweats under his blanket, he suddenly sees—like someone who opens a hotel window in the middle of the night and looks out at the unfamiliar view overlooking an emptied village—how bleak and mirthless his life has been, how it's always missed its mark and cut corners at every turn, straying like a ghost ship from harbor to haven without ever stopping at the one port he's always known was home, because, in the middle of this fateful night, he suddenly realizes something else as well: that the very thought of home turns out to be little else than stopgap, everything is stopgap, even thinking is stopgap, as are truth, and joy, and lovemaking, and the words themselves he tries to land on his feet with each time he feels the ground slip from under him—stopgap, each one. What have I done, he asks, how sinister my joys, how shallow my crafty roundabouts, which cheat me of my very own life and make me live quite another, what have I done, singing in the wrong key, saying things in the wrong tense, and in a language that speaks to everyone I know but moves me not a whit?

Who is he when he opens his window and looks out to Bellagio and is all alone at night and no one watches—not his shadow self, not his chorus of lampposts with their heads ablaze, not the person who now sleeps in his bed and has no sense that what he's staring at with so much gall in his heart is his life on the other bank, the life that's almost there, the life we spend staring at and grew to think was only meant to be stared at, not lived, the life that never happens, because, unbeknownst to us, it's being stared at from the bank of the dead to the land of the living? Who is he when the very language he disclaims is the only one he speaks, when the life he cheats is the only one there is?

I wanted to think of Muffy and her two *gemelline*, trying to coax laughter in my heart. But no laughter sprang. I could feel the tears streaming down my cheeks again, but I was in too much agony to think whether they were tears of pain, of sorrow, gratitude, love, shame, panic, revulsion—for I felt all these at once, the fear of crying, and the shame of crying, and the shame of my own shame, and the fear of my body giving out on me each time it blushed, and hesitated, and spoke out of turn, or couldn't find something to say instead of nothing—always looking for something instead of nothing, something instead of nothing.

So that it all came down to this, didn't it—this moment, these tears, this dinner in a greenhouse, this party, this woman, this fire in my gut, this roof garden, and this glass dome a world apart with its visionary expanse of the Hudson in midwinter and that tireless celestial beam, which kept resurfacing each time you thought someone had finally pulled the plug on it and which now traveled the sky like a lazy presage of the many wastelands in store for me and of the wasted landfills straight behind—all of it added up to one thing: that if to some, being human comes naturally, to others, it is learned, like an acquired habit or a forgotten tongue that they speak with an accent, the way people live with prosthetic pieces, because between them and life is a trench that no footbridge, no *corvus* can connect, because love itself is in question, because *otherpeoples* are in question, because some of us—and I felt myself one in the greenhouse—are green card–bearing humanoids thrust among earthlings. We know it, they don't. And part of what we want so desperately is for them finally to know this—but not to know. And what kills us in the end is finding that they've always known, because they themselves feel no differently, which is why if knowing all this had passed for a consolation once, now it was a consolation from hell, for then, in my father's words, there was no hope and things were far worse than we feared.

All I could think of as I sat there with my eyes still closed was fear—fear exposed, fear of daring and being caught daring, fear of wanting and hoping so badly, but never badly enough to dare anything worth getting caught fretting for, fear of letting Clara know everything, fear of never being forgiven—fear of spitting out this piece of Mankiewicz as though it were a lie I'd choked on all evening long but didn't know what to replace it with, fear that I might mull this lie a while longer, as I'd done all life long, until it lost its pungency and became as ordinary as the water of life itself.

"This is so awful," I heard Clara say.

I looked at her imploringly as if to say, Give me a few more minutes, don't start the sparring yet, wait for me, just let me catch my breath.

I heard the hubbub of voices coming nearby.

Hans rang a bell for water.

It took me a few seconds to realize I must have fainted or done something quite like it, because when I opened my eyes, I saw that others had joined Hans and Clara and were already taking their seats at the adjoining tables.

"You shouldn't talk," said Clara, as one might tell someone lying on the sidewalk that he shouldn't move until an ambulance arrived.

The waiter had already brought a glass brimming with ice cubes and handed it to Clara. On her face sat the mildly impatient, steady gaze of a skilled torturer who is long familiar with the undesirable effects of interrogations and who always finds a vial of smelling salts nearby, to bring back the prisoner to his pain.

I held the glass in my hands. Then took short, gasping, almost sobbing sips.

I watched her face again. *Just one more sip*, she seemed to say, and then another, and another again—she was talking to a baby, not a drinking buddy. She bore the look of worn-out daughters by the bedside of a very sick parent who for weeks has refused to eat. A second later, and that same mournful, worried look hardened into something cross, as though she'd shrugged me off but was going on with tedious motions of caring until the next shift.

Why the turnabout? The sudden hostility? The feigned indifference, even? Or the quipping with Beryl and Rollo in the background while I lay dying? Stop pretending you do not care.

"Drink more water. Please, just drink." As I was drinking: "What is it with you?" she said. It was the sweetest thing she might ever have said to me, *What's with your mouth, here, let me rub your lips, let me kiss your lips, your lips, your poor, sweet, wretched, God-given burning lips*. I'd take pity in a second.

•

Eventually my eyes began to clear. My mouth was still burning, and I could feel that my lips were quite swollen, but at least I could speak. To every dreamer who's had a nightmare, this was like dawn. Soon daylight would come, when every chimera withdraws and dissolves into the morning dew like milk in a large cup of warm English Breakfast tea. Perhaps this was not even the end of the ordeal—and part of me, even while I struggled to put it as far behind me as I could, was already hoping that it wasn't quite over and had begun to miss the confused and silent outpouring of panic and grief that I knew was my way of asking her to take a hard look at what anyone with half a brain would have guessed right away.

It was as though I had finally shown her my body, or done something with it to touch hers. As clumsy as my gesture was, I felt no less relieved than a wounded soldier who is seized by a sudden impulse for his nurse, grabs her warm palm, and holds it to his crotch.

"Better?"

"Better," I replied.

And as I looked at all of those who had gathered more or less around us, some with their plates and their rolled-up napkins containing silverware dating back to the time Hans's parents had fled the Old World, I realized that, despite all their banter and their teasing about my reaction to Mankiewicz's appetizer, this was still one of the most beautiful evenings I'd spent in a very long time. Hans, Pablo, Pavel, Orla, Beryl, Tito, Rollo, unknowns all of them.

Clara reminded everyone it would soon be time to head out to the Midnight Mass. "Just for an hour or so," she explained.

Next year, someone said.

"We're also missing Inky," said Pablo.

"He's gone." Rollo was obviously coming to Clara's rescue.

"Yessssss," said Clara, to mean, *Okay, everyone stop asking.*

"I can't believe it." This, she later told me, was Pavel.

Someone was shaking his head. *Clara and the men in her life!*

"Does anyone have any idea how fed up I am with men, each with his little Guido jumping to attention like a water pistol—"

"God spare us," said Pablo. "We're back to Clara's I'm-so-fed-up-with-men routine."

"Which includes you, Pablo," she snapped, "you and your puny flibbertigibbet."

"Leave my dousing rod out of this. It's been in places where no man's Guido's been before. Trust me."

"How about him?" asked a petulant Beryl, meaning me. "Fed up with him already?"

"I want nothing to do with *anyone*, not this winter, not this year, I'll kiss a woman before I kiss another man. I'll sleep with a woman before I so much as let a man touch me with his stinkhorn." And to prove her point, she walked up to Beryl's table, sat next to her, brought her lips very close to hers, gave a few soft pecks, and then began to kiss her deep in the mouth. Neither resisted, both shut their eyes, and the kiss, however whimsically begun, could not have seemed more passionate or more acquiescent.

"There!" said Clara, disengaging without giving Beryl time to recover. "Point taken?" It was not clear which man she was addressing. "And she kisses well too," said Beryl.

It was a savage kiss. I had assumed lying low meant *I am not ready, I want to go home, take me elsewhere, I want to be alone, let me find love without others, let me go back to my walls, my staunch, loyal, steadfast walls.* Instead, her kiss had been brutal. We can fuck, but we won't find love, I won't find it in me, for you, with anyone. Which is why you're in my way. She was speaking to me, I was almost certain now. Even your patience wears me out. Everything about you—your silence, your tact, your fucking restraint, and the way you give me slack, hoping I don't notice, everything rushes me, it's not love I need, so leave me alone. The two women kissed again.

When they had stopped kissing, Hans spoke first.

"All this is starting to look like a French movie. Everything always makes more sense in French movies."

Trying not to look too unsettled by the women's kisses, I said I wasn't sure. French movies were about not life but the romance of life. Just as they're not about France but the romance of France. Ultimately French movies are about French movies.

"Your answer is like a French movie too," Clara said as she made her way back to our table, speaking with impatience in her voice, meaning, *Enough with the mind games.*

"My life as a French movie—there's an idea," said the party girl, who was tired of mind games. "Maybe I should see it tonight." Then, on second thought: "No, I've seen it too many times already. Same plot, same ending."

"French movies are about urbane Parisians," said Hans, "not dyspeptic Upper West Side Jews on antidepressants." There was a stunned moment of silence. "And on that," he said, standing up and turning to me to shake my hand, *"enchanté."* He was leaving the greenhouse. "Come for New Year's. I mean it. But not a word of it to Monique."

"Who is Monique?" I asked Clara after he had gone and left us alone at our table.

"His flame-no-longer-his-flame," explained Clara.

I pondered the information.

"Were you his flame once?"

"I could have been."

"—but didn't want to?"

"It's more complicated."

"Because of Gretchen?"

"Gretchen would have driven me to it, not stopped me. *Because of Gretchen*, seriously!"

"I was just curious."

Then, after a pause: "For your nymphormation, namphibalence strikes women too."

"And do you feel any now?" I asked, delighting in my own boldness, knowing that she'd know exactly what I was referring to, "because right now I feel absolutely none," I added.

"I know you don't." This was the closest she had ever come to me.

"How do you know?"

"Because I just do."

"You don't miss a beat, do you?"

"No. But then that's why you like me?"

"Remind me never to have anything to do with women who never miss a beat."

"When do I start reminding you?"

"Start now. No, not now. Now is too lovely and I'm having such a good time."

And then, before I could add anything more, came the one gesture that could change lives. She brought her hand to my face ever so slowly and, with the back of it, caressed my face on both sides.

"I'm lying so very, very low, you've no idea. Not like your typical French movie, I'm afraid. In magazine lingo, I'm *this close* to being not a well person," she said, bringing her thumb as close to her forefinger as possible.

"Perhaps you shouldn't read magazines."

She let the comment pass.

"Can I say something?"

"By all means," I said, feeling a knot tightening in my stomach.

"I'd be so wrong for anyone these days," she added, meaning *for you*.

I looked at her.

"At least you're honest. Are you honest?"

"Seldom."

"That's honest."

"Not really."

After that, people began to interrupt us, and unavoidably Clara's attention was drawn to the others in the greenhouse, which was when she reminded us of the Midnight Mass.

•

We arrived at the Cathedral of St. John long after Mass had started. None of us minded being late. All we did was join the thick crowd bottlenecking the entrance and then just stood there, watching people file through the nave looking for an empty spot among those who were already seated and taking the chalice. The atmosphere was dense with candlelight, music, banners, and the shuffle of infinite footsteps working their way up and down the central aisle. "We're staying ten minutes, not more," said Clara as she and I went as far as the cordoned-off ambulatory, then back the way we'd come, squeezing through the crowd, finally running into those of our group who were headed toward the transept. "Runcible Jews," she said, meaning all of us. We found a tiny free corner to lean on in one of the vaulted chapels and stared at the tourists, as we listened to a New Agey organ piece struggling to sound inspirational.

Perhaps it was the combination of Clara, church, snow, music, our romance with France, and the votive tapers we each lit in silent wish-making that made me think of Eric Rohmer's films. I asked Clara if she'd ever seen his films. No, never heard of him. Then she corrected herself. Wasn't he the one where all that people did was talk? Yes, the very one, I replied. I told her there was a Rohmer retrospective playing on the Upper West Side. She asked where. I told her. "To some of these tourists it must be magical indeed, coming all the way to New York City from who knows where and stepping into this Midnight Mass," she said. She'd been coming here as far back as she could remember. I pictured her with her parents, then schoolmates, lovers, friends, now me. "One day they'll open up the transept and finish building this cathedral." I remembered reading somewhere that the cathedral had run out of funds, fired its stonecutters, its masons, put away their tools. In a hundred years they might—but then might not—start rebuilding. "The man who'll lay the last stone here isn't even born yet." These were the party girl's last words before rounding everyone up and herding us to the main portal. It put things in perspective, I thought. The gas jets of a century ago and the last stonecutter a century from now. Made me feel very, very small—our quags, our party, our unspoken darts and parries, our night on the terrace watching the beam pick its way through this silver gray night as we spoke of eternity, in one hundred years, who'd know, who'd want to know, who'd care? I would. Yes, I would.

On our way back through the snow, she and someone from the party whom I hadn't met yet darted ahead, holding hands, then started throwing snowballs at each other. There was no traffic headed uptown, which was why we all walked on Broadway itself, feeling like privileged pedestrians reclaiming their city. Finally, when we were about to cross Straus Park, Clara came back to me, put her arm under mine, and insisted that she and I walk through the park, her favorite spot in the world, she said. Why? I asked. Because it was in the middle of everything but really nowhere, just elsewhere—tucked away, safe, nothing touches it, a private alcove where you come to turn your back on the world. Or to lie low, I said, trying to make fun of her, of us—even the statue of Memory was lying low, she said. Indeed, the statue was lost in thought, drifting elsewhere, wrapped in Hopkins's *wiry and white-fiery and whirlwind-swiveled snow.* I want a strong, ice-burning shot of vodka, she said as we were leaving the park. And then I want something sweet, like dessert. But yes, like Hopkins, she added. Why am I so happy tonight? I wanted to ask. Because you're falling in love with me and we're watching it happen, the two of us together. In slow, slow motion. Who'd know? you ask. *I* know.

•

We all crammed in the elevator, dropped our coats at the coat check, and rushed upstairs, back into the greenhouse. Our tables had been cleaned and were laid out for dessert and more drinks. After vodka was poured for everyone, I resolved to wait awhile and after the second round of desserts began to make signs that it was time for me to go. It was already long past two in the morning. The more I feigned veiled uneasiness to signal my imminent departure, the more I felt compelled to hasten it. Perhaps all I wanted really was for Clara to notice and ask me to stay.

Eventually she did. "Are you really leaving?" as if it was something she couldn't have imagined unless she'd thought of it first.

"What, leaving already?" exclaimed Pablo. "But you've just arrived."

I smiled benignly.

"*I*"—and there was a loud emphasis on the *I*—"will pour him another drink." This was Pavel. "Don't want you leaving on an empty stomach."

"We certainly don't want that," added Beryl.

"So are you staying or you're leaving?" asked Pablo.

"Staying," I conceded, knowing that I wasn't conceding, since I was doing exactly what I wanted.

"Finally, a decision," said Clara.

How I loved these people, this greenhouse, this tiny island away from everyone and everything I knew. This shelter from time itself. It could last forever.

"Here," said Pavel, offering me a large snifter. Just when I was about to take it from him, he withdrew it ever so slightly, and as I got closer to take it, he applied a kiss to my cheek. "I had to," he said loud enough for everyone to hear. "Besides, it'll make *him* so jealous, and I love Pablito when he gets jealous."

"I must instantly apply the antidote," said Beryl. "The question is: will he let me?"

"He might."

"Oh, he definitely might," said Clara, with implied indifference that unmoored me totally.

"Well, before I plunge, I had better ask," tittered Beryl.

"It's not you he wants. But then that's why he'll let you kiss him the way she kissed you, big frontal *mit* frotting too." Rollo again.

"Who does he want, then?"

"Her," said Rollo.

"Then I don't want him," she retorted.

"*She's* lying low," said Clara, referring to herself.

"And *he's* on ice," I said.

We looked at each other. Mirth and collusion in our heady, seemingly levelheaded words.

"By the way," she said, "I never told you my full name. It's Clara

Brunschvicg, spelled the French way. And since you did ask, yes, I am listed."

"Did I ask?"

"You were going to. Or should've. Academy two . . ."

She read me so well, whereas I couldn't begin to scratch her surface.

Brunschweig. Brunschwig, I thought to myself, how does one spell that? Brunswick, Brunchwik, Bushwick.

"Shall I write it down for you?"

"I know how to spell Brunchweig."

Once again, though reluctantly, I made renewed motions to leave. But it must have been so obvious that I was begging to be asked to stay that one word from Pablo and Beryl and I was seated again with yet another something to drink in my hands.

Beryl dawdled past me, then stopped in front of me.

"Are you angry with me?" I asked.

"No, but we've a score to settle. Later, maybe."

Eventually we came down the spiral stairs together to find the party in full swing, the crowded living room huddled around the pianist with the throaty voice who'd probably taken a long break and was now back to his old spot singing exactly the same song he'd been singing hours earlier. There was the Christmas tree. There the same old bowl of punch. There the spot where Clara said I looked lost. There, Clara and someone whom she introduced as *the* Mankiewicz asked everyone to be quiet, stood on two stools, and began singing an aria by Monteverdi. It lasted two minutes. But it would change my life, my way of seeing so many, many things, as the snow and the beam and the empty snowed-in park had already changed me as well. Minutes later, the singer with the throaty voice took over again.

·

Past three in the morning, I finally said that I did have to leave. Handshakes, hugs, kissy-kissy. When I went to the coatroom, I could see that the party was giving no signs of letting up. As I passed by the kitchen, I thought I made out the sweet, chocolaty yet vaguely fried scent of what might easily have been yet another squadron in an endless procession of desserts if it didn't bear a suggestion of early breakfast.

Beryl followed me to the coatroom. I had lost my stub, and the attendant let me inside the large superpacked coatroom with Beryl. Was she leaving too? No, just wanted to say goodbye and tell me how happy she was we'd met. "I like you," she finally said, "and I thought to myself: I must tell him."

"Tell him?" I knew I was smiling.

"Tell him that I'd been looking at him and thinking, If he ever gets around to it, I'll tell him. Tomorrow, when I'm totally sober, I'll pretend I never said this, but right now it's the easiest thing in the world, and I just wanted you to know—*voilà!*" She was, I could tell, already backtracking. I would have spoken the exact same words to Clara.

I did not speak. Instead, I put an arm around her shoulder and pressed her toward me in an affectionate, friendly hug. But she was yielding to an embrace, not a hug, and before I knew it, I was pushing her behind one of the overstuffed wobbly coat stands and then farther into the inner jungle of fur coats that thronged the room like unstripped hanging carcasses in a slaughterhouse, and hidden behind the packed racks, I began to kiss her on the mouth, my hands all over her body.

No one saw or would have paid us any mind. I knew what she wanted, was glad to show I knew. Neither held back. It would have taken no time.

"Thank God there are others to stop us," she said in the end.

"I suppose," I repeated.

"Don't suppose. You don't really want this any more than I do."

There had been, neither on her part, nor on mine, the slightest passion between us, just juices.

When I left the coatroom with my coat, I saw Clara talking to someone in the corridor. Something in me hoped she had seen us together.

"You do know she's head over heels for you," said Beryl to me.

"No."

"Everyone noticed."

I thought back and couldn't remember Clara giving me the slightest hint of being head over heels. Was Beryl perhaps making it up to mislead me?

"Must you really go? I've been looking everywhere for you," said Clara, holding a glass in her hand.

"*Ciao*, lover," said Beryl, leaving me alone with Clara, but not without a wink meant to give away part of our secret in the coatroom.

"What was that all about?" Clara asked.

"Her way of saying goodbye, I suppose."

"Did you two have a Vishnukrishnu Vindalu moment, is that it?"

"A what?"

"Never mind. Are you really leaving in this snowstorm?"

"Yes."

"Did you come by car? It'll be impossible to find a cab on a night like this."

"I came by bus—I'll go back by bus."

"The M5—my favorite bus in the world. Come. I'll show you to my bus stop."

"I—"

There, I was about to do it again, trying to dissuade her, when nothing would have pleased me more.

It took another twenty minutes to find Hans and say goodbye to everyone all over again.

Then the elevator came. We entered it in total silence, strangers wondering what to say, yet dismissing each subject as an obvious silence filler. "This, for your nymphormation, is thirteen," she said, as if she were talking about a friend we'd brought up earlier and whose building we were now passing by car. "You saw me get off at ten." She smiled. I smiled back. Why did I feel that another minute of this could crush me? I couldn't wait for our ride downstairs to be over. But I also knew that our remaining minutes were numbered, and never wanted these to end. I would have wanted her to press the stop button as soon as the doors had closed and say she'd forgotten something, and would I mind holding the door for her. Who knows where all this might have led, especially if some of her friends spied me waiting for her by the open elevator door—Just take off your coat and enough with this going-once, going-twice routine. Or the old, jiggly elevator could stop between floors and trap us in the dark and let this hour be a night, a day, a week, as we'd sit on the floor and open up to each other in ways we hadn't done all evening long, in the dark, for a night, a day, a week—to sit and listen to the sound of the superintendent banging away at cables and pulleys and not care at all, seeing we were back to Dostoevsky's "White Nights" and Rilke's Nikolai Kuzmich, who ended up with so much time on his hands that he could afford to squander it as much as he pleased, in big bills or small—spend,

spend, spend, and like him I would ask time for a huge loan and allow this elevator to be stuck forever. They'd lower down food, drinks, a radio even. Our bubble, our dimple in time. But our elevator kept going down: seventh, sixth, fifth. Soon it would be over. Soon, definitely.

When we reached the lobby, I saw the same doorman. He was wearing the same large brown overcoat, whose shaggy long sleeves with yellow piping I still remembered from the time he had pressed the elevator button for me, making me feel at once honored and inept. He was now opening the heavy glass door of the lobby to let new arrivals in. Stamping their feet, shaking their umbrellas, giving their names to two young fashion-model types leafing through page after page of the same single-spaced list of guests on which I'd pointed out my name inscribed by hand on the very last page. The afterthought guest. The afterthought party. The stopgap, afterthought, adventitious night.

I'd been one of these guests hours ago. I was leaving, they were coming in. Would Clara return to the party, find a new stranger standing by the Christmas tree, start all over?

I am Clara. I can do this forever, once more, and once again, and many more times again, like the beam over Manhattan, and the singer with the throaty voice, and the corridor leading down paths unseen till, by miracle, it took you right back to where you'd started.

Before heading out, she undid the knot of my scarf, wrapped it around my neck once, then doubled up the scarf and looped it on itself. *Her knot.* I loved it.

"You're not going out like this, are you, Miss Clara?" asked the doorman in a gravelly voice.

"Just for a minute. Would you lend me your umbrella, Boris?"

She was wearing nothing over her crimson blouse. "I call him Boris, after Godunov, or Feodor, after Chaliapin, or Ivan, after the Terrible. Faithful as a Doberman."

He had meant to hold the umbrella for her. "It's okay, stay inside, Boris."

I wanted to lend her my coat. But then my gesture might be deemed overbearing. So, in an effort not to fuss or seem intrusive, I had basically resolved to let her freeze in her see-through crimson shirt. Then, on impulse, I took off my coat and put it around her—intrusive-obtrusive, I didn't care. I liked doing this.

Leaning on my arm as she held Boris's extra-large umbrella for the two of us, she walked past the Franz Sigel memorial statue, both of us hesitating down the stairway that was entirely buried in snow. I used to go snowboarding here, she said.

The quiet, empty Riverside Drive, piled with heavy snow, had grown so narrow it reminded me of an unpaved country road leading to nearby woods that extended for miles before reaching the next small village with its adjoining manor house. You could even stand in the middle of the Drive and never once have to worry about cars, as though on nights such as these a friendlier, quieter, picture-book Manhattan took on life-size dimensions and cast a spell on its otherwise hardened features.

The bus stop stood just across the road. "You might have to wait awhile, I'm afraid," she said.

Then she took off my coat, gave it back to me, put out her hand, and shook mine.

I am Clara. The handshake.

That coat would never be the same.

Some of her was on my coat now.

Try again: some of me had stayed with her.

Isn't this why I'd made her wear it?

Correction: there was more of her in me than there was of me.

Yes, that was it. There was more of her in me than there was of me.

And I didn't mind. If she owned me, I didn't mind. If she'd read my thoughts because she'd worn my coat and could spell each thought out, one by one now, I didn't mind. If she knew everything I knew, together with all I had yet to know and might never know, I wouldn't mind. I wouldn't mind, I wouldn't mind.

Soon I saw myself crossing the street. She stood still for a moment, as if to make sure I had gotten there safely, her left arm crossing her chest and clutching her right ribcage to suggest she might turn to ice any moment now but was trying to hold out awhile longer. I had an impulse to say, "Let's go back—it's too cold, let's go back to the party." I know she would have laughed—at me, at the suggestion, at the sheer joy of it. Just ask me to ask you to go back upstairs. Just ask me and see what I'll say.

Then, her right hand holding the giant umbrella, she managed to wave a brief goodbye with her left and, turning in the other direction, headed home like the owner of a manor who has kindly escorted a guest to a small unassuming gate, a last farewell chimed by a hidden bell once the gate closes behind him.

•

When the bus came, I'd sit in the seat nearest to the front door, opposite the driver, and watch the scene unfold before me, as I had watched it unfold earlier this evening, except in reverse order. I already wanted to return by bus again, and again, for who knows how many months. I'd take this bus on Sunday mornings, on Saturday afternoons, and Friday nights, and Thursday evenings. I'd take it in the snow, on sunny days in spring, and on the way back on late-autumn evenings when the cast of fading light still glistens on the buildings of Riverside Drive, and I'd think of Clara writing her thesis on Folías and of Clara speaking of Teaneck and "White Nights" to me on the terrace as we watched the beam circle Manhattan. The bus ride would become part of my life. Because it would lead to this very building, or pass by it each time and remind me that any moment now I'd get off two stops up in a fairy-tale blizzard and walk back to a Christmas party where my name was permanently penciled on the guest list. I'd take this bus perhaps long after Clara and Hans and Rollo and Beryl and Pablo and all the rest of them had moved out of New York, because in thinking of this ritual bus ride through time at this very moment, I might finally make myself forget that Clara was still upstairs, that I hadn't asked how to spell her name, that it was always easier to think of vanished worlds and lost friendships and party leftovers than look forward to Hans's repeated invitation that I return in seven days.

After waiting five minutes by myself at the bus stop, I began to give up on the bus. I was also afraid I'd look terribly stupid if anyone upstairs saw me waiting like this for a bus that was clearly never going to come.

I looked up at the rooftop. Scarcely four hours ago I'd been sitting in that same greenhouse. Now it stared down at me as if it didn't even know me. On our way there she'd opened up a bit and told me about Inky and how, for a while at least, he had put out the darkness in her life. What an odd way of saying it, that was. I had looked outside and promised to remember all this. I was remembering it now. Turn your back on things and they become Bellagio.

Seeing no hint of traffic from behind the bend farther up the Drive, I

walked past the Franz Sigel memorial statue back to Clara's sidewalk and
dawdled there awhile, as if looking for an excuse to linger in her neighborhood, examining each of the surrounding buildings like a latter-day
Joseph scoping out lobbies and their doormen while Mary waited in the
car, hoping all along that someone might eventually open a window
upstairs, yell out my name on this silent night, and utter a peremptory
Just come back upstairs—it must be freezing out there.

I imagined myself immediately heading back into the building, overlooking Ivan's or Boris's formalities at the door so as not to appear unen-
thusiastic to those who'd opened the window and called out my name,
all the while trying to retain the hesitant, undecided air of someone who
was only acquiescing in the spirit of fellowship with the casual *Why not,
but just for a short while* of a parent about to concede five more minutes of
television time.

Just look at you, you could use a warm drink. Here, let me take your coat,
they'd say.

And before I knew it, I'd shake the very same hands I'd shaken goodbye, including those of the latecomers I'd seen downstairs, as if I were an
old friend who made the party just in time for breakfast.

There, and all this rush to get away from us.

So why did you leave tonight? as she hands me the same glass she's
been drinking from all evening. That glass, that glass, in a moment I'd be
holding that glass.

I left—I don't know why I'd left. There are so many reasons. There
are no reasons. To strike an attitude. To leave something for later. Didn't
want to overstay the welcome. Didn't want to show I enjoyed it so much,
or that I never wanted it to end.

Perhaps I had other things to do—

At four in the morning?

I have my secrets.

Even from me?

Especially from you.

Remind me never to have anything to do with men who have secrets
at four in the morning.

Remind me never to be tempted to say everything, because I'm dying to.

Start now. Why did you come back?

If you ask, Clara, it's because you know already.

Tell me just the same.

Because I didn't want to go home yet. Because I didn't want to be alone tonight. Because I don't know. My heart beat faster and faster as I thought of adding, Because of you.

Because of me? Spoken in Hans's slow, deliberate manner.

How lovely to say *Because of you* or *Because I didn't want to be alone tonight*. Hello, I don't want to be alone tonight. I want to be with you. And with your friends. In your world. Your house. And stay after everyone's gone. Be like you, of you, with you—even if you're lying low, as I'm lying low, as Hans is lying low, as Beryl and Rollo and Inky and everyone else in this city, alive or dead, lies low, low, low, shipwrecked, damaged, and wanting, alone with you till I smell of you, think like you, speak like you, breathe like you.

Breathe like me? Are you serious?

I got carried away.

From the middle of the street I looked up again and made out the partying silhouettes of so many people resting their backs against the frosted windowpanes upstairs, everyone with outstretched elbows, meaning they were holding wineglasses and plates in their hands—would they really be serving breakfast soon, as in some demented intercontinental red-eye?

Why had Clara taken me downstairs? To end up walking in the snow with me? Or had she meant something else and I had upset her plans by pressing the L for lobby button before she'd had a chance to press her floor? Did I do this to show that her apartment hadn't crossed my mind? Or was I just trying to make it difficult because it would have been so easy to say, *Show me your place.*

Or did I not want to be with anyone tonight? *Want to be alone. Want to go home. Yet want to be loved. For the distance between you and me, and, while we're at it, between me and me, is leagues and furlongs and light-years away.*

I want love, not others. I want romance. I want glitter. I want magic in our lives. Because there is so little of it to go around.

I thought of others in my place, so many young men, eager and selfless in their love, like Inky, traveling all the way to or back from wherever to stand outside her home, throwing clumps of snow at her window at night till their lungs give out and they waste and die, and all that stays is a song and a frozen footprint.

As I stood there, I put my hand in my pocket. It was filled with tiny paper napkins. I must have been nervous throughout the evening and, without thinking, stuffing napkins in my pockets each time I put down my glass or finished eating something. I remembered the hand-kerchief she'd given me during my bout with pepper. What had I done with it?

In my pocket I also felt the folded oversized invitation card on which the address of the party was printed in spirited filigree. I vaguely recalled, while talking to Clara at the party, that I'd frequently encounter this card in my pocket and would absentmindedly twiddle its corners, experienc-ing a sudden burst of joy when I put two and two together, and, in the fog of distracted thoughts, remembered that if the card was still damp from the storm, this could only mean I'd just come in from the snow, that the party was still young, that we were hours away from parting, and that there'd be plenty of time for anything to happen. And yet, even if behind these bursts of joy lingered something like light resentment for being dragged to this party, only to be stood up by my father's friend, still, it may not have been resentment at all but yet another cunning way of allowing my thoughts to stray from where they wished to linger, only to be pulled right back to Clara and to the uncanny suspicion that Pooh might even have orchestrated a bit of what had happened tonight. *Father died. I promised to look out for him. Lonely. Doesn't know what to do with himself. Meet people.*

I began to make my way toward Straus Park on the corner of West End and 106th Street. I wanted to think of her, think of her hand, of her shirt in the cold, that look when nasty humor twisted everything you mistook for harmless and straightforward and reminded you that *I sing in the shower* was drab, ordinary, flat-footed stuff. I wanted to think of Clara, and yet I was afraid to. I wanted to think of her obliquely, darkly, spar-ingly, as through the slits of a ski mask in a blizzard. I wanted to think of her provided I thought of her last, as someone I couldn't quite focus on, someone I was beginning to forget.

And as I approached one of the lampposts to examine this feeling better and could almost see the lamppost lean its lighted head over my shoulder, as though, in exchange for helping me see things better, it sought comfort for trying so hard to give comfort, I began to think of the lamppost as a person who'd know what this twined feeling of near-bliss and despair was and explain it to me, seeing it had known me for years and surely would understand who I was or why I'd behaved the way I had tonight. It might tell me, if I asked, why life had thrown a Clara my way and watched me thrash about like someone reaching for a buoy that kept sinking. So you know, I wanted to say, you do understand? Oh, I do know and I do understand. And what do we do now? I asked. Do now? You travel all the way to a party and then can't wait to leave when you're dying to stay. What do you want me to say? You want guidance? An answer? An apology? There aren't any. Distemper lacing its voice. The only other person I would speak with, and he is dead.

On the spot where West End Avenue converges with Broadway, I realized there'd be no way to find a cab here either, and as for the downtown M104, chances were no better than with the M5 on Riverside. Thick, luminous, untouched snow lay everywhere. Not a car in sight, while the borders between sidewalks and streets, or between the streets and the park, or between the park and this invisible moment where Broadway and the northernmost tip of West End Avenue converge, all had disappeared. The snow mantled the entire area and made the city look like a boundless frozen lake from which protruded trees and strange undulations, the buried hoods of cars parked around Straus Park.

Inside the park, frozen, speckling boughs reached out heavenward, a cluttered show of stripped, gnarled, outstretched, earnest hands beckoning from Van Gogh's olive groves like the tortured *shtetlers* of Calais huddling in the cold, while the intense white pool reflected at the base of each lamppost made everything seem unsullied, wholesome, and ceremonial, as though the streetlamps had filed up one by one to clear a landing spot for the lost Magi who alight on Christmas Eve.

How serene and silent the snow—*candid* snow, I thought, thinking back to Pokorny's reconstruction of the Indo-European root of the word: **kand*—to shine, to kindle, to glow, to flare, from which we get incense and incandescent. There was more candor in snow than in me. Let me light a candle here and think of Clara and of that moment in church, ages ago, when we put in a dollar each and lit candles for God knows whom.

I undid her knot and rewrapped my scarf around my neck, crossing both ends of the scarf snugly under my coat, the way I'd always done it. It wasn't cold. I began to wonder whether the snow would stick and hold out till tomorrow. It never did these days. Slowly, as I made my way through the park, I found a bench and came up with a crazy notion. I must sit here. With my glove, I brushed off the snow and finally sat down, extending both legs in front of me like someone taking the sun on an early afternoon after a hearty midday meal.

I liked it here, and I loved the way both avenues and their adjoining streets seemed to blend in this one spot and, by disappearing in the snow, suddenly revealed that the Upper West Side had undercover harmonies and undisclosed squares that spring on you like stalls in movable market-places, new squares that come out with the snow and vanish no sooner than it melts. I could spend the night here and hope the snow stayed all night and all day tomorrow, so that I could return tomorrow night as well and find it lingering still, sit here on this very bench again, as if I had found a ritual and a hub all my own, and wait for the luster of the moment to wash over me again, even if I knew that the luminous patina I was projecting on Straus Park was weather-induced, and alcohol-induced, and love- and sex-induced, an accident and nothing more perhaps, like sitting on this and not another bench, or finding so much beauty because I couldn't find a cab, or ending up here instead of on Riverside, or biting into a peppercorn instead of crème fraîche, standing, not in the library, where I might have met Beryl first and lived through an entirely different, perhaps better evening, but behind a Christmas tree—suddenly all these incidentals were filled with clarity, radiance, and harmony, hence joy—joy, like snow, that I knew would never last, joy of small miracles when they touch our lives, joy like light on an altar. I knew I would revisit this spot tomorrow night.

All this in one little word that went far back to a language no one had probably ever spoken: *kand—. The candor of women.

Yet I knew nothing about her. I knew her first name, could not spell her last, and I'd seen her kiss a man and then a woman. Who was she? What did she do? What was she like? What did others think of her? What did she think of herself, of me? What did she do when she was alone and no one was looking?

Perhaps all I wanted was to sit and think, and think of nothing, sink into myself, dream, find all things beautiful, and, as I'd never allowed myself to do during the entire evening, to long for her, the way we long for someone we know we don't stand a chance of meeting again, or of meeting on the exact same terms, but are all the same determined to long for, because longing makes us who we are, makes us better than who we are, because longing fills the heart.

Fills the heart.

The way absence and sorrow and mourning fill the heart.

I didn't know what all this meant, nor did I trust myself with this, but as I mused over these stray thoughts, I didn't move, as though something timeless and solemn was taking place, not only in the park itself as I sat there on a cold bench, but in me as well for having entered this deserted, solitary spot called Straus Park, where people like me come to be one with themselves and with everything around them. With the city, the night, and the park, and the loud neon sign hanging over the pharmacy across the park and over the fried-chicken restaurant to the right. The way she stubbed her cigarette and then gently pushed it off the ledge with her shoe, the haunting image of her crimson shirt with its buttons so visibly undone past the sternum that one could guess, and was meant to guess, the shape of her breasts as she spoke to me and tweaked me gently when I'd spoken of love in quags and trenches, only to lure me back into the selfsame quags and trenches and remind me that, with all her confiding airs, she was, in case I forgot, very much the off-limits party girl who just happened to place her elbow on your shoulder when she spoke to you and let you think you and she were one and the same, but not the same, but yet the same and never the same.

I wanted to feel sorry for myself, wanted to feel sorry for always wanting, wanting, wanting, and never knowing what to do or where to go beyond wanting. I wished to light a candle in Straus Park, as one does in church when one isn't sure whether one's praying to ask for something or to give thanks for having gotten it, or just for knowing it exists, for seeing it at such close quarters for the short time it is given us to see that the simple wish to hold on to the memory of its passage in our lives bears all the features, not of longing, or of hope, or even love, but of worship.

Tonight she was the face I put on my life and how I live it. Tonight she was my eyes to the world looking back at me.

Tonight I had come so close—one more glance and I'll kiss you, Clara, as you kissed Beryl, your tongue in her mouth, which is why I kissed Beryl, my tongue, her tongue, your tongue, everyone's tongue.

If I had my way, I would plant this imaginary votive taper right here and dig it into the snow as Clara had dug her glass in on the terrace, and

I'd let it stand there. And I would light not just one but many such tapers, and stand each one along the rim of the dried flower bed girding the statue of Memory, and I would cover the statue itself, from head to toe, with slim tapers, as they do with Madonnas and saints in tiny street altars in the villages of Spain, Italy, and Greece, till they all glimmered around Straus Park like will-o'-the-wisps on those damp and marshy cemetery grounds where the souls of the dead rise up at night and wander about like glowworms clustering together to stay warm until daybreak, because the dead are good to one another.

I would sit here and never budge. I would freeze for her. Because tonight she was the face that I put on my life and how I hadn't learned to live it.

·

Perhaps it was the cold that finally brought tears to my eyes; perhaps I'd had too much to drink to know the difference. But as I stared at one of the streetlights nearest me, I began to see double, and the lamppost, from seeming to lean, began to sway, as if it were trying to dislodge itself and would eventually drag itself toward me, shuffling like a beggar on misbegotten limbs, doing what could only seem an imitation moonwalk. He stood there, leaned to and fro, as if to make sure it was indeed me he had spotted, then withdrew and shuffled back and became a streetlamp again. Who was he? And what was he doing on this senseless night? What was I doing out in the cold? Was he another me trundling about here, saying he was taking over, seeing how I'd messed things up for us? Or was he an unfinished me, and how many of these were there who hadn't seen the light of day yet and might never see it, and how many ached to come back from the past if only to give me garbled solace and distempered advice, not realizing that the crib notes we sneak through time are written in invisible ink, all of these selves thronging around me like a penned-up legion from the underworld thirsting to taste what was so effortlessly and perhaps undeservedly given to me and only me: lifeblood.

Perhaps I'd light candles around Straus Park for them as well, as ritual stand-ins for what I couldn't see within me and wished to behold as candles outside of me.

Then I saw it and touched the speckling twig hanging just above my head. It was crystallized. I tried to pull at it, but it was impossible to break

off. What would happen if I pulled harder? The twig might tear somewhat, and I'd probably cut myself. I pictured the blood welling up on my
finger and spilling on the snow. I leaned my head all the way back and
thought of what my father would say: *This isn't new. You've been like this
for years. And there's no one can help you. Life in my blood, soul of my life.*

What would Clara say if she'd seen the state of my bleeding finger? I
pictured her coming up to me in her maroon shoes and standing right
before me in the snow.

What is it with you? Let me take a look at this.

It's nothing.

But you're bleeding.

Yes, I know. Soldier in the trenches, you know.

Feeling sorry for yourself?

I did not answer. But, yes, feeling sorry for myself. Hating myself.

She rips off a swatch of cloth from her red blouse and swaddles it
around my finger, then around my wrist. I am thinking of the Princesse
de Clèves wrapping a yellow ribbon around a wooden cane that belonged
to the man she loves. That swatch around my stick, my flesh, my Guido,
my everything on your hem, on your hand, on your wrist, your wrist, your
wrist, your sweet, stained, blessed, God-given wrist. Now look what
you did—she smiles—I'm trying to concentrate. You could get a serious
infection.

And if I did?

Let me focus here—as she tends to my wound.

Then, when she's done being my nurse: So why did you do it? she
asks.

Because of everything I wanted and never had.

Because of everything you wanted and never had. You'll catch your death
of cold sitting here.

So? To sit out this cold night and in the morning be found frozen
blue, think I'd mind if it's for you?

For me or for you?

I shrugged my shoulders. I didn't know the answer. Both answers were
right.

Amphibalence, she says.

Amphibalence, I say.

And it hits me that more was being said in this short conversation between our shadow selves in this lonely park than anything we'd spoken all night. A lovers' colloquy, as in Verlaine's poem, where both our shadows touch, the rest just waits, and waits, and waits. This wasn't new. I'd been doing this for years.

•

"Something wrong?" It was a uniformed policeman who had just shut the door of his car and was crossing the park toward me. He looked like the only other being left on this planet.

I shook my head and pretended to look elsewhere. Had I been speaking to myself all this time?

"Are you all right?"

"Yes, Officer. I was just trying to collect my thoughts."

Collect my thoughts—people get arrested for speaking like this.

"Not thinking of doing anything stupid, are you?"

Again I shook my head, smiling. Second time tonight.

"Been drinking?"

"Too much. Way too much."

"Merry Christmas."

"And to you too, Officer—?"

"Rahoon."

"Rahoon, as in 'She weeps over Rahoon'?"

"Don't know that song."

"Not a song—poem. Irish."

"You don't say!"

I was about to say *youbetya* but figured, better not.

"So what you got, woman trouble?" He crossed his arms. I could see the edges of his bulletproof vest bulge under his tight blue jacket.

"Nope. Not woman trouble. It's just the old man's gone. Was just thinking about him tonight, soon it will be exactly a year ago." And suddenly I remembered his very own words, *Soon I won't even know I ever lived*—and if my shadow bumps into yours on a busy sidewalk, my heart won't jump as it did that night when you peeked into my room. So much love and all of it a waste, so many books and verses stored, and all of it gone. I look at this hand, and I know, soon I'll no longer see it, for it's no longer quite mine, the way my eyes are not quite mine, I'm not even here, my feet have already gone before me and found a cozier spot at God

knows what time zone beyond Lethe and Phlegethon. I won't even
remember Lethe or Phlegethon, or the mutinous Shannon waves, or
Phaedo, or brave Aristides and those long speeches by Thucydides we
read together. All these immortal words, gone; Byzantium, gone. *Pff!* Part
of me is no longer mine, the way life was never really mine, the way my
clothes and my shoes and the smell on my body were never really mine,
the way even "mine" isn't mine any longer, my thoughts, my hair, my
everything have drifted from me, and love too is no longer mine, just
borrowed, like an umbrella from a tattered old coatrack—you and me,
umbrellas on a coatrack, though you're closer to me now than the blood
in my neck, the breath of my life. I look at myself in the mirror and all
I'm doing is saying goodbye to both my face and yours. I'm leaving you
piecemeal, my love, and I don't want you to grieve, I want to take this
picture of you now to wherever they're forcing me to go now and hope
that once I've shut my eyes this will be the last thing to go, for the last
thing you see they say is the one you take forever, if "take" means
anything beyond Lethe and Phlegethon.

"Do you know Lethe and Phlegethon, Officer?"

"Who're they?"

"No matter." The worst part of dying is knowing you'll forget you ever
lived and ever loved. You live seventy or so years, and you die forever.
Why can't it be the other way? To be dead for seventy years—and throw
in another seventy for good measure—but to live forever. What purpose
does dying serve, anyway? I don't care who says no human could endure
living more than a lifetime. Ask the dead and see what answer you get—
ask the dead what they wouldn't give to be here and catch tonight's
snow, or have a week of starlit nights like these, or fall for the world's
most beautiful woman. Ask the dead.

" 'Just promise me this,' he would say, 'that when the time comes,
you'll help me—but only if I ask, not before, and so long as I can hold
out, but not sooner.' "

"And did he ask?"

Was the lawman being cunning with me?

"He never asked."

"They never do when the time comes. So what you so broken up for?"

"He went to sleep for a few hours and I walked about the neighborhood like a lover waiting for a girlfriend to clear every last thing she

owns from his home, hoping she'll change her mind, until I passed by a park and I knew, by the hiss of the wind through the trees in the cold, that he'd arrived safely. I was to read Plutarch to him. I let it happen."

"Intentionally?"

"I'll never know."

Tell me I'm not cruel, Officer Rahoon. Tell me that he knew, Officer Rahoon.

"Just look at this moon."

"Good night, moon," I said.

"Good night, moon," he repeated, to humor me, shaking his head, meaning, *You people!*

A beggar woman had crossed the street and was coming toward us. The park was probably her bedroom. Her bathroom. Her kitchen. Her parlor. "Mister, some bread."

I put my hand in my pocket.

"Are you out of your mind!?" said the policeman. Then turning to the beggar, "Beat it, *mamacita.*"

"Don't be cross with her. It's Christmas."

"She puts her grubby fingers on you—and see how Christmasy you feel."

The beggar woman who had spotted a soft heart kept her gaze on me, begging silently.

Just when I was about to leave Straus Park, I took out a five-dollar bill and snuck it into the hand of the beggar woman. *Por mi padre.*

"Seriously?"

"Let it rest, Officer," I said. You never know, I wanted to say. In another age, the old hag would have asked me to sit on one of these benches, brought a bucket to wash my feet, spotted something, and I'd be home. *Y por Clara también.* I should have added.

Rahoon and his car were gone, everything was quiet again.

As I crossed what must have been the street and not just the sidewalk, I looked back at the park, knowing now that I'd give anything to start the evening all over again exactly as it had turned out—do with time what Romans did when they gorged themselves on food—regurgitate time, wind the clock back to seven o'clock, and start right here in Straus Park again. It is snowing. I am still very early for the party. I'll stop and have tea in this little coffeehouse. Then I'll head to the building, pretend I am not sure that this is the correct address, shake my umbrella, watch the burly Russian with the stentorian voice open the door for me, and walk into the elevator, whose Gothic doorway doesn't give a hint of where things are headed tonight. I wanted to start the evening all over again, and many more times again, because I did not want it to end, because, even if something wistful and unfinished hung over the entire night, I would take it, wistful and unfinished night that it was, and consider myself twice blessed.

Tomorrow night I would come and relight each candle all over again, one by one, and, looking around me, almost feel how every corner of the park still echoed with Clara's presence, with me, my life, and how I live it, and with my father, who, unbeknownst to me, had been trailing me from the very start this evening and to whom I was holding on as to a shadow that is any moment about to dissolve but then comes back to take a last look, as if he'd forgotten his keys, then back again because he'd forgotten his glasses, and once again because he'd forgotten to check the gas, and would be coming back many more times again like the poor, restless, tormented man who'd known scant love in his life, as I would be coming back to this spot, fearing I'd left something behind, knowing that what we leave behind is a shadow self, but that this shadow self is the truest and most enduring of all our selves.

Looking back one last time, I thought to myself how much I'd always liked this little park, and how easy it would be to come back tomorrow and sit here awhile, and in the whiteness of the hour preceding sunup, contemplate once more, as ever again, the imperishable silence of the stars.

SECOND NIGHT

I spotted her right away. She was standing outside the movie theater. A crowd was gathered around the box office, and the line of ticket holders extended halfway down the block. From the island in the middle of Broadway, I dove across even before the light changed. When I looked at the crowd again, she was gone. I was almost certain it was Clara.

I had spent the whole day thinking of her, and already twice—at lunch, and later at Starbucks—could have sworn I'd seen her drift in and out of my field of vision, as though wishful thoughts had raced ahead of me and pasted her features on anyone bearing a resemblance. Now running into her a third time today would ruin the spontaneity and allow me to say things I'd had plenty of time to rehearse hours earlier—anything from the initial shock and bliss of bumping into her to the pretense that I was having a hard time placing her—*Oh yes, last night, Hans's party, of course*—to a desperate, overzealous desire to restore that initial shock and resist all camouflage by blurting out something seemingly unstudied: *I've been thinking of you all day, all day, Clara.*

All day I'd been doing just that. Looking for one store that was open on Christmas Day and finding all of them closed, lunching with Olaf, who badmouthed his wife in one unending screed, in the packed greasy spoon because everything else was closed, trying to shop for Christmas presents on Christmas Day, the whole day punctuated by hazy premonitions that last night might happen all over again. I had spent the entire day totally spellbound by our parting in the snow, wearing, but not wearing, my coat, saying goodbye with a handshake after she'd walked me to the bus stop and rushed back to her building, handing the doorman the umbrella she had borrowed, not turning, but then turning back at the last moment, every last part of me clinging to the memory of her elbow resting on my shoulder at the party, her burgundy suede shoes kicking off the snow, the cigarette, the ex-boyfriend, the Bloody Mary she had scarcely touched and later abandoned on the balcony while I'd stared at her open blouse, wondering all night why in someone so tanned was the base of her breasts so fair. I've been thinking of you all day, all day.

Would I have the courage to say this?

I caught myself making a wish: I would tell her I'd been thinking of her all day provided she materialized on Broadway and Ninety-fifth tonight. Humbled, hopeful, happy, I'd tell her however it came out.

Or this: I was just thinking of you—with a waggish smile in my voice, almost as though I wasn't sure I was telling the truth. She'd know how to read this.

For good measure, I already assumed a flustered, unfocused air allegedly caused by my bold dash across Broadway—which would also justify my failure to notice her any sooner.

I was hoping it would be you—but then I said it couldn't be—yet here you are.

While I was trying out these phrases like someone matching neckties to a shirt, I made every effort not to look in the direction of the crowd. I didn't want her to know that I had already spotted her and was simply pretending. I wanted to think she'd recognize me first and be the first to seek the other out.

But there was another reason for not looking in her direction. I didn't want to dispel the illusion or undo the thrill of running into her. I wanted to hold on to that illusion and, like a well-behaved Orpheus determined to keep his end of the bargain, I wanted to think that she'd already seen me and was just now making her way toward me, provided I didn't look back. I wanted to cup my hands around this tiny, furtive, shameful hope as if all I had to do then was look away, keep looking away, and so long as I kept up with the pretense, she'd come behind me, place both palms on my eyes, and say, *Guess who?* The more I resisted turning in her direction, the more I could feel her breath graze the back of my neck, closer and closer, the way she had let her lips almost touch my ears at the party each time she'd whisper to me. There was something so enthralling about waiting and hoping, without so much as giving a hint I knew I was being watched, that I even caught myself trying not to

hope so much—she couldn't possibly be there tonight, what was I thinking!—realizing all along that this sobering strain of counterhope was not
just my way of seeing that life seldom grants us what it knows we want,
but also my own twisted way of courting its goodwill by pretending to
forget it likes nothing better than to grant us our wish once we've all but
given up and embraced despair.

Hope and counterhope. First you think you've spotted her, then you
can't quite bring yourself to believe it, and in between both options
you're instantly rummaging for things to say, for an attitude to strike—
hide the joy—show the joy—show you're hiding the joy—show you're
showing every last strain of joy. Then you spot someone who simply
looks like her. The illusion is shattered. It's someone else.

But then, because the things you thought you'd say thrilled you and
seemed to blanket the cold evening around you, you suddenly catch
yourself wanting to undo the thrill yourself rather than have others do it
for you. Perhaps, you begin to think, it's just as well this way; such
encounters never happen, it's pointless to think they might, and besides,
the quiet evening at the movies you'd been looking forward to all day
was finally being given to you, and just as you'd planned. You and the
movies are going to sit and spend hours together, though, because of a
face half perceived in the crowd, perhaps something might indeed happen between you and the film, as though the film could in its own strange
way bring to life the very things you've been asking by granting them on-
screen instead.

Later, after seeing the film, I'd probably find the lingering mirage of
her presence around the box-office window. The mirage had already
begun to cast its radiance around the whole evening, and I knew that if
the illusion of having seen her was something I could take with me to
the movies and snuggle up with for a few hours, the movie in return
would allow me, once I stepped out onto the sidewalk, to take home with
me the sense that the thing that happens between men and women in
films had indeed happened to me tonight.

Perhaps this last illusion was nothing more than a desperate attempt
to buoy my spirits before giving up on the day and locking myself in the
theater for five hours. By midnight, I thought, it would be tomorrow
already—and this strange Christmas Day that had started in a fairy-tale
greenhouse and couldn't have felt more aimless afterward was finally

being let go of, like an unmoored punt starting to drift with the rising tide of the day-to-day.

After the movies, I'd take a bus, or walk home, or take a cab farther downtown, or stop somewhere along the way, if for no other reason than to see faces before calling it a night.

To see faces as opposed to not seeing any at all. Faces. People. Midnight people, *otherpeoples* who'll brave a storm to buy cigarettes, walk a dog, grab a bite, get the paper, or, like me, see faces.

I began to think of places I'd wander to after seeing the film. A bar-and-grill. Or Thai Soup.

I had good memories of Thai Soup.

Trench soup she'd have called it, with *beef pandangst*. How I missed her way of taking something, then turning it upon itself, and then turning it back to how it was before, knowing it would never be the same afterward.

Then I saw her.

I wanted to sound surprised—but not totally thrown off—as if I'd expected something of the sort but had let the matter slip and never given it another thought.

Perhaps I would find a way to tweak the conditions of my initial wish now that it had been granted and no longer feel bound to tell her how I'd been thinking of her *all day, all day.*

"Clara?" I asked, exaggerating my surprise, as people do when they rush to greet you first, for fear of being caught trying to avoid you.

"There you are. Finally!" she shouted. "I tried calling you a million times, but you're never ever home"—it almost sounded like a lover's reproach—"I thought you had changed your mind and weren't going to come."

To show she wasn't exaggerating, she displayed two tickets clasped tightly in between flushed knuckles. "I've been waiting and waiting and waiting. And. It. Is. Freezing," she said, as if all this was my fault. "Here, feel." She brought her palm to my cheek to prove how cold. "I've called you so many times I know your number by heart. Here—" She turned her cell phone toward me and began to scroll down row after row after row of countless friends. It took a few moments to recognize the numerals on the colored screen. Under the phone number I saw something else that looked uncannily familiar: my name—last name first, first name last. Was I officially on her A-list? "Why don't you answer your *télyfön?*" I didn't know why I didn't answer my *télyfön.*

In her place I would never have entered someone's name that way. Putting a totally new name on my permanent list would have nipped every hint of uncertainty, chilled the flustered hesitation with which we palpate a stranger's name before admitting it into the ledger of our lives; I would have placed it in abeyance, in limbo—until it had "proven" itself. The inadvertent misspelling on a paper napkin, the name hastily plunked down in the cold, the intentional absence of a surname to show we're not so sure we'll call—all these are not just markers of inner diffidence and hesitation along the twisted path to others, they are also loopholes in every exaltation, the shallow wetlands we leave behind for speedy backtracking. I would never have listed her under Brunschvicg. Nor would I have entered her name or her number in my cell phone's memory. I'd have made every effort to unremember her number if I caught myself already knowing it by heart.

It hit me that she said exactly what I'd have said under the circumstances. But I would have said it for exactly the opposite reason. I would have been overly demonstrative, as she was, to show how lightly I took these matters. Was hers the voice of diffidence cloaking itself behind hyperbolic complaints about the weather, about my phone, about me— or was she making no secret of something most people are reluctant to reveal too soon? Was it too soon?

Was she thinking like me?

Or was she telling a man what he'd give anything to hear a woman say to him on their first night out?

Was this our first night out?

I wondered if she'd rehearsed saying any of it.

I would have.

Then I thought: Better yet if she'd rehearsed it. It meant she'd cared to rehearse it.

Then I remembered I had never given her my number. Nor was my number listed.

She must have read what was going on in my mind. "You'll never guess who gave me your *télyfön*."

"Who?"

"I told you, you'll never guess. I brought us this," she said, and produced a white paper bag containing food and things to drink.

"I'm—overwhelmed."

Pause.

"He's overwhelmed." She puckered her lips and looked away, as though to signal stifled exasperation at some strange mannerism in my speech. I instantly recognized the mock chiding of last night's banter on the veranda. I missed it, welcomed it back, had been away from it too long. "A million times," she repeated, seemingly speaking to herself.

There was, in her word, both the open-faced boldness of those who know how to make difficult admissions to people they scarcely know, and the specter of irony, which comes to their rescue when they find the difficult admission not difficult at all.

Anyone else would have read the most reassuring signals in this.

I couldn't have been more pleased to find her standing there, waiting for me, with two tickets in hand and snacks to boot, in an attitude suggesting that she might have planned this all the way back to the moment in church when I'd brought up the Eric Rohmer festival. I had an image of her waking up in the morning and, instead of thinking of Inky, already making plans to meet me in the evening. First she would have tried to obtain my number. Then, having found it, she would have called. Late morning. Early afternoon. Eventually she would have had to leave a message. But no one had left a message.

"People on ice check their voice mail, I guess," she said, remembering my words.

"And those lying low?"

"People lying low still make an effort to call. I stopped calling until a few minutes ago."

"How did you know I was going to be here?"

What I meant to ask was how did she know I was going to come alone tonight. "What if I hadn't come?"

"I would have gone in. Besides," she added, as though the thought had never occurred to her before, "we had a date."

Did she know I knew we didn't have a date, and that if I suddenly pretended to remember that we had one it was less to let her save face than to put off deciding what sort of attitude to strike myself?

Or was this simply her way of spelling out my unspoken reason for bringing up the Rohmer festival last night? Had we perhaps firmed up something that remained undefined in my mind simply because I couldn't bring myself to believe it could have been so easily arranged?

"Clara, I'm so glad you're here."

"You're glad! Imagine how stupid I'd feel holding these two tickets in the cold. Do I go in, do I keep waiting, what if he doesn't show up, do I give away the tickets, keep one, give the other to some man who's going to think he's entitled to speak to me through both films if I last that long? I just hope they're good films," she added, as if she hadn't quite believed they might be until she'd seen the line and managed to get two tickets minutes before the show sold out. Or was this her way of paying me a compliment, because, left to her, she would never have stepped out into the cold for a Rohmer film unless she trusted the man who loved these films.

We barely had time to say anything more when she proceeded to whisper curses at the management, launching into a mock tirade against the very notion of a 7:10 show. Seven-ten was too early. Seven-ten was for those who needed to go to bed before midnight. Seven-ten was dolt time. "What did I do on Christmas Day in the year of our Lord such-and-such? I went to the movies at seven-ten."

"I too ended up going to the movies that day."

"You don't say."

There it was again. Mock-rebuke—like someone suddenly slipping an arm under yours as you're walking together. It was her way of saying that her hunch had paid off. I would remember this. *On Christmas Day in the year of our Lord such-and-such*—how I liked that beginning. It went with the snow outside the theater, with the light haze around traffic lights down Broadway, with everyone shivering in line, eagerly awaiting *My Night at Maud's*.

"I didn't have a chance to eat anything. I suppose you haven't, either," she continued as we stood in line, muttering muffled curses at the weather with spirited feigned anger. I told her about Thai Soup and their *garlique*-infested prawn broth. It made her laugh. Perhaps she enjoyed how I'd used her word from last night. Her laugh was high-pitched, which drew the attention of one of the ushers, who scowled at us. "Just look at that face," she whispered, indicating his sharp crew cut and broad shoulders. "And his teeth. People with faces like his invent times like seven-ten." I laughed. "Quiet, he's seen us," she hissed, as though playing cat and mouse, slipping her white paper bag under her coat. The burly usher with the bouncer's gait and the clip-on tie walked up to us. "Youse waiting for the seven-ten show?" he asked. "Affirmatov. We is," she replied, staring at his face and handing him our tickets. He took them in one palm and, rather than tear them in two, dropped into her hand what looked like two crushed spitballs.

"What's this?" she said, holding the mangled stubs in an open palm. The man did not answer. "He chewed them with his hands," she added as we took our seats. Once again she revealed the white paper bag. "I got coffee." "Did you get one for me too?" I asked, pretending I hadn't heard the first time. "No, I only do things for me," she snapped as she handed me mine, with a look that said, *Needs constant reassurance*. I watched her remove the plastic cover, add the sugar, stir it, and, after placing the cover back on the cup, lift the tab. "I like coffee."

It sounded like a bashful admission.

I liked coffee too, I said. It was good coffee. I liked coffee in movie theaters. I also liked where we were seated. This is just perfect, I caught myself saying.

"Do you think I was mean to him?"

"Who?"

"The bouncer. Gave me the dirtiest look since last he boozed Stolies in Bratislavovich. He mad."

We waited for the theater to grow dark. Another surprise. She dug deeper in the same paper bag and produced two halves of a large sandwich. "*Very très goormay*," she whispered, taking an indirect swipe at Manhattan's love affair with the finer things of the palate. The sudden smell of garlic cheese and prosciutto was overpowering. Once again she burst out laughing. Someone asked us to be quiet.

Then we sank deeper into our seats. "This isn't going to be boring, is it?" she said as the credits began to roll.

"Might be deadly."

"Good. Just wanted to make sure we're in this together."

An abrupt "Shush" shot out from behind us again.

"Shush yourself!"

Then suddenly we were in the black-and-white universe I'd been longing for all day. The town of Clermont-Ferrand around Christmas, the man studying Pascal where Pascal was born, the drive down the crowded narrow streets of a provincial French town lightly decorated with Christmas lights. The blond girl. The dark girl. The church. The café. Would Clara really like this?

I didn't dare look in her direction. Did people go together to the movies to see movies or to be together, or because they liked each other and this is what one did sometimes when one liked someone—one went to the movies with her, as if it was the most natural thing in the world. Did one switch from watching the movie to being together, and at what point did one stop switching from one to the other? Why was I even asking all this? Did asking automatically put me in the camp of those who wonder about being natural and who suspect others do not nurse the same doubts about themselves, or did others secretly hope that everyone was as diffident as they were? Was she thinking about being natural? Or was she just watching the movie?

She was staring intently at the screen, as though resolved to ignore me now. Then, without warning, she ribbed me with her elbow, all the while sucking in her cheeks and looking straight before her, chewing words that were sure to be nasty. I had seen her do it with Rollo on the terrace in a moment of suppressed anger. Why had she nudged me that way?

Then I got it. Clara was not upset at all. She was struggling not to burst out laughing, and by ribbing me as she was doing a second time now, she was making sure I was aware of her struggle and, better yet, passing it on to me.

"What possessed me to ask for *garly* cheese—what was I thinking?"

I was about to throw in a possible guess when she ribbed me yet again, waving me away with her hand, as though anything I might breathe was sure to make her explode. Tears of suppressed laughter were welling up in her eyes—which finally gave me a case of the giggles as well. "Want more *garly?*" she began. It was my turn to brush her away.

It took me a few seconds to note that she had spun out a new version of a word I thought was intimate kitchenspeak between us. Can't get too cozy with her.

The film. Blond girl. Dark girl. Blond girl is virtuous, dark girl a temptress. Catholic man refuses to be snared. Snowbound on Christmas Eve, the man is forced to spend the night in dark girl's apartment, in her bedroom, finally in her bed. Nothing happens, but toward dawn, when the flesh is weak and he is just about to make a move, she jumps out of bed. "I prefer men who know what they want." That same morning, outside a café, man runs into blond girl.

At intermission, Clara suddenly got up and said she had to make a phone call.

·

Left alone, I looked around in the dimly lit darkness of the movie theater, watching people arrive, mostly in pairs. A group of four men and a woman filed in, each drinking from a huge cup, unable to decide where to sit, until one of them pointed to the back and whispered, "How about there?" A couple stood up to let them squeeze through. One of the five turned to the other and said, "Say thank you." "Thank you," played along the other. The atmosphere was charged with subdued excitement. People had come from all around the city for this film and, despite their differences, knew they shared something, though it was impossible to tell exactly what. It might have been their love for Eric Rohmer's films. Or their love of France, or of the idea of France, or of those confused, intimate, random moments in our lives that Rohmer had borrowed for an hour or so; he'd drawn them out, scaled down their roughness, removed all accidentals, given them a rhythm, a cadence, a wisdom even, and then projected them onto a screen and promised to return them to us after the show, though slightly altered, so that we'd have our lives back, but seen from the other side—not as they were, but as we'd always imagined they should be, the idea of our lives.

I tried to imagine these five friends huddled in a corner at the Starbucks next door as they waited for the first film to end and then rushing to catch the last show. Here they were now. One of them produced a bag of doughnuts, which he had smuggled into the theater under his coat and was now passing around. Within a minute or so, another girl holding a giant container of popcorn wandered into the theater, looked momentarily lost, then spotted her group and walked up the stairs toward them. "I also got these," she said, producing two large yellow boxes of M&Ms.

I liked being lost in this crowd, liked these people who had escaped the swarming, cold, floodlit city to this quiet oasis on the Upper West Side where each hoped to catch a glimpse of an imaginary, inner France. I liked knowing that Clara was out in the hallway somewhere and would be coming back—liked thinking that the world could be shut out for a few hours and, as soon as she was back from wherever she had gone to make her phone call, sitting close together like passengers in a crowded ferry boat, we would once again drift into this strange, beguiling fantasy world of Rohmer's invention that might be more in us than in the films themselves. I looked around at the groups and couples in the theater: some were clearly happier than others—happier than I, than people who were not lovers, though it was still good to be among them. I liked the idea that dropping Rohmer's name in the wee hours of the morning last night had made her want to see this film with me.

This was not how I had imagined my evening. Now I was thrilled that this was the course it had taken, that someone had unexpectedly turned up, and that this someone should be Clara, Clara with whom laughter was easier than with anyone else, Clara who knew how to make things happen long before I was aware of wanting them, and who, with two theater tickets purchased before my arrival, had given me the best Christmas present I'd received since childhood—a present that could turn into air, for Clara could have gone to phone another man at this very moment and, being impulsive, could just as easily come back to pick up her things and leave me stranded in my seat. *Sorry, have to run, enjoyed the film— great seeing you.*

But as I sat there, worrying about this, I knew that worrying was also my way of paying token tribute to unfounded fears before admitting that tonight I was indeed happy. Waiting for her made me happy. Coddling the thought she'd even spurn my way of waiting for her made me happy. Rehearsing her abrupt goodbye as soon as we'd leave the movie theater in two hours made me happy. And what made me happier yet wasn't just that we were together again after scarcely spending the day apart, but that her presence made me like the way the day had turned out, made me like my life and the way I lived it. She was the face of my life and how I lived it, my eyes to the world staring back at me. The people in the theater, the people I had known, the books read, lunch with Olaf, who bad-mouths his wife, the places I'd lived in, my life on ice, and all the things I still wanted, all had suddenly turned a dearer and more vulnerable face under her spell—for this was a spell, and struck like a spell, and, like all spells, ushered in new colors, new people, new scents, new habits, un-veiling new meanings, new patterns, new laughter, a new cadence to things—even if, all along, a small unseen, untapped part of me was per-fectly willing to suspect, as though for good measure, that I could just as easily have preferred the spell more than the person who cast it, the coded sparring between us more than the person I was sparring with, the me-because-of-Clara more than Clara herself.

Clara had left her coat on her seat. I let my hand rest on her coat, stared at its lining, touched the inner lining. Clara. It was also my way of remembering I was not alone, that she would very shortly come back and take up her seat again and tell me—or perhaps not—why she had taken so long. Sometimes just placing my coat next to my seat when I am alone in a movie theater is itself a way of conjuring a presence in the dark, of imagining that someone has stepped out for a second and will any moment come back—which is what happens in the dead of night, when those who have left our lives suddenly lie next to us no sooner than we've whispered their name into our pillow. Clara, I thought, and there she'd be, taking the seat next to mine.

And as I listened to the violin sonata by Beethoven, which always appears in this theater as soon as the intermission lights come on, I remembered that no more than three winters ago I had done the very same with someone else's coat while she had gone to buy sodas at the concession stand. I'd pretended we had broken up or that she had never even existed, only to be surprised when she returned and pushed down the seat next to mine. Afterward, we had left the movie theater and had bought the Sunday paper and ambled home in the snow, speaking of *Maud* and of *Chloé*, improvising dinner somewhere after visiting a bookstore. It seemed so long ago. And I thought back to a much younger *I* who had come to this very theater alone one Saturday night and, while looking for a seat without disturbing too many people, had overheard a man ask a woman, "Do you like Beethoven?" The woman, who had let her coat hang on the backrest of her seat, slouched over it and, turning to him, had replied something like "Yes, very much, but this sonata I hate." They were, even I could tell, on their first date.

That night I'd hurled a hopeful and mystified glance to the future, asking who would the woman be in my life who'd sit next to me and listen to this piece by Beethoven and say, *Yes, but this sonata I hate.* They knew so little about each other that the man needed to ask whether she liked Beethoven. It had never occurred to me until now that all he was trying to do was make conversation.

Yes, but this sonata I hate, I had repeated to myself, as though the mildly miffed tone of her words held a key that might unlock a passageway to where I wished my life to go one day—words that seemed fraught with intimations that were as stirring and reckless as a compliment I had never heard before and desperately wished to have repeated. *Yes, but this sonata I hate* meant, *I can say anything to you. It's good to be together on this cold night. Move closer and we'll touch elbows.* Now, reexamining her unguarded response years later, I realized that I knew no more about the shoals between men and women than I did then; nor did I even know what my mystified wish had been that night when I sat alone thinking ahead of myself, hoping to trace the pattern my life might take, and never for a moment realizing that the questions I had asked of life then would come bobbing back to me years later in the same bottle, unanswered.

All those years, and all I'm still trying to do is make conversation!

All those years, and all I want to show is that I'm not scared of silence, of women.

I thought of the lovers again. I had caught sight of them once more outside the theater as everyone waited for the rain to stop. Then the years went by. Then someone came along, and perhaps on our first date I too had asked what she thought of Beethoven and, by so doing, put a check mark next to the question that signaled entrance to the rose garden. We too had waited for the rain to subside. Then I went alone to the movie theater. Then with others. Then alone. Then with others again.

Had I seen more films alone or with others? And which had I liked more? I wondered.

Would Clara say *alone* was better, but then, just when I was about to agree with her, turn around and say that, in the dark, she still needed *otherpeoples*, an elbow to rub against?

The road once traveled seemed filled with potholes now.

Perhaps I would tell her all this.

The pleasure of peeling back the years and laying myself bare before her aroused me. The pleasure of telling her anything about me aroused me.

To tell her: For a moment I made myself fear that I was only imagining you were with me tonight. Want to know why?

I know why.

Would I tell her I'd thought about her the whole day, or would I suggest something a bit tamer, that our meeting outside the theater seemed lifted from every film I'd seen and presaged the course of many a Rohmer tale? I could tell her I'd walked many blocks in search of open stores, and all I could think of was her, looked for her, stopped somewhere for coffee, almost certain I had spotted her, but, knowing better than to hope, had given each place a cursory glance, then walked away, just as she was calling me a million times? Should I tell her that I'd rehearsed telling her all this?

I remembered the failing late-afternoon sun and how gradually it began to spell loneliness and dejection after I'd lunched with Olaf, its waffling light taking me down with it as I watched the day put an end to its misery—and yet, in the background always that unwieldy hope that the clock would turn back twenty-four hours and take me to exactly where I'd been yesterday evening, before boarding the uptown M5 bus, before buying two bottles of Champagne, before leaving my mother's home on my way to the liquor store . . .

I'd been heading uptown all afternoon. Scoping out her territory, on the fringes of her territory. You always run into the one person you'd give anything to run into, baiting them with desire, your own.

But, then, fearing she might run into me and guess why I'd wandered so far uptown, I decided to head home instead. By the time I left again and arrived at the movie theater, the show was sold out. I should have known. Christmas.

•

When she finally sat down next to me, the lights were already dimming. She wasn't her jovial self any longer. She seemed agitated. "What's wrong?" "Inky's crying," she said. Did she want to leave? No. He always cried. Why had she called him, then? Because he was leaving too many messages on her voice mail. "I shouldn't have called." Someone again shushed us from behind. "Shush yourself!" she snapped.

I thought I liked her irked and groused manner, but this was too much. I began to think of poor Inky, and of his tears over the phone, and of the men who cry for the Claras they love—a man who weeps on the phone must be in the bowels of despair. Had she told him she was with me?

"No, he thinks I'm in Chicago," she whispered.

I looked at her with baffled eyes, not because she had lied, but at the absurdity of the lie. "I'm just not going to answer my phone," she said. This seemed to ease her mind, as though she had suddenly stumbled on the one solution capable of dispelling all her worries. She put her glasses back on, took a sip from her coffee, sat back, and was clearly ready to enjoy the second film. "Why would he keep calling if he thinks you're in Chicago?" I asked.

"Because he knows I'm lying."

She was staring straight in front of her, making it clear she was intentionally not looking in my direction. Then with a huff—

"Because he likes to hear my voice on the outgoing message, okay? Because he likes to leave long messages on my answering machine that I erase no sooner than I hear them and are sheer torture when I'm there with someone and he knows I am, but goes on yapping and yapping away until I lose my patience and pick up. Because he knows I'm fed up. Okay?"

This was rage speaking.

"Because he lingers on the sidewalk and spies on me, and waits for my lights to go on."

"How do you know?"

"He tells me."

"I don't think I want to touch this," I said with marked, overstated irony, meaning I didn't want to risk adding anything that would further upset her, and was now graciously backtracking with a hint of humor to ease our passage into movie mode.

"Don't." She cut me short.

Don't stung me to the quick. She'd spoken this word once last night, and it had had the same chilling effect. It shut me up. It stayed with me for the remainder of the second film, a cold, blunt admonition not to meddle or try to ingratiate myself with the intrusive goodwill of people who pry and wheedle their way into private zones where they aren't invited. Worse yet, she was mixing me up with him.

"He prowls downstairs, and whenever he sees my lights come on, eventually he calls."

•

"I feel for him," I said when we sat after the movie at a bar close to her home. She liked Scotch and french fries. And she liked coming here, occasionally, with friends. They served Scotch in a wineglass here. I liked Scotch and ended up picking at her fries.

"Then *you* feel for him." Silence. "Feel for him all you want. You and everyone else."

Silence again.

"The truth is, I feel for him too," she added a moment later. She thought awhile longer. "No. I don't feel a thing."

We were sitting at a small, old, square wooden table in the back of a bar-restaurant that she said she liked because late on weeknights, especially when the place was empty, they would sometimes let you smoke. She had a wineglass in front of her, both elbows spread on the table, a cigarette burning in the ashtray, and between us, a tiny lighted candle, sitting in a paper bag like a tiny kitten curled in a rolled-down sock. She had pulled the sleeves of her sweater up, and one could make out a shade of down along her bony wrists, which were red from the cold. It was an oversized home-knit sweater made of very thick, brushed wool stitches. I thought of heather, and of large winter shawls, and of flushed naked bodies wrapped in sheepskin. "Let's talk of something else, can we?" She seemed mildly annoyed, bored, vexed.

"Like what?" I asked.

Did she actually believe in choreographed conversation?

"Why not talk about you."

I shook my head to mean, You're joking, right?

She shook her head to mean, *Absolutely not joking.* "Yes, that's it," she said, as she dismissed any possibility of hesitation on my part. "We'll talk about you."

I wondered whether she suddenly perked up and was leaning over the table toward me because she was truly curious about me or because she was enjoying this sudden turn from pity-the-woman-with-the-wrong-ex-boyfriend to hard-nosed cross-examiner.

"There's so little to say."

"Tell!"

"Tell . . ." I repeated her command, trying to make light of it. "Tell what?"

"Well, for one thing, tell why there's so little to say."

I didn't know why there was so little to say. Because there's so little about me I care to talk about before knowing it's quite safe to—and even then . . . ? Because the person I am and the person I wish I were at this very moment in the bar aren't always on speaking terms? Because I feel like a shadow right now and can't fathom why you can't see this? What was she really asking me to say?

"Anything but bland pieties."

"No bland pieties—promise!"

She seemed thrilled by my reply and was eagerly anticipating what I was about to say, like a child who's just been promised a story.

"And?"

"And?" I asked.

"And keep going . . ."

"Depends what you charge."

"A lot. Ask around. *So, why is there so little to say?*"

I wanted to say that I didn't know where to go with her question and that, because its candor made evasion an unworthy option, I was drawing a complete blank—a complete blank that I didn't want to talk about so soon, the complete blank sitting between us, Clara, that is crying to be talked about. A Rosetta stone in the rose garden, that's what I am. Give me a pumice stone, and it'll be my turn to bash every evasion in my mouth. My pumice stone, your pumice stone, I should have brought mine along tonight and dumped it on the table and said, "Ask the pumice stone." Did she want to know what I'd done in the past five years, where I'd been, whom I'd loved or couldn't love, what my dreams were, those at night and those by day, those I wouldn't dare own up to, a penny for my thoughts? Ask the pumice stone.

"And don't give me the *obituary you*. Give me the real you."

Ask the pumice stone, Clara, ask the pumice stone. It knows me better than I do myself.

I raised my eyes, more flustered than ever. It was then that I felt the words almost slip from my mouth. She was looking at me longer than I expected, I returned her gaze and held her eyes awhile, thinking that perhaps she was lost in thought and had absentmindedly let her glance linger on mine. But her silence had interrupted nothing, and she wasn't absent at all. She was just staring.

I averted my eyes, pretending to be absorbed in deep, faraway thoughts that I didn't quite know how to confide. I watched her fingers fold the corners of her square paper napkin around the base of her wineglass. When I looked up, her gaze was still glued on me. I still hadn't said a thing.

I wondered whether this was how she was with everyone—simply stares, doesn't stuff silence with words, looks you straight in the face, and then bores through each of your frail little bulwarks, and, without shift-ing her glance, begins smiling a lukewarm, impish smile that seems almost amused that you've finally figured she's figured you out.

Should I stare back? Or was there no challenge in her gaze, no unspo-ken message to be intercepted or deciphered? Perhaps it was the stare of a woman whose beauty could easily overwhelm you, but then, rather than withdraw after achieving its effect, simply lingered on your face and never let go till it read every good or bad thought it knew it would find and had probably planted there, straining the conversation, promising intimacy before its time, demanding intimacy as one demands surrender, breaking through the lines of casual conversation long before preliminary acts of friendship had been put in place, daring you to admit what she'd known all along: that you were easily flustered in her presence, that she was right, all men are ultimately more uneasy with desire than the women they desire.

For a moment, I thought I caught a mild, questioning nod. Was I imagining things? Or was she about to say something but then thought better of it and retracted it just in time?

Still, someone had to say something. I'd brace myself before taking the bold plunge.

"Do you always stare at men like this?"

I nipped the words just in time. But a moment more under her gaze and I would have broken down and said something more desperate, any-thing to ward off the silence and choke the chaos of words welling up inside me, words that were still totally unknown to me and seemed to skulk in the backdrop like tiny unfledged, unsprung, jittery creatures caught in their larval stage and that, given the opportunity, would spill out of me and reveal more about me than I knew myself—how I felt, what I wanted, what I couldn't even suggest or hint at, opening a door I dreaded but was willing to venture through if only I knew how to shut it afterward. Was I going to say anything simply to say something? Is this what people do? Say something instead of nothing, go with the moment? Or, in an effort to avoid taking chances, was I going to utter something unintended and irrelevant: "Do you always ask people to tell you about themselves?" I nipped this as well.

"What a silly, unrealistic movie," I found myself saying, not sure why I had said it, or to which of the two films I was referring, especially since I knew I liked both films and didn't necessarily consider realism a virtue. I had said it with an air of resigned gravity and preoccupation, attributing the vague dismay in my voice to something awkward and disturbing in the films themselves.

I was simply trying to conceal my inability to come out and say something that didn't bear on the two of us.

She misunderstood me completely. "Unrealistic because no one sleeps together in Rohmer's films?" she asked.

I shook my head with a hint of troubled irony, meaning she was so off base that I'd rather erase my misguided attempt at casual conversation and start all over with something else. She let a moment pass.

"You mean because we're not sleeping together tonight?" she said.

It came from nowhere. But there it was. She hadn't misunderstood a thing. Or, if I thought she had, it was only because she had taken the words from my mind and given them a spin that wouldn't have occurred to me so soon but was the only one eager to be heard.

"It had occurred to me," I said, pretending I wasn't startled by her thunderbolt. I was attempting an amused smile that meant to overstate her reading of the situation and by so doing to suggest how far off the mark it fell—my way of parrying her dart with an equally pointed admission of my own. She right away dismissed it with an arch smile to mean *I thought as much*—a variation on what the woman on the terrace had asked her companion when he put an arm around her while holding a cigar in his other hand. *Are you hitting on me?*

The silence that rose between us as quickly as steam from a sprinkled clump of dry ice made it clear that neither had anything to add and that we both wanted the subject swept aside by whatever means. "Nev-er mind," she intoned, with the self-mocking strain of people who have ventured too far but who, to smooth ruffled waters, are merely pretending to be unhinged by their boldness. Her smile either underscored her outspoken remark or suggested she did not believe I was as unfazed by it as I wished to seem. "That was just *in case*," she said, raising her eyes at me once more. And then it came: "In case I hadn't made it clear last night. I'm just lying low," she added, something almost helpless and modest in her voice. She had used the exact same tone last night, lacing, as she always seemed to do in difficult moments, straight talk with double-talk, blandspeak with sadspeak. But this time she wasn't saying it about herself or about her reclusion from those around her; she was saying it to me, staving *me* off, shooing *me* away. It occurred to me that if she was with me on this Christmas night, it was precisely because she *was* lying low. We would never have met, or spoken, or stood on the terrace together, much less been to the movies or sat in a bar as we were doing now, if she wasn't in *Rekonvaleszenz* and if I hadn't taken on the role of night nurse, the visitor who stays long past visiting hours, the last hand that gently turns the lights down after the patient's finally dozed off.

As she explained when I walked her home later that night and watched her look for ways to underscore the words *lying low*, she was always *this far* from crying, she said, indicating, as she'd done last night, the distance between her thumb and her forefinger. But when we finally reached the entrance to her building, the girl who could come this close to crying would suddenly turn on me and remind me, with goading raillery, not to look so glum. I'd been forewarned, hadn't I? Suddenly the distance between us was wider than the distance between ice poles.

·

I had tried, at the bar, to open up and tell her why I liked Rohmer. How I'd discovered him at an age when I knew next to nothing about women or about myself—

"You're sitting too far away, I can't hear you," she had said. Which is why I brought my face closer to the candle, realizing that I had been sitting almost a whole table width away from her. She didn't like you to drift. At one point I noticed that while talking to her all you had to do was to sound vaguely tired or let your thoughts seem to stray during a moment of silence and she would immediately look hurt. If I persisted, however, she would punish my distraction first by pretending to be lost in thought herself and then by looking bored or far too interested in what the people next to our table were saying. She played this game better than anyone. "Maybe I should be thinking of going home," she said, before suggesting we have a second drink. Then: "Finish what you were saying." This was how she flattered you. The films, I thought, were about men who loved without passion, for no one seemed to suffer in them. "Rohmer's men talk a good game around love, the better to tame their desires, their fears. They overanalyze things, as though analysis might open up the way to feeling, is a form of feeling, is better than feeling. In the end, they crave the small things, having given up on the big ones—"

"Have *you* known the big ones?" she interrupted me, honing once again on the unstated subject of our conversation.

I thought awhile. There was a time when I could have sworn I'd known them. Now, in truth, I didn't think I had. "Sometimes I think I have. Have you?" I asked, still trying to stay vague.

"*Sometimes I think I have.*" She was mimicking me again. I loved how she did this.

We both laughed—because she had mimicked me quite well, because my answer was indeed hollow, and was meant to sound hollow, because by laughing she herself was hinting she'd have tried to dodge the question, seeing that she too might never have known the big ones and that we had both lied about knowing them to sound a touch less icy than we feared we seemed.

Last call came. We ordered a third round. Not one thing had gone wrong.

"Promise me something, though," she said after I'd just repeated I was pleased we'd met tonight.

I looked at her and said nothing, not entirely certain I understood, trying to look surprised at whatever she was about to say, even if the use of her "though" was like an uneasy warning of gunfire to come.

She hesitated before speaking. Then she changed her mind.

"I don't think I need to spell it out," she said.

She knew I knew.

"Why?" I asked.

"I don't know, it might just ruin things."

I took my time, sensing that my initial assumption had been totally correct. It had never occurred to me that we had so many *things* that could be ruined if I failed to promise what she was asking of me. I thought we had a scatter of small disconnected things between us—not *Things* with a capital *T*, and certainly not as many as she was implying!

"*Things?*" I asked, with something like an amused expression on my face, as though I had considered but then hushed an impulse to mimic her word. I knew I was being disingenuous and that I was desperately trying to find something else to say, perhaps to stave off what I was inferring from her and wished might remain ambiguous yet. But I didn't want to deny it either.

"Things," I repeated, as though her meaning had finally sunk in and that I was going to comply with her wishes.

"It won't ruin *things*," I replied. I tried to soften the conscious irony I was spreading on her words even before they had left my mouth, as though her concerns about us had never occurred to me before and, come to think of it now, were a touch amusing. Perhaps I was trying to dispel her doubts about me but didn't want them totally dismissed either. I was taking cover in the truth. "Besides, you might be entirely wrong," I added.

A short silence.

"I don't think so."

There was almost a note of apology in her eyes—apology for the unspoken slight directed at me. "Point taken," I said. "Admonition forbidding mourning noted," I conceded.

She squeezed my hand across the table and, before I could return the grasp, withdrew hers. She seemed relieved that she had finally set things straight between us and proceeded to light another cigarette by raising the stump of the candle and bringing it close to her face, determined to enjoy her third glass of Scotch. That face in candlelight, I thought!

I had never seen her face in such light before. Smoking, which she did by turning her face away from yours without ever averting her eyes, gave her silence a willful, omniscient air that I found difficult to hold.

We clinked glasses three times. Then three times again. And a third set of threes, "for good measure," she said, "three times the Trinity." "Repeat after me: *Ekh raz, yescho raz, yescho mnogo, mnogo raz . . .*" She repeated the Russian phrase once more, slowly, word for word. Once more, and once again, and many more times again. I remembered her toast with Hans. Who knew in whose arms she'd learned it?

•

This was when I made that passing comment on Rohmer's movies. I had said it to fill the silence, but it gave our conversation a strange spin. Her impulsive reading, brutally frank, had simply exposed the drift of our conversation. Not sleeping together—this was the missing term. It unsaddled and deflated everything. I tried to rescue appearances.

"What is unrealistic is that in Rohmer love may just be an alibi, a convenient metaphor—but as for love, none of his characters really trusts it, much less believes in it, or feels it, including the film director, and even the spectators, though all of us keep going through the motions of knocking at love's door, because outside of love we wouldn't know what to do with ourselves. Outside of love, we're out in the cold."

She thought awhile. Was she going to make fun of me again?

"Is everyone out in the cold, then?"

"I suppose some more than others. But everyone knocks."

"Even if love is an alibi . . . a metaphor?"

She *was* making fun of me.

"I don't know. Some knock at a door. Others at a wall. And some keep tapping gently at what they hope is a trapdoor, even if you never hear telltale sounds from the other side."

"Are you tapping now?"

"Am I tapping now? Good question. I don't know, maybe I am."

"Any telltale sounds?"

"None so far—all I'm hearing are *lying low* sounds."

"*That* was no gentle tap." She laughed uneasily.

I ended up laughing as well. For a second I thought she was reproaching me for using *lying low* against her. I was already trying to come up with some form of apology when I realized she was simply deriding what I thought was a deft and delicate pass.

"Trenches are empty, land scorched, all things *lite*, I thought I told you."

Was this reproof in her stare? Or was it apology? And why did she keep staring at me?

It was to stop blushing that I finally found myself saying, "Here I am looking at you, Clara, and I don't know whether to tell you that I love staring at you as I'm doing now or whether I should just keep quiet, say nothing, and curl up into the most abstinent silence."

"A woman would be crazy not to let you go on."

"And a man would be crazier not to ask you to stop him."

"Is this Rohmer, or you?"

"Who knows. I stare at you and my heart is racing and you're staring back at me, and all I keep thinking is: Trenches are empty, land scorched, keep it *lite*, and Mind the road signs."

She made a motion to interrupt. I immediately stopped.

"No, keep going."

What an amazing woman.

"And now I've been made to feel like a street performer."

"Oh, stop. We've had our intensely spiritual Vishnukrishnu Vindalu moment for tonight." She stood up, took out a dollar bill from her purse, walked over to the jukebox, and right away pressed a series of buttons— obviously "her" song. I had expected her to come back to our table and finish her drink, but she stood by the jukebox as though inspecting the list of songs. I stood up and went to her. The music started, it was a tango.

The raucous words of the song cast a spell as soon as I heard them. They rose out of the late-night stillness in the almost emptied bar like a wool blanket being unfolded from a linen closet on a cold night, when the only sound you hear is hail and rattling windowpanes. Clara knew the words, and before I saw what was happening or had a chance to resist or even make a show of resisting, there I was, being asked to lead in a dance I vaguely remembered from my early college days. We danced by the jukebox not three yards away from the entrance to the bar, and we danced much slower than a tango is meant to be danced, but who cared, for there we were, the jukebox and us and the rare faces of passersby on the sidewalk who happened to look in from behind the frosted windows, dancing, as in a Hopper painting, under a lighted green Heineken sign, while one or two of the remaining waiters went about the business of refilling ketchup bottles—we thought we danced perfectly, we thought this was heaven, we thought tango had brought us closer in three seconds than all the words we'd been sparring with since 7:10. And then it happened. After the song, she stood still for a second and, with her hand still in mine, almost in jest—or was it in jest?—said *Perdoname*, and right then and there began singing out the words in Spanish, and she sang them for me, a cappella, with that voice that tore everything inside me, staring at me the way singers do when they unhinge you totally as you stand there helpless and bared, and all you have is a shaken self and tears running down your cheeks. And she watched this, and she didn't stop singing, as if she knew, as she began to wipe my eyes with her palm, that this couldn't have been more natural and was exactly what should happen when one human being stops dancing, holds your hand, and then sings to you, for you, sings because music, like a machete in the jungle, cuts through everything and goes straight to that place still called the heart.

"Don't, please, don't," she whispered, then, changing her mind, went back to "Perdoname," her song.

"*Perdoname,*" she said,

> *Si el miedo robó mi ilusión*
> *Viniste a mi*
> *No supe amar*
> *Y sólo queda esta canción*

I knew I'd never forget this. It's the story of a man who, fearing love, chose to "protect his heart." "You came to me but I didn't know how to love, all I have now is this song," he says. Was Clara speaking to me—or was this coincidence? Did I have Juan Dola, she asked? Who was Juan Dola? "One dollar! Really!" Feigned exasperation. I took one out and watched her push the same buttons on the jukebox. "One more time," she said.

Is it me she's dancing with?

It is me.

Why wasn't there a thing about her I disliked?

"It's a good thing I'm not your type and you're not mine either," she said, as we took our seat after the second dance.

I laughed at the maneuver.

"So, I'll live with it. Let it be *my hell.*" I was trying to echo her words from last night.

I helped her with her coat. As she turned around and wrapped her shawl over her head, there was a fleeting moment when all we'd been saying seemed to come to a point. She hesitated. "So you're not going to listen to me, are you?"

"Listen to what?" I was going to say, feigning once again not to have followed her drift for fear of admitting we were always, always on the same wavelength. Or I could have said, "You know I can't, and I won't."

Instead, I ended up saying something so totally unlike me that it scared and enthralled me at once, as if I were suddenly wearing not my regular clothes but a soldier's uniform, with saber, stars, medals, and epaulettes, but no boots and no undies. I liked being *unlike me*, hoped that this being *unlike me* was not an ephemeral visit to a costume ball or a day trip into an unknown landscape that would vanish as soon as my return ticket expired, but an indefinite voyage out that I had neglected to undertake all life long, and now its time had come. Being unlike me was being me. Except that I didn't quite know how to yet. Perhaps this was why I'd been so tongue-tied with her; part of me was still discovering in erratic starts and sallies and in all manner of inadvertent ways, this unknown new character who had been waiting in the wings so long and who, for the first time in his life, was going to risk stepping up. Part of me didn't know him yet, didn't know how far to go with him. I was still trying him on for size, as if he were a new pair of shoes that I liked but wasn't sure went along with the rest of me. Was I learning to walk all over again—learning to become human? What had I been all this time, then—a stilt walker? A reversible human?

It took me a second to realize that I was afraid of something else as well: not just of growing to like this new me, of becoming totally attached to him, of giving him more and more slack and, with him, discovering all manner of new worlds, but of finding that he existed only in her presence, that she, and only she, could bring him out, and that I was like a genie without a master who recoils into his millennial spout, condemned to wait and wait for a chance to come out and see daylight when the next right person comes along from behind a Christmas tree and says her name is Clara. I did not want to grow attached to him and then find that he wouldn't last longer than Cinderella's livery. I was like someone who doesn't speak French but who, in the presence of a Frenchwoman one evening, turns out to be the most loquacious French speaker, only to find that she'd gone back home the next morning and that, without her, he'll never speak a word of French again.

The way she faced me with her wool shawl covering her ears and part of her face made me answer her warning with something uncharacteristically reckless.

"So, you're really not going to listen to me, are you?" she asked.

"Don't want to listen."

"Doesn't want to?"

"Doesn't want to at all."

This could easily have been our last moment together. "Just don't fall in love with me, please!"

"Won't fall in love with you, please."

She looked at me, drew closer, and kissed me on the neck. "You smell good."

"Walk home with me," she said.

Outside the bar, it was snowing. A faint, quiet amber glow had fallen on Broadway, coating the dirty sidewalks of 105th Street with a sense of quiet joy that reminded me of the film we'd just seen and of Pascal's own words: Joy, joy, joy. Traffic was scarce—buses and cabs, for the most part—while from a distance, as though emanating from neighborhoods far away, came the muffled metallic clang of a snowplow quietly plying its way downtown. She slipped her arm through mine. I had hoped she'd do just that. Was this just fellowship, then?

When we walked past the Korean twenty-four-hour fruit vendor, she said she wanted to buy cigarettes. "Read this," she added, pointing to a misspelled sign that read TANGELINES and right next to it MERONS. She burst out laughing. "Just fancy how they'd spell blueberries and blood oranges," she said, laughing louder and louder before the befuddled Mexican helper pruning flowers at this ungodly hour of the night. It scared me to think what she'd find about me the moment my back was turned. No, she'd do it to my face.

We reached her building sooner than I wanted. I decided there was no point in tarrying, and although I buttoned the last button of my winter coat to show that I was indeed heading into the cold after dropping her and was already bracing myself against the weather, she seemed to be trying to linger awhile longer as we stood outside, pointing to a view of the Hudson, finally saying that she would ask me upstairs but she knew herself and thought that perhaps we had better say good night now. We hugged—it was her idea, though the embrace seemed a bit too expansive to suggest anything more passionate or less chaste. I let the hug wane on its own. It was a friend's or a sibling's embrace, a feel-better gesture followed by a hasty send-off kiss on both cheeks. She lifted up my coat collar to cover my ears, staring me in the face, almost hesitating again, like a mother saying goodbye to a child who'll probably have a terrible time on his first day at school. "You don't mind?" she said, as though alluding to something we had been discussing earlier. I shook my head, wondering to myself how, even in saying as simple a thing as good night, she could still remain cryptic and explicit in one and the same breath.

"Let me walk you to where we said goodbye last night."

Was she into replaying scenes too? Were we pretending it was last night? Or was she doing it for me? Or to get me away from the lobby of her building? I told her I was taking a cab tonight. "'Cuz, bus, he no show up last night."

"He no show?"

"No show."

"Then you should have come back upstairs."

"I was dying to."

"Party went on till morning. You should have stayed."

"Why didn't you ask me to?"

"After your little performance? Me so pressed, me so busy, misosouporsalad. Get me my coat, get me my scarf, must rush, must go, flit, flit, flit."

She walked me to the statue where we'd parted last night. My turn, I said. I walked her back to her building. Her face swaddled in the shawl, her hands in her coat pockets, shivering. Posture: vulnerable and beseeching, could break your heart if you didn't know better.

"Just don't do it," she added, with that same touch of apology and fair warning in her voice, shattering our momentary elegy in the cold with the caustic snub of a love sonnet carved on granite with barbed wire. She placed a palm on my cheek, and without thinking, I kissed it—soft, soft palm of her hand. She removed it—not swiftly, as if I had crossed an imaginary line, but almost reluctantly, so as not to call attention to it, which stung me more, for it made her lingering gesture seem deliberate, as though her way of censuring my kiss was to overlook it, gracing withdrawal with tokens of indecision—not unflattering, but chastening just the same.

Whoever minded having the palm of his hand kissed? Even if last night's beggar woman kissed the inside of my hand, I'd have let her. I gave her an awkward glance, meaning, I know, I know, lying low.

"You did it all wrong," she explained.

I was dumbfounded. What now?

"Scarf!"

"What about scarf?"

"I hate this knot."

She untied my scarf and redid the knot the way she liked.

The knot will stay with me till I get home, I know myself. I'd probably want to keep it awhile longer, even with the heat full throttle at home. Get naked with Clara's knot, get naked with Clara's knot. Tied me up in knots, that's what. Last night I'd intentionally undone my scarf to show I had my own way of doing things, thank you very much. But that was last night.

Ivan-Boris-Feodor opened the door for her. I said I would call. But I wanted her to think I wasn't sure I would. Perhaps I wanted to think so myself. Then she went inside. I watched her step into the elevator.

I remembered the scent of loud perfumes in the corridor fused to that vague, old-elevator smell that had welcomed me to her building. Last night.

I stood there gathering my thoughts, trying to decide whether to walk up to the 110th Street train station or simply hail a cab, wondering which of the dark windows in her building would light up within minutes of our goodbye. I should stay awhile and see which window it was. But what I really wanted was to see her rush out the door looking for me. Something even told me the same impulse had crossed her mind and that she was debating it right then and there, which could be why she hadn't turned on her lights yet. I waited a few seconds more. Then I remembered I didn't know which side of the building her apartment faced.

I walked to the corner of 106th and West End, convinced more than ever now that I must never see her again.

I crossed over to Straus Park, following the flakes of snow that were massing like a frenzy of bees swarming in the halo of a streetlamp, growing ever more dense as I looked beyond them uptown and over toward the river and the distant lights of New Jersey. I pictured her in that oversized sweater. All evening long, even at the movies, it had made me think of a rough wool blanket with room for two in it. I wondered what the world smelled of under that blanket, was it my world with its usual, day-to-day odors or a totally alien, unfamiliar world with scents as new and thrilling as those of equatorial fruit—what did life feel like from Clara's side, from under her sweater, how different was our city when stared at through the lattice of her stitches—how did one think of things when one was Clara, did one read minds, did one always stare people down when one was Clara? Did one shush people when they complained? Or was one like everyone else? What had I looked like when she stared at me with her shawl covering all but her face, thinking to herself,

Ah, he's dying to kiss me, I know, wants to put his hands under my shirt the
way Inky did last night, and he thinks I can't tell his Guido's up to no good.

•

It felt good to be alone and think of her and coddle the thrill in my mind
without letting go. Here, before crossing the street, she had spoken to me
of Leo Czernowicz's lost pianola roll of Handel's arias and sarabandes as
one speaks of unsolved crimes and missing heirlooms. I wondered if the
bootprints before me were hers. No one else had stepped on this side of
the park since we'd headed toward her building. She had hummed the
first few bars, the same voice I'd heard last night. Just a voice, I thought.
And yet.

"I'd love to," I'd said when she asked if I wanted to hear Czernowicz's
lost pianola roll one day.

When I walked into the park from the same exact spot where I'd
entered last night, I knew that I would once again step into a realm of
silence and ritual—a soft, quiet, limelit world where time stops and
where one thinks of miracles, and of quiet beauty, and of how the things
we want most in life are so rarely given that when they are finally granted
we seldom believe, don't dare touch, and, without knowing, turn them
down and ask them to reconsider whether it's really us they're truly being
offered to. Wasn't this what I had done when I prematurely buttoned up
my coat in front of her doorman—to show that I could take my leave
and not say anything about meeting again, or coming upstairs, staying
upstairs? Why go out of my way to show so much indifference, when it
would have been obvious to a two-year-old . . . Strange. No, not strange.
Typical. The distance of a day had changed nothing between us. I was no
closer to her now than I'd been last night. If anything, the distance was
greater now and had solidified into something more pointed, craggier.

As I loitered about the park and looked around me, I knew I didn't
mind the sorrow, didn't mind the loss. I loved lingering in her park, liked
the snow, the silence, liked feeling totally rudderless and lost, liked suffering, if only because it brought me back to last night's vigil and
enchantment. Come here as often as you please, come here after every
one of your hopes is dashed, and I'll restore you and make you whole, and
give you something to remember and feel good by, just come and be with
me, and I'll be like love to you.

I cleared the snow off the same bench I had used last night and sat down. Let everything be like last night. I crossed my arms and, at the risk of being seen from her window, sat there staring at the bare trees. No one in the park. Just the statue, its lean, sandaled foot hanging from the pedestal, snow resting on her toes. Behind me, I made out the rhythmic rattle of a tire chain, reminding me of old-style patrol cars. A police car did appear from nowhere, turned on 106th, and sidled up to a parked bus. A silent greeting between the two drivers. Then the patrol car swooped around, made a brisk U-turn, and began speeding down West End. Officer Rahoon and two other cops. Good thing he didn't see me. Officer Rahoon, Muldoon, and Culhoon—three cops in a carriage, three beers and a cabbage. Was that it, then, the magic gone, Cinderella's back mopping floors?

Total silence descended.

The lamppost nearest me stood upon its gleaming pool of light and, once again, seemed to lean toward me as it had done last night, as eager to help, though still without knowing how.

What had it all meant? I wondered—the staring, the chummy-chummy hug-hug and perfunctory two kisses, French-style, the bit about how she knows herself, and telling me not to look so glum, and so much talk of lying low, and mournful hints of love and admonition laced into the sad tale of lost Czernowhiskeys, all of it capped with a bitter *I don't think I need to spell it out, it might ruin things*, like venom at the end of a love bite.

Ruin what things? Do me a favor!

Just don't fall in love with me. Which is when she planted a kiss under my ear—*You smell good*, uttered almost like a jeer and an afterthought. Venom, venom, venom. Venom and its antidote, like the warm, puffed taste of newly baked bread on a cold morning when the crust suddenly cuts into your gum and turns the most wholesome taste on earth into rank and fulsome gunk. *No things, okay? meaning, No sullen faces, no sulky-pouties, no guilt stuff, okay?* Because it could turn into her hell. Get real, *Schwester!* The mopey heiress from Maine didn't rattle so many keys before unlocking the fortress. The small-time hussy speaks the lingo of eternity—do me a favor! And all that talk of lying low—what prattle and claptrap!

I heard the bus driver turn on his engine. The lights inside the bus flickered on. How snug the foggy orange glow behind the glass panes, a haven from the cold. Just me and the bus driver, the bus driver and me.

Perhaps it was time for me to leave as well, though I didn't want to yet. And suddenly it came to me. I should call her, shouldn't I? Just call her. And say what? I'd figure something out. Time I did something— always waiting for others to do—tell the truth for a change, engage, for crying out loud. *I don't want to be alone tonight.* There! She'd know what to say to that. She'd keep the conversation going; and even if she had to say no, it would be a kind no, as in: Can't, lying low, you see? Ah, but to hear her say it that way, *Can't, lying low, you see?* like a reluctant caress that starts but then lingers on your face and shoots straight to your mouth and unbuckles your heart. I reached for my cell. She was the last person to call—hours ago. We'd exchanged numbers while still waiting on line, and she said, Let me call you instead, this way you'll have my number too. This was before the admonition, before Affirmatov had taken our tickets and crushed them in his fist. There was her number. My heart instantly sank, for the task seemed beyond me. What else were you planning to do with me but call? asked my phone, now that I held it in my hand. I imagined the sharp sound of her ten numerals chiming away like metal spikes hammered into splintering rock, followed by the grumbling, minatory drumroll of the ringing itself. *Academy 2*—fancy people still using Academy as a prefix, I'd said to her, to tease her or imply there was something willfully dated and archaic, even a touch precious in the way she'd given me her phone number. Now it was her number's turn to make fun of me, like a tiny reptile that looked totally docile in the pet store when the salesman made you rub its tummy with the tip of your finger but that now bites into your fingernail and then tears it out. She justified giving out her telephone number that way, because, she said, this was how her mother would say it and how, to very few people whom she felt *comfortable* with, she continued to say it—with the implication that you ranked among those who instantly understood that her Old World and your Old World shared a lineage in common, though not necessarily on the same branch, because what was defunct and obsolete in you was retro-swanky-cutting-edge in her, and, despite great-grandparents in common and a language in common, we might not have belonged on the same tree at all. So there! Academy 2 for the happy few.

I thought of her phone number—generations of phone calls from desperate boyfriends. How did it ring when you called her late at night? Could she tell by its ring whether it came from hopelessness or guilt or anger and blame or from shyness that hangs up after three rings? Did jealousy have a telltale ring that shouted louder truths than are dreamt of in caller ID?

Oh, Inky, Inky, Inky. How many times had he called tonight? He'd be calling right now. As I would myself. I imagined calling her. Ringing once. Ringing twice. Suddenly she picks up. Huffing. I can hear the water running in the background. Party's over, Cinderella's mopping floors. Inky? No, it's me. It's you. It's me. Me trying not to pull an Inky. But clearly doing just that. How do you say I don't want to be alone tonight now that I can't think what to say next? Just like that: I don't want to be alone tonight. Maybe with a question mark? Maybe not. A woman would be crazy not to let you say all this.

An M104 bus stopped on the corner of 106th and Broadway. I caught it just in time and, before sitting, watched the triangular park fade into the snowstorm. I may never see this place again in the snow. And just as I was beginning to believe it, I knew I was lying to myself. I'd come back tomorrow night, and the night after that, and after that as well, with or without her, with or without Rohmer, and just sit here and hope to find a way to avoid thinking that I'd lost her twice in two nights, sensing all along that hers was the face I'd put up around this park to screen me from myself, from all the lies I round up by night if only to think I'm not alone at dawn.

•

Later that night, I was awakened by the loud bang of a snowplow scraping my street. Suddenly I was filled with a feeling so exquisite that, once again, I could only call it joy, Pascal's word spoken in his solitary room one night at Port-Royal.

It reminded me of that moment when we'd walked out of the bar after last call and found the snow blanketing 105th Street. Our arms kept rubbing each other until she slipped hers into mine. I'd wished our walk might never end.

I got out of bed and looked out the window and saw how peacefully the snow had blanketed the rooftops and side streets of Manhattan. It was—perhaps because it reminded me so much of Brassaï—a stunning

black-and-white spectacle of the rooftops of Paris or of Clermont-
Ferrand, or of any French provincial town at night, and the joy that suddenly burst within me cast so limitless a spell in my bedroom as I tiptoed
my way to another window next to my desk to glimpse a different view of
the world by night that I caught myself trying to avoid making any
sound: not let the wood floor creak under my feet, or the old counter-
weights on the sash give their telltale thud when I'd raise the window
just a crack and let the cold air in, not do anything to disturb the silence
that had glided in as on the wingtips of an angel, because, as I stood
watching the night, I could so easily make believe that hidden under my
comforter lay someone whose sleep was as light and restive as mine.
When I'd come back to bed, I'd try not to move much, find a spot on the
right side and lie still and wait for sleep, all the while hoping it wouldn't
come until I'd smuggled the image of her naked body into my dreams.

Tomorrow, first thing, I'd rush out, have breakfast, and try to see my
friends and tell them about Clara. Then I'd take a stroll through a
department store, lunch at the Whitney among throngs of tourists snapping pictures with their jet-set grandparents, shop for Christmas presents
on the day after Christmas, all of it punctuated by the diffident premonition that tonight might happen all over again, must happen all over
again, may never ever happen again.

Once again, my mind drifted back to that moment when we'd walked
out of the bar after last call and found fresh snow on 105th Street. She'd
kissed me on the neck and, after telling me never to hope for anything,
snuggled her arm into mine, as though to mean *Never mind all this* but
Never forget all this. Now, in the dark, with the memory of her body leaning on mine, all I had to do was say her name and she'd be under the
covers, move an inch and I'd encounter a shoulder, a knee, whisper her
name again and again till I'd swear she was whispering mine as well, our
voices twined in the dark, like those of two lovers in an ancient tale
playing courtship games with one and the same body.

THIRD NIGHT

I was in the shower the next morning when I heard the buzzer downstairs. I jumped out of the bathtub, raced past the kitchen door, and yelled a loud "Who is it?" into the intercom, water dripping everywhere.

"It's me" came the garbled voice in the box, not the doorman's.

"Me who?" I shouted, exasperated at the deliveryman, as I began frisking for loose bills, first on my dresser, then through last night's trousers hanging on a chair.

"Me" came the same voice, followed by a moment's pause. "Me," it repeated. *"Moah."* Another pause. "Me, Shukoff. Me, lying-low. Misosouporsalad. *Me, goddamnit!* How quickly we forget."

Silence again.

"I'm driving to Hudson," she shouted.

I demurred a moment. What about Hudson? Did she want to come up? I asked. The thought of her coming upstairs swept through me like an indecent and almost guilty thrill. Let her see my crumpled world, my socks, my bathrobe, my foul rag-and-bone shop, my life.

"Thanks, but no thanks." She'd wait in the lobby, she didn't mind, just don't take too long—was I sleeping?

"No, shower."

"What?"

"Sho-wer."

"What?"

"Never mind."

"Just hurry," she cried, as if I had already agreed to come.

"Actually—" I hesitated.

There was a dead silence.

"Actually, *what*? Are you *that* busy?" she blurted out.

The static on the intercom couldn't muffle the irony crackling over each syllable.

"Okay. Okay. I'll be down in five."

She must have grabbed the phone from the doorman.

There goes my regular breakfast at the corner Greek diner, I thought. Newspaper waiting by the cash register, crossword puzzle I never care to finish, thimble-sized glass of orange juice as soon as they spot you trundling through the snow, omelet, hash browns, and small tinfoiled packets of very processed jam—they know me there—speak a few words of *Helleniki* with the waitress, pretend we're both flirting, which is flirting twice-removed, then stare out and let your mind drift. I could almost hear the sound of the door, with its thumb lock permanently stuck down, followed by the bell and rattle of the glass panel as you shut the door behind you real fast, rubbing your palms from the cold, scanning for an empty table by the window, then sit and wait for that magical moment when you'll stare out and let your mind drift.

Six hours ago, just six hours ago I was standing outside her building watching her disappear into the elevator.

Now she was standing outside my building, waiting. Suddenly the words I'd spoken to her last night in bed came back to me, word for word. *You know that walk on 106th Street? I wish it hadn't ended.* I wish it had gone on and on, and that we'd kept walking all the way to the river, then headed downtown, and who knows where else by now, past the marina and the boats where she'd once told me Pavel and Pablo lived, to Battery Park City all the way over and across the bridge to Brooklyn, walking and walking right until dawn. Now she was downstairs. *You know that walk . . .* The words coursed through me like a secret wish I'd failed to expiate last night. I wanted to take the elevator downstairs and, tying the knot of my bathrobe, drip into the main lobby and tell her, *You know that walk on 106th Street? I wish it hadn't ended, never ended.* Just the thought of saying these words to her now as I was hastily drying myself made me want to be naked with her.

When I finally saw her downstairs in the lobby, I complained that eight o'clock was an unseemly hour to drag people out of their homes. "You love it," she interrupted. "Hop in, we'll have breakfast on the way. Take a look."

She indicated the passenger seat of a silver BMW. Two *grande* coffees stood at a precarious angle, not in the cup holders below the dashboard, but right on the passenger seat itself, as if she had plopped both down in what I took to be her typical impatience with small things. There were also what appeared to be neatly wrapped muffins—"Purchased just around *your* block," she said. She had bought them with me and no one else in mind, it seemed, which meant she knew she'd find me, knew I'd be happy to come along, knew I liked muffins, especially when they had this vague scent of cloves. I wondered whom else she'd have barged in on if she hadn't found me. Or was I already the standby? Why think this way?

"Where to?" I asked.

"We're visiting an old friend. He lives in the country—you'll like him."

I said nothing. Another Inky, I figured. Why bring me along?

"He's been living there ever since leaving Germany before the war." She must have inherited this from her parents. They called it *the war*, not World War II. "Knows everything—"

"—about everything." I knew the type.

"Just about. Knows every piece of recorded music."

I pictured a fretful old *garmento* type hobbling on frayed slippers around a large gramophone. *Tell me, Liebchen, what watch? Do you know that land where the citrus blooms?* I wanted to make fun of him. "Another Knöwitall Jäcke," I said.

She caught my skepticism and my attempted humor.

"He's lived more lives here and elsewhere than you and I put together multiplied by eight to the power of three."

"You don't say."

"I do say. He goes back to a time when the world ganged up on every last Jew, and all that was left of Europe was a tiny spot off a magical lakeside town overlooking a canton in Switzerland. There, my father, Hans, and Fred Pasternak met in elementary school, which was why my father insisted I go to school there for a while. There, for your nymphormation, Max turned the pages for the man who'd once turned them for the man who'd turned them for the last of Beethoven's pupils. Maybe I worship him."

I hated her blind adulation. No doubt she hated my senseless wish to deride him. "So don't *you* be the knöwitall." She repeated my word to soften her censure. "We're going to hear some stuff he's unearthed—pretty amazing too, if you care to know."

A chill suddenly hovered between us. To fend it off, we kept quiet. Let the fog pass, let it disperse and drift away and spill out of the car like the cigarette smoke being sucked out of the tiny crack in her window. Our silence told me not just that our thoughts were temporarily elsewhere, or that anger was blocking something between us, but that she, like me, and without wishing to call attention to it, was desperately scrambling to make last-minute repairs to save the moment.

A good sign, I thought.

This is when she took out a recording of Handel's piano suites. I said nothing, fearing that mentioning music might suddenly bring up her aging cyborg with the giant phonograph. She's putting on the Handel to fill the silence with something. To show she is aware of the tension, to show she isn't aware of it, to smooth the ruffles the way a beautiful woman in an elevator once rubbed a hand across the front of my sports lapel to undo a fold in my collar. A conversation opener. Not a conversation opener.

She must have realized what I was thinking.

I smiled back.

If she cradled a mirror version of my unspoken *You know that walk, last night*, what would it be? *I know what you're thinking. It's nothing like yours. It's only the tension makes you want to read my thoughts.* Or was it harsher yet: *You had no right speaking of Herr Jäcke that way—look what you've done to us now.*

We were on Riverside Drive. Soon we would near the 112th Street statue, where, for a while that seemed to last forever two days earlier, I'd enjoyed feeling stranded in the snowstorm. I tried to remember the evening and the snowed-up hillock and the St. Bernard coming out of nowhere, then the elevator, the party, the tree, the woman. Now I was riding in Clara's car, eager to put the tension behind us. I watched Tilden's statue come and go. It had seemed so timeless, so blissfully medieval under the snow two days ago; now it scarcely remembered who I was as I sped by in the sports coupe, neither he nor I able to share a thought in common. Later, I promised, maybe we'll reconnect on my way back, and I'll stop and ponder the passage of time. *See this statue, it and I . . .* I would have told her, my way of reminding her how we'd stood on a balcony and watched eternity the other night—the shoe, the glass, the snow, the shirt, Bellagio, almost everything about her aching to turn into poetry. It was poetry, wasn't it, the walk that night, and the walk last night, *You know that walk on 106th Street? I'd been thinking about you all day, all day.*

"Ugly day, isn't it?"

I loved overcast gray days, I said.

Actually, she did too.

Why say *ugly*, then?

She shrugged my question away.

Probably because it seemed the easiest thing to say? Because we'll say anything to defuse the tension? For a moment she seemed elsewhere and far away.

Then, within seconds and without warning—as though this was where she'd been headed even before putting on the Handel, before the tension in the car, perhaps even before buzzing me or before buying the two *grandes* around the corner—"So"—and right away I knew what she was going to say, I just knew—"Did you think of me last night?" she asked, staring straight before her, as if too busy to look in my direction, though it was clear she'd see through anything I said.

There was no point beating around the bush. "I slept with you last night."

She didn't say anything, didn't even cast a sidelong glance.

"I know," she replied in the end, like a psychiatrist pleased to see that the medication prescribed almost absentmindedly at the end of one session had had its intended effect by the start of the next. "Maybe you should have called."

That came out of nowhere. Or was this her way of pushing what I presumed was the limit between strangers? She was frank when it came to delicate issues. Like me, perhaps, she found admissions easy and bold questions easier yet, but working up to them was probably *torment and torture*, the way it's not passion people hide but progressive arousal. Truth jutted out like shards of glass; but it came from an inner skirmish, perhaps because its origin was closer to fear than violence.

"Would you have wanted me to?" I asked.

Silence. Then, just as abruptly: "There are muffins and bagels in the white-gray paper bag to your left."

She knew how to play this.

"Ah, muffins and bagels in the white-gray paper bag to my left," I echoed, to reassure her that her intentionally obvious evasion wasn't lost on me, but that I wouldn't press any further.

I took forever to examine the contents of the white-gray paper bag. The last thing I had eaten was Clara's garlic cheese sandwich almost half a day earlier.

"Permission to eat in car?"

"Permission granted."

I broke off part of the crusty top of the buttery cranberry muffin and held it out to her. She took it and, with her mouth full, bowed twice, to signal thanks.

"Permission to try other muffin for sake of variety?"

With her mouth still full and, on the brink of laughter, she simply nodded I go ahead.

"Must absolutely ferret out the other contents of . . . this here white-gray paper bag to my left."

She seemed to shrug a shoulder in mock-laughter. We were over our moment of tension.

Her cell phone rang.

"Speak," she said.

It was someone asking her a question. "Can't, I'm in the car. Tomorrow." She clicked off. Then turned off her phone.

Silence. "I like this breakfast-on-the-go situation," I finally said. But she spoke at the same time as I did. "And you didn't call last night because . . . ?"

So we're back to that, I thought. She wasn't letting it go—was this a good sign, then? And if it was, why did I feel this rush of something terribly awkward and uneasy between us, especially since I had nothing more to be ashamed of after my avowal of moments earlier. Or had I made the avowal to shock her enough that it would freeze the subject on the spot, show I could speak the whole truth if I wanted to, but also on condition we slammed the door on it? The last thing I wanted was to tell her why I hadn't called, though this and only this was the thing I wished to tell her most now. I wanted to tell her about last night too, how I'd woken up to her when I remembered the light down on her skin at the bar and how the thought of it was still with me when she buzzed me downstairs and I'd wanted to run down in my bathrobe and expose the effect of her voice on my body.

"Because I wasn't sure you'd want me to," I ended up saying.

Why hadn't I called her? Was I simply pretending not to want to tell her? Or did I not even know how to begin telling her? What could I tell you, Clara? That I'd abide by your rules even though I didn't want to? That I didn't call because I didn't know what I'd say after It's me, I don't want to be alone tonight?

"Why didn't I call?" I finally repeated in an effort at candor. The words that unexpectedly came to my rescue were her very own from last night: "Just lying low, Clara. Like you, I suppose. Don't want to disturb the universe." I knew it was a cop-out. I was looking straight in front of me, as she was doing, trying to give my admission a tongue-in-cheek air of premeditated but all too visibly suppressed mischief. Had I meant to scorn *lying low*? Was I using it against her? Or was I taking my fragile cop-out back by suggesting they were copycat words, not mine, just hers? Or was I trying to show we had more in common than she suspected— though I couldn't begin to know what that was? Or did I have nothing up my sleeve but desperately needed her to think I did, so that I might believe so myself?

It did not occur to me until I'd uttered her *lying low* that I was far closer to the truth about my condition in the car or last night or at the party or in life even than I wished to convey with my mock-struggle to affect an impish look.

But I also sensed that I hadn't yet told her why I never called and that perhaps she was waiting for an answer.

"Look, I think I'm going to need to say something," I finally began, not knowing where I was going with this, except that saying it with protest and gravity in my voice gave me the impression I was obeying an impulse to speak out meaningful and inexorably honest words that were sure to banish all ambiguity between us.

"You're going to *need* no such thing," she snapped, making fun of the verb to need, which I'd forgotten she hated.

"I was just going to say that most of us are in a repair shop of one sort or another."

She looked at me.

"No, you weren't."

Had she, once again, seen through me before I could? Or, as I preferred to think, was she thinking I was making fun of her in a delayed revenge for last night's cold shower when she cautioned me not to *ruin things*?

To undo the damage I added, "Everyone lies low these days, including those who live happily ever after—they're lying low too. To be honest, I no longer even know what the phrase means." Had she asked, I would have found a way of explaining that I had simply taken cover in her words like a child snuggling under a grown-up's blanket in the middle of a cold night. Borrowing your words, to burrow in your world, in your blanket, Clara, that's all. Because they explain everything and they explain nothing, because, much as it hurts me to say it, there's greater truth when you breathe than when I speak, because you're straight and I'm all coils, because you'll dash through minefields, unblinking, while I'm stuck here in the trenches on the wrong bank.

"I think I'm going to *need* to start asking you for another piece of muffin."

We laughed.

.

We were not far from the Henry Hudson and would be sidling the river all the way north, she said, especially since she hated the Taconic. And as we drove, eating breakfast on the fly, the way we'd had dinner on the fly last night, I began to think that perhaps what brought us together was none other than a longing to lie low with someone desperate to do the same, someone who asked for very little and might offer a great deal provided you never asked—we were like two convalescents comparing temperature charts, swapping medications, one and the same blanket on both our laps, happy we'd found each other and ready to open up in ways we'd seldom done before, provided each knew convalescence didn't last forever.

"So, did you think of me last night?" I tossed the question back at her.

"Did I think of you?" she repeated, seemingly puzzled, with the air of an unspoken *How totally inappropriate!* "Maybe," she finally replied. "I don't remember." Then, after a pause, "Probably not." But the look of guile that I myself had affected a moment earlier told me she meant the exact opposite as well: "Probably not. I don't remember." Then, after a pause, "Maybe."

In this game, which had once again erupted between us, did one score more points by feigning indifference? Or by feigning to feign indifference? Or by showing she had cleverly spotted but sidestepped what was an obvious trap and, in doing so, had managed to throw it back at me war-in-the-trenches style just before it exploded in midair? Or did she score higher points by showing that she was, yet once more, the bolder and more honest of the two, if only because scoring points was the farthest thing from her mind?

I looked at her again. Was *she* counterfeiting a repressed grin now? Or was she simply grinning at the scoreboard I was busily checking in my desperate attempt to catch up to her?

I held out a piece of muffin for her, meaning, *Peace*. She accepted. There was now less to say than when there'd been tension between us. So I stared out at the river till I caught sight of a large, stationary cargo ship anchored right in the middle of the Hudson, with the words *Prince Oscar* painted in large mock-Gothic red-and-black script.

"Prince Oscar!" I said to break the silence.

"I'll have another piece of Prince Oscar," she replied, thinking I had for some reason decided to call the muffin Prince Oscar.

"No, the ship."

She looked to her left.

"You mean Printz Oskár!"

"Who is he?"

"Never heard of him. An obscure royal cadet in a Balkan country that no longer exists."

"Except in Tintin books," I added. Or in old Hitchcock movies, she countered. Or he's a short, stubby, monocled South American *dictatóremperadór* type who tortures prepubescent girls in front of their fathers, then rapes their grandmothers. Neither of us was succeeding in making the joke come alive. We were speeding along the Drive when a car suddenly swerved into our lane from the right.

"Printz Oskár up your mother's," she yelled at the car.

Her BMW swooped over to the fast lane and sped up to the car that had cut in front of us. Clara stared at the driver in the adjacent car and mouthed another insult: *Preeeeentz-os-káááááááááááár!*

The driver turned his face to us, leered, and, exhibiting his left palm, flicked and then waved his middle finger at us.

Without wasting another second, Clara smirked back and, out of the blue, shook her hand and made a totally obscene gesture. "Printz Oskár to you, dickhead!" The man seemed totally trounced by the gesture and raced ahead of us.

"That'll teach him."

Her gesture left me more startled than the driver. It seemed to come from an underworld I would never have associated with her or with Henry Vaughan or with the person who'd spent months poring over Folías and then in the wee hours sang Monteverdi's "*Pur ti miro*" for us. I was shaken and speechless. Who was she? And did people like this really exist? Or was I the weirdo, so easily shocked by such a gesture?

"Any Printz Oskár left?" she queried, holding out her right hand.

What on earth did she mean?

"*Un petit* Printz muffín."

"Coming up."

"I think there might be another Printz left," she said.

"Already eaten up."

She stared at the two cups of coffee.

"Mind putting one more sugar in my Oskár?"

She must have sensed her gesture had upset me. Calling everything Printz Oskár was her way of defusing my remaining shock over her gesture. But it also reminded me how easy it was to create a small world of our own together, with its own lingo, inflections, and humor. Another day together and we'd add five new words to our vocabulary. In ten days we wouldn't be speaking English any longer. I liked our lingo, liked that we had one.

Just ahead of us another large barge came into view. It reminded me of the giant barge anchored among the floes off 106th Street on the night of the party. I'd been thinking of the word *worship* back then.

"Another Printz Oskár," I said, my turn to speak our lingo.

"This is more like King Oskár," she corrected as we watched what turned out to be a dinosaur barge with a very tiny, cocky head jutting at its very, very back, immense, ugly, brainless. There was no way such a thing could have crossed the Atlantic on its own. Probably came down another river. Clara sipped her coffee. "You stirred it good."

She removed the Handel.

"Bach?" she said, as if to ask whether I minded Bach.

"Bach is good."

She slipped the CD in. We listened to the piano. "We'll be hearing this very piece again when we get there, so get ready."

"You mean at Herr Knöwitall's house?"

"Don't be a Printz, will you. You'll like him, I promise, and I know he'll like you too."

"We'll see," I said, seemingly absorbed by the Bach and all the while pretending I was struggling to withhold a dismissive comment about Herr Knöwitall.

"What if he turns out to be a total bore?" I finally said, unable to hold back.

"What if you turn out to like him? I just want you to know him. Not too much to ask. Stop being so difficult."

I liked being told to stop being difficult. It brought us closer, as though she had thrown five or six sofa cushions at me before laying her head on me. What I liked wasn't just the air of familiarity and reproof that brought us closer; it wasn't even the sarcasm with which she finally said "You're a terrible Printz Oskár!" meaning a terrible snob, terribly childish, obtuse—but because "Stop being so difficult" is precisely what everyone had always said to me. She was speaking my language from way back. It was like finding the sound of one's childhood in an emptied apartment, or the scent of cloves and grandmother spices in the muffin bag Clara had brought this morning.

"Here, take this piece," I said, on finding a small, hidden muffin.

"You have it."

I insisted. She thanked me exactly as she had the first time, by nodding her head in front of her.

Clara liked speeding in her sports car. The Saw Mill Parkway in the light fog suddenly opened up, an endless stretch to places unknown and unseen and that I wished might remain so forever.

"Are you good at math?"

"Not bad." Why was she asking?

"Finish this sequence then: one, two, three, five, eight . . ."

"Easy. It's the Fibonacci sequence. Thirteen, twenty-one, thirty-four . . ."

A few moments later. "How about this one: one, three, six, ten, fifteen . . ."

It took a while.

"Pascal's triangle: twenty-one, twenty-eight, thirty-six . . ."

Always curt and snappy. "Now try this sequence: fourteen, eighteen, twenty-three, twenty-eight, thirty-four . . ."

I thought hard for a moment. But I couldn't solve it.

"Can't."

"It's staring you in the face."

I tried all sorts of hasty calculations. Nothing. Why was she always good at making me feel so clumsy and clueless?

"Can't," I repeated.

"Forty-two, fifty, fifty-nine, sixty-six . . ." She was giving a few hints.

"How do you figure?"

"The stops on the Broadway local. You don't see what's right in front of you, do you?"

"Seldom do."

"Figures."

Clara Brunschvicg, I wanted to say, what is the Brunschvicg sequence? "Clara, I didn't call last night because I chickened out, okay? I'd even taken out my *télyfön*, but then thought you wouldn't want me to. So I didn't."

"So you made love to me instead."

"So I made love to you instead."

●

She had picked the right day. Everything was white. Not a chance that the sun was going to break through today. And yet despite the hoarfrost, which cast a chill layer around us from the sloping hood of her silver-gray car to the silver-white lane, something warm had settled between us in the car—part Clara's mood, part the breakfast she had brought along, part Christmas, and part the afterglow of last night that seemed to have gathered around *Did you think of me last night?* like an aura on a saint's figure, solemn and speechless.

"And I kept hoping you'd call."

"Instead, you showed up."

"Instead, I showed up."

Still, what gumption to drop in on someone with breakfast-on-the-go and never a worry he'd say no. This was how she'd introduced herself. This was how she waited at the movie theater. This is how she lived, did everything. I envied her.

This is how she behaved with everyone. Skipping out on people, then barging back in. Speak, she'd say, and then as suddenly click off. Something told me that as late as it got last night and as often as she'd avoid picking up her phone while with me, she'd still found time to call Inky after I'd dropped her off. Then there was the old man we were visiting. He had no idea she was going to show up that morning, much less with a stranger. You mean you'll just idle into his driveway, honk a few times to give him time to wash his face, comb his hair, and put in dentures, and shout Yooohooo, guess who's here!

No, she was going to call him as soon as we left Edy's.

Who's Edy? I asked, more baffled than ever. You'll see. Silence. Did I like not knowing anything? No, I didn't. Actually, I loved nothing better and was just discovering it. This was like playing blindman's bluff and never wanting my blindfold removed.

Perhaps I got to love having my hours messed and tousled with, because dicing up my days and my habits into scattered pieces that you couldn't do anything with until she was there to put them together for you was her way of shaking things up, spinning you around, and then turning you inside out like an old sock—your heart a laundered sock looking for its mate—I didn't just think of you last night, Clara, ask me, make me tell you and I will, I'm dying to anyway.

I didn't know where we were headed, or when we'd be coming back. I didn't want to catch myself thinking about tomorrow either. There might not be a tomorrow. Nor did I want to ask too many questions. Perhaps I was still fighting back, knowing that fighting back is the dead-giveaway gesture of those who've long ago already surrendered. I wanted to seem totally nonchalant in the car, but knew that the stiffness in my neck and shoulders had started the moment I'd gotten in. It had probably been there last night at the movies as well. And at the bar. And on our walk. Everything was urging me to say something, not something bold or clever, but something simple and true. A strange narrow door was being left open, and all I had to do was flash my pass and push through. Instead, I felt like a passenger timorously walking up to a metal detector. You deposit your keys, then your watch, your change, your wallet, belt, shoes, télyfön, and suddenly realize that without them you're as bare and vulnerable as a broken tooth. A stiff neck and a broken tooth. Who was I without my things in their tiny, little places, without my little morning rituals, my little breakfast in my crammed little Greek diner, my cultivated sorrows and my cunning small ways of pretending I hadn't recognized that the woman downstairs screaming Me, Shukoff. Me, goddamnit! was the very one I'd taken to bed with me last night and, in the dark, thrown every caution when I'd asked her not to take her sweater off so that I might slip into it as well, because, in thinking of our naked bodies shrouded in wool together, part of me knew it was safe to break down the sluices and let my mind run wild with her, now that I'd blown two chances two nights running and had, in all likelihood, lost her for good?

"You're drifting."

"I'm not drifting."

She too hated people who drifted.

"You're quiet, then."

"I'm thinking."

"Tell it to the barges." She paused. "Tell me something I don't know." Still looking straight ahead of her.

"I thought you knew everything there was to know about me."

I was trying to remind her of last night's admonition at the bar.

"Then tell me something I want to hear."

The privilege of drivers: to say the boldest things without ever looking at you.

"Like what?"

"Like I'm sure you can think of something."

Did I get where she was going with this? Or was I just imagining?

"Like walking you home last night and hoping to think of one more way to avoid saying goodbye because there was still so much to say? Like not knowing why the film seemed tied to us in so many knots? Like wanting everything all over again? Like that?"

She didn't answer.

"Like do you want me to go on, or should I stop?"

I meant it to sound both as a warning of an avalanche to come as well as to show that I was just playing with her, that however close I got, I would never be the first to remove the specter she had put between us.

"Like you can stop whenever you please," she said.

That would teach me to ask for help in navigating the shoals between us.

"Where do they make people like you, Clara?"

At first she did not answer. "Where?" she asked, as though she didn't understand the question. "Why do you ask?"

"Because it's so hard to figure you out."

"I have no secrets. I lay my cards out. I have with you."

"It's not secrets I'm thinking of. It's how you get me to say things I'd never tell anyone."

"Oh, spare me the Printz Oskár!"

I let a few seconds elapse.

"Spared!" as though I was conceding the point to humor her only, though I felt at once snubbed, yet relieved.

She laughed. "I can't believe it's me who's blushing, not you," she said.

"Permission to change subject?" I said, handing her the last piece of muffin found at the bottom of the paper bag.

"The things you come up with, Printz."

•

I loved these little towns along the Hudson, especially on such an ashen, white day. Two decades ago, some of them may have been no bigger than industrial hamlets with sunken wharves and skeletal jetties. Now, like everything else around the city, they had blossomed into picturesque weekend villages. Off the road and perched on an incline was a little inn. I envied its occupants, its owners, those sitting in small dining rooms reading the morning paper this Christmas week.

No. I liked being in the car.

Yes, but to be in the dining room with her in one of those bed-and-breakfasts. Or better yet: to be there waiting for her to come downstairs and take her seat right next to mine at our table. And suppose it snowed heavily tonight and we had nowhere to sleep but here . . .

"So tell me something else—anything, Printz."

"Clara B., it's difficult keeping up with you. You're constantly changing lanes on me."

"Maybe it's because you're headed to one place and one place only—"

" and have been warned repeatedly there are major repairs up ahead—"

"—and don't forget the roadblocks," she corrected, seemingly jesting as well.

Clara was a fast driver, but not reckless; I caught her several times changing lanes to allow impatient drivers through. But she didn't let them through out of courtesy. "They make me nervous." I had a hard time picturing her nervous.

"Do I make you nervous?"

She thought for a moment.

"Do you want me to say yes—or no? I can go both ways."

I smiled. I couldn't think of a nerve-racking moment in my life I'd enjoyed more. I nodded.

"Deep, very *très* deep," she said. "Way too much Vishnukrishnu Vindalu Paramashanti stuff going on between us."

I said nothing. I knew what she meant. But I had no idea whether she welcomed the intimacy or wanted it stopped.

"Cemetery town," I interrupted, pointing out the row of cemeteries in Westchester. "I know," she said.

I looked outside and realized we were in fact fast approaching the cemetery where my father was buried. I knew I was not going to raise the subject and would let it drop as soon as we'd passed the town. Had I known her better or felt less cramped, perhaps I would have asked her to take the next exit, turn around, find a florist along the way, and join me for a short visit there.

He would have liked her. Pardon me for not standing, frankly this here is really not good for anyone's back. And turning to me, At least this one, with her spunk and her pseudo-hussy airs, is no ballbuster heiress.

I wondered if the day would come when I'd trust asking Clara to park the car and take a few minutes to stop by his grave. Why didn't I? She wouldn't have hesitated to take me to her father's, or to mine if I'd asked. Why hadn't I called last night? Why couldn't I just say, Will you let me tell you about my father someday?

I'd never spoken about him. Would I remember to think of him again on our way back? Or would I choose to hate myself for burying him with a second death, the death of silence and shame, which I already knew was a crime against me, not him, against truth, not love. The wages of grief are paid in large bills and, later, in loose change; those of silence and shame no loanshark will touch.

•

A while later, and without warning, she veered right onto an exit and entered what seemed a tiny old fishing village with an antique masthead signaling the center of town. Then, in front of a secluded 1950s candy store not ten yards from a gas station, she parked the car. "We'll stop for a short while." A faded shingle up a brick staircase announced a place called Edy's.

I liked the nippy air that greeted us as soon as we stepped out of the car.

Edy's was a totally deserted blue-collar luncheonette. "Norman Rockwell goes Podunk," I said. "Tea?" Clara asked. "Tea is good," I said, determined to play along. Clara immediately dropped her coat on a Formica table by a large window facing the Hudson. "I'm going to the bathroom."

I always envied people who never thought twice about saying they were going to the bathroom.

The fifty-plus waitress, whose name was embroidered in cursive pink on a striped blue apron, brought two empty thick mugs from which dangled two Lipton tea tags. Her left index finger was stuck through the handles of the two mugs, while her other hand held a round glass pitcher of hot water. "Edy?" I asked by way of thanking her. "That's me," she replied, depositing the mugs on the Formica table and pouring the boiling water.

I took the seat facing the least appealing of the two outside views: a floating shed, which looked more like an abandoned ice-fishing hut. Then I changed my mind when I realized that Clara's side featured a tilted, rusted, trellised pier. Then I changed my mind again: perhaps the view of the floating barge at the bottom of the gully wasn't so ugly after all. I couldn't make up my mind until I sensed a fireplace with a burning log in the back of the coffee shop. Suddenly the illusion of bay windows. I picked up both mugs and moved them to the sheltered corner booth by the fireplace. Even the view was better from here. Two tiny paintings hung between the relics of a sextant and an oversized meerschaum pipe: an imitation Reynolds portrait and a picture of a lurching bull with a matador's saber pierced up his spine.

When Clara came over, she sat down and cupped the mug with both palms in a gesture suggesting she loved nothing better than the touch of a warm mug between her hands.

"I would never have discovered this spot in a million years," I said.

"No one would."

She sat, as she had last night, with both elbows on the table.

Your eyes, your teeth, Clara. I had never been stirred by her teeth before, but I wanted to touch them with my finger. Never seen her eyes in daylight before. I sought them out and feared them and struggled with them. Tell me you know I'm staring at you, that you just know, that you want me to, that you too are thinking we've never been together in day-light before.

Perhaps I was making her uncomfortable, for she resumed the affecta-tion of trying to relieve something like frostbite on her hands by caress-ing her mug. An arm around her shoulders, an arm around her oversized sweater hanging off her bare, cashmered shoulders. That could be done easily enough, why not with Clara?

She sat up, as though she had read my mind and didn't want me to stray down this path again.

I said something humorous about the old Jäcke. She didn't answer, or wasn't paying attention, or was simply brushing aside my limp attempt at blithe chitchat.

I envy people who ignore all attempts at small talk.

An arm to touch your shoulder. Why weren't we sitting next to each other instead of face-to-face like strangers? Perhaps I should have waited for her to sit first and then sat next to her. What idiocy my changing seats and the commotion about the view of the floating barge and of the trellised pier, back to the floating barge—what did views have to do with anything?

She leaned her head against the large sealed windowpane, trying to avoid touching the dusty tartan curtains. She looked pensive. I was about to lean my head against the window as well, but then decided against it; she'd think I was trying to mimic her, though I'd thought of it first. It would have seemed too premeditated an attempt to seem lost in the same cloud. Instead, I slouched back, almost touching her feet under the table.

She crossed her arms and stared outside. "I love days like this."

I looked at her. I love the way you are right now. Your sweater, your neck, your teeth. Even your hands, the meek, untanned, warm, luminous palm of each hand resting cross-armed, as if you too were nervous.

"So talk to me."

"So talk to you."

I fiddled with a sugar packet. For a change it seemed it was she who needed to fill the silence, not I. And yet it was I who felt like a crab that had just molted its shell: without pincers, without wit, without darting steps, just a hapless mass with aching phantom limbs.

"I like being here like this too," I said—being here, with you, having tea in the middle of nowhere, next to an abandoned gas station in the heart of soddy, cabin-town America—does it matter? "And this too, I like," I added, letting my gaze land on the iced white shore and the bluffs beyond, as though they too had something to do with liking *being here like this*. "Being here the way we are right now," I threw in as an afterthought, "though all this might have absolutely nothing to do with you, of course," I added slyly.

She smiled at my attempted *afterthought*.

"Nothing to do with me at all."

"Absolutely not," I insisted.

"I couldn't agree more."

She started laughing—at me, at herself, at the joy that came from being together so early in the day, at both our willfully transparent attempts to play down the joy.

"Time for a third secret agent," she added, taking a cigarette and proceeding to light it.

Teeth, eyes, smile.

"If it's any consolation, I like this too," she said, staring over at the distant woods across the river, as if they had more to do with our enjoyment of the moment than we did ourselves. Was she doing exactly what I had just done, paying us a compliment while undoing it by redirecting her gaze to the spectacle of bluffs beyond, or was she trying to raise the subject in a manner I didn't dare to yet?

"I'm sure you couldn't care less, but I used to come here with Inky."

"What, chez Edy's?" Why did I keep making fun of the place, why?

"When they were kids, he and his brother would ride their boat here, fish, get drunk, then head back home before dark. Inky and I would drive up here, park the car, loll about awhile, and I'd watch him miss the old days, till we got into the car again and rode back to the city. Such a lost, lost soul."

"You're a lost soul too?"

"Nope!" she snapped without letting me finish what I didn't even know I was attempting to ask. It meant, *Don't even try.* Trenches, pits, the dales of pandangst were party talk.

"Are you here now to be with him?"

"No. I told you already. We're over."

Dumb, dumb question.

"So why are you bringing him up now?"

"No need to be upset."

"I'm not upset."

"You're not upset? You should see yourself."

I decided to joke about it and picked up the tiny metal milk dispenser and, as though to determine what an upset face looked like, examined my reflection in it, once, twice, three times.

Then I saw it. In the rush to meet her this morning, I had completely forgotten to shave. This, after making a deliberate effort to take my time in coming down, to show I wasn't racing down the stairs to meet her.

Did she want me to say I was upset? Was this, then, an "opener" of sorts, her way of forcing me to admit what I felt each time she spoke of him, so that she might yet again remind me that I had overstepped the bounds? Was she using her constantly resurrected ex to remind me of the trench between us?

"I don't look upset at all," I said, pretending to argue with her remark.

"Just let it go."

Why did she bring me to the brink each time I thought it was safe to take a step closer?

"Inky would just sit here and simply stare at the bridge over there."

"Stare at the bridge? Why?"

"Because his brother jumped off it."

I felt for the three of them.

"And what did you do while he stared?" I asked, not knowing what else to ask.

"Hoped he'd forget. Hoped it would stop haunting him. Hoped I could make a difference. Hoped he'd say something. But he'd just sit there and stare, blank, always blank. Until I realized he was telling me in his own subtle, tormented way that if I wanted to and kept at him, I could make him jump too."

Yes, I could see how Clara could bring anyone to jump.

"So why do you come here?"

"I like the salty-dog grunginess." She too could affect being intentionally flippant.

"Be serious. Do you miss him?" I proposed, as if to help her see the answer staring her in the face.

She shook her head—not to mean no, but as though she was shaking me off, meaning, *You'll never catch me, so don't try.* Or: *You're way off, pal.*

"So this place has Inky written all over it," I finally said after waiting for her answer.

"Not Inky."

"Who, then?" I asked.

"That's a Door number three question. How much do you charge per hour?"

But she didn't wait for my answer.

"Me, that's what's written all over it. Because this is the spot where it finally hit me that perhaps I didn't know what love was. Or that I'd practiced the wrong kind. That I'd never know."

"Did you bring me all the way up here to tell me this?"

This caught her totally by surprise.

"Maybe. *Maybe*," she repeated, as if she had never considered the possibility that she'd brought me along to reopen old wounds and help her witness where truth had felled her. Or perhaps she simply wished to see if she'd feel differently with another man. Or was it too soon yet? Lying low and all that.

"I'd sit and watch him drift and drift and drift, as if he were taking me up to that bridge and was going to jump on condition I jumped with him. And I wasn't going to go up that bridge or jump from it, not with him, not for him, not for anyone, unfortunately; nor was I going to sit around and watch him think of it each time we came here while he stared and said he'd die for me, when the one thing I wanted to tell him the most I couldn't even say."

"And that was?"

"So I *am* paying you by the hour!"

She paused for a moment to catch her breath, or to collect her thoughts—or was she smothering the start of a sob? Or was it a grin?

"That he could go ahead. Mean and nasty. Not that I didn't care, but that I was never going to love anyone—not him, at any rate. I'd have jumped after him to save him. Maybe. No, not even." She was playing with her spoon, drawing patterns on the paper napkin. "The rest let's not talk about."

"I would have rushed in to save you, wrapped you in all the coats hanging on Edy's coatrack, screamed for help, breathed into your mouth, saved your life, brought you tea, fed you muffins." I knew it was the wrong thing to say the moment I'd said it, a lame pass sandwiched in soft-core wit.

"The tea and the coats and muffins I like. The mouth-to-mouth, no, because it's as I told you last night." .

I stared at her with a startled face. Why say such a thing? I felt I'd been led to the bridge and pushed. Just when she was most vulnerable, most human, at her most candid, out sprang the barbed wire and the serrated fang. *Because it's as I told you last night.*

How long would it take me to live this moment down? Months? Years?

We were sitting in what was one of the coziest corners in the world—fireplace, tea, unhindered view of the ancient docks, dead foghorns, quiet coffee shop that probably went back to the days of Coolidge and Hoover and where the distant sounds you heard from deep behind the narrow kitchen window reminded you that there were others on this planet—all the dreamy warmth of a black-and-white romantic film sequence slung along a mean and nasty Hudson. I was tense, awkward, dismayed, trying to seem natural, trying to enjoy her presence, sensing all along that I might have done far better at my local Greek diner, chatted the waitress up, ordered my favorite eggs, read the paper. All of it was wrong now, and I didn't know how to fix it. It kept breaking.

"Just do me one favor, though, will you?" she said as we were walking along the unpaved icy path toward her car, both of us staring at the ground.

"What?"

"Don't hate me either."

The word *either,* which so clearly subsumed the word we'd been avoiding, struck my pride—just my pride and nothing else—as if pride lined every ridge on my backbone and her word had struck it dead with the quick fell stroke that sends a bull lurching to the dust before it knows what hit it. No weakening of the limbs, no buckling, no teetering in the knees—just dead, pierced, in and out. Not only had I been found out, but what was found out about me was being used against me, as if it were a source of weakness and shame—and it became one precisely because she made me feel she'd used it this way. Does pride bruise more easily than anything else? Why did I hate having everything about me found out, exposed, and put out to dry, like soiled underwear?

I was ashamed both of the hatred I knew myself perfectly capable of, and of the opposite of hatred, which I did not wish to stir up just yet, because I suspected how much of it there was, though placid, like lakes and rivers under ice. Her *either* had made whatever I felt seem like an indecent breach, a suggestion of slop. Suddenly I wanted to blurt out, "Look, why don't you go ahead to wherever you're going, I'll catch the first train back to the city." That would have taught her a lesson right there and then. I'd never see her again, never answer the doorbell, never go on drives upstate to rinky-dink luncheonettes where a hungover Captain Haddock is as likely to peep from behind the kitchen curtain as would be an old abortionist come out to dram a shot of rum before whetting his tools on Edy's broken marble slab by the cash register. Why bother coming this morning, why the ride to God-knows-where, why the simpering *Did you think of me last night?* when she was telegraphing *hands off*, now and forever?

"I didn't upset you, did I?" she asked.

I shrugged my shoulders to mean, You couldn't if you tried.

Why did I still refuse to acknowledge that she had—why not say something?

"Twice in the same morning—you must think me a real Gorgon."

"A Gorgon?" I teased, meaning, A Gorgon only?

"You know I'm not," she said, almost sadly, "you just know I'm not."

·

"What is your hell, Clara?" I finally asked, trying to speak her language.

She stopped cold, as if I'd thrown her off, or offended her, and had put her in the mood to tell me off. I had asked something no one seemed to have asked before, and it would take a long time before she'd either forgive or forget it.

"My hell?"

"Yes." Now that I'd asked, there was no turning back. A moment of silence fell between us. The fences, so hastily broken down, had come back up again, only to be pulled down the next minute, and were being raised right back up again.

Was ours a jittery, easy, shallow familiarity, and nothing more? Or did

we share the exact same hell, because, like neighbors on the same apartment line, I knew the layout of her home, from the hidden fuse box
down to the shelves in her linen closet? "Maybe our hells are not so different after all," I finally said.

She thought about it.

"If it makes you happy to think so . . ."

In the car she took out her cell phone and decided to call her friend
to tell him that *we* would be there in less than twenty minutes. "No," she
said, after a hasty greeting. Then: "You don't know him. At a party." I
fastened the seat belt and waited, trying to look nonchalant as though
drifting to sleep in the comfort of my reclining seat. "Two days ago." A
complicit glance, aimed in my direction, meant to pacify me. Pause.
"Maybe." He must have asked the same question twice. "I don't know."
She was growing impatient. "I won't, I promise. I won't." Then, clicking
shut her cell phone and looking at me: "I wonder what all that was
about," she said, trying to make light of the questions I'd clearly inferred
by her answers.

To change the subject: "When was the last time you saw him?" I
asked.

"Last summer."

"How do you know him?"

"My parents have known him forever. He's the one who introduced
me to Inky."

"A friend of a friend of a friend?" Why was I trying to be funny when
I clearly hated having Inky's name thrown at me all the time?

"No, not a friend. His grandfather."

She must have loved scoring this point. She caught the missing question. "We've known each other since childhood. If you must know."

Clara never spoke of Inky in the simple past, as someone permanently
locked away in some hardened, inaccessible dungeon of the heart whose
key she had tossed in the first moat she crossed no sooner than she left
him. She spoke of him in a strange optative mood, the way disenchanted
wives speak of husbands who can't seem to get their act together and
should try to pass the bar exam again, or grow up and stop cheating, or
make up their minds to have children. She had spoken of him with a
grievance that seemed to reach into the present from a past tense that
could any moment claim to have a future.

Where did I fit in all this? I should have asked. What on earth was I

doing in the car with her? To keep her company so she'd have a warm
body to chat with in case she got drowsy? Someone to feed her muffin
bits? Was I to devolve into the best-friend sort—the guy you open up to
and bare your soul to and walk around naked with because you've told
him to put away his Guido?

I had never seen it as clearly as I was seeing it now. This was precisely
the role I was being cast into, and I was letting it happen, because I
didn't want to upset anything, which was also why I wasn't going to tell
her how much of a Gorgon she'd really been to me. Rollo was right.

"Music?" she asked.

I asked her to play the Handel again.

"Handel it is."

"Here, this is for you," she said as soon as she turned on the engine.
She handed me a heavy brown paper bag. "What is it?"

"I'm sure it will bring bad memories."

It was a small snow globe bearing Edy's name at the bottom. I turned
it upside down, then right side up, and watched the snow fall on a tiny
log cabin in an anonymous postcard village. It reminded me of us,
shielded from everyone and everything that day.

"But they aren't bad memories for me," she added. She must have
known I'd give everything to kiss the open space between her bare neck
and her almost-shoulder when we were sitting in our warm corner at
Edy's. She must have known.

"Romance with snow," I said, as I stared at the glass globe. "Do you
already own one of these?"

It was what I ended up asking instead of Why do you turn on and off
like this?

"No, never owned one. I'm not the kind who stows away ticket stubs
or old keepsakes; I don't make memories."

"You savor and spit, like wine experts," I said

She saw where I was headed.

"No, my specialty is heartburn."

"Remind me never—"

"Don't be a Printz Oskár!"

•

We arrived at the old man's house sooner than we figured. The roads
were empty, the houses seemed shuttered, as though every family in this

part of Hudson County was either hibernating in the city or had flown off to the Bahamas. The house was located at the end of a semicircular driveway. I had imagined a shack, or something unkempt and broken down, held together with the insolent neglect that old age heaps on those who have long given up touching up the world around them. This was a mansion on top of a hill, and right away I guessed that the back overlooked the river. I was right. We stepped out of the car and made our way to the front door. But then Clara had a change of heart and decided to enter by way of a side door, and sure enough, there was the river. We stood outside a large porch with a wrought-iron table and chairs whose cushions had either been removed for the winter season or that disuse and sheer age had totally ruined and which no one bothered to replace. But the wooden path down to the boat dock seemed to have been rebuilt recently—so these people did care for the house, and the cushions on the porch were probably being carefully stowed away during winter. From the porch Clara attempted to open a glass door, but it was locked. So she tapped three times with her knuckles. Once again she put on her lit- tle freezing-shoulders performance by rubbing her arms. Why didn't I believe her? Why not take her at face value? The woman is cold. Why go looking for that something else about her, why the hunt for subtexts? To remember to be cautious? To disbelieve what she'd said to me last night and repeated at least twice this morning?

"Don't you think it would be wiser to ring the front bell?"

"It just takes them a while. They're scared of wolves. But I keep telling them all they have here are wild turkeys."

Sure enough, a Gertrude-type old woman opened the door ever so gingerly. Arthritic hands, bad limp, scoliotic back.

They exchanged hugs and greeted each other in German. I shook the arthritic hand. "And I am Margo," she said. She led us indoors. She'd been working in the kitchen. A large tabletop displayed scattered hints of a lunch to come. Max would be with us soon, she said. They contin- ued to chatter in German.

I felt totally lost in this house, a stranger.

I wished I had taken the train back to New York. Wished I had never stepped out of the shower, or answered the buzzer, or gone to the movies last night. I could undo all this in a second. Excuse myself, step outside the house, take out my cell phone, call a local car service, dash back into their house, utter a hasty toodle-oo—and then be gone, *adiós, Casa-blanca*. You, Margo, Inky, and your whole tribe of limp, pandangst kultur wannabes.

I ducked outside on the pretext of wanting to glimpse the scenery. Then I realized I wasn't interested in their scenery either, came back in, and shut the kitchen door.

"I just made you coffee," said the arthritic Margo, handing me a mug with her right hand and, with the other, offering me a packet of sugar held between her thumb, forefinger, and middle finger, her bent and troubled arm almost beseeching me to come closer and take it from her before she dropped it and then fell trying to catch it. I wondered why she was offering me coffee and not Clara; but then I saw that Clara had already helped herself to some and was about to sit at an empty corner of the large kitchen table. The old woman's pleading, beckoning gesture, at once humble and contrite, had touched me.

"Clara always complains I make very weak coffee," she said.

"She makes the worst coffee in the world."

"It's not bad at all!" I said, as if I'd been asked an opinion and was siding with the host.

"*Ach*, Clara, he's so polite," she said. She was still sizing me up and, so far, approved.

"Who is so polite?" came the voice of an elderly man. Mr. Jäcke Knöwitall himself.

Kisses. Just as I'd expected. Firm handshake, hyperdecorous Old World smile that doesn't mean a thing, slight bow of the head as he hastened, indeed rushed, to take my hand. I recognized the move instantly. Deference writ all over, except when you turn your back. And yet, unlike his wife, not a trace of a German accent, totally Americanized—*A real pleasure to meet you!*

"What are these ugly shoes, Max?" asked Clara, pointing at what were obviously orthotic contraptions with rows of Velcro fasteners. It was, I realized, her way of asking about his health.

"See, didn't I tell you they were ugly!" He turned to his wife.

"They're ugly because your legs and your knees and every other bone in your wobbly, weather-beaten body is out of whack," she said. "Last year your hips, this year your knees, next year . . ."

"Leave that part of my anatomy alone, you pernicious viper. It served you well enough in its time." This, it took me a second to realize, was all for Clara's benefit. "Sir Lochinvar may no longer be among us, may he rest in peace, but in the middle of the night you can hear his headless torso galloping above our bedroom in search of a dark passage, and if you paid attention, you toothless daughter of scorpions, you'd open your window, offer him your sagging pan-fried eggs, and put your mouth to work."

Everyone laughed.

"*Ach*, Max, you've become downright lurid," said his wife, looking in my direction as though imploring me to pay no mind to his latest outcry.

"Dear, dear Clara, I am out of whack with myself, that's what I am."

"Complain, complain. His new thing now is he wants to die."

He ignored her.

"Do I really complain all that much?" He was holding Clara's hand.

"You always complained, Max."

"But he complains even more now, all the time" came back old arthritic.

"It's the Jewish way. Clara, if I were younger," he began, "if I were younger and had better knees and a better charger and steed—"

Margo asked me if I could help. *Naturlich!* Would I mind going with her outside? "Put your coat on. And you'll need gloves."

Soon I discovered why. I had to get some wood for the stove and bring it into the kitchen. "We love cooking with wood. Ask my husband. What am I saying—ask me."

Together we walked out toward the shed where the gardener stored the firewood. She complained about the deer, sidestepped their droppings, cursed when she stepped on something that wasn't mud, then scraped the bottom of her shoe against a boulder. I wasn't sure whether she was speaking to me or just muttering. Finally, out of the blue: "I am happy to see Clara." Perhaps it was an opener of sorts, making conversation, or she might just have been talking to herself, so I didn't respond.

I returned with two logs. In the kitchen, Margo opened the stove and displayed several halved golden butternut squashes glistening with oil and herbs.

Max uncorked both a red and a white. "To while away the time," he said, and proceeded to pour the white wine into four glasses. Then, pinching the base of his glass between his thumb and his index finger, he swirled the liquid a few times and finally brought it to his lips.

"A sonnet, a miracle," he said. Clara clinked glasses with Margo and Max and then three times with me, and twice three times more, repeating the old Russian formula in a mock-whisper. No one said anything until he spoke: "All it takes is a senseless round fruit no bigger than a baby's testicle and you have heaven."

We were all tasting his wine.

"Now try the other," he said, proceeding to decanter the pinot into my glass once he saw that I had downed the sauvignon.

"Another small miracle."

We all tasted, swayed approbation on our faces. Inky's grandfather was staring at me. He suspects they've broken up already. He's trying to feel her out before seeing if he can patch things up between them. I'm now definitely the one-too-many in this crowd. I should have called a cab. I'd be in the station and far away by now.

"I think both wines are wonderful," I said, "but I'm such a boor when it comes to wines that I very often can't tell one from the other."

"Oh, just ignore him, he's just being his usual Printz Oskár." She was speaking to them, but seemed to be winking at me, or neither winking at them nor at me. Just winking, or maybe not at all.

She is far too clever for me, I thought. Too, too clever. How she shifts and beckons and rebuffs and then switches, and just when you're about to give up and head for the first train back to the city, she'll throw you a Printz Oskár for you to chew on, and dangle it way over your head to see if you'll try to yap and jump, yap and jump.

"Has she said why she's here?" he finally asked me.

"No, I didn't," she interrupted.

"Well, prepare yourself. You've come for Leo Czernowicz, Czernowicz playing the Bach-Siloti. Then we'll hear him doing the Handel. And then we'll be in heaven, and we'll have soup and wine, and, if we're truly, truly lucky, one of Margo's salads with these strange mushrooms she'll use to shut me up for good if one more bawdy comment comes out of my mouth."

"Sit," he said. I looked around at the many chairs and armchairs in the living room. "No, not over there—here!"

He opened the pianola and began fiddling with it before inserting the head of what turned out to be a long, unfolded strip of something like perforated yellowed parchment.

"Is he familiar with the Bach?" he asked.

I looked at her and nodded.

She was made to sit right next to me on a narrow love seat. I'd wait for the music, and then I would just let my hand rest on her shoulder, that shoulder which now, more than ever, seemed to know and to second and to want me to know it knew everything I was thinking.

"Well, even if he knows the prelude, this is something you've never heard in your life. Never. Nor will you ever hear it played this way. First you'll hear him play the Bach prelude on the pianola and then Siloti's transposition of that Bach prelude. Then you'll hear it as I've had two students from one of the colleges nearby remaster it. And if you behave, and you don't interrupt too many times, and eat your soup, I'll let you listen to Leo's Handel. Ladies and gentlemen, this is Leo Czernowicz, just a few years before the Germans found him and took him away and didn't know what to do with him, so they killed him.

And there it was. At first a very faint drone, then the sound of a gasp, like air sputtering and hissing its way through a congested windpipe, and then it came, the prelude I'd heard who knows how many times before, but never once like this: hasty, tentative, and ever so deliberate. Then we heard the Siloti.

"The prelude is too solemn," said Clara, "too somber, too slow perhaps." She had to find something wrong with it. Why wasn't I surprised?

"Not to worry, we've had to speed it up, of course, because those of us who heard Leo play remember he was very fast, too fast. But it doesn't matter. Art is about one thing: speaking directly to God in God's language and hoping He listens. The rest is pipi caca."

He put on the CD, and sure enough, I finally saw why we'd traveled for two hours on this freezing day to get to this house.

"Shall I play it again?"

Clara and I glanced at each other. Sure.

"Then I'll go and look after the lunch," said Margo.

Without hesitating or even waiting for our response, he proceeded to play the Bach-Siloti a second time.

Deftness and dexterity, something so easy, lambent, and yet ever so contemplative in the face of what lay in store for the likes of Czernowicz, who was, so many, many decades later, still speaking to God. I kept thinking of his playing this piece as the piano cut holes into the very piece of cardboard in front of us—how could he not have known that in a few years he'd drink of the black milk of dawn? The more I listened, the more it seemed to become more about him than about Siloti, more about Jews like Max who outlived the Holocaust but would never live out its sentence, more about the fugue of death than about Bach's prelude and fugue. I knew that this would never be undone, that from this too there was no turning back, no coming back, just as I knew that without Max and this old house, without winter on the Hudson, without Clara and our three days together, the prelude would remain the glistening empty shell it had always been for me until now. It needed the Shoah for it to come alive, it needed Clara's voice in my intercom, Clara's laughter as she waved obscene gestures in her car, it needed *our being here like this* in Edy's warm corner by the lurching bull, and her admonitions forbidding so many things; it even needed my inability to focus on the music, as though not focusing on the music while thinking of reaching out to her would end up being part of how the music needed to be heeded, registered, remembered. If art were nothing more than a way of figuring out the design of random things, then the love of art must come from nothing less random. Art may be nothing more than the invention of cadence, a reasoning with chaos. It will use anything, just anything, to loop itself around us, and around us again, and around us once more till it finds its way in.

Could one ever listen to the Bach after the Siloti?

No one answered.

I asked if I could hear it once more.

He looked pleased. I was hooked, he thought.

Then, when the glorious beginning swept over us again, he excused himself to go help Margo out with lunch.

Left alone with her, I began to feel a sense of total discomfort. All of these empty chairs around us, and yet here we were, Clara and I, squeezed tight together on this narrow love seat. I wanted to find an excuse to move away, perhaps by making a show of wanting to get closer to the music. But I stayed put, did not breathe, did not budge, didn't even show I had thought of budging. She too must have felt awkward before noticing my own discomfort. But she masked it better than I, for she didn't even stir. Perhaps she hadn't noticed anything, and my reading of her discomfort, as my reading of the Siloti prelude, or of what she meant by Printz Oskár each time she used the words, or of our awkward love seat arrangement right now, was nothing more than another misreading, my startled gaze to the world looking back at me. Was there any way for her to know what I was feeling, thinking? Or hadn't it even crossed her mind? She was so distracted by the music that she hadn't even noticed that her thigh was touching mine, from hip to knee, hip to knee, which is to say, almost 20 percent of our bodies. What if I told her that while the prelude was streaming over us, my thoughts were focused on the hip-to-knee, joined at the hip, you and I, Clara, for we're of one kidney too, and all we need is a slight tilt in our seating, and it could just as easily be my hips against your hips, me inside you, as we listen to this music, again and again, the smell of you on my skin, everywhere on my skin, because I want to be bathed in your smell, rub it on my back, your wetness on my neck and everywhere on my body, you and I, Clara.

I knew that the slightest stir in my body, even moving a finger, would suddenly rouse her from her own thoughts and tell her that our bodies were touching, hip to knee. So I didn't move a thing; even swallowing became difficult, as I grew conscious of my own breathing, whose pace I tried to steady to a monotonous rhythm, and finally, if I could, to a halt.

But then another thought rushed through me: Why not tell her what was happening to me, what I felt, why not move, stir, budge, and show at least that I liked being glued together on this love seat and that all I had to do was touch her knee, part her knees, and just place my hand there, and, as in so many paintings of the Renaissance, let her slip a leg in between mine in a posture that speaks legends, like Lot's with his daughters'? Was she with me? Or was she elsewhere? Or was she one with the music, her mind in the stars, mine in the gutter?

With all these feelings tussling within me, I knew I would never dare anything, especially now that we were alone together. Gone was my resolve, my wish to put an arm on that shoulder, as we listened to the music, and let a hand land ever so lightly and caress her there, and then bring my mouth where it ached to be, not to kiss, or even lick, but to bite.

I sensed her tense up. She knew.

Any moment now, Clara will stand up to help in the kitchen. Or should I be the first to stand now, to show that I wasn't committed to this love seat arrangement, that I wasn't trying to feel her up, that I couldn't really care?

"Do you want to hear it again?"

I stared at her. Should I tell her now once and for all, just tell her and let the chips fall where they will?

"The music—do you want to hear it, or have you had enough?"

"Let's hear it one more time," I finally said.

"One more time it is."

She stood up and pressed the play button, then after standing by the CD player came back and resumed her seat right next to me.

Do we touch hands, or what?

Just be natural, a voice said.

Which is what?

Be yourself.

Meaning?

Being myself was like asking a mask to mimic a face that's never been without masks. How do you play the part of someone trying not to play parts?

We were back to hip-to-knee. But it felt mechanical, heartless, cold. I'd take that moment last night anytime, when she stopped before crossing the park and told me about Czernowicz as our arms kept touching, inadvertently.

This was all in my head, wasn't it?

Suddenly I caught myself thinking of wanting to come back here again—if only to touch this moment again: the cluttered room, the frost, the dead pianist, she and I seated unusually together in this snow-globe cabin of our invention, and all this stuff around us, the soup, Inky's brother, last night's Rohmer, the snow on Manhattan and on Clermont-Ferrand, and the fact that if Czernowicz never knew what awaited him after playing the Siloti here, he'd never have guessed that, two nights after staring out to his world in prewar Europe, we'd be sitting in this room like the oldest and closest of friends, listening to a pianist that my grandfather and Clara's grandfather might easily have heard in their youth, never once suspecting that their grandchildren . . .

When the music stopped, I said I wanted to step outside for a few minutes. I didn't ask her. "I'll come with you," she said.

"Where are you two going?" asked Margo, when she saw us leave through the kitchen door.

"To show him the river."

•

The ground underfoot was hard, with patches of brown earth under the snow. Clara cleared away a tricycle that she said belonged to one of the grandchildren. Miles was his name. "Secret agent?"

"Secret agent," I said, accepting a cigarette.

"Let me light it for you."

She lit my cigarette, then took it back before I could even draw my first puff in ages.

"Not on my watch!"

So I wasn't going to be allowed to smoke.

"What do you think they're talking about now? Me? You?" I asked.

"Us, most likely."

I liked our being called *us*.

In the summer, she said, Hudson County was lush, and people simply sat around here and whiled away entire weekend hours on lounge chairs, while food and drinks kept coming. She loved sunsets in the summer here. She was, I could see, describing Inkytimes in Inkyland.

We ambled through a narrow alley flanked by tall birch trees. White was everywhere. Even the bushes were a pallid, pewter gray, except for the stonework around the house and for the wall lining the length of the wood, verdigris bordering on livid gray. I imagined a carriage stopping here a century ago. As we walked, we began to near what seemed a dirty wooden fence that led to a wooden gangway and farther off to a withered stairway. "The boat basin is down there. Come."

They had cleaned the Hudson years ago. Now, if you didn't mind the undertow and the eels, you could swim. Still more trees, bare bushes, more sloping walls lining the property.

Then we spotted the river and, beyond it, the opposite bank, all white and misty, an Impressionist's winterscape.

It made me think of Beethoven's late quartets. I asked if she'd ever heard the Busch Quartet play. Maybe as a child at her parents', she said.

As we approached the river, we began to hear crackling sounds that became louder and louder, clanking away like iron rods being hammered on an anvil. Crick, crack, crack. The ice on the river was breaking, clacking and clattering away, one floe knocking into the other, wrecking that neat white sheet of ice we had been seeing from the distance of the house, block after block of iced Hudson whacking its way downstream, with dark, dirty, glutinous black water underneath. Perhaps the Hudson was giving us its own version of the Siloti—crick, crack, crack, crack.

"I could listen to this for hours," I said. What I meant was: I could be with you for hours—I could be with you forever, Clara. Everyone else has been make-believe, and maybe you are too, but right now, as I hear our music served on ice, my heart isn't on ice, as I know yours isn't either. Why is it that with you, for all your stingers and thistles, I feel so much at home?

"I could listen to this all day," I repeated.

I had forgotten that in Clara's world one didn't rhapsodize about nature, sunsets, rivers, or songs in the shower. One didn't hold hands either, I supposed.

"You don't like this?" I asked.

"I like this fine."

"Oh, just tell me you like it, then."

She turned toward me, then looked at the ground. "I like it, then," she said. A mini-concession no sooner made than instantly withdrawn.

How long would lying low last?

And then I don't know what possessed me, but I asked her: "How long will all this lying low last?"

She must have seen this coming, or had been thinking about it her-self, perhaps wondering at that very moment how long before I'd say something like this. Which is perhaps why she didn't ask why I was asking.

"All winter, for all I know."

"That long?"

She picked up a stone and hurled it far into the river. I picked one up too and did the same, aiming mine as far as I could. "Bellagio is a stone's throw away," I said. "And yet."

She said she loved the sound of stones striking the ice, especially the heavier ones. She threw another. I lobbed another and another. We stood and watched where they landed.

"Maybe I need time."

She didn't quite finish her sentence. But I knew right away.

"You're an amazing woman, Clara," I said, "just amazing."

She didn't say anything.

"It's good to hear someone say this." Then having heard her sentence, she couldn't help it. *"It's good to hear someone say this."* She parodied her own words.

"Amazing all the same."

We threw more stones at the ice floes and listened to the ice bark back as though there were penguins who'd hopped up on the floes to forage for their young and thought we had thrown them bread, and what we threw was ice and stones.

On our way back, I held out my hand to her. I hadn't even thought of it. She gave me hers as we went up the wooden stairs that led to the gangway. Then she let go, or I let go, or we both did.

When we returned, the soup was ready. Margo liked to add cream to the thick golden brew. So did Clara. It was a soup for cold weather, said Margo. A rustic, rectangular table had been set up, Max sitting at the head, Margo to his left, Clara to his immediate right, and I next to her. "I would have wanted Clara at my left," said Margo, who seemed to be in a happy, chatty mood, "but I didn't want to separate you."

What on earth were they thinking? What had they been told?

I tried to give Clara an inquisitive look, but she must have anticipated this and was focusing intently on her soup, trying to show she hadn't heard the comment I knew she couldn't have missed. She raved about the soup and, better yet, about the crème fraîche, raved about the curry. "I believe in sixty-minute-not-a-second-more cooking. And that includes dessert," said Margo. "And I," interjected Max, "believe that a good wine will rescue anything you dish out with your sixty-minute chow even raccoons won't touch."

"Be grateful I'm around to feed your rotting gums."

"And I to down what we'll call food in front of our guests."

Clara was the first to laugh, then Margo and Max, then me.

This was family business as usual, I guessed.

I am sitting where Inky sits, I thought.

The soup and the bread and the cream and the wine, which kept coming, were extraordinary, and soon enough we were being regaled with Max's latest complaint. His knees. He'd been on archaeological digs in his youth and was now, in his nineties, paying the price for his follies near Ekbatana. "With most people my age, it's the mind that goes. Mine is intact. But the body's checking out."

"How do you know your mind is so intact, old man?" said Clara.

"Do you want me to tell you how?"

"Please."

"I warn you, it will be obscene, I know him," cut in Margo.

"Well, about a month ago, because of these damned knees—which incidentally are about to be replaced, so this is the last time they'll be seeing you—I had to get an MRI. They asked me of course if I wanted to be sedated and if I suffered from claustrophobia. So I laughed in their faces. I survived the Second World War without so much as taking aspirin, now I'm to be sedated simply because they'll put me in a box with a hole in it? Not me. So in I go. But no sooner am I in there than I realize this is what death must be like. The machine starts such a ghoulish pounding and gonging that I want to ask for sedation. Problem is, I'm not supposed to move; if I do, they cancel the procedure. So I decide to brace myself and go on with it. Except I know my heart is racing like mad, and I can't think of a single thing but the noise, which, more than ever now, reminds me of the hellish pounding of the dead statue in *Don Giovanni*: dong, dong, dong! I try to make myself think of the Don, but all I can think of is hell. This is death. I need to think of something quiet and soothing. But quiet and soothing images fail to come. This is when memory rescued me: I decided to count and name every woman I'd slept with, year by year, including those who brought me so little pleasure in bed that I've often wondered why they parted the Red Sea if they had no manna to give and certainly wanted none of mine. This, to say nothing of those who wouldn't take off their clothes, or would do *this* but certainly not *that*, or who always had engine trouble, so in the end, though you might have been in bed together, and even fallen asleep, it was never clear whether you had scaled the summit. In any event, I counted them and they added up to—"

"One thousand and three!" exclaimed Clara, referring to the number of Don Giovanni's mistresses in Spain.

At which we all clapped.

"Or was it ninety-one?" asked Clara, the Don's mistresses in Turkey.

"Six hundred and forty," added Margo, referring to those in Italy.

·"Two hundred and thirty-one, and not a woman more!" thundered Max, the Don's mistresses in Germany.

"*Madamina* . . ." I began, deepening my voice till it growled with comic gravity the way Leporello catalogs the number of Don Giovanni's mistresses around the world.

It was so unlike me to hurl a joke among people I barely knew, much less with song, that I was surprised to hear Clara laugh the loudest, and more surprised yet when she took up what wasn't even meant as a cue and began humming the opening bars of the aria, and then actually singing the aria, with a voice that, once again, came unannounced and was more lacerating than the one I'd heard at the party or by the juke-box, because this time it seemed to palm my neck with its breath, once, twice, every syllable a caress. "*Madamina, il catologo è questo, delle belle che amò il padron mio* . . ." A few verses more and her voice had so totally shaken and moved me that, in an effort to keep my composure, I found myself putting an arm around her and then, pressing my head against her back, squeezing her toward me. She didn't seem to mind, because, more surprising yet, she held my hand on her waist and, turning to me, kissed me on the neck, letting her hand linger there, the way she'd done last night, as though the hand was part of the kiss.

Her kiss unsettled me more than the singing. I had to keep quiet, focus on the soup, show that this third wine was far better than the first two. But I was too flustered for words. I had touched her sweater, and its softness belied every cutting inflection in her speech, in her face, her body.

By then we had each already finished two servings of soup and begun eating the marinated greens. More wines.

After the salad, Margo got up and came back with a cake. "It's a *strudel gâteau*. I hope you all like it."

She also brought to the table more crème fraîche. "This is everyone's favorite."

She had probably meant to say, *This is Inky's favorite*, but had caught herself in time. Or perhaps I was making this up. But Clara's determined focus on her slice of the turned-over apple pie told me once again that she had intercepted the very same backpedaling and was passing over it in silence.

"Max, want some *strudel gâteau?*"

"Silly woman. Must you always call it *strudel gâteau?*"

"Behave," whispered Clara.

Who knows what existed between Clara and the old couple. I would have to ask her at some point, probably on our way back, during one of those long silences that were bound to crop up between us. But part of me was tired of so many reminders of Clara's past with Inky. Had they grown up together? Would his shadow linger forever between us? If she was done with him, why go visit his grandparents? To show she was with another man now, hoping they'd tell him? But anyone with half a brain could instantly spot by our behavior together that we were not together. Was her kiss meant to suggest we were? Is this why she'd brought me along? Getting me out of the shower, bringing me breakfast, making me feel special, giving me all this nonsense about lying low, which she knew would stoke anyone's curiosity, calling herself a Gorgon—all this just to send Inky the message that love was dead?

I wondered what kind of evil monster she turned into when her love died—did she tell you it was finished: *Just let it go?* Did she drop you back into the fish tank where you sank or swam, or did she release a few bubbles at a time and throw you tiny pellets of food as she did with Inky that night at the party, so you wouldn't go belly-up, though you know and she knows it's only a matter of time before they pick you up and flush you down where all fish souls end when they go back to the greater scheme of things? Was I making all this up, or was I myself gradually being put in a straitjacket before being dunked in a pickle jar as I looked up at the hole that was about to close on me?

I could always escape. The train to the city. My beloved Greek diner. Doing the *New York Times* crossword puzzle. I still had Christmas presents to buy, the stores would still be open if I left now. Was there a limit to how late one could give Christmas presents?

"Another slice of *strudel gâteau?*" asked Margo.

I looked at her and wondered where she stood on the Inky front. Then I remembered that they'd sat us near each other, not once but twice.

Yes, I would take another slice of the *strudel gâteau.*

"All young men like this cake," said Margo.

I looked over at Clara. Once again, her face was neutral.

"Ladies and gentlemen, it's been nice," said Max. "Come, Margo."

I looked up at them, totally baffled.

"I need to take a nap. Otherwise I age by five years, and that, dear friends, takes us to unreal numbers. Or I start dozing in public, and frankly, no one enjoys watching old people nod and drool and mutter things that had better be left unsaid."

"As if he ever watches his speech."

"*Ach*, Margo, it's not like you don't nod in the afternoon either."

"—and leave our guests?"

"Come and cuddle and don't fuss so much, woman."

"Cuddling, he calls it—phooey."

"Fie and phooey to you too, besotted harridan; come upstairs, I said, and watch me be daring in love and dauntless in war—"

"—and dangle your bonnet and plume? I'm not sleepy."

"Don't bother about us," interrupted Clara. "I'll make coffee and put the dishes away."

"Esmeralda will do it. Otherwise we pay her for what?"

"On second thought," Clara said, "we might as well say goodbye now. We're leaving in a short while. It might snow again."

"Yes, you don't want to be snowed in."

Clara suddenly turned to me. "Do you want to be snowed in?"

What an amazing, amazing woman.

"You know damn well I would love nothing better," I said.

"Margo never asked if I wanted to be snowed in. You're a lucky man."

"Upstairs, Lochinvar," said Margo. "Upstairs, with your old bonnet and plume."

Clara kissed the two of them more affectionately than when she'd greeted them.

"You'll see, you'll be your dashing self in no time," she added, knowing he was worried about his operation.

"Just don't forget to listen to the Handel. With all this talk of soup, wine, and bonnets, I forgot."

"Don't blame the wine or my soup, you forgot because you're old."

"*Because you're old.* Those are probably the last words I'll hear before I head out to the eternal landfill. But don't forget the Handel. That Handel was worth waiting seven decades for."

•

"Let's make coffee first."

I watched her open one of the kitchen cabinets and take out the espresso maker. She knew exactly where to find it. She tried to twist it open, but it was shut tight. "Here, you open it," she said, handing it to me. "They don't drink coffee anymore," she added, as though registering yet another instance of their decline. The packet of ground coffee was also where she knew it would be, in the freezer. Even the silver spoon with which she spooned out three heaping spoonfuls was in an old wooden drawer that rattled first before suddenly dipping at a precarious angle once you pulled it out—a cemetery of old cutlery that hadn't seen sunlight in who knows how many years. "Here," she said, handing me two mugs. "Spoon. Sugar. Milk?"

"Milk," I said.

I liked how she made everything seem normal, habitual, routine, as if we'd been doing this for ages.

Or should I be on my guard: people who make you feel unusually at home when you know you're just a guest can, within seconds, show you to the door and remind you you're no better than a deliveryman who rang a doorbell on a hot day asking for a glass of water.

I wondered if we were going to sit next to each other at the large table, as we'd done during lunch, or across from each other, or at a right angle. At a right angle, I decided, and put down the spoons accordingly. "I am sure she has tiny sweets somewhere," said Clara, who began rummaging through the fridge and the old kitchen cabinets. "Found 'em," she said.

"Ach, Liebchen, not sweets after the strudel gâteau," she said as she helped herself to a box of Leibniz chocolate cookies, tore off the cellophane wrapper, and put four on a dish, which she placed right between what were going to be our seats. She had mimicked the old woman's accent so well that I couldn't help laughing, which made her laugh as well. I asked her to repeat what she'd just said.

"No."

"Come on."

"No."

"Why not?"

"Because I'm embarrassed, that's why."

"Just say shtroodel ga'tow."

"Shtroodel ga'tow."

I felt my stomach muscles tighten. I was dying to kiss her. She could say anything and I'd want to kiss her, make any gesture and I'd be pulled toward her, and if she happened to lean toward me as we tried to speak softly so as not to wake the old couple upstairs, then I'd have to struggle not to put my arm around her as I did at the dining table, but this time I'd let my palm rub her face, once, twice, just keep rubbing that face, and touch those lips, that mouth, and let my face rub against hers; what wouldn't I give to touch her teeth with my hand, with my lips. We were standing in the kitchen rinsing the dishes.

"Are you happy you came?" I asked.

"Yes. I liked seeing them, I always do. They are like two coiled snakes corkscrewed unto their last. You watch: when one goes, so will the other, like a pair of old slippers."

"Is that what love is like—a pair of slippers?"

"Don't know about the slippers. But they are identical, Max and Margo. Inky and I, on the other hand, couldn't have been more different. Inky doesn't have a devious bone in his body. Inky wants you to be happy; Inky misses you when you're gone, runs errands if you ask, fixes things when they break, will die for you if you so much as hint that you want him to jump from this or that ledge. He is kindness and health personified—which is why he'll never understand me."

"Because he is not all twisted?"

"Not like us, he isn't."

I liked this.

"So you said no to Inky because he's a healthy human being?"

"So I said no to Inky." Pause. "Here, eat this cookie, otherwise I'll eat it, and when I get fat, trust me, I get even more bitter and depressed."

"Bitter and depressed, you?"

"As if you hadn't noticed. You're like me. We're chipped all over. Like these dishes. Jewish dishes." She smiled.

I did as I was asked with the dishes. Then we loaded them into the dishwasher. We were standing almost hip to hip, neither budging, until our hips were touching. Neither of us moved away.

She asked if I'd split another Leibniz cookie with her.

"Promise not to be bitter and depressed."

"I'm already bitter and depressed."

"Because of me?" I had said it in complete jest and couldn't possibly have meant what she heard. But she turned to me with her wet pink hand and, with the back of it, touched me once on the cheek, and then again and again. And then she kissed me so close to my lips that she might as well have kissed me all the way. Which is when I let my lips touch hers, once, twice, rubbing her face with my own wet palm as I'd been craving to do all through lunch.

She let me brush her lips, but there was forbearance in her lips, and I knew not to push.

"So you will split another chocolate Leibniz with me."

"I have no choice."

"Inky calls these chocolate lesbians. We used to think it was funny. I wonder if there's anything we can take for the road."

She ferreted through the cabinets. Nothing. Just M&Ms, probably bought for the grandchildren or for Halloween. The large yellow bag was sealed with a giant clasp. "Let's take a few."

We found a small ziplock bag and transferred M&Ms into it with the pantomimed complicity of amateur safecrackers.

"Thank you," she said.

"For the M&Ms?"

"No, for coming here with me. For knowing. For everything else. And for understanding."

"Especially for understanding," I repeated with emphasis and mock-humor.

Thank you for understanding. What a way with words she had. Saying everything and saying nothing.

"I told him I was the wrong woman for him. But did he listen? Then I told him he was the wrong man for me. And he still wouldn't listen. And he'll keep fighting it. I know him; he'll call them tonight and ask if I came by. And they'll say yes. And he'll ask if I came alone. And they'll say no. And he'll ask who with, and they won't know, and he'll call me, and it'll never end. Happy you came now?'"

"You answer."

"I think you still are."

She dried her hands, passed me the towel, and began putting the wine away.

"Clara?"

She turned back. "Yes."

"I want to tell you something."

She was putting the corks back into the two bottles. This was going to be it.

"You want to tell me something"—again the same restraint in her voice, in the way she held her body and stared at me now—"don't you think I know?" She looked me in the face. "Don't you think I know?"

The way she said it broke my heart. I could almost feel a sob rising in my chest. *Don't you think I know?* It's what one said in lovemaking: *Don't you think I know? Don't you think I know?*

I was about to add something, but there was nothing else to say; she had said it all.

"Let's hear the Handel, then," she said.

We walked into the living room. She turned on the CD player, then lowered herself to the floor and sat on her knees on the rug. She was already wearing her winter coat. I sat across from her on a chair against the wall. In the same room, saying nothing. And then it started.

I couldn't understand what it was about this sarabande that had made us come all the way up here to hear it. Perhaps because I had never heard it before. "Isn't it played a bit too slowly?" I finally ventured to say, trying to suggest that I too could tell it could use some mechanical acceleration.

She shook her head once and said nothing, dismissing my comment for the simple, intrusive thing it was. Then, for no reason, or for a reason I couldn't begin to fathom, she raised her eyes and began to stare straight at me, but in a vague, lifeless manner, which made me suspect that though she was looking at me and wasn't looking away, she wasn't really looking at me either. There was no doubt, though; she was staring. I stared back with the same seemingly unfocused gaze, but she didn't register my gaze, or didn't register me, and I thought, This is what happens to people who are entirely rapt by music, whereas I am almost just pretending, the way I almost just pretend to be rapt by food, wine, scenery, art, love. When others listened to music, they became one with music and just stared at you, past you, through you, and expected no reciprocity, no implicit eyebrow signal, because they were already one with things.

Were we just going to stare at each other for however long it took to hear the music?

So it seemed.

So I left my chair and, all the while continuing to stare at her—she was still following me with her gaze—kneeled down right next to her on the rug, my heart racing, neither of us taking our eyes off each other, I not knowing whether I was breaking some tacit understanding I hadn't altogether agreed to, she not knowing what I was up to—except that suddenly I caught her nether lip give a tremor, her chin seemed to cramp ever so slightly, and, before I knew what was happening, her eyes were filled with tears and she began crying. I envied her even this freedom.

"Clara," I said.

She shrugged her shoulders, as if to mean, *Can't be helped.*

"I don't know what's come over me. I don't know."

I reached out and held both her hands in mine.

"I'm a total mess, aren't I?"

"It's the Handel."

She said nothing, just shook her head. I should have kissed her right there and then.

"Or maybe it's Inky," I threw in. "Or seeing Max and Margo," I added, trying to help her narrow down the cause of her tears, the way a parent might help a child find the exact spot where his arm hurts.

"We're taking the CD. He made other copies," she finally said. She was trying to show she was quite able to compose herself. "Poor man, him with his dead music and his rotting body and all that talk of eternal landfills—"

She began to cry again, this time in earnest.

"You left out *strudel gâteau.*" I was trying to distract her and make her laugh, though I wouldn't have minded if she continued crying. Tears seemed to have removed every barb from her body and, better yet, to have humanized her the way I'd seldom seen someone be so human before. It left me feeling totally rudderless. I attempted another joke, this time at the expense of art and pipi caca art.

She gave a mild laugh, but wasn't falling for the diversion.

"Does music always make you cry?"

But my question was a weak diversion, and she wasn't falling for it either.

"I'm not ready," she finally said.

I knew exactly what she meant. Might as well bring it out into the open.

"Because I am?" I asked, as though to undo any pretense that I might be.

Were we saying yes by saying no?

Or was it the other way around? Saying no to mean yes to say no?

"What messes," she said.

"Well, at least we know we're safe messes."

She took this in. I thought I had finally comforted her.

"I don't know that I am—safe, that is. Perhaps neither of us is."

Even in the midst of tears, I could heed the light, windblown cheep of rusted barbed wire dangling on a long country fence.

I took out my handkerchief and gave it to her.

She grabbed it as though it were a jug of ice water in July, wiped her tears several times, then crumpled it tightly in her fist.

I feared she might hold this moment against me.

"You're the only person I know"—she hesitated a moment, making me think she was about to say something ever so sweet about me—"who still uses handkerchiefs."

"What do most people use, their fingers?" I asked.

"Some do. Most use tissues. Others gloves."

I could sense that maybe humor wasn't going to work.

"I'm just afraid I may never see this house."

She was on the verge of tears again.

"What if we promise to be back here in a week—together?"

She looked at me point-blank and said nothing, the same vague, absent look on her face, which told me she either didn't trust my motives or that she simply lacked the will to remind me how quixotic was my plan. For all I knew, she had other things lined up for next week, things I wasn't part of—for all I knew, this should have been the time to bring up her admonition yet again, but she didn't have the strength or the heart to do so now.

"Why not, you'll pick me up, bring me breakfast, and sing for me in the car."

"You're such a Printz Oskár."

When she gave me back my handkerchief, I could feel its dampness. I put it back in my pocket, hoping it might never dry.

"You're the best person to have Vishnukrishnus with," she finally said. "Today was my turn; yesterday, yours."

"Keep talking like this and you'll make me have one this minute."

"What wrecks," she said.

•

On the way back we listened to Handel's sarabande again and again. I knew that this would be our song, the song of December 26, and that wherever I'd be in the years to come, if, like a traveler in the desert I should lose my bearings one night, all I would have to do was think of this sarabande as played by a man who had disappeared into the hinterland of time, and like an anthropologist piecing bone fragments together one by one, I'd be able to bring back who I was on this day, where I'd been, what I'd wanted most in life, and how I'd fallen for it and almost touched it. As we listened to the music quietly, I thought of how she and I had stepped down the ramp onto the riverbed and heard the ice break, and how that too was forever laced into that moment on the rug when I realized, as I'd never done since meeting her, that the remainder of my life could hang on that tune and that it would take nothing but a misplaced breath to make my life go one way or the other.

"Clara Brunschvicg," I said.

"Yes, Printz Oskár?"

"Clara Brunschvicg, I'll never forget you," I was going to say. But then I thought it sounded too wistful. "Clara Brunschvicg, I could so easily fall in love with you—if I haven't already." No, too laden. "Clara Brunschvicg, I could do this for the rest of my life—me and you, alone together, whenever, wherever, forever. Spend every minute the way we've done today, winter, car, ice, stones, soup, because one hundred years from now, those minutes are all we'll have to show for ourselves, all we're ever going to want to pass on to others, and frankly, in one hundred years they'll all forget or won't care or know how to remember, and I don't want to end up like my father with dreams of love and of a better life he'd been robbed of or is still sailing out to. I don't want to pass by your building in thirty years and, looking up, say to myself or to the person I'll be with that day, You see this building? There my life stopped. Or there my life split. Or there life turned on me, so that the person looking at the building right now and talking to you is, ever since that one winter so many years ago, still *on hold*; the hand holding your hand is a phantom limb, and the rest of me is prosthetic, too, and I'm a shadow and she's a shadow, and, as in Verlaine's poem, we'll still speak shadow words of our shadow love while the decades trawl past us as we stay put and hold our breath. The real me is frozen on this block and chances are will outlive me by many years until he turns into one of those family legends that gets retold on ritual anniversaries and from tragedy become a font of laughter and ridicule. *So, tell me the one about the man who was named after a large tanker*, they'll say, the way I'd ask my father about ancestors who'd had their heads lopped off."

"What were you going to say?" she said.

"Nothing."

"That's not what you were going to say," she said.

"Yes, I know," I replied.

At which we laughed. "Aren't we so very, very clever, Printz."

"We are, we are."

•

The same thing happened twice again that day.

We were speeding down the country road on our way back to the city. It was past sunset, and we watched a pale, listless color line the white Hudson we'd been staring at all day. We'd been driving for around half an hour when the tiny town began to come into view. Neither of us said anything, and it seemed we'd both forgotten and were going to pass in silence. Clara, who was driving, looked at me. Then she began to pick up speed, and I could tell she was smiling. She was bluffing.

"Want to pass it up?" she asked.

"No. I was going to ask you to stop."

"Lipton tea *that* good?"

I nodded.

"You know we're not being very good," she said.

"I know. But a cup of tea never hurt anyone."

We parked the car exactly where we'd parked that morning. I ordered two teas just as I'd done before. Clara went to the bathroom. I chose the same spot by the wood-paneled wall. The fire was still burning in the fireplace. And she knew exactly where I'd be. Except that this time as soon as she sat down I told her to scoot over, because I wanted to sit next to her. She didn't seem to mind. She didn't let much time go by before asking, "So tell me about her." Did she really want to know? I asked. Yes, she really wanted to know. And as though to entice me, she snuggled into the corner between the end of the seat and the glass panel with the darkling view of the Hudson right behind her. I met her right after college, I said. The love of your life? No, not the love of my life. So why are you telling me about her? You'll see if you let me finish. She was a dancer, but by day an editor, a good cook, and three times a week a single mother. She was older than I was. By how much? Ten years—and don't interrupt. She cooked meals for me that I'd never eaten before, with sauces that would seem to require chefs and sous-chefs days to prepare but which she'd whip up in a matter of minutes. Here I was almost a vegetarian eating steak dinners every night. It took me a while to realize why she was feeding me so much protein. She, on the other hand, never ate. She smoked all the time. So we'd have those fabulous dishes on the tea table, and I would eat and eat and eat, while she sat next to me on the floor and watched me chomp away. She was probably bulimic, or anorexic, or both, except that you'd never know it, because she was always bingeing in secret. She was also addicted to sedatives, laxatives, antidepressants.

"What was good about her?"

"For a while everything."

"Then?"

"I stopped loving her. I tried not to stop, but I couldn't. From not loving her I started not wanting to listen to her, then to not wanting to touch her, to hating the sound of her laugh or the rattle of her keys when she came home, or the sound of her slippers when she woke up in the middle of the night and went into the living room for a smoke, and sat there in the dark because I said the light bothered me, down to the click of the television when she'd turn it off, which meant she was coming back to bed. It was horrible. I was horrible. So I left her."

"Are you not good for people, either?"

"I don't think I am. And she knew it. One day, toward the end, she said, 'I'm someone you won't remember having loved. You'll walk out on me and won't give it a second thought.' And she was right."

I fell silent.

"Well, go on with your story."

"Late last winter, out of the blue, one evening I got a call from her. We'd not spoken in three or four years. She said she wanted to see me—no, *needed* to see me. Well, I knew she hadn't borne me a child in secret, I knew she wasn't short of money, and I knew she hadn't uncovered an STD she had to tell all her old lovers about. She just needed to see me, that's all. The man of my life, she called me. It tickled me somewhat. We made a lunch date, but it fell through, then another, which also fell through. And then she never called again, and I didn't either. A few months ago, through a series of coincidences, I found out she had died. The news of her death still haunts me, or perhaps I want it to."

"And?"

"And nothing. She'd found out she was very sick and needed to reach out to someone who'd mattered and say a few things she'd never had the courage to say before. Now that the veil was shed and there was no room for pride or other nonsense, all she wanted was to spend a few hours together."

There was a moment of silence between us.

"I thought she was lonely and had run down a list of old flames, old friends," I added.

"I wonder whom I'll call when my time comes. Not Inky, that's for sure. Who would you call?"

"That's a Door number three question. And we don't do those in diners and grills."

"I hear pandangst."

I gave her a look that said, You should know.

She replied, *I most certainly do know.*

She straightened up and sipped from her tea, holding both palms around her mug.

I wanted to grab both her hands, put them together, and hold them in between my own and then spread them open as one opens the pages of a hymnal and kiss each palm.

I told her I liked watching her drink tea.

"And I love your forehead," she said.

I looked out the window, feeling that this working-class diner had something unbelievably magical, as if it understood that for us to be together and feel comfortable here it had to be as ordinary and unassuming and as run-down as anything in a Hopper painting, like Lipton tea, like the plaid faux-linen curtains that kept rubbing her hair, and the thick chipped earthenware mugs we drank from. I wondered if she and I were not like Hopper's perpetual convalescents—Hopper people, vacuous, stunned, frozen Hopper people, resigned to hidden injuries that might never heal but that have long since ceased to stir either sorrow or pain. I wasn't sure I liked the Hopper analogy. But this, I realized, was exactly what she meant by lying low. Staying put like Hopper's people, sitting upright at a slight distance from things like jittery lemurs scoping out an all-too-familiar landscape called life with neither interest nor indifference.

"I can see why she called you, though."

It took a few moments for me to realize she was referring to my old flame.

"Why?"

"No why. I can just see it."

·

"It's getting late," I said.

And suddenly, as soon as I'd said this, I knew she knew why I'd said it.

"At what time does it start?"

"Seven-ten, didn't you know?"

"Am I invited?"

I looked at her. "Who's the Printz Oskár now?"

"So we're going to the movies?"

"Yes," I said, as if I were finally yielding to a request she'd been struggling to make all day.

"So we're going to the movies."

It took me a while to understand what the near-imperceptible lilt in her voice meant when she said "So we're going to the movies." She was either enacting or genuinely expressing the excitement of children whose parents on a bleary Sunday afternoon suddenly decide to put on their coats and herd everyone to the movies. We're going to the movies, I repeated after her, the way a schoolmate who'd been visiting me after school, rather than being sent back to his parents in the evening, was invited to come along to the movies.

We had less than an hour to drive to the city and find a parking space. Or we could park in her garage and hail a cab. "It could be done," she said. Or I could jump out and buy tickets while she parked nearby. Could we call the theater and have them save two spots under our name? Which name? Your name. My name. "You know what name," she said.

We were now speeding along the highway, and in no time spotted the lights of the George Washington Bridge glimmering over the vast and

tranquil Hudson. "The city," she said, the way anyone might say on spotting a familiar lighthouse signaling the way home. I remembered the tension in the car earlier that morning, and the muffins and bagels in the
white-gray paper bag, and the Bach version we'd listened to and how it
all belonged to another time warp. "Look to your right," she said, having
spotted it before I did. And there it was, exactly where we'd left it earlier
this morning, anchored smack in the middle of the Hudson, the *Prince
Oscar*, our beacon, our lodestar, our emblem, our double, our namesake,
our spellbound word for the things we had no words for—love of my life,
my dear, dear *Prince Oscar*, dear, troubled ship that you are, lord of all
ships in the catalog of ships, give us a sign, tell us, oh, boatswain, what of
this night, tell us of this land of dreams you ferry passengers to, tell us
what's to become of us, what's to become of me—can you hear?

It had seen us come and go and, for a minute now, seemed to light up
its deck to hail us from far away across the Hudson, as if to say, You mor-
tals, you lucky, holy pair who remembered me tonight when you could so
easily have looked the other way and made light of my years, take a good
look at this damp, ferruginous, scrap-metal tub stuck out in the middle of
my hoary winters, don't think I don't know what it means to be young, to
hope, to fear, to crave, as you come and go, and may come and go again
on this drive, I who have seen riversides aplenty and gone up and down
the world like so many phantom ships before me, oh, never become
ghost ships, marking your years with layers of rust till the water seeps
through and you're nothing but a slough and a hollow hull stranded after
many wrong turns and shallow bends, till the rudder is no longer quite
yours, and the rust is no longer quite yours, and you won't remember you
were a ship once—yours is the real journey, not mine. Oh, don't take me
away and unbolt me as they unbuckle the dead, but think of me as both
the light and the way, and remember this day, for the time comes only
once in a lifetime and the rest, in thirty years, is good for nothing except
to remember that time.

"Printz Oskár," she finally said.

"Yes," I answered.

"Printz Oskár."

"Yes!" I repeated.

"Nothing, I like saying it."

The girl is in love with me, and she doesn't even know it.

•

I thought of the evening awaiting us. Two films, the walk in the snow to the same bar, where we'd take the same seats, though side by side this time, and order the same drink, talk, laugh, dance to the same song, maybe twice, and then the dreaded walk home past my spot in Straus Park, where I'd want to tell her, or maybe not, about my spot in the park, all of it followed by the perfunctory good-night kiss at her door, which would most likely try to seem perfunctory, though maybe not, and finally, after watching her disappear into her elevator with Boris minding the foyer, my walk back to the park, where I'd stop tonight as well, sit on my bench if it wasn't wet, and just stare at the fountain, look at the trees in the middle of this nothing park off Broadway, and wonder which part I liked best, spending the entire day with Clara or coming all alone here to think of the Clara I'd just spent the entire day with—hoping not to have an answer, because all answers were right till they turned and proved the question wrong, the way so many things were right and then wrong and then right again, till all we had was our nightly colloquy, with the candles lit around us and our shadow selves rubbing shoulders as we'd done at Edy's, and in our pub, and during lunch, and when we listened to the music, and washed the dishes, and sat together in the theater, shoulder to shoulder, speaking shadow words each to each.

On my way home that night, I received a text message.

PRINTZ OSKAR ONE DAY I'M GOING TO HAVE TO SEND YOU A TEXT MESSAGE

FOURTH NIGHT

What is your hell?" I had planned to ask her. It would have been my way of drawing her out and helping her lower her defenses. I liked it when she spoke about herself. I liked when she cried, liked when we sat inside the booth at Edy's in the dark and I had almost held her hand and kissed both palms at the same time, liked her when, past midnight after the movies, she said they made good fries at our usual place, because she knew I wanted to be back there and, better yet, be at the same table, side by side, and pick up where we'd left off our talk of Rohmer and the men and women who were all about the obvious but had lost their way around it. I liked the way she skipped out of the movie theater in between films and found an open newspaper vendor who sold M&Ms, because we'd forgotten those we had poured out into a small ziplock bag in Margo's kitchen. Meanwhile, she had also found the time to buy two *grandes*. Morning and evening, she said. I assumed she'd also taken the time to check her messages. How many times had he called? I asked. Just eight— and that's not counting the messages he left on her home phone. Wasn't she curious to know what he'd said in them? She knew what he'd said in each. I would much rather have seen her pity and kiss him than prove she could churn kindness into venom.

After we'd said goodbye at night, I'd made myself promise not to expect her to call me the next day, not to expect to see or hear from her in who knows how long, and certainly never to think of calling her. Unless I had good reason to. The best reason sprung on me hours later, but I didn't heed it.

At first I wanted to call her and tell her that . . . that I was happy to have spent the day with her and, in the process, make a few references to

the day's markers—Bach, *strudel gâteau*, Rohmer again, and the sudden
appearance of the *Prince Oscar* along the Henry Hudson lying in wait for
us, or the goodbye kiss it was no less awkward to seek than to avoid.

But call and say what? That I took back every joke made at Herr
Jäcke's expense? That I'd spent an amazing day precisely as she foretold?
That there's so much to say? So, say it. I don't know where to start. Is
this going to take forever? I just wish you'd come home with me now, tonight, this moment. Why didn't you ask me then, Oskár? Because I just
couldn't, because you're so fucking forbidding with your hot-cold, fire-
ice, speak-don't-speak airs. Because I can't make out where you are, who
you are. Printz Oskár! Clara Brunschvicg! Good night. Good night.
There'd be a moment of silence. Clara Brunschvicg . . . What? Clara
Brunschvicg— Don't say it, she'd interrupt. Don't want me to say it? No.
Then *you* say it. Printz Oskár, let's not do this now. Tell me why you
don't want us to say it, tell me, tell me, tell me.

I could have called on my way back home.

I could have called in the cab.

I could have called once I got home.

I could have called you while you were in the elevator, called your
name while you were speaking to Boris, shouted "Clara!"

I could have answered her message as soon as I got it. *One day I'm
going to have to send you a text message*. Written in typical Claraspeak, in
stone, like a glyph that no one can decipher, not even its author. What
could *One day I'm going to have to send you a text message* possibly mean?
That this is not the text message she means to write, that the message
she will write *one day* will say much, much more, and that this was just a
teaser, a stay-tuned signal, with or without sequel? Or did it mean: I wish
I had more to say, I wish I had the courage to say more, I wish I could tell
you what I know you want to hear—why don't you ask me, why don't
you just ask me, goddamnit? I wish you would read in between the lines,
as I know you will and love to do, because you'll take nothing I say at
face value, which is why I must speak in double-speak, though I do not
want to speak in cipher, especially to you, but am reduced to speak in the
bleakest of codes.

I kept reading the text message for at least an hour, as if it had come
with a crib note I had accidentally lost. I should have answered something right away. But by three I had not answered, and I didn't want her
to think that I was the sort who checks messages in the wee hours of the

morning. By four, when I awoke from a dream I couldn't even remember, I thought I should answer with something witty: "*Ceci n'est pas un message non plus. Go to bed.*" But then I thought: Let her stew awhile.

It did not occur to me that of the two of us I was and would always be the one stewing, not Clara. She *didn't do* stewing. She'd written her SMS off the cuff and then gone to bed. Or did she just want me to think she'd written it off the cuff, then gone to bed?

And why would she want such a thing? To hide what? To suggest what? To have me suspect or second-guess what exactly?

No, this was me, just me.

Then I was seized by a terrible anxiety. What if she had stayed up waiting to hear from me? What if, left by herself, she finally did pick up the phone when it rang for the nth time that night and had one marathon tug-of-war session with Inky that always led to a listless *Okay, come over if you really want*? I wonder if she would have picked up the phone on seeing it was I calling?

At eight in the morning, when, contrary to every absurd expectation, it finally became apparent that she was not going to buzz me downstairs, I decided it was time to give up hope and head out to the beloved-no-longer-so-beloved Greek diner. Now yesterday's missed opportunity to be alone with eggs and the paper came back like a reminder of failure and despair. Before stepping into the shower, I eyed the telephone. No, you do not call the Claras of this world just to say hi. You call them with a purpose, with a plan—even if it is a makeshift purpose. Do you have a plan? I do not have a plan. But you want to call? I want to call.

Lunch, I thought. No, a late lunch. Not too loud, not too many people. A late lunch in a nice place.

CB HOW ABOUT LUNCH PO

Let her think this is my natural texting "voice." Breezy, untrammeled, happening.

By the time I came out of the shower, she had already answered. Here was someone not reluctant to show she was eager to respond.

WHERE WHEN WHAT HOW WHY

She had seen and raised me.

It meant: *So you want to play curt and lapidary, here's curt and lapidary. See who'll fold first.*

The *why* she'd thrown in as an afterthought was the thorniest part of the equation.

PIRANESI 2 PM ITALIAN 67 & MADISON CUZ
TERRIBLE REASON
YOU DON'T WANT TO KNOW THE REASON
NAME ONE
HANDEL ROHMER LAST NIGHT
THAT WAS YESTERDAY
I WANT TODAY TO BE LIKE YESTERDAY DO I NEED TO GO ON

I was on the verge of acknowledging something, though I had no idea what.

SMS is at once more intimate and more distancing. More so sometimes than the spoken word. The accent is there, but louder, sharper, clearer, a reef of curt intentions, easily mistaken but seldom misinterpreted. One more round and we'd be quarreling, not kissing.

I KNOW OF A BETTER PLACE PICK ME UP AT 2

I was going to utter a determined "Great," but then decided to soften the tone to the more upbeat but formulaic "Done," which I altered to the more compliant "I'll be there," to the mock-imperative "Be there," but which, at the very last second, I wanted to mollify to the more gentle and evasive "Until then," opting in the end for my original "Done."

All so very guarded and shifty. Posturing. On both our parts? Or just on mine?

Afterward, I went to my Greek diner and did exactly what I'd longed to do yesterday. Sat by the large frosted window. Managed to exchange the exact same words with the Greek *kukla* who is no longer a *kukla*. Had my bottomless insipid coffee, ate all my hash browns, read the paper and yesterday's as well.

Then I went to a music store and bought CDs of all of Handel's piano suites and of the Bach-Siloti. I would put on the music as soon as I got home and try to remember how the ice had cracked to the beat of a prelude that cast a haunting spell all day.

I walked into a Starbucks, ordered the same coffee infused with mocha she had brought along yesterday, and opened one CD box after the other. I liked the post-Christmas crowd, tourists milling around Lincoln Center and so many New Yorkers off for the day. I still had two presents to buy. Then I realized that what I truly wanted to do was to buy Clara a present. *Why buy me a present?* Because. *Because is a terrible reason.* Because you changed everything, because as soon as you touch a day in my life, it changes color, like one of those mood rings, because if you so much as graze my skin that part of me is burned forever. Here, see this elbow? You tapped it once when we walked back from the bar. It hasn't forgotten. See this hand? It held the tips of all your fingers when you cried. And as for my forehead, you once said you liked it, and ever since my thoughts are no longer the same. Because you make me like my life, who I am, and if everything stops here, not to have met you would be like having lived in a north country and never tasted a single tropical fruit. Cherimoya, mango, guava, papaya, I'll name them all like the Stations of the Cross, or the towns to Campostella, or the stations on the Broadway local line, including the ghost station under Ninety-first Street, which is where you and I, Clara, drink of the same blood like two shades from the underworld who need to time-out together before heading back to what are called the living.

And then it hit me: I'm someone you'll forget having known, aren't I?

I'm someone you'll never remember meeting.

I could die and you wouldn't know.

I bought her a copy of the Busch Quartet playing Beethoven's A minor. With an indelible marker, I scribbled my dedication: *The Heiliger Dankgesang is for you. It's me.*

Dramatic.

Subtle.

Sweet.

Fatuous.

Happening.

I liked it.

Something told me she'd laugh and still forget.

At two in the afternoon, when I came by, Clara was already waiting for me downstairs.

"Last night's film does not make sense at all," she said as soon as the other Boris opened the door for her. "He didn't desire her knee, he wanted her, but knew he'd never get her, so the insidious little perv went for the knee. A cheap diversion. Actually, he desired her but didn't want to own up to it. Or—and it gets worse—he never did want her but thought he should, which put him in the double-bind position of wanting her and not wanting to want her, without perhaps ever having wanted her—"

"How are you?" I interrupted.

She started laughing.

"I'm very well. But do you think I'm wrong?"

"I think all of Rohmer's men—oh fuck it!"

She wrapped her huge multicolored wool shawl around her head and tucked it under her chin.

"Scarf!" She wasn't budging.

"Scarf," I repeated, undoing my scarf and fumbling with the knot she liked.

"I'll do it," she said.

Then she put her arm in mine and suddenly began walking north. We could take a cab, or we could take the bus—very scenic route, she said. Let's walk, she wasn't cold, she said. I immediately felt dismayed and began wondering whether this was going to be another outing that would require work or turn out to be one of those restaurants where she and Inky were regulars, where she and Inky did this, ate that, met So-and-so. "I know exactly what you're thinking, it has nothing to do with it." "That's a relief," I said. "I have to think of everything, don't I. We don't want no pouting." "Who pouts?" "Someone I know gets easily worked up." "I wouldn't talk," I replied.

On our way up the totally deserted sidewalks of Riverside Drive, we finally remembered the barges and the giant tankers. "I see something up higher," she said. "Do you think it's what I think it is?" "Might be. Just might be." But we both knew it couldn't be. It was just our way of resurrecting yesterday.

As we walked, I kept looking at all the buildings along Riverside Drive. I hadn't walked on this sidewalk for years, and it hadn't changed a bit. Now they had Clara written all over them.

At some point along the way her phone began to ring. She looked for it in every pocket of her thick coat and finally found it. "I don't have my glasses, who is it?" she said, handing over her phone. "It says Ricardo." She grabbed the phone from me, turned it off, and put it away. "Who is Ricardo?" I asked. I'd always felt that she was surrounded by men, but why had she never mentioned Ricardo before?

"It's Inky." Spoken abruptly.

"Named after a ship, perhaps?"

"No." She didn't think I was funny.

The restaurant was empty. At one of the large tables closest to the kitchen, the help was already busy having lunch. One of the waiters was sitting at a small table all by himself reading the *Corriere dello Sport*.

As soon as Clara walked in, she greeted him by his first name. He was the co-owner. Was there pasta? Plenty. He didn't look up. She snuck behind the bar, opened what must have been an old fridge, produced a bottle of chilled wine and two glasses, asked me to uncork it, and headed into the kitchen, all the while removing her coat and undoing the complicated shawl wrapped around her head.

Timidly, I uncorked the bottle, poured wine for the two of us, and joined her in the kitchen. The water, apparently, was still hot, so she asked Svetonio to "throw" in the pasta and begin heating the sauce. There were also some slices of chicken waiting to be sautéed if she wanted. "*Grazie*, Svetonio." She turned to me and, without making introductions, explained that their friendship went back a long way. Should I read anything into it? Svetonio lets me come here and do my thing. I get him the best opera tickets all year. Believe me, I get the raw end of the bargain, *non è vero*, Svetonio? "Who's to argue with Clara?" he said.

She found the dry frying pan she was looking for, took out the sliced chicken wrapped in cellophane from the large refrigerator, then poured some olive oil into the pan. Svetonio produced some sliced vegetables. "Are you going to just stand there?" "No, I'm observing," I replied.

"Observe away. Lunch in no more than nine minutes. Better than anything you'd planned, right? . . . I need lemon and some herbs." But she was talking to herself, not me.

I watched as one of the waiters set a table that was far away from everyone else, but right by one of the French windows. I took out the CD and placed it on her side of the table.

"What's this?" she said when she came out to see if everything was ready. "*Ein Geschenk.*" "*Für mich?*" "*Für dich.*" "*Warum?*" I looked at her and couldn't help saying: "Cuz."

She took the wrapped CD with her into the kitchen. I joined her again and stood by as she watched Svetonio remove the pasta and ladle it into two deep dishes. Sauce, cheese, and what she called *some-pepper-please* in imitation of waiters in restaurants. He then placed the sautéed chicken in a dish, covered it with another, produced the vegetables, and within seconds we were seated across from each other. Someone had even found time to bring a large bowl of salad for the two of us.

"So what's this?"

"It's my favorite piece of music."

"Yes, but what do you mean by *It's me?*"

"My moods, my thoughts, my hopes, everything I was before hearing this music and everything I became after hearing it—it's all in there. Just better. Maybe it's how I want you to see me."

We drank the wine.

"And you want me to have this why?"

"I can't explain."

"You can't or you won't?"

"I can't explain that either."

"We're doing real good, Printz. Let me ask you different, then."

Suddenly I felt at risk, exposed, about to be caught off guard.

"Why give *me* this?"

"Because I've bought almost everyone I know a Christmas present except you."

"And that's the real reason?"

"No, it is not."

"Printz Oskár!" There was mock-reproof in her voice.

"Clara Brunschvicg, you make it very difficult for me both to lie and to tell you the truth. Everything seems twisted in an elaborate cat's cradle."

"How?"

"We say the things that matter as though they didn't matter. And we let tangents take us off course to save us from lingering on the stuff that really matters. But then what matters comes back again, and we're off on tangents and detours again."

She was staring at me. She was silent.

"What stuff that matters?"

I should have known.

"Do I really have to tell you?"

"Someone walking on eggshells?"

I shook my head to suggest that I wasn't. But I *was* walking on eggshells, and there was no point denying it. "Me feet is bleeding and me tongue is tied."

"Will you please just tell me and let's move on to the pasta."

"Well, how shall I say this? Suddenly it feels so difficult—"

"Why?" There was tenderness and no impatience in her voice.

"Partly because I've never known anyone like you. I've never wanted to be known by anyone the way I want you to know me. I want to fake nothing with you and, yet, without meaning to, when I'm with you, I always feel I'm ducking and dodging. And yet you're like the twin I never had. Hence this piece of music. The rest is all Vishnukrishnu Vindalu stuff, which I'll spare you."

"No, I want to hear the chicken vindaloo stuff too."

"Not over spaghetti."

"We can have Indian food for dinner if you like."

"So you're free tonight?"

"Aren't you?"

I saw her lean her right side against the French window. I leaned against it with my left. This was just like yesterday, except better. I did not mind the silence. It brought to mind that time when we'd listened to the Handel together and had stared at each other for so long. She rested her chin on a fist and, looking at me, asked, "So go on with the vindaloo stuff."

I could feel my shoulders bunch up again. This was beginning to make me feel very uncomfortable, as if I were hiding something but didn't have a clue what it was. I couldn't even look her in the eye. The disconnect between our sentences, between her candor and my diffidence, was being rubbed in my face. Why did I feel I was being shifty with her when I was dying not to hide anything from her?

"About the Beethoven-Vindalu," I said, as if this was really what I'd been trying to say ever since watching her unwrap my gift, "maybe all I wanted was someone to speak for me—"

"And say what?"

"Clara, every subject we touch on, from boats to Bach to Rohmer, to *tangelines* and *strudel gâteau*, takes us to the same exact place each time, as though everything between us seems fated to keep prowling and scouring and knocking at one door—and that door we've decided—*you've* decided—stays shut. Right?"

"I'll answer when it's my turn."

"Maybe Beethoven is my way around this door. Or maybe I should learn from Rohmer's people, who get an indecent thrill from talking intimately about things that most people who've just met find awkward and prefer to pass over in silence."

I was running for cover, not realizing that I had just given away my hiding place.

She interrupted me. "So this is awkward for you?"

The *this* was us, I presumed. There was something savage and cruel in her question, as though she was striking back at something I'd said that had offended her. But it also seemed that all she wanted was to expose me, to expose me for the sheer, perverse pleasure of doing so. Two nights ago she'd warned me not to hint at any of this—why was she raising the subject when I was clearly trying to avoid it? Her six clipped words *So this is awkward for you?* were a straight indictment of everything I was; they made me feel like a slithery trickster who should be punished for beating around the bush when he'd already been warned to stay off the grass.

And yet I knew she was right. She'd seen through me and zeroed in on the one thing I feared most: the awkwardness that sprang up between us each time she looked me in the eye and made it so difficult to speak to her or find the courage not to deny that awkwardness did indeed exist between us. I didn't even want her to see how easily I blushed the instant I felt I'd strayed from indirect speech. Was I hiding desire? Or that I didn't feel I deserved to desire?

Why had she ever asked me this? To unsaddle me even more, in case I presumed too much? To egg me on, if I presumed too little? To rob the moment of its luster? To bring out the truth? To make me doubt everything about us? Or, as I was perfectly willing to accept, was all this taking place in my head only?

I looked at her. I knew I could risk everything by saying something marginally wanton or clever. The Claras of this world seldom give men second chances. Say the wrong thing and they're gone. Say nothing and they're equally gone. She'll put on a dark skirt, a crimson blouse, and, with her daunting good looks and many shirt buttons undone, find any man at the first party she'll care to get herself invited to. I was staring at her unbuttoned light green shirt now. No wonder she was wearing such a heavy shawl. There was nothing underneath. Why the unbuttoned shirt? Do I look or do I look away? I'll look.

"Now this is getting really awkward, Printz. Is this another Vishnukrishnu Vindalu moment?"

Keep a lid on and out fly the barbs, I thought.

"You mean my silence?" I asked.

"I meant your staring. But the silence too."

"Let's change the subject, then," I said.

"And run away? No, talk to me about awkwardness. I want to learn."

I cleared my throat.

She removed the cover dish from the chicken plate and served me two slices of chicken and herself two. "Three tiny potatoes for you, three for me, one more for you, because every man about to make a speech deserves a potato, five sprigs of asparagus for you, three for me, because I need to make room for what I'm about to receive from him, and finally, a bit of gravy for you and some for me to wash things down with. Okay, I'm listening." Then, realizing she'd omitted something, she added, "And don't ruin the moment."

"I was thinking of how lucky I was to have gone to Hans's party."

"Ye-es." Cautious encouragement to keep going.

"Lucky for me, I mean, not for you."

"Of course."

We laugh. We know why we laugh. We pretend not to know. Realize we're both pretending. Standard fare. I love it. *Aren't we so very, very clever.*

"Maybe I don't feel awkward at all with you, but feel that I should. Maybe the twinge of awkwardness sitting between us right now is nothing more than intimacy deferred. Or waiting to happen. Or failing to happen."

"And?"

"And something tells me we both feel that this could easily be the best part, which is why we're both reluctant to fight it. This may just be the rose garden. What comes after could be trenches."

"And?"

Was I even speaking the truth? Was I lying? Why couldn't I believe a word I was saying?

"And?" she insisted.

"And this is where I wish Beethoven might step in and make this moment last forever, this lunch, this conversation, even these twinges of awkwardness. I want nothing to change and everything to last."

"And?" At this point she was teasing, and I was loving it.

"And here's a thought: In a year from now, when we go to Hans's party, will we go there as strangers?"

"Well, I am no stranger to Hans."

"I didn't mean Hans and you."

She elbowed me.

"I know what you meant. Chances are we will have had a few arguments, maybe strong disagreements, ratted on each other—I'm almost certain—and probably hung up and sworn never to speak again—but I harbor no grudges and make up way too easily, so the asshole who'll ruin things will be you, not me."

"Ruin? Ruin what?"

I had finally managed to corner her.

"See—you're doing it now—ruining things, this time by pretending."

So there was no boxing her in anywhere.

"Well, what if I am an asshole? What then?"

"You mean will I make allowances, and try to understand, and get under your skin and feel your pain, and see the world with your eyes and not through my own blinkered, selfish point of view?"

Why was she sidetracking?

"Put it this way: What if *things* suddenly die, or are about to, and with their death the desire to keep them alive dies as well—what will you do then?"

Without meaning to, I felt that I had cornered her once again.

"I will let you know they're about to die, but I won't do a thing more."

"So, it is conceivable that we will meet at Hans's party next year— what am I saying?—next week, and though we'll stand this far apart, we could be total strangers."

I was sounding peevish.

"Why are you doing this?"

Suddenly she wasn't being flippant at all. "We're having this most wonderful lunch, probably one of the best I've had all year, and look at us: we're playing chess—worse than chess, because chess pieces move, but you're freezing us on the spot, like two blocks of ice stuck under a bridge. The idiots get past all our roadblocks and find all manner of shortcuts. The one or two lifemates end up ruining things, and I'm the one who's blamed. Shall I keep going, or shall I flip channels?"

"Please, please, keep going and don't change channels."

"Unlike you, you mean." A little dart—light and swift. Light and swift, just as I liked her. I let it slide. "See, I know what you want, and the funny thing is, I can bring it to you, but I also know you: you want promises more than what I have to bring, and promises I can't make. Nor, for that matter, can you—not these days. Let's not fool ourselves; this ain't the rose garden."

I was stunned by her candor.

"Have I spoken out of turn?" she asked.

"Nope. As always, you've nailed it on the head. Sometimes I wonder why I can't speak like you."

"Want to know why?"

"Dying to know why."

"It's very simple, Printz. You don't trust me."

"Why don't I trust you? Tell me."

"Really, really want me to tell you, Mr. Vindalu?"

"Yes."

"Because you know I can hurt you."

"And you know this for a fact?" I was trying to recover my dignity.

She nodded.

Why couldn't I be like her?

I reached out and held her hand in mine, then lowered my head, opened her palm, and kissed it. How I loved that hand, exactly as it was, as I felt it, as it smelled. It belonged to that shirt which belonged to that face, to this woman who had always been *me* but might never want *me*. I felt her hand go limp in mine; she was suffering me to touch it and would do no more.

"Why?" I said.

She shrugged her shoulders to mean, *God knows.*

"I don't always think I'm a good person. But telling people this only makes them want to prove me wrong, and the more they try to prove me wrong, the more I want to push them away, but the more I push them away, the guiltier I get, the nicer I become, the more they think I've changed. It never lasts. In the end I learn to hate both myself and them for things that should have lasted no longer than a few hours." She reflected on this. "Maybe a few nights. Inky and I could have stayed friends."

"This is the most twisted thing you've said so far."

"What, that being kind to people makes me want to hurt them? Or that hurting them makes me want to be kind?"

"Both. I won't ask you why you're telling me all this—"

She didn't let me finish. "Perhaps my hell is having to say all and not knowing if I should be quiet instead, and yours, unless I'm all wrong, is to listen and not know whether I mean it."

"Amphibalence?"

She looked at me with something like gratitude in her gaze.

"Amphibalence indeed. But let me put this on the table, but you can't raise me, okay?"

So typical. I nodded.

"I said you don't trust me. And I'm sure you have your reasons, and I won't ask what they are. But I also know you: you'll never ask me what we're doing here together. And one day you're going to have to."

"And when that day comes?"

She pursed her lips, gave another wistful shrug of her shoulders, said nothing.

She wasn't answering. "Door number three?" I asked.

She nodded.

"That's my hell," I said.

"Unfair. It's mine too."

I thought I understood. But she was right. One day I'd have to ask her what she meant. And that day, it suddenly hit me, was today, was now. And I didn't have the courage to ask.

·

"On the house," said one of the Mexican waiters who, along with the other waiters and cooks, had long finished lunch and cleared the staff's table. He had placed two squares of what looked like tiramisu and two cups of coffee on the table.

"Do you know what time it is?"

We were both dumbfounded. It was 4:30.

She said she needed to walk. I did too. After coffee we put on our coats, she did her complicated shawl knot, said goodbye to Svetonio, who was back to the sports pages, and we walked out to find a cold setting sun. Everything about her, about today even, was totally unusual. Not paying for lunch, helping the cook in his own restaurant, walking into places and taking over—a home, a kitchen, a restaurant, a life—all these gusted through otherwise ordinary days. This was not just Clara's style, it was Clara's world, a life that seemed boundless, extravagant, and every inch festive and unlike mine. And yet here we were, two beings who, for all our differences, seemed to speak the exact same language, liked the exact same things, and led almost identical lives. How could we be in two different rooms, let alone live streets and blocks apart, when we were made to share the same chair? Then I thought of Inky and caught a glimpse of his hell. He too must have thought they were identical beings, and yet there he was, living with the awful proof that being similar, and thinking the same thoughts, and feeling inseparable from someone was nothing more than one of the many screens that loneliness projects on the four walls of our lives.

I told her it was doubtful we would have time for Indian food tonight.

"Why?" she asked.

We laughed. She knew exactly why.

We had slightly more than two hours before 7:10. On the way down Broadway, she stopped by a botanica and asked, in Spanish, if the owner was there. The girl, who was hardly older than fourteen, went in, called her mother, who soon after appeared. "Together or separate?" she asked. "You decide," said Clara to the fortune-teller. The woman asked me to produce my palm, which I did, reluctantly, never in my life having done anything like this before. It felt no different than entering a slovenly tattoo parlor or opium den, something slightly disturbing, because I might never be the same person on coming out. Worth a shot, I thought. The beefy woman took hold of my left palm with one hand and with the pinky of her other seemed to point at things I wasn't seeing. Someone very dear to me had bad leg troubles, no, just the right leg. A sibling— and moments later—no, a parent, she said. Very serious leg trouble, she said, raising her head and staring at me. It's over, she corrected. I withdrew my hand before she had time to say anything more. But you have a good line, she said, by way of compensating for the bad news. She asked for Clara's hand. The bucket is full, but I see nothing anywhere. Was this a metaphor? Then she whispered something in Clara's ear. Clara raised her shoulders, to suggest either indifference or that she didn't know. We walked out humbled and crestfallen creatures.

"What did Madame Sosostris whisper to you?" I asked once we'd left the palm reader's parlor.

"You don't want to know."

"Unfair."

"Actually, you do, but you really don't."

"Inky?" I asked, knowing that, after our lunch, my cards were all on the table.

"Not telling."

Clara wanted to buy a candy bar, she said. It was five o'clock.

We had two hours, yet strangely enough neither of us felt they were hours we had to kill. We could have walked, stopped in stores, bought presents, kept going, kept going—till when, Clara, till tomorrow, next year, forever?

"I can make tea," she said.

I couldn't resist. "You mean walk into a coffee shop, dash into the kitchen, and produce two mugs with Lipton tea bags?"

"No, at my place."

I had to control a sudden surge of instant panic and bliss. Part of me didn't wish to go upstairs for fear of what I'd be tempted to do. The other for fear that I'd never even dare.

Boris—if he remembered me—must have suspected that something like this was bound to happen. She stamped her feet as he was holding the door; I did the same, and thanked him with a semiflustered greeting. I was, without realizing it, uneasy and trying not to show it.

We stepped into the elevator. This was where I'd met the woman in the blue overcoat.

The elevator felt and smelled different. I didn't know this smell. A mid-afternoon-in-a-strange-new-place smell. I had wanted to pretend I was coming here for the first time, that the party had already started, and that I was about to meet Clara any moment now. But before I knew it, we had already reached her floor.

She unlocked the door. Then she removed her coat, unwrapped her complicated shawl, and showed me into the living room, which overlooked the Hudson. I felt that I was back at the party, except that everything had been cleaned up and put back together to look totally different. Partitions had come up where none existed upstairs, furniture had been moved, the artwork looked different, older, the Hudson felt closer, and when I neared the bank of large windows, it seemed to me that even Riverside Drive felt different, more accessible than the far-flung vista that had made me think of Gogol, Byzantium, and Montevideo.

"Give me your coat."

She took my coat, and what almost moved me—because it seemed so unexpected—was her manner of handling it, as if it were going to break or crease if she didn't take deferential care of my stupid old coat. Was this a sign? There are no signs, I kept telling myself.

"Come, let's go to the kitchen. Then I'll show you around."

Was she going to show me her bedroom?

The kitchen, like the entire apartment, hadn't been touched up in decades. Her parents, she explained, had lived there until the day of the accident, and ever since, she'd never had the heart or the time to fix much. There were walls to be broken through, others to put up, wiring to pull out, so many things to be given away. To prove her point, she showed me the gas range and asked me to light it. "Don't you just turn a knob or press something?" I asked. "No, you use this," she said, taking out a match from a large matchbox. "Does this thing whistle when the water boils?" "No, it chimes." She pointed at a very contempo-designed teakettle. A gift. But major renovations would take so much time. "Plus I don't think I want it changed." Her whole apartment, it occurred to me, was lying low too.

We stood in the unlit kitchen waiting for the water to boil.

"I have no cookies. I have nothing to offer."

Girl on perpetual diet, I thought.

She was standing with her arms crossed, leaning back against the kitchen counter, looking, as I began to notice during similar moments of silence between us, mildly uneasy. I wondered why. Was she always curt and abrupt and agitated to cover up her uneasiness—was this her way? Or was she really curt and abrupt, which sometimes coincided with her uneasiness? I felt for her, which was why, as I watched the westering light fall on her figure, I said, "All you need is a dead pheasant and a bruised pomegranate sitting in a blue-rimmed bowl near a clear jar of aquavit and you get a Dutch master's *Girl Leaning against Kitchen Counter*."

"No, *Girl Making Tea with Man in Kitchen*."

"Maybe girl suspicious of man in kitchen."

"Girl doesn't know what to think."

"Girl very beautiful in kitchen. Man very, very happy."

"Girl happy man in kitchen."

"Man and girl talking real stupid."

"Maybe man and girl seen too many Rohmer films."

We laughed. "I haven't spoken to anyone the way I speak with you. You're the only one I laugh with nowadays." There was nothing to add to this except to look her straight in the face.

She opened one of the cabinets to get the sugar. I saw an assortment of about two dozen different steel butcher knives. Her father, she explained, loved to cook on weekends. Now they were all bundled up and heaped on the top shelf. One teaspoon for me and two for her. I could tell she was uneasy.

"Girl will put on CD man gave her," she said, "then the two will *go to France*." This was how she referred to Rohmer's films.

The chime of the teakettle, I said, sounded like a World War II air-raid siren. She said she hadn't noticed, but, yes, it did sound like an air-raid siren.

I asked if she had a teapot available, because I was going to make tea as in *My Night at Maud's*. She had tea bags only, she said, though surely there must be a teapot around—probably very old and very dirty.

Tea bags would do, I said, and proceeded to pour hot water into two mugs, one bearing the name of a city in Umbria, the other of a store in SoHo. "Let it sit a moment, then we'll pour the water out."

"Do you know what you're doing?"

"Not a clue. But I will drop an Earl Grey tea bag into each mug."

The scent filled the kitchen.

Let's go into the living room, she said, carrying her mug and the CD. She opened a cabinet, turned on the CD player, and before long there it was, the hymn from the Adagio in all of its piercing, heartrending beauty. I love Earl Grey tea, I said. So did she. "Time for a secret agent."

The sofa, which was new, was placed directly in front of the bay of windows, so that one could see the Hudson while drinking. What a view, I said. I loved the tea, I loved the Hudson, loved the Beethoven, and I loved the Rohmer tea-in-the-afternoon thing. Outside, where the snow was still untouched by tires or footmarks, was where Clara used to sled with her friends after school.

"Now tell me why the Beethoven is you again."

"Again with the Beethoven!" I was enjoying this.

"Just try, Printz. It's you because . . . ?" she asked, imitating bated breath.

"Because the *Heiliger Dankgesang* was written while Beethoven was convalescing and, like me, like you, like everyone really, was lying very low. He had come close to dying and was grateful to be alive."

"And . . . ?"

"And it's about a simple handful of notes, plus a sustained, overextended hymn in the Lydian mode, which it loves and doesn't wish to see end, because it likes repeating questions and deferring answers, because all answers are easy, because it's not answers and clarity, or even ambiguity, that Beethoven wants. What he's after is deferral and distended time, a grace period that never expires and that comes like memory, but isn't memory, all cadence and no chaos. And he'll keep repeating and extending the process until he's left with five notes, three notes, one note, no note, no breath. Maybe art is just that, life without death. Life in the Lydian mode."

The silence between us told me that, in her mind, Clara had right away substituted the word *life* with another word. Hence her silence.

"Tea in the Lydian mode. Sunset in the Lydian mode . . ." I added to stir some humor between us, at which she almost snickered, meaning: *I know what you're doing, Printz.* "Yes, that too," she said.

I looked over the room. There must have been twenty pillows on the sofas and armchairs, and, in one of the corners by the window, two large plants. The armchairs looked old, but not dowdy, as if the rest of the room were trying to adjust to the new sofa without straining itself. Every electrical outlet seemed packed with what looked like a grape bunch of plugs sticking out of it.

"Is this where you did your homework as a little girl?"

"Homework I did in the dining room, right over there. But I liked this spot for reading. Even when we had guests, I'd sit on an ottoman in the corner and slink away to St. Petersburg. This is also where I played the piano."

"Perfect childhood?"

"Uneventful. I don't have bad memories, or great ones either. I just wished my parents had lived longer. I don't miss them, though."

I tried to imagine her bedroom. I wondered why she had decided to write her master's thesis in Hans's apartment instead of right here.

"Because they made me breakfast and lunch. You'd be surprised how quickly time flies when people cook for you and look after you. I spent six months up there writing away, paying attention to no one."

I remembered the desk and the room upstairs where I'd waited for her to bring back appetizers, fearing she'd never return, though come back she did, bearing goodies, as she called them, arranged in a Noah's ark formation—two by two, meaning one for you and one for me, and another for you and me—a room where I kept thinking, Let's just sit here in this tiny alcove all our own and reinvent the world in our image, with our own firmament extending no farther than the table where all these strangers stood confabulating around the singer with the throaty voice, like aliens who had dematerialized around us and whose shadow was all that remained of them. I had promised to wait another fifteen minutes and not a minute more before leaving the party, but on seeing Clara return with the large dish in her hand, I'd begun to think that this was better than a dream and who was I to meddle with dreams, as I watched those fifteen minutes extend past three in the morning, which was, as everyone led me to believe even on my first night here, yet too early for anyone to leave. That little room seemed the closest I'd ever get to Clara. Now I had come back to the same spot, down by a few flights, a few sunken city layers deeper, and we were still on the surface, still above sea level. I wondered how much farther underground Inky's soul roamed in this building's netherworld.

"Above that little room, however, was the balcony."

The poet was Vaughan and the spot Bellagio and, in between, a lady's suede shoe stubbing a cigarette that tailspun its way down onto the snow-banked driveway where Igors and Ivans stood smoking like displaced double agents recalling the Cold War.

Remember? Could I ever forget?

The rooms and balconies stacked one on top of the other seemed like versions of a vague and mysterious design presaging something about me or about her or about our time together that I wasn't quite grasping yet. Was I closer to that something on her floor or was I farther from it than I'd been there three days earlier? Did each floor point to a weaker or to a louder echo of itself? Or was it the echoing effect that was beckoning me right now, rising and falling from floor to floor, like snakes and ladders, like Beethoven's overextended hymn, which comes on and then withers and then comes back again, timeless, spellbound, and imperishable?

So this is awkward, she had said at the restaurant. I wouldn't touch that, but I knew she was pleading with me to speak, to go beyond, just say something.

The arrangement of rooms and windows on the same corner line made me think of the elements of the periodic table, all of them lined up in neat rows and columns according to a logic that is totally cryptic and yet, once arranged numerically, no less predictable than fate itself to those who know the cypher. Sodium (atomic number 11) is the uppermost floor with the greenhouse, and right under it is potassium (19), where I nearly passed out, and right under it rubidium (37), the floor with the balcony and the Bloody Mary, and under that cesium (55), Clara's world. Couldn't one organize one's life along a periodic table under the assumption that if one calculated the rule behind the 11, 19, 37, 55 sequence, one could easily predict that the next element would be number 87—francium? Weren't we going to Rohmer's France in less than two hours?

She liked things improvised; I liked design.

"And what does this room correspond to on the ground floor?" I asked. "The lobby." "And below that?" "Storage room, superintendent's digs." "And below that?" I asked, as if trying to determine where fate might take me if I were to roam from floor to floor like a flying Dutchman trapped for eternity in the freight elevator. "Bicycle room. Laundry room. China," she replied.

Here I am trying to determine that there is no below after rock bottom, no after-omega, that beyond the person I see in Clara there is no other person, and yet how like her to tell me that rock bottom does not exist, that there are as many Claras as there are buried tiers and legends on our planet. And how about me?

"Man thinking about first night, wondering what would have happened had he gotten off on wrong floor and gone to a different party."

"Man would have met different Dutch lady."

"Yes, but what does present Dutch lady think of that?"

"Man is fishing, so Dutch lady says *Go fish.*"

How I loved her mind. To every north, my south, to every secret, its sharer, to every glove the partner.

"Printz," she said. She had stood up to put away our two cups in the kitchen and had momentarily looked out to the darkling view of the Hudson from one of the other large windows in the living room.

"What?" I asked.

"I think you should come and have a look. Here," she said, producing to my complete surprise a pair of what looked like World War II binoculars. "Look over there." She pointed toward the George Washington Bridge.

"Is it what I think it is?" I asked.

"I think it might be."

"Let's give it five minutes. Maybe it will pass by."

We waited in suspense, listening to the closing segment of the Beethoven.

But the ship was not drawing any closer, and for all we knew, it might have been stationary; it was already too dark to make out its name. It was also late, and unless we hurried, we'd miss the movies. So she tied her shawl, told me where to find my coat. From the bathroom, I heard her strum a few bars of the Handel on her piano. It meant—or so I wished to think—we could stay indoors, we could order in, we could sit still till it got dark, yet never budge to turn on the lights, because just moving a muscle would break the spell. We should take a cab, I suggested. Absolutely not, we're walking, she replied.

"So this was you," she said in the elevator. It took me a moment to realize she was still harping on the Beethoven.

"This was me," I said almost shyly, without conviction, as though held to an admission I'd made without thinking earlier in the day and now wished I could take back.

"Next time I'll play you a few sarabandes on the piano. They too have me written all over them."

"What do you mean?"

"Sarabandes are fast and slow. Someone once said sarabandes are danced two steps forward and three steps back—story of my life, if you ask me."

•

We took a shortcut down West End Avenue, which, unlike Riverside, had already been plowed, with the snow gathered in high banks along the curbs. The walk was all downhill, and when we got there, the ticket holders' line was longer than we'd anticipated. Someone said they weren't sold out. When we got our tickets, all I hoped was that we wouldn't be separated. And if we were? We walk out, she said. We recognized some faces from the previous evenings. Clara, as became her habit, said she'd try to get something from a nearby Starbucks. We liked the slice of lemon cake she had bought last night. In line, I started talking with a couple standing in front of us. She had seen many Rohmer films; he had seen only a few. They had come the night before as well, but he wasn't convinced. She thought that tonight's films might actually persuade him of the director's genius. Did I think he was a genius? He could be, I said. But real people never behaved, much less talked, that way in the real world, he said. "Well," interrupted Clara, who had gathered the gist of the man's objections as soon as she joined me on line, "Monet's paintings look nothing like the real world, nor would we want them to. What's the real world got to do with art, anyway?"

That seemed to shut him up.

Perhaps the poor man was trying to make conversation. They were so clearly on their second date.

"I wonder where seven-ten with the sloping crew cut is tonight. Oh, there he is."

I gave him our tickets, and she smiled at him. *"Danko, filo donka,"* she said in mock-German, a clownish simper on her face. He growled in silence as he had done two nights before. He could sense she was making fun of him.

"I don't like your attitude," he finally said. "I love yours," she retorted. She didn't know whether to call him Fildanko or Fildenko. So she decided to call him Phildonka, with a *ph*. She was laughing all to herself, until we saw Phildonka's face peer at the audience through the slit in the thick, dark curtain and, with the beam of his flashlight, point to an empty seat behind us. "Madam, the seat," he said, which Clara instantly parodied into *madamdasit*. "Can you see?" I asked when the credits came on. "Not a bit." Then she repeated *Phildonka madamdasit*, and neither of us could stop laughing.

Midway through the *Le rayon vert* the situation became totally untenable. She opened her purse and produced a nip, which she twisted open and pressed on me to drink from. "What is it?" "Oban," she whispered. My neighbor turned his head to me, then looked at the screen, as though determined never to look our way again. "I think we got caught," she whispered. "He tell Phildonka, you watch, Phildonka get furious." Suppressed laughter.

Later, the film stopped rolling. At first people sat quietly in their spots, then they began to grow impatient, finally erupting in hisses and

taunts that grew louder and louder, as in a high school auditorium. I told
her that Phildonka was all at once ticket collector, usher, popcorn maker,
and projectionist, which sent her roaring out loud, shouting, "Phildonka,
fixitdamovie!" Everyone was now staring at us, and the more they stared,
the more she laughed. "Fixitdamovie," she hollered, everyone joining in
the laughter. This the woman who leaned against her kitchen counter a
few hours ago and looked so uneasy during an awkward silence between
us that all she could do was speak in pidgin English. Same Clara, new
Clara, old Clara, the Clara who shut people up and put them in their
place, the Clara who stares and weeps, the Clara who, on weekday afternoons after school, would dash out of her building on 106th Street and
scamper down the stairway by the Franz Sigel memorial statue to join the
other children and sled down the hill or head toward Straus Park, where
they all sat on one bench, ratting on their parents—Clara who mourned
her parents in silence when she heard the news, but then changed
clothes and went to a party—Clara never outgrew the comfort of those
hours when her parents drank tea with friends by the large bay of windows facing the Hudson and all she had to do was sneak in among them
with a book, and all, all was well and safe in this medieval town along
the Rhine which her parents and grandparents had resurrected this side
of the Atlantic. Was there a periodic table for her, as she floated her way
up, down, and across her various little squares, her Folía and her solemn
sarabande wrapped in one and put under a panino press like a *sandwich
cubano* sold on the corner of her block? Or was she like me—but so much
better than me?

"What do we do now?" I asked. "I dunno. What do you want to do?"
"I think we should have a real drink." In our rush to leave the theater
before something might make us change our minds, she barely had time
to throw her scarf over her head or tie her knot. "What happened to the
complicated knot?" I asked. Leave the complicated knot alone, she said
as she snuggled under my arm, then under my armpit, before I could even
put my arm around her. "Let's catch a cab," I said. "Usual place?"
"Absolutely."

But the cabs were not coming on the uptown side, so we walked
across to catch those headed downtown. This was exactly the corner
where I'd spotted her two nights ago. The light was red, so we had to
wait, and in the island in the middle of Broadway she began chanting

with teeth clattering in the cold, "Phildonka, Phildonka, thy 'larum afar / Gives brings hope to the valiant, and promise of war." "Who?" I asked. "Byron." She couldn't let go of the word until she saw a cabbie drive by wearing a turban the size of a pumpkin, so that instead of shouting "Hey, cab," she yelled out, "Da cab, da cab, madamdacab," into the night, watching the bearded cabbie speed by us with a fare in the backseat no less turbaned than the driver himself. This brought us to such a paroxysm of laughter in the freezing cold that I caught myself thinking, This is all nonsense, but this nonsense is the closest I ever got to happiness or to another human being, and without thinking turned to her and kissed her on the mouth.

She pulled back immediately. Even a hand accidentally put over fire could not have recoiled this fast. She uttered the word *no* almost before my lips had touched hers, as if she'd been expecting something of the sort and had an answer already prepared. She reminded me of someone who has her thumb already poised on the head of the mace spray can in her coat pocket, determined to spray and ask questions later, only to realize that the man who walked over to her one night was none other than a lost tourist who'd meant to ask for street directions.

For the first time in my life I felt as though I had tried to assault a woman, or was judged to have attempted it. Had she accompanied the gesture with a slap, I would have been less stunned.

This was not only the first time that I had ever met with resistance while trying to kiss a woman, but the first time where the kiss had come so spontaneously and in so involuntary and unrehearsed a manner that to have it thrown back at me so brusquely felt like an affront to every moment we'd shared for the past four days, an affront to candor, to friendship, to our humanity itself, to everything I was, to the me I was only too happy to let her see. Could my kiss have come so unexpectedly as to have shocked her? Could it have been such an offense? Could it—or could I—have been so repellent?

I did not know how she was taking all this and wanted to make sure it wouldn't spoil things between us. So I apologized. "I hope I didn't offend you."

"No need to apologize. I should have seen this coming. It's my fault."

It seemed I was less guilty than I feared. But my innocence was more galling yet. I had misread our giddiness for something it was not.

"Clara, I really hope you're not offended."

"I am not offended, I said. You behaved like a fourteen-year-old. No need to apologize like one too."

That was it. I was apologizing from my heart. This was a gratuitous snub.

"I think I'm going to get you a cab," I said, "then I'm going to head home as well."

She was more flummoxed by this than by my kiss.

"Don't go home like this."

"You didn't have to put me down."

"You didn't have to kiss me."

"Yes, I did."

"Just don't go home, don't do it." She looked at me. "It's so fucking cold. Let's have a drink. I don't want this to happen."

"Why?"

"Why? Because we were having a good time together. Because if you think it's a marvelous thing we both ended up at Hans's party, don't you think that I think so too? Don't you think that if you've never wanted to be known by anyone the way I know you it's because I may want the same from you?"

"So why not let me kiss you?"

"I don't have to explain. I don't even want to try. I'm cold. Let's grab a cab."

"Why not tell me you'd rather not kiss me instead of pushing me away as if I'd tried to rape you or had the plague."

"You scared me, okay? You wouldn't understand. Could we not talk about it now?"

"We never talk about anything."

"That's not fair."

She listened for me to say something. But I didn't know what to think, except that I was happy to be heading back home.

"This is my hell. This is my hell," she kept repeating, "and you're making it worse."

"Your hell? Think of mine!"

I shook my head, at myself, at her. "Well, it's too cold. And we both need a drink."

I couldn't understand, but she snuck right back under my armpit and put one arm around my waist, as if nothing at all had happened. "There's a taxi coming."

We hailed a cab, got in, watched the cab suddenly skid in the snow as it made a totally unflappable U-turn and was soon speeding uptown. "It got terribly cold, horrible weather," uttered Clara through the glass partition. The man was quietly and serenely putting out his cigarette, listening to soft jazz. "Amerikon wezer," he replied. "You don't say," she commented, trying to sound earnestly intrigued by the cabbie's view of American weather. "Did you hear that," she turned to me, "*Amerikon wezer.*"

When we got out on 105th Street, we were in stitches.

We rushed indoors, found our usual shoulder-to-shoulder spot on the bench which she called *our banquette*, where I ordered two single malts and french fries, while she hastened to the bathroom.

Minutes later, she was back. "You won't believe what someone left in there," she said, this time truly bursting with laughter. "It's too disgusting, as if the entire Third World had come to take a dump in this bathroom."

Did she need to go elsewhere?

No, she had used the men's room.

Were there any men in the men's room?

"Yes," she said. "This guy."

And she pointed to a lanky-looking young man at the bar who probably needed a drink to recover from the shock. "And don't look at me like that," she said out loud to him. "You didn't see nothing, and if you did, consider yourself lucky."

Cheers, we said when our drinks came, once more, and once again, and many more times again.

I looked at her and couldn't help asking, "Are we just laughing or are we really very happy?"

"Did you by any chance see a Rohmer film tonight? Just give us Juan Dola, mista. And let's dance."

•

As had become our habit every night, we left the bar well after two in the morning. The walk home never lasted long enough, and the cold didn't help. What was not unpleasant was watching how the two of us, while very conscious of the windchill, tried not to pick up our pace. We had drunk more than usual, and as we walked, my arm was around her shoulders. Was anything ever going to be unconscious between us?

The problem was how to say goodbye. Kissing was out of the question. Not kissing, too staged. A normal peck, totally perfunctory. "I know this is awkward," she said, "but I think we'd better not say good night." As always, on the same wavelength.

So we shouldn't kiss at all and forgo all motions of saying good night—that's an idea, I thought, almost admiring her ability to avoid a yet more awkward moment at her door. Meanwhile, not a word about my aborted kiss, not a word about the song, nothing about the tango we'd danced four times tonight. Why wasn't I surprised? "Maybe you're right," I said. And maybe she was. With her hands deep in her coat pockets, she darted forward to where Boris stood, while I, after waiting a few seconds to see that she got in, spun around and headed toward Broadway. "Well, it's been nice," she had said, clearly aware she was using formal Holly-wood dating lingo. But without a trace of irony.

Later, when I reached the park, I began to think that perhaps it was time not to see Clara any longer, that this had gone far enough and should go no further. Too much chaos, too many doubts, and far too, too many jabs and darts, everything bathed in a caustic brew that could peel off the outer layers of your body and leave you no less denuded than a newborn mollusk. End it, I thought, just end it. She'll mind, probably, but of all people, she'll recover faster than you ever will. Within hours, she'll forget to remember, then forget she's forgotten. As for me, it would take a while. Perhaps it was time to reconsider my own lying-low practice.

For the first time in weeks, I found myself itching to buy a pack of cig-arettes. Was I going to call them secret agents? Yes, why not, at least for the time being. But my name would never again be Oskár.

The park by night, as always, felt as welcoming as a church on a rainy day when you have an extra ten minutes to yourself during lunch and, because you don't belong to the faith and have no ritual to perform there, simply step in as you please, asking for nothing, expecting noth-ing, giving out nothing—just an empty pew, where you sit and think, just sit and think and hope you can intone something like a silent hymn.

I had passed by here just before one o'clock today, thinking to myself that tonight, after walking her home, I would indeed stop by here. If things went better than that, then I'd send the park good-night thoughts. The park would understand. As Tilden understood. As my father understood when I failed to send parting thoughts on rushing back to the city last night. But things had not gone well. Now I was back, no closer to her than I'd been on our first night. Two floors up, and three floors down. Just treading water, as always treading water. How I hated this feeling. I sat in the freezing cold for a few moments, knowing I'd have to leave soon, trying all the same to summon up the splendor of the party and how everything seemed touched by luster and legend that night. No more magic, none left, none here. My Magi with their heads ablaze—gone home. Go home, Oskár, go home.

I stood up and watched the city at three in the morning, the city I loved at three more than at any other time perhaps. It knew nothing about any of this, did it? Nor could it do anything to help, except watch and go about its business and from time to time look up again, the way zebras continue to graze and watch as their predators quietly scour the plain for their young. Go home, Oskár.

I decided to get another drink at our pub and sat at the bar. Perhaps all I wanted was to stay in her neighborhood. There was almost no one left inside, just the waitress and two men sitting at the bar, and a couple farther down. Would I ever in my life be able to come back here and not think of her? Or come back here and not hate my life, myself?

I was, I recalled, sitting exactly where the lanky young man had been standing after inadvertently sharing the bathroom with Clara. I had enjoyed her cutting words to him. Even he was far better off than I was right now. I looked over to what had been our table. They had already snuffed out the candles in that corner. The whole place reminded me of an emptied theater where a manager still allows you to go back to retrieve the small umbrella left under your seat—but all the actors, from King Lear to Lady Windermere to the cleanup crew, have gone home already, including the underpaid mopping crew who's already taken the subway and is on its way to the outer reaches of town, counting the minutes before each man can sit to eat the food his good wife has kept warm for him.

Traces of our presence were everywhere. This is where she and I had talked of Rohmer's films, ordering more drinks than either of us was in the habit of drinking, her head on my shoulder, my arm sometimes around her shoulders, neither daring to go beyond that. Just looking at the bench with the cushion that might still be bearing the imprint of our bodies brought everything back.

I ordered a drink. "Fucking winter," the barman said. The old tooth-less man sitting at the far end of the bar liked that. "Fucking winter," he repeated, "you bet!" I immediately thought of *Amerikon wezer* and almost choked on the laughter as it worked its way up my throat. Had I ever laughed so much with anyone lately? And what was it about laughter that I loved so much—silly, slapstick, childish, fatuous laughter that it was. *Amerikon wezer*, she had repeated to the cabbie, making a face as if to say, *Fancy that*, Amerikon wezer! How I'd wanted to kiss her then.

I took out a dollar and put it in the jukebox. It would be just like me to come back and play our song again. I stood there, transfixed by the door of the bar, listening to the song, not caring a bit what the people who'd seen us dance together might think I was doing now, all by myself, *en soledad. So she didn't let him have his way with her, did she, and after all their dancing and boozing*—not caring, because nothing mattered to me now but that moment when she put her hand to my face two nights ago with so much kindness—yes, kindness—that thinking of it now could make the tears come again—not tears of self-pity, or of self-hatred, or self-anything, or even love, though it must have been something like love, because two beings, two objects, two cells, two planets cannot come so close and not be altered by a hindrance and a disturbance called love. I could have let myself cry because prolonged confusion could do this each time. And perhaps being all alone here and wanting to remem-ber the doleful tenor of her gesture when she rubbed her palm along my face after singing the words in my ear, only to ask for another dollar sec-onds later, made me think, almost against my will, that all this must surely be love and had always been love, her love, my love, our love. I played the song once more. Strange how she hadn't said a word about it on our way home. Not a word about my kiss either. And certainly noth-ing about the way we'd held each other at the bar. Nothing. The whole thing swept under, forgotten, not talked about—as if they were all just tangents and detours.

We hadn't taken a step forward since this afternoon, when we stood in the kitchen wrapped in a cloud of awkwardness. Who had put the cloud there, and why, with all our experience in matters of intimacy, were we so frozen and unable to shoo it away? *I think we'd better not say good night*—who ever says something as cramped and flat-footed as that? *I think we'd better not say good night.*

·

I sat at the bar and had started drinking my Scotch when it finally hit me.

What a dreadful fool! I kicked the stool next to mine. Then to cover the kick I made it seem that I had accidentally banged it while crossing my legs. *I think we'd better not say good night* did not mean we shouldn't kiss goodbye, it meant I don't want us to say goodbye *yet*. Why hadn't she said *yet*? Is *yet* such a hard word to say? Why hadn't she said it clearly? Or had she said it more than just clearly and I had simply failed to hear it because I couldn't believe I was being offered what I'd always wanted and, because I'd wanted it, felt unworthy of it.

Or had I understood her meaning exactly but pretended to disbelieve it so as to have her repeat it a second time, perhaps with greater emphasis—which Claras don't do?

Suddenly, and more than anything right now, I wanted to call her and hear her raucous sleepy voice and, in hearing it, say to that raucous sleepy voice what I would with difficulty have said to her sparkling daytime voice, things one only mutters in unfettered half-sleep to those who'll heed it in half-sleep themselves: I don't care if I wake you up, I want to be with you now, in your bed, under your blanket, in your sweater, life is so very cold tonight, I'll sleep in the next room if I have to, but I don't want to be without you, not tonight.

Should I call her now? Past three in the morning?

After our walk it might have been okay to call. But at three? Only in emergencies do people call at three. Yes, but wasn't this an emergency? Only drunks call this an emergency. Well, I am drunk, and if ever there was an emergency, this was it. There! Call her and say, I can't think of being without you tonight. That sounded more like a suicide note, or a marriage proposal. Aren't both the same? I asked, thinking of Olaf, already suppressing a chuckle.

What I couldn't wait to read was the e-mail or text message I knew was bound to come any moment now. Surely it would be cruel and tart in that typically off-putting, cutting, Clara way of hers. But if only not to do what she'd already done last night, she wouldn't send an e-mail right away. She'd keep me waiting long enough so that I wouldn't find sleep, and when I did find it, I'd still wake up to check. Then I realized that if my sense of her—or of fate—was in any way accurate, she would not send me a text message at all tonight. Let silence have its full effect, let silence be the poison, let silence *be* the message.

But she had another torture in store for me, one that allowed me to suspect, without knowing for certain, that all this was happening in my mind, and in my mind only, and that these twisted riddles being spun around me had nothing to do with her and personified my gnarled relationship with myself, with her, with life itself.

But I wasn't going to fall for this. I wasn't being paranoid, I thought—she's the one who's doing this to me. So I decided to turn off my phone—to show her.

Then, snuffing these thoughts from my mind, sprung the quantum theorem from hell. Two options, but not both at the same time. If I turned my cell phone back on, I would find either no message from her or one that said such cruel things that it would leave me stunned and reeling for days. But if I didn't check and kept my cell phone off, I would never read the message that started with,

DEAR OSKAR DONT BOTHER CALLING OR WRITING OR TAKING OFF YOUR SHOES JUST BRING YOURSELF OVER AS QUICKLY AS YOU CAN I DONT CARE WHAT TIME IT IS I DONT CARE IF YOU WANT TO OR NOT DONT CARE WHAT I SAID TODAY OR YESTERDAY OR THE NIGHT BEFORE I JUST WANT YOU WITH ME TONIGHT AND I PROMISE I WONT SLEEP UNTIL I HEAR THE RING OF MY BUZZER DOWNSTAIRS DONT BOTHER CALLING OR WRITING OR TAKING OFF YOUR SHOES JUST THE BUZZER THE BUZZER THE BUZZER DOWNSTAIRS.

Like Orpheus I could not resist turning on my phone and checking my messages. But, as with Orpheus, no sooner had I checked than the message she would have sent disappeared instantly.

FIFTH NIGHT

The one question I woke up to and couldn't shake off and took with me to the shower, to my corner Greek diner, and then on the long way back home without ever being able to answer was: Is she not going to call me at all today or is she just pretending not to call?

After breakfast, to stop myself from hoping—or was it to spite myself for hoping?—I decided to turn off my phone again and found myself dawdling on Broadway under the pretense that I had plenty of time and nothing to do this morning. But my reason for not wanting to get back too soon was too obvious to ignore: I wanted to prove—to myself, to her, to the gods themselves—that I was in no rush to know whether she had written or called or come by, because the last thing I wanted to know this morning was that she had made no effort to call or see me. In the end, what brought me to the brink of shame—because it was the one thing I wanted most—was to hear her admission that she was going through the exact same *torment and torture* herself. Had she come by car, she would have found my buzzer silent; had she called, she'd have reached voice mail; had she run into me and asked where I'd been, I would have been evasive. Then it hit me that this was exactly what she wanted me to go through—and I found comfort in this. She wanted me to juggle all these doubts because she herself was juggling them at this precise moment.

In my mind—and perhaps in mine only—it all boiled down to one question: Who was going to pick up the phone and call first; who was the author, and who the victim of silence? And was hers just silence or, like mine, was it disguised chatter? Where did tacit end and silent start? Clearly, a Door number 3 question.

There was, however, one last hope, even if it came at the end of what would surely be a long and twisted day: the unspoken 7:10. Not saying anything about 7:10, however, was either a sign or no sign, but no sign was itself a sign as well.

How to break this radio silence?

I could take the Staten Island ferry, and as soon as I stood on the freezing deck before the Statue of Liberty, call and say, Guess where I am—and send her a picture to prove it. But I also imagined her reply: gruff and unresponsive, *Your point being?* Or I could stand on the Brooklyn Bridge or sit on one of the pews inside the Cathedral of St. John, scarcely ten blocks from her home. *And your point being?*

Or—and this is what I did—at around 2:00 p.m. I sent her a picture of the statue of Memory in Straus Park. This is where you can find me. I'll wait awhile, a very long while. But by then bring an ice pick.

I waited for her to call me back. But she did not. So things had degenerated far worse than I feared. She wasn't talking to me. Perhaps she had turned off her phone. But then that too was a sign, wasn't it?—especially if she kept hers turned off for the same reason, which would make it the loudest sign of all.

I ran through a series of wished-for scenarios. The best consisted in her sending me a picture of where she was at this very instant. No text. Just her way of explaining why she couldn't meet me. For some reason I imagined her sending me a photo of the Temple of Dendur. Bergdorf's. The road to Darien. A bathroom bowl.

Then I began to wish that her reply might come in the form of Leo Czernowicz playing the Bach.

Then that she'd call me back, saying, What?

What do you mean "What?" I'd reply.

You called.

Are you free?

Why?

If you're busy, I'll call some other time.

What did you want?

I called to apologize.

For?

You know exactly what for.

You already did. What else?

Nothing else.

•

"It's freezing cold, and I can't believe you made me leave my house."

She knew she'd surprise me. But no sooner did I see her materialize at Straus Park than we burst out laughing hysterically. Partly because she was making fun of our overdrawn radio silence; or because it was obvious that our embattled stillness was nothing more than a clash of wills, a bogus cold war. What a relief to admit it with laughter—and move on.

"Were you working?" I was hoping she'd say no.

"Yes. But it was taking too long, and with all you made me drink last night, I could barely focus."

"Are you still pissed?"

"Depends what for."

"Did you eat?" She made it clear she was changing a delicate subject, though I was not quite sure what precisely that subject was. Standard MO.

"No."

"Me neither."

"Want to do ethnic?"

Within minutes, I knew, there'd be new people in our lives, new ways of naming things, new foibles to pick up on in a storehouse of characters sprung out from the mind of a girl I couldn't begin to understand except by thinking she was my spitting image, but my image in reverse, the mirror image of her own replica.

We walked down Broadway, examining several places along the way as possible restaurants for lunch, and yet, for one reason or another, did missing each. The truth is, neither of us was hungry and would have settled for an intimate café. I missed the sextant and the oversized meerschaum pipe and the picture of a lurching bull. There were, as usual this time of the year, lots of people about, lots of tourists and young residents of the many two-star hotels that had sprouted around the neighborhood. Every place was full, and there was a ferment in the air, which gave our walk its hasty, spirited pace.

Clara decided she needed to buy candy. Did one really buy candy at her age? "I like candy, okay?" At some point, we decided to take the crosstown bus and head to the East Side. But did we want to run into more crowds of people? There's the Guggenheim, I said. Did we really want to go to the Guggenheim? Actually no. We could *go to France*, I suggested. But at this time in the afternoon? It would be all wrong.

"Yes—about the movies," she started, "I know this will upset things, but I don't think I'm going to be able to make it tonight," she said.

Did she mean *upset things* or *upset me*?

"Bummer," I said, trying to show I'd taken the news with no less equanimity than if I'd received a "regrets only" from someone I'd invited reluctantly. "It won't be fun without you." I couldn't have found a dumber comeback.

It hurt. The question was where. I didn't mind going alone—I had always liked going to the movies alone. I just didn't like having to cancel what, without totally admitting it to myself, I'd taken 'for granted. I didn't like finding, as I always knew I'd eventually find, that she had another life, that I played no part in that life, and that the part I played in her lying-low phase was so small that no one, other than Max and Margo, and the few who'd seen us together at the party, had the slightest inkling I existed. Perhaps what I didn't like was having to change my life back to what it had been before Clara. Four nights, and I'm hooked. Is that it?

A dead silence had fallen between us.

I was afraid this would happen. But so soon?

"I'll live. Trust me."

Silence again. "Well, aren't you going to ask me why I can't come? With most people not asking means they're dying to ask."

I was trying not to ask so as not to seem curious or cranky. Nor did I want to sound indifferent. I didn't know what to do. Perhaps I didn't want to know what she did when I wasn't with her. I cared only for what we did together—or so I wished to believe. What she did with others didn't matter, especially if it did not interfere with our being together. In this, it took me a while to realize, I was thinking and behaving like every jealous man.

"You really don't want to know?"

"Doesn't matter. Obviously you're dying to tell me."

"*Otherpeoples,*" she said. Her way of remaining vague and all too specific at the same time.

But it hit me hard, as though she'd finally taken a large spade and with it shoved dirt at my face. The streets became gray, and the sky became gray, and the festive people crowding the stores around the crosstown stop on Broadway lost their color and became gray, and life, having lost the dimple in its smile, had turned sullen and gray.

Once again, I decided to have nothing more to do with her. This was the time to put that resolution into effect. This is when it should happen: man may be buckling at the knees, man may have aimed too high, but man splits now. Why bother having lunch under the circumstances?

"Do they serve tea in your house?"

I looked at her in total surprise.

"Yes, all the Twinings in the world. It's just that the pre-check-in crew arrives tomorrow, so the place is a mess."

"Is there a clean corner?"

"There should be."

"And il y a things to eat?"

"Very old ham, green-flecked cheese, and the potatoes in the bottom drawer have grown trees. Always wine, though."

How could she do this? From ice to scalding hot. Suddenly a party erupted in our lives.

On Broadway we stopped and decided to stock up on food. The store was mobbed, but neither of us minded. Two cheeses, one, no two, baguettes, one ripe avocado, some ham, raw and cooked. Why the avocado? Goes with the ham and mustard. Did I have mustard? Yes, but very old. By God, when were you last in the rose garden? Told you, aeons ago. Some fruit? Winter or summer fruit? Does it matter, they're all imported from faraway places whose fruit matures nowhere but on board the giant dark containers piled on beaten-down tankers called *Prince Oscar* that shuttle up and down the Atlantic to bring berries of all colors and no taste to people ready to sit around Yule logs and sing carols over spiked fruit punch. "All right, all right, je get it," she said. Did we have milk? We did, I said, and made a humbled shame-face, but it might have turned to yogurt. At the last minute we remembered what would have made all the difference in the world: caviar and sour cream. We were, once again, playing house. How about some junk? Junk and candy, she said.

By the time we were done, we had filled two large grocery bags. "Suddenly I'm hungry," she said. I was starving.

"Before we go any farther, is the kitchen clean?" she asked as we entered my building.

Was she asking if my sheets were clean?

"Señora Venegas comes twice a week. But she is not allowed to touch anything in the refrigerator or in my study."

I got out of the elevator, forgot to tell her that its doors shut very, very quickly, and suddenly saw Clara with her package violently shoved out of the elevator by the closing door. "The fucking door. The fucking nerve." She kept cursing at the door all the way down the corridor to my apartment.

She fell in love with my rug. She had an idea, she said. "Let's picnic in the corner room. I'll take care of everything, you take care of the wine and the music." For a second we stood next to each other, looking out at the view of the park. Another overcast white day bursting with inner joy.

She found a tablecloth in the linen closet. "What's this?"

"From Roussillon. Bought it as a present, never gave it, things fizzled, kept it instead."

On her way to the kitchen she spotted a photograph of my father and me when I was four. It was taken on our trip to Berlin. We're in the Tiergarten, he and I. And next to it is a black-and-white picture of him with his father on the same exact spot. "Return of the Jew."

"Revenge of the Jew."

"You look like him."

"I would hope not."

"Didn't you like him?"

"I was crazy about him. But I don't think he knew happiness."

"With what happened after this picture was taken, difficult to imagine happiness anywhere."

"He had his chance. I think."

"You think."

"I know."

"And?"

"He let it go."

"Meaning?" Why the sudden interest in my father?

"Meaning he didn't think he was worthy enough. Meaning he knew love once and only once, yet never got close enough or risked enough to go after someone who might have asked for nothing more than his love. Meaning he had waited too long but didn't know that life was willing to wait out the hurdles it had thrown his way."

"Amphibalence Senior?"

"If you wish."

"When did he die?"

"Last year."

She got closer to the picture.

"I was born the summer this was taken," she said.

"I know."

Let her know that I too had done the math, that I'd already thought, Did I know, as I was ambling in a small park in the Tiergarten with my father, that somewhere in a hospital in Manhattan someone who'd be named Clara . . . ?

What I didn't tell her and would never have dared hint at was that I was also thinking, Did he know, as an anonymous photographer was busy snapping our photo, that the one person I wished he'd meet someday would stand before his picture and ask me about him? Did he know that the Persian rug we bought together at an auction sale one Sunday five years ago would inspire Clara to make a picnic?

"How do you know so much about his private life?"

"Because we had very few secrets. Because he was so unhappy sometimes he couldn't afford secrets. Because he went over all mistaken turns in his life so I wouldn't make the same ones myself when the time came."

"And have you?"

"That's a Door number three question."

"Has the time come?"

"That's another Door number three question."

"And?"

"And—since we're into ramming doors open—let's say the matter is being weighed even as we speak."

"Deep. Very, very *très* deep."

We uttered it at the same time: "Vishnukrishnu!"

She took the tablecloth from Roussillon, threw it briskly on the rug with one determined flap that made the cloth rustle like a pennant on a windy day. I put on my favorite recording of the *Goldberg Variations*, uncorked a bottle of red, and watched her bring plate after plate from the kitchen. Then came the puzzling moment. There were no napkins, neither cloth nor paper ones. We looked everywhere. That Venegas woman probably uses them to wipe her nose with. Was there a roll of paper towels anywhere? "I looked everywhere," said Clara, "*es gibt kein* paper towels." She'd checked all the cabinets in the kitchen—*Nada*, she said. There was, I said, only one solution left. I hadn't even finished saying it when she burst out into hysterical laughter.

"Can you think of a better option?" I asked.

She shook her head, still unable to contain the laughter.

"It's your house, you get it."

So I found a full roll and brought it to our picnic, placed it next to her.

"I can't believe you're making me eat with a roll of toilet paper staring at me. To your health and a Happy New Year." I reached over and placed what turned out to be a prolonged kiss below her ear. "And many more times again, many, many."

I loved the way she had removed her boots and was reclining on the floor facing me, with one bare tanned foot on the other, staring at me with her lingering, sometimes sullen gaze. Once or twice she'd caught me staring at her feet, and I could tell she liked that; she knew what I was thinking, and I knew she knew, and I loved it. A week ago they were on sand, now they're on my rug. We were no longer just friends, and there was clearly much more between us than ordinary man-woman friendship, but I didn't know what any of this was or where it was headed or whether it had already crested and this was all we were ever going to be together. For the first time in days I was willing to see that what stood between us was not a gray, barren no-man's-land littered with craters and mines but something else, though uncharted and as silent and snow-hushed as the Nativity itself, filled with the hopeful, aching mirth that lasts no longer than improvised truces when guns go silent on December 25, and enemy soldiers climb out of their trenches to light a cigarette, but then forget to light another.

At some point I said I'd let her hear all the Silotis I'd been able to buy.

"Which is the best?" she asked.

"Yours."

"My point exactly."

•

Our picnic lasted over two hours, especially since she turned on the television and, without either of us meaning to, we watched *The Godfather*, starting from the murder of Sollozzo and of the crooked policeman till the near-end, when Michael Corleone has everyone eliminated and tells his brother-in-law, whom he's about to have killed as well, "Ah, that little farce you played with my sister. You think that would fool a Corleone?" "Ah, you think that would fool a Corleone?" she repeated. Afterward, we listened to my new versions of the Handel. We discussed Rohmer again, but stayed clear of tonight's films. I didn't want to know where she was going after our picnic, did not want to ask, did not want specifics. Knowing might hurt more than aching to know.

"What is it that he says?" I asked.

"Ah, you think that would fool a Corleone?"

I loved how she said it. "Say it again."

"Ah, you think that would fool a Corleone?"   .

But then, just as she was about to pour me more red wine, she tipped over her glass, which had been standing quite steadily on a large dictionary. The little that remained in her glass left a small red pool on the carpet that soon disappeared into the dark-hued lozenges of the Persian rug. Her sudden apologies reminded me of the spontaneous and effusive Clara I'd seen when she had turned around and kissed me in Max's dining room. I tried to calm her, told her not to worry, and rushed into the kitchen to find a rag.

"Dab, don't rub. Dab," she repeated.

I tried to do as told.

"You're still rubbing, not dabbing."

"You do it, then."

"Let me," she said, first imitating my rubbing motions far from the rug, then showing me how it should be done.

"Now I need salt," she said.

I gave her the salt shaker.

She laughed at me. Where did I keep the salt?

I brought her a giant box of kosher salt. Clara poured a generous mound on the wine stain.

"Why on earth do you have such a giant box of salt but no food in the house?"

"Rose garden lived here and cooked a lot—which also explains the very large containers of spices. Food's lying low these days," I added.

"What did she do?"

"Cooked big dinners."

"No, I mean what did she do to get booted from the rose garden?"

"Told me I should dab, not rub."

"And where is she now?"

I shrugged my shoulders. "Gone."

I looked at the neat little mound she'd carefully evened with the flat of her fingers and which bore four finger-length furrows that I knew I'd never have the heart to remove. I shall keep this forever and ask Mrs. Venegas not to even think of touching or of vacuuming the salt. And if she does remove it, I'm sure I'll have the stain to remember this day by, the way people put plaques at the site where a meteor struck the earth but left no trace of itself save for the crater bearing its name now. She was the meteor, I the gaping hollow. On December 28 Clara and I picnicked on my floor, and here's the proof. As soon as she'd leave—I knew myself—I'd stare at those tiny creases marking the spaces between her fingers and say to myself, Clara was here.

"Hopefully there won't be a stain."

"Hopefully," I said, "there will."

"Printz," she said reproachfully. Both of us understood. After a short pause, she suddenly added, "Dishes!"

We brought the dishes back to the kitchen, and she dropped them in the sink.

"We forgot dessert," she said.

"No, we didn't. I bought chocolate lesbians."

"I didn't see."

"Surprise! But on one condition—"

"What condition?" Concern rippling down her face. I knew I'd made her nervous.

"On condition you say, 'Ah, you think that would fool a Corleone?'"

My heart was racing.

"The things you think of!"

She opened the three packs of cookies and laid them out by twos. If you wedged each one in between your toes, I'd bring my mouth there and bite each one—*The things I think of*, you said?

"Still want tea?" I asked.

"Quick tea," she said. "I have to get going soon."

I don't know what had made me think she'd forget about her date

with *otherpeoples*. How silly of me. But how totally insensitive of her to
remember. Part of me went so far as to believe that she enjoyed breaking
our little routine, enjoyed throwing me off, enjoyed watching me hope
she'd forgotten, only then to yank me back to reality and remind me that
she hadn't.

But I also knew that to ascribe such motives was like attributing an
intention to a storm or looking for a meaning behind the sudden death of
a friend with whom we'd been playing tennis just two hours earlier.

We boiled water in the microwave oven—two minutes. Then dipped
Earl Grey tea bags in the boiling water—one minute. Within seven minutes, we were done with tea. Bad sex tea. Very, very bad sex tea, she
repeated, not Lydian at all.

Then she stood up and went to one of the windows to watch yet
another white cold gray winter day wear itself out. She didn't say anything about Rohmer. I didn't say anything either.

I left the door to my apartment ajar and walked her to the end of the
corridor, where we waited in an awkward silence for the elevator to
arrive. We never made plans when saying goodbye, and this was no different, except that not saying anything about tomorrow had strained the
air between us and given an unnatural, almost hostile cast to our silence,
as though what we were hiding was not our reluctance to formalize our
friendship or to reinvent it each time it brought us closer; what we were
hiding was the guilty diffidence of those who have no intention of meeting again and are desperately avoiding the subject. When the elevator
did come, we were back to an abrupt and hasty peck.

"Soon," I said.

"Soon," she mimicked.

As the door began to shut between us, I knew I was seeing her for the
last time.

"The fucking door," I heard her yelp once the door had slammed into
her. I'd forgotten to remind her about the door again. I could hear her
laugh all the way down.

•

Once in my apartment, I was back to that moment earlier this morning
when I didn't know if we'd ever speak today, let alone continue this
hybrid friendship for another day. The late-afternoon hour, which I

remembered having set as that time of day when I'd finally let myself break down and make the dreaded phone call, had come and gone, and yet I was no better off now, after spending a few hours with her, than I'd been in the morning when my resolution stood out like the last beacon, the best morsel you leave for last, because after that there's nothing left to look forward to.

I looked out the window. Dreary, dreary, dreary.

Teatime, I thought. But I had just had tea with her. I could feel the air closing in on me, as it does in everyone's image of London in this unnamed, predusk hour that could last anywhere from fifteen minutes to an entire day. Time to get out. But there was nowhere to go. I should call a friend. Half of them were out of town. The other half might not be free. There were Rachel and her sister, but the first thing they'd do was give me a hard time for lacking courage, gumption, and, above all, honesty. Besides, I didn't want to see them again without bringing Clara to meet them.

I decide to head out to the gym, take a book, get on the treadmill, maybe swim a few laps, and by 7:10 be where I had always planned to be, except that now it felt as though I'd be doing it failing anything better. Maybe I'd have dinner after the movie—ironically at Thai Soup, of all places. Sometimes it's not bad to be alone.

She had cut the avocado into thin slices and superimposed a series of green half-moons obliquely on the baguette, then added two layers of ham, then the cheese, then a drop of hot mustard, finally flattening the bread down a bit under the panini grill, licking the excess mustard that had stained her fingers. "This is for you, Printz," she had said, handing me the sandwich on a plate with something any halfwit wouldn't have called just friendship.

But there was the caviar too. She insisted on spreading it on the sour cream herself. Why? I'd asked. "Because you don't know how to do it." "I can do it just fine." "Then because I want to."

•

The words *Because I want to* simply undid everything protecting me from her and shot straight to my heart.

•

The afternoon went faster than I expected. What surprised me was the sense that things hadn't turned out as badly as I'd feared. One could always live through this. All I needed was to overcome the haunting regret of having come so close, only to lose her. I'd live. Or was she, like John the Baptist, a sign, a precursor of worse things to come, of sorrows, like photographs, that hadn't even been developed yet, much less hung out to dry?

When I arrived at the movie theater, I noticed that the line was shorter than usual. These were not Rohmer's better films, and the thin audience tonight confirmed it. After purchasing a ticket, I decided to get a *grande* coffee next door and, without bothering to ask myself why, bought a candy bar. Then I bought her brand of cigarettes. Time, I wanted to think, had stopped last night at the movies, and like a sports trainer, I was intentionally holding the stopwatch down to mark the moment when the race ended, to mark the high point of the week, of the year.

Phildonka Madamdasit was there, unchanged and stout, same haircut, same scowl, same shirt. Without her, though, he was not funny, simply smug and thuggish. He took my ticket, stared me down with a *Stood you up, didn't she?* then grabbed someone else's ticket.

I found a spot three seats away from people at either side and sat down. Coffee at the movies was her invention; I'd always had a cold drink, never coffee, and certainly not a nip. I wondered which of her many ex-boyfriends had taught her to bring nips to a movie theater. How many times had she resurrected with me habits picked up with old flames?

In the dark before the film started, I suddenly remembered how I had put my coat on the seat next to mine the first time with Clara when she'd gone to make a phone call, trying to pretend that I had come alone that night the better to enjoy waking up to her presence when she returned. Had I squirreled away the memory for this evening, the way a time traveler on a mission to alter history buries an automatic pistol now, to retrieve it in Ancient Rome tomorrow?

Then came the film credits, and my mind tried to drift and think of someone else with whom I'd been to see this film a few years earlier. This was not bad—not great, but not bad. The opening sequence was exactly as I recalled it, and I was happy to see that for all my ability to recall it in detail, the film still seemed very fresh and would have carried me exactly where I wished to be taken had there not been more noise than usual in the theater, a latecomer unable to decide where to sit, a couple chitchatting about changing seats, Phildonka's beam traveling over my head, and finally the banging of the door, and behind it the repeated clank of a soda dispenser that seemed to be stuck. There was a rumble of voices. I heard someone try the dispenser again—clank, clank, and clank again—then I heard the thud of several cans crashing into the dispenser's bottom tray. "You've hit the jackpot," someone shouted. The audience laughed. This should have been Clara's line, I thought. But just as the film was starting, the door opened once again and another couple walked in, both their heads cowered in typically considerate, Upper West Side self-effacement. The light from outside intruded for a second but disappeared when the door shut. Another intruder was having a hard time finding a seat—that too distracted me. Then I heard the cough. Not a nervous cough, but an intentional cough, as when people cough to remind others of their presence in a room. Again the damned cough interrupted both the credits and the voice-over that had begun as soon as the credits had run their course. Cough, cough. I was convinced I was making it up—but the cough was whispering, "Printz Oskár"—I couldn't be making it up, but what wouldn't I give . . . Seconds later, without the cough this time, but whispered all the same, almost as an inquiry to mean, *Are you there? Can you hear me?* "Printz Oskár?" The whole audience turned in the direction of the door. This was unbelievable, but who else would say such a thing in a movie house once the film had started? I raised my arm, hoping she'd spot it. She did, and walked immediately in my direction. "Very sorry, most very, very sorry indeed," she said in mock-apology to those standing up as she tried to reach my seat. "The fucking Phildonka wouldn't let me in"—and right there and then she burst out into uncontrollable laughter, arousing universal hisses from everyone in the theater, while I couldn't let go of her as soon as I embraced her, holding on to her head and kissing her head and pressing her head against my chest as she quietly began to remove her shawl.

"Can I watch the movie now?"

My lips must have been all over her neck. "Do you have any idea how happy I am?"

She took off her coat, disturbed more people, sat down, took her glasses out. "Yes, I do know."

I knew, however, that I'd have to let go of her. I didn't want to let go of her. I liked being like this. I knew that, once released, she'd be impossible to touch again, and that soon enough the water that had bubbled between us for a few seconds would freeze and, for miles of cracking ice, would loom the old no-man's-land between her mainland and my distant shore. So I let my hand rest almost casually on her shoulder, knowing, though, that she'd spot the studied nonchalance of the gesture and in all likelihood make fun of it. *So this is awkward for you, isn't it?*

When she spotted my coffee, she immediately reached over and drank from it. Why hadn't I put sugar in? Because I never do. I can't believe you didn't buy me coffee. So this is your revenge—not buying the poor girl coffee? Anything to eat?

I handed her the candy.

"At least that!"

She chuckled.

"What?" I said.

"Nothing."

The man behind us asked us to lower our voices.

Clara turned to him and threatened to wash his hair with her coffee if he didn't take his feet off the seat next to hers.

·

Until she appeared in the movie theater, I'd been more or less resigned to an evening by myself. I was even able to stare straight ahead and not be too scared of the bleakness awaiting me as soon as I walked out into the empty street. It was not going to be so terrible, I'd been telling myself, just as it wasn't so terrible that she had found yet another cutting way to remind me she had a life outside of mine, other friends, *otherpeoples*—not terrible that a day that started poorly should end no less poorly, not terrible being so thoroughly alone now and watching the hours stretch into tomorrow, and other tomorrows, and more tomorrows pitching their way back-to-back like blocks of ice crick-cracking down the slow Hudson till they'd leave all land behind and head to the Atlantic and out toward the glacier of the Arctic Pole. Not terrible that everyone was wrong, wrong as my life, as this day, as everything can seem so thoroughly muddled and disjointed and yet so easily tolerable.

After the movie I'd already resolved to head uptown, perhaps even walk past her home, especially now that I knew which side her windows faced. Walk uptown to replay and relive the scene uptown. Or was this all an excuse to stalk her building, her street, her world? Was I really the type who stalks buildings, windows, people? Follow her, spy on her, confront her? Aha, see! Or better yet, bump into her. Fancy running into you at this time of the night!

Or was heading uptown to 106th Street simply a pretext to stay busy and give myself something to do at night, the way buying Christmas presents three days after Christmas might give me something to look forward to once I'd run out of things to stuff my hours with?

Sitting next to her now on our usual banquette, I realized that all I'd done since hearing she wouldn't be going to the movies with me was try to keep a straight face, with her, with me, with everything—try not to enjoy too much our moment together on the rug so as not to feel it was the highlight of the year, keep the moment on ice, keep friendship on ice, and live with each of my tiny, minuscule hopes, like caviar always chilled.

As soon as we walked out of the theater, neither of us said anything about where we were headed. Instead, we started walking in the same direction as always and, in case there were any doubts, crossed over to the right side of Broadway to show we had no other place in mind but that one. I couldn't wait to get there and go back to our ritual by the banquette and order our first drink. Perhaps she too was eager to bring things back to where we'd left them—though there was no telling where her thoughts were. Once we crossed Broadway, though, all she did was slip her arm into mine and say she couldn't wait for our Oban.

"You're becoming an alcoholic under my influence."

"That, and other things," she said. I thought she was referring to her growing fondness for Eric Rohmer and didn't bother asking her to explain. Then it occurred to me she might have meant something else, but for fear of finding it out, I didn't press her to explain.

But no sooner were we sitting at our spot and had signaled to the waitress, who immediately assumed we were ordering the "usual," than things began to trickle forth. At first I thought she'd already had something to drink before coming. But that was almost four hours ago, long enough for her to have sobered up. As was her habit, she ordered crispy fries, which she liked to drown in salt and mounds of ketchup. I would have ordered a salad, but decided to go with a side order of fries as well. I liked mine with mayo. Once the matter of ordering was taken care of, she extended her palm.

"Give!" she said.

I gave her a dollar.

"More."

She walked over to the jukebox, and soon enough we began hearing the few bars of Chopin that prefaced our tango.

I had made myself promise not to ask her anything about where she'd been, what she'd done, whom with. But she almost resented my silence, and after we'd danced, she finally blurted a "Well, aren't you going to ask me what happened?"

"This time I don't dare ask."

"Because you're too polite to ask, because you don't care, because you don't want to know—or other?"

"Other," I said.

She was in a strangely sparkling mood tonight, and I feared the worst. She was going to tell me something I knew I didn't want to know. I would gladly have steered her away from it. I could sense it was probably going to be something like "We've decided to get back together," or "I'm having his child," or—and this was a road I didn't even want to travel on, though scoping out its signposts before she'd even hinted the matter might blunt the shock—she'd remind me I was doing precisely what she'd warned me not to do, Printz. Knowing Clara, she'd still manage to surprise me. "I think we shouldn't be together so much." She would not say "seeing each other," which might implicate her more than she wanted, but "be together," which would leave things vague enough and not give a deeper meaning to the whimsical, improvised beauty of our five days. I was already anticipating the flustered stammer in her smile as she let an earnest, longing gaze precede the tenderness of the five words she would most likely say, all the while gauging their effect on me: "You're not upset, are you?" Damned if I'm upset, I'd say, fuck damn I'm upset! But I knew myself: I'd say nothing.

The drinks arrived. We clinked glasses carefully, because if you miscounted, you'd have to clink another nine times. We uttered the Russian words in unison.

"Do you or don't you want to know?"

I said I wanted to know, almost listlessly, not just to dampen my curiosity, but to dampen the frisky tone in her voice.

"I was with Inky."

"So you two are an item again?"

She looked at me in wonder.

How had you guessed? she seemed to ask. It was obvious from the start, I would have said.

"I had promised to have dinner with him. We started with early drinks, which is why I had to leave your place early. Then it fell apart— I knew we were going to quarrel. So I left."

"Just like that?"

"Just like that."

"You *wanted* to leave?"

Clara gave me a fearless stare.

"I'm not going to lie to you: I *was* looking for an excuse, and he gave it to me in no time. I knew I'd find you at the movie theater."

I couldn't put together the reasoning behind what she'd just said.

"Are you two over, then?"

"So very over."

I was on the verge of asking if she was sorry things had taken this course, but she seemed so bubbly, there was no point in asking.

"Now it's your turn," she said, leaning sideways toward me.

I knew what she meant, but pretended not to understand. "My turn for what?"

"What did you do after I left?"

"Went to the gym, swam, went to the movies—that's all."

She wanted something from me, and I wasn't responding. She started doing what she'd done the first night: wrapping her napkin around the base of her wineglass. It was her way of collecting her thoughts before speaking. I knew exactly where she was headed. *There should be others in your life, not just me. I don't want to mislead you. And besides, I am still lying so very low.* I didn't know the exact order, but these were going to be the highlights of her little talk, because, from long experience with my father, I could sense a little talk coming.

No sooner had the waitress passed by than Clara ordered another round. That was fast, I thought.

"So I'm the one who's going to have to say it, then?" she said.

All I could do was stare her in the eyes till she looked down.

Was this how she had started with Inky? *Want me to be the one to say it, then?* Twice in one day? I hated conversations that threatened to leave me totally exposed—even when I didn't know what exactly I'd be exposing, even when I knew that exposure, as an abstract concept, was far better than being so bottled up. What was I hiding that she didn't already know?

"I was going to say it in an e-mail two days ago."

What was she being so cagey about?

"Why didn't you send it, then?"

"Because I know you: you'd read it this way, that way, turn it around 180 degrees, 360 and 540 degrees, and still come out with nothing. Tell me I'm wrong."

"You're not wrong."

"See, I know you." She was going to accuse me of not heeding her warnings, of wanting from our friendship things she'd never promised, much less be able to deliver. She'd said it before already, didn't have to repeat it, it hovered over every minute we'd spent together. Now it was going to come out in the open. I knew the it's-not-you-it's-me speech. I'd given it myself many times.

"You asked me the other day if we could end up at Hans's party and be total strangers. I've run into people I no longer speak to. I can live with that. I don't even mind having to hate them if that's what it takes to dump leftover baggage. I know how quickly I change. But if we do become strangers, and I do learn to hate you, and watch you turn your back as soon as I walk into a room, just know this: that no part of me will ever forget this week."

"Why?"

"For the same reason you won't."

"This is starting to sound like a lopsided goodbye."

"Let's say then that maybe this is *our* hell. The closer we draw, the farther we drift apart. There's a rock standing between us. I obey it. Or let's say: I don't have it in me to fight it, not these days. Frankly, I don't think you have it in you either."

"Don't say that."

"Why? It's the truth."

"You're the one who put the rock there four nights ago, not me."

"Maybe. But I had no idea it would turn into such a convenient rock for you as well."

Was this the truth, or had Clara seen something I'd been avoiding? Did the rock between us really work for me? Was my habit of deferring and doubting and reading into so many things simply my way of keeping my distance by drawing closer? What doubts, what fears was I cloaking? Had I, perhaps, been blaming her flippant mood, or her string of *other-peoples*, or her caustic tongue, the better to blame the tip of an iceberg that hardly stood between us when it was really my miles and masses of hardened ice underneath that would cause the real damage?

"Look," I began, as I shifted in my place. Perhaps I was trying to change the drift of our talk, or perhaps I wanted the two of us to think I was finally about to say something momentous that might stem the downhill course of where we seemed to be headed. Perhaps I wanted to throw her off by sounding very solemn and serious—this was going to be a time for calling a spade a spade. In fact, I had no idea what I was about to say.

"The other night I read you loud and clear, and ever since, I have not strayed. I haven't even raised the subject. I said it already: we're like two blocks of ice trapped under a bridge—you're lying low, and I'm too frozen on the spot to risk anything. Let me just say, though, that this is unlike anything I've known. You read me better than I read myself, and part of the joy of being together is just that: discovering that you and I are the same person in two bodies, like identical twins."

This was worse than *I sing in the shower*. The same person in two bodies—seriously?

"We're not twins." Clara overlooked nothing. "I know you'd like to think it, but we're not. We're very similar, but we're also very different. One of us will always lapse into wanting more—"

"And this someone is me, of course, right?"

"It's me too, if you cared enough to look."

"I do care enough to look—what did you think?"

"Then you should have seen it coming, Printz."

Clara made me order another round of fries.

"You're not going to eat more fries by yourself?"

"You order a pecan pie and we'll share both. With whipped cream—the kind that comes in a spray can." The carefree gesture with which she threw her hair back said she was going all out tonight.

The waitress must have grimaced at the suggestion of the spray can. But then something told me that Clara asked for it precisely for its shock value.

Then she did something she'd never done before. She took my hand and placed it on her cheek. "Better," she said, as if she were just speaking to herself, or to a friend with whom she was trying to make up. I let my hand rest on her cheek, then caressed her neck, right under her ear, the exact spot where I had kissed her so feverishly when she arrived in the theater a few hours before and, in the heat of the moment, must have caught her totally unprepared for my kisses. Even now, she didn't seem to mind; she leaned into my hand, like a kitten whose cheek you might have rubbed absentmindedly but who then wants more of the same. "But I have to tell you something." All I could do was stare at her, saying nothing, just keep caressing her face now that I saw I could. Then, without thinking at all, I let my finger touch her lips, and from her lips let it move to her teeth—I loved her teeth, and though I knew that this had crossed the line and gone beyond the harmless *hand on a cheek* she'd asked from me, still, I was no longer the owner of that hand, she was, for she kissed my finger first, then held it delicately between her teeth, and then touched it with the point of her tongue. I loved her forehead and rubbed it as well, and the skin of her eyelids, I loved it too, everything, everything, and that smile that made silence come and go and made my heart skip the instant it left her face. What were we doing? "I want us to speak," she began, "because I want you to know something." I had no idea what she meant, but knew that if she seemed to be yielding with one side of her, she was just about ready to take back everything with the other. "Time for a secret agent," she said.

"Wait." I put my hand in my coat pocket and pulled out a sealed packet of her brand.

"You're joking!" She tapped the pack, then opened it. "I won't ask what this was doing in your pocket."

"Don't bother, you know already."

I've always envied people who put their cards on the table—even when they don't have a hand—people who are willing to call a conveniently ambiguous situation by its name if only to clear the air. She was right: I didn't trust her, I feared being set up. Any moment now, she'd tell me the one thing I dreaded most. *You do know what I want to say?* I think so. *What?* And I'd fall for the oldest trick in the world. Chastened by her frank gaze and by that hint of reprobation to come, I caught myself tempted to preempt her, if only to say it myself and not hear it from her. That we should cool it, maybe see other people, not misread this for what it's not, it's not you, it's me—I'd been expecting this speech for days already. Then, by way of capping all this, I finally said, "I know you have a whole life outside of Rohmer and me." It was meant to show I harbored no jealousy or illusions. But I also wanted her to read that the same might be said regarding aspects of my life about which she knew very, very little.

"Can I be blunt?" So she wasn't going to let me diffuse what she had started to say. "Yesterday afternoon when you came by I could have asked you and I know you would have said yes—but it would have been more by way of consent, just as had you insisted after you tried to rape and bludgeon me last night, I'd have agreed, but that would have been no more than a lukewarm yes. By the time we left the bar last night, you knew I was of two minds anyway—and don't deny it."

I was about to affect surprise. But she cut me short. "Don't bother. You knew."

This was more frank than anything I'd expected. She was honing in on everything, and I suddenly felt this wave of anxiety wash over me, because I didn't know yet whether she was about to bring out into the open everything we'd left tactfully unsaid during our evenings together or whether she was simply going to eviscerate me and expose me for the shifty, jittery, wanting man I'd always known I was.

"Why call it consent if we're both willing?" I threw in.

"Because you and I both know there is something holding us back, and neither of us knows what it is. If I cared less, I'd say I didn't want to get hurt, but I don't give a damn about getting hurt, just as I don't care if you get hurt. If I cared less, I'd also say it would ruin our friendship. But I don't give a fuck about friendship either."

"I thought we did have a friendship, or were working up to one."

"Friendships are for other people, and neither of us wants friendship. We're too close for friendship."

Was there no hope for anything, then? Suddenly all I could think of was the word *heartbreak*. You're breaking my heart, Clara, and these are cruel and cutting words that cause heartache, and rupture of blood vessels. My heart was indeed racing. This was so sad that, for the first time in my life, I suddenly found myself on the verge of crying because a woman had said no to me before I'd even had a chance to ask anything. Or had I asked her already? Hadn't I been asking for days now? Did men really cry like this—and if they did, where had I been all my life? I'll always hate you for this, for bringing me to the abyss and forcing me to stare down, the way they force a detainee to watch the brutal execution of his cellmate, only to be told after, but not before he's witnessed the atrocity, that they had no plans to execute him at all, in fact he was free to go.

She must have noticed. Maybe she'd already seen it once this very afternoon with Inky. "Please don't," she said, as she had the last time, "because if you start, I'll start, and once this happens, then all signals get crossed, all systems go down, and we'll be back to even before we started this conversation."

"Maybe I'd rather be where we were before we started. This talk is going to places I'm not going to like."

"Why? You're not surprised. I'm not surprised."

It swept through me before I knew what was happening. This was going to be totally out of order, and it might bring everything we'd been saying down to a crappy, hackneyed plane, but I had nothing left to lose, no dignity, no ammunition, no water in my gourd, and I felt it was worth throwing this last vestige of pride into the fire the way, on very cold days, a freezing bohemian poet might throw his manuscript into the fire, to stay warm, find love, spite art, and show fate a thing or two.

"Let's just face it," I said, "you're just not attracted. Just say that the physical thing isn't there. I don't do it for you. Say it. It won't tear me up. But it will clear the air."

"You're always playing, even when you're serious. It has nothing to do with physical attraction. If anything, it's because I am attracted that we've come this far."

This was news! Had I so thoroughly misread her that it had to hit me in the face—or was this her turn to play with me, play any card, so long as she averted the silence she probably hated as much as I did.

"So, according to you, all this should flatter me," I said. I was being ironic. Or perhaps I wanted her to say it once more in clear and plain language.

"Flattery is irrelevant. I don't give a fuck about flattery, and neither do you. It's not what either of us wants."

"Why, do *you* know what you want?"

"Do *you?*"

"I think I do. I've wanted it from the very first, and you've known it."

"Not true. You're knocking at a door, but you're not even sure you want it opened."

"How about you?"

"I'm not knocking, I've pushed open the door already. But I can't say I've stepped in either."

"Maybe it's because you don't trust me."

"Maybe."

And then it hit me. "You're not afraid of getting hurt, or of being rejected, are you?" I said. "You're terrified of what you may not find. You're afraid of being disappointed."

"Aren't you?" she asked right away, as though she'd known it all along.

"Petrified," I replied. I was exaggerating.

"Petrified," she repeated. "This doesn't flatter either of us, does it? Or maybe we're just two grown-up scaredy-cats. Just scaredy-cats."

I didn't like where this was going either.

"Petrified or not, let me say this, then," I said. "I think of you all the time. All the time, all the time, all the time. It's a fact of life. I'm just happy this is a magical, snow globe, holiday week—but I've been with you every minute of every day. I eat with you, I shower with you, I sleep with you. My pillow is tired of hearing your name."

It didn't seem to surprise her.

"Do you call it Clara?"

"I call it Clara, I tell it things I've told no one in my life, and if I have more to drink tonight, what I have to tell you will make it difficult to face you again tomorrow."

The heavy silence brooding between us told me I had overplayed my hand and made a dreadful mistake. How to backpedal now?

"If you need to know, it's hardly any different here," she said, almost reluctantly, something like halting sorrow straining her voice, the equivalent of a helpless shrug during a moment where words fail. Was she bluffing? Or was she raising the stakes? "I say your name when I'm alone."

Was this the same girl who didn't sing in the shower?

"Why didn't you say anything before?" I asked.

"*You* never said anything, Mr. Amphibalence, me-Door-number-three man."

"I was playing by your rules."

"What rules?"

I looked at her more baffled than ever. The admonitions, the roadblocks, the subtle warnings—were they nothing?

The fries arrived. She squeezed a dollop of ketchup onto them, and then added more. She was about to say something. Before speaking, though, she picked up a fry with her thumb and forefinger and, while it awaited its baptismal ketchup, she kept staring at it, lost in what looked like stray thoughts and misgivings, as though her fry had become an amulet or a sacred relic or a bone fragment from a patron saint who was being asked to guide her in this difficult pass. "I'll say this much, and you're free to believe me or not, to laugh at me or not, but I'm ready to go all the way with you," she said. "This afternoon I left your home feeling I was making the worst mistake of my life, because I didn't feel I'd ever be able to repair it. The minute I saw Inky, I had to run away on any pretext, not sure I'd find you, not sure you'd be alone, not sure you'd even be happy to see me again, but I chanced it and I came. I left a million messages, if you care to check."

I hadn't checked, precisely because I did not want to find none waiting.

"I kept hoping you'd call, which is why in the end I left the house and went to the gym."

"Now that makes perfect sense, doesn't it? And you turned off your *télyfôn* for the same reason, I suppose."

There was no point denying it.

"It's as I said, Printz: I'm ready."

I didn't know what she meant exactly, but was afraid to ask. What was clear was that her sentence had the assertive dare of a *Your move*.

"Could you just kiss me now and not argue so much?"

She leaned over toward me, reached for my neck, lowered my turtleneck, and kissed me straight on the neck—something unusually long and sensual for a first kiss.

"I've been staring at your skin for an hour. I needed to taste it," she said, palming the skin around my eyes.

"And I've been staring at your teeth for days now."

This was the first of many kisses. Her breath tasted of bread and Viennese butter cookies.

·

Last call was on the house, courtesy of the waitress, who'd been working the late shift every night this week. We were sitting on the banquette, unable to move, fearing that any movement or change might break the spell and pull us back to doubts and heartbreak waiting around the corner. When Clara returned from the bathroom, she put her arms around me and immediately resumed kissing me on the mouth. I could not believe how fast things were moving. "You taste fantastic," I said.

Then she told me: "Just don't make me think this is happening in my head. Because I know you," she said. "And I know myself. I want this, but I also know what you'll drive me to do, and I pray, pray, you don't." I had no idea what she meant. "Don't you have any trust, any faith?" I asked. "None." In moments of extreme tenderness she spoke with a serrated tongue.

It occurred to me she must have thought the same of me. Had she asked me if I trusted anyone, I would have said the exact same thing.

As some point I said I had to go to the bathroom. "If you take more than one minute, I'll go into high pandangst and think you've escaped through some back, rat-infested alley, and I'll just leave—because I know I can't take it."

"I'm just going to pee, okay?"

But on the way to the bathroom the thought did occur to me: I'll sleep with her tonight, then tomorrow we'll see. I wondered if she could get even more passionate in bed than she'd been already on the banquette, or would she suddenly turn out to be the type who needed this done, and that done, and more of this and less of that, and no biting please, or was it going to be beastly lovemaking where we'd tear each other's clothes off as soon as we were behind the elevator door and out of her doorman's sight? Or would there be candlelight, with Straus Park behind us and the *Prince Oscar* looking after us outside our window as we stood naked together and watched the night like two sleepless starlings listening again and again, and many more times again to Beethoven's "Song of Thanksgiving"? Or would it be as it always was with her: chill winter gusts in a minefield of scalding geysers? In the bathroom I caught

sight of my face in the mirror and smiled at myself. I had drunk three, no
four Scotches. "Hi," I finally said out loud. "Hi," he responded. Then I
looked down at Signor Guido, my patient foster-child of silence. "Who's
the man?" I finally asked. "You're the man," I said as I watched him perform his ancillary function. "Who loves you?" "You do," he said, still
wearing a simper on his bald pate. "This is your moment, and tonight is
your night, you intrepid scalawag, you."

While standing in front of the urinal, I rested my forehead against the
cool, glistening steel pipe connected to the flusher, where condensation
had collected, and simply stood there, enjoying its cooling feel as I
pushed my forehead into the large hexagonal steel nut, now smiling at
myself each time I heard the words repeated in my mind: Who's the
man? You're the man. Who's the man? You're the man. I was almost on
the point of bursting out laughing. The most beautiful moment of my life
happened before a urinal. Just please, please don't make me stop loving
her, don't make me squelch this or wake up sated and indifferent. Don't.

When I returned to Clara, she looked totally alarmed.

"What did you do to your face? Did you fall?"

I had no idea what she was talking about. I was too busy trying not to
look unsteady as I sat back down. "You have something that looks like a
gash—no, a bruise—on your forehead. She was touching it, lovingly.
Could this woman who could cut me with two syllables show such tenderness for my forehead? I touched my forehead. No doubt about it; there
was an indentation in my skin. Was I bleeding badly? How could this
have happened? Then I remembered. The steel nut—I must have been
leaning forever against the large nut on the steel pipe.

"Just looking at it makes me want to touch you. What took you so
long? What were you really doing in there, Printz?"

"Clara Brunschvicg, you shock me."

And we kissed again. In the fog of our caresses and lovemaking, I
understood why people bring their mouths together. This is why people
kiss, I kept thinking, the way an alien from distant constellations might
say to himself, after trying out a human body, *So this is why they do it.*
What had I been doing before? I wanted to ask. Whom had I filled my
life with all this time? And what had all these women been doing in it?
Why, for which reason, what pleasure, what end, when it was so very
clear that small love was taken and less given back? Had everyone been a

Sunday filler? What rose gardens had I slumbered through and what could we have been swapping in the din-filled Exchanges of Love? Or did it not matter, so long as we kept the ships coming and commerce going and the piers bustling—people, action, places, cargo, buy, sell, borrow— yet everyone, in the end, always, always alone when night falls on the dale of pandangst.

Why even bother asking why this was different?

In the men's room I had taken a moment to check if there were messages for me. She had called eight times but never left a message. Why did I assume that she'd lied to me when she claimed she'd called so many times? Because you don't trust me, because you're afraid of me. Afraid of what, though? Afraid. Afraid because I could be better than you. Afraid because, unlike love with others, you've no clue where this is going. Afraid that, contrary to what you desperately want to believe, you'll never want this to end. Afraid—and you're only beginning to get a glimpse of it now—that I'm the real deal, Printz, and that this hindrance and disturbance we thought was a rock between us is what bound us from the get-go. Today you like me more than you know. But what you're scared to death of is wanting me more tomorrow.

I'd known her for only five days, but I already knew that this was the stuff of planets and of lives moved by fate, gods, and by the nebulae of ghosts who have come and gone, keening over loves that time won't expiate or pleas bring back. You've sprung like a curse on my land, Clara, it will take my blood generations to wash you away.

Clara, I was lying, I am not afraid of being disappointed, I am afraid of what I'll have and don't deserve or wouldn't know what to do with, much less learn to fight for each day. And yes, afraid you are better than I am. Afraid I'll love you more tomorrow than I do tonight, and then where will I be?

"Tomorrow is *Full Moon in Paris*," she said.

I did not reply. She intercepted my silence before I did.

"Are you thinking what I think you're thinking?"

She knew, she knew.

"You don't know if there'll be a tomorrow?"

"Do you know?"

"I make no promises."

"Neither do I." I was boasting.

"Printz, sometimes you don't know what you're saying."

Our knives were drawn again.

"For the record, though—"

"Yes . . ." There it was, as always, the little threat that pricks your pulse and sends it racing into panic mode.

"Just for the record, so you won't fault me for not saying it now: I'm more in love with you than you know. More in love than you are."

We kissed again. Neither of us cared who was watching. No one bothered to watch when it came to couples in this bar. This was the woman who was going to make love to me tonight. And she was going to make love to me, not like this, but more than just like this. All that stood between us was our sweaters. Then we'd be naked together, her thighs against my thighs, face-to-face, very face-to-face, and we'd pick up just where we'd have left off at the bar and go on talking and laughing and talking as we'd make love, and go on and on till morning and exhaustion. This was, and the thought came from so far away that I could easily put it on hold for a while, the first and only woman I'd ever wanted to make love to.

•

It had snowed outside. The snow on the stoop to the bar made me think of our first night together when we'd left the party and she wore my coat for a few minutes and had then given it back to me, after which I slogged my way down the stairs by the monument onto Riverside Drive, thinking to myself that perhaps I'd left the party too soon and should have stayed awhile longer, who cares if they think I've enjoyed the party and am eager to stay for breakfast! Later, I had changed my mind and walked to Straus Park, where all I did was sit and think and remember the minutes when we had come back after Mass and she'd pointed out her bench to me. So many years on this planet, and never once felt anything like this.

"Wait," she said, before leaving the bar. "I need to tie my shawl."

Soon her face was almost entirely wrapped in her shawl. All one could see was the top of her eyes and part of her forehead.

At the corner of the street, I put my arm around her and let her mold into me as she always did when we walked together. Then, without caring how long it had taken her to cover her face, I snuck my hand into the shawl and held her face, pushing the shawl all the way back to expose her head and to kiss her again. She leaned her back against the bakery store window and let me kiss her, and all I could feel then was my crotch against hers, pushing ever so mildly, then pushing again, as she yielded first and then pushed back, softly, because this is what we'd been rehearsing all along, and this too was a rehearsal. This was why they'd invented sex, and this was why people made love and went inside each other's body and then slept together, because of this and not for any of the many reasons I'd imagined or been guided by during my entire life. How many other things would I discover I didn't know the first thing about tonight? People made love not because they wanted to but because something far older than time itself and yet way smaller than a ladybug ordained it, which was why nothing in the world felt more natural or less awkward between us than for her to feel my hardness rubbing against her or our hips caught in a rhythm all their own. For the first time in my life I wasn't out to seduce anyone or pretend that I wasn't; I had arrived there long before.

But perhaps I had arrived too soon, and my mind was lagging behind, like a limping child slowing down those who had gone ahead of him.

"This is my bakery. I buy coffee here," she said.

Why did it matter? I thought.

"And the muffins?"

"Sometimes muffins too." We kissed again.

Inside the park, she stood by the statue. "Isn't this the most beautiful statue in the world?"

"Without you it means nothing," I said.

"It's my childhood, my years in school, everything. We met here this morning, and here we are again. It has so much of you."

Clara's world.

In the cold night I began to dread our arrival and was hoping to defer it—not, as I had hoped on previous nights, because arrival meant saying goodbye after perfunctory pecks and the perfunctory hug—but because tonight I'd have to say what I lacked the courage to say, what I wasn't even sure I wanted to say: "I'm dying to come upstairs, Clara, I just need time."

She looked at me as we approached the door to her building. She'd sensed something. "Did I do something wrong?"

"Not a thing."

"Then what is it? What's happened?"

I was the girl, she was the man.

I stopped on the sidewalk with her still in my arms. I couldn't find the right words, so I blurted the first thing that came to mind.

"It's too soon, too sudden, too fast," I said.

"What do you mean?"

"I don't want to rush it. Don't want to mess this up."

Perhaps I didn't want her to think I was like everyone else, and was determined to prove it to her.

Or was it boorish Boris and his so-you're-finally-gonna-get-some-tonight smirk that I wished to avoid?

Or was it just that I wanted to let the romance last awhile longer and ripen on its vine?

"So you'll leave me alone and go home in this weather? Sleep on the couch if you must."

"We've seen too many Rohmer movies."

"You're making such a terrible mistake—"

"I just need a day."

"He needs a day."

She had withdrawn from my arm. "Is there something I should know?"

I shook my head.

"Are you . . ." And I could tell she was looking for the right words but couldn't find them: "Are you damaged? Am I not what you like?"

"For your nymphormation, I am not damaged. And as for that other thing—you're so off track."

"Still, such a mistake."

We were both very cold by then, and it was good that Boris had opened the lobby door a crack.

"Kiss me again."

Boris's presence for some reason cramped me, but not her. Still, I kissed her on the mouth, then once again, and as though she remembered the gesture that had brought us closer than we'd ever been before, she lowered my turtleneck, exposed my throat, and placed a long kiss there. "I love your smell." "And I love everything, just everything about you—that simple." She looked at me. "*Idiot*." She was quoting Maud from the film. "I know." "Just don't forget. First thing tomorrow morning—call me," she added, making a gesture she often parodied by extending her thumb and index finger. "Otherwise, you know me: I go into high pandangst, and there's no telling what can happen." I tried to humor her. "Printz, I shouldn't tell you, because you don't deserve it, but you're the best thing that's happened to me this year."

SIXTH NIGHT

That night, in Straus Park, I almost did light a cigarette. It was too cold to sit and it had started snowing, so I could stand there for only a short while before moving on. One day, I'll grow tired of this. One day, I'll pass by and forget to stop.

I called her as soon as I arrived home. No, she wasn't sleeping. Didn't want to lose the feeling either. No, same spot, by the window, men's pajamas. She sounded sleepy and exhausted, but no different than when I'd left her. I can still smell you, she said, and it will be like sleeping with you. I felt she was drifting off, perhaps I was keeping her up. "No, don't go yet, I like that you called." Maybe I'd done the right thing, she said. "Calling?" I asked. "Calling too."

There were long silences on the phone. I told her I'd never felt anything like this for anyone. "I have," she said, and, after a momentary interruption, added "for you." I could see her smile rippling on her tired features, the dimples when she smiled, her hand when she rubbed her palm over her forehead. I want to be naked with you. It's not like you weren't asked.

We said good night, but neither got off the phone, so we kept urging the other to hang up, and each time we said good night, a long silence would follow. Clara? Yes. You're not hanging up. I'm hanging up now. Long silence. But she wouldn't hang up. Did it take you an hour to get home? Almost. What crazy ideas you have, Printz, going home like this, you would have made me happy, and I'd have made you happy too. Good night, I said. Good night, she said. But I didn't hear a click, and when I asked if she was still on the line, I heard a smothered giggle. "Clara B., you're crazy." "I'm crazy? *You're* crazy." "I'm crazy for you." "Obviously not crazy enough."

I did not want to miss her by calling too late the next morning. But I didn't want to call too early either. I waited to take my shower for a while, but then, for good measure, took both my phones into the bathroom in case she called either one. As for breakfast, no way I was going to leave home before speaking to her. This was when I came up with the idea of buying an assortment of muffins and scones nimbly stacked in a white paper bag folded at the top. That's right. Two coffees and an assortment of muffins, scones, and goodies, nimbly stacked . . .

On my way to the shower I spotted the mound of salt on the carpet still bearing the grooved imprints of Clara's fingers. My God, she had been here less than twenty-four hours ago—here, in this very apartment, sitting on this very carpet, barefoot, with chocolate cookies wedged in between her toes. The idea seemed unreal, impossible to grasp, as if some higher order had suddenly descended to pay a visit to my arid, dull, sublunary landfill. Yesterday we were together, I kept repeating.

I watched the stain and feared that it might lose its luster and meaning, that she too, as a result, might begin to retreat, ebbing like a lakeshore town when just hours earlier it seemed a stroll away.

When I bought this rug, the idea of a Clara couldn't even have crossed my mind, and yet that Sunday in late May with my father when I bid on the rug at an auction before moving here is now indissolubly fused to this spill, as though she and the rug and my father, who wanted me to learn how to buy things at an auction, because one had to learn these things, had run on three totally seemingly unrelated paths that were destined to converge on this very stain, the way the pictures of the cages in the Tiergarten would lose their meaning now unless joined to that of a baby born that same year one summer thousands of miles away.

I loved reading my life this way—in the key of Clara—as if something out there had arranged its every event according to principles that were more luminous and more radiant than those of life itself, events whose meaning was made obvious retrospectively, always retrospectively. What was blind luck and arbitrary suddenly had an intention. Coincidence and happenstance were not really chaotic but the mainsprings of an intelligence I had better not disturb or intrude upon with too many questions. Even love, perhaps, was nothing more than our way of cobbling random units of life into something approaching meaning and design.

How nimble, how natural, how obvious her suggestion that we have lunch at my place. It would never have occurred to me. How simple her way of coming up to me at the party. Left to my own devices, I'd have spent the whole evening trying to speak to her and finally given up on hearing her tell someone something casual, caustic, and cruel.

I looked at the salt on the rug and renewed my promise never to touch it. This was proof that we'd been happy together, that we could spend entire days and not once grow tired of the other.

Of course, I feared that the joy I felt, like certain trees, had taken root at the edge of a craggy cliff. They may crane their necks and turn their leaves all they want toward the sun, but gravity has the last word. Please don't let me be the one to pull this tree down. There is so much sarcasm and drought in me, to say nothing of fear, pride, disbelief, and an evil disposition ready to spite myself if only to prove I can do without so many of the things that life puts on the table that I'll even be the first to push the poor sapling into the water. Don't do it. If anything, let her.

I thought once again of last night and how our hips had moved together. *Too soon, too sudden, too fast.* What an idiot!

Compare this to: *You're the best thing that's happened to me this year.* You could take these words to a broker and buy put options in a bullish market and still make a killing—words whose hidden luster I recovered and would let go of so as to recapture them over and over, the way someone finds his fingers returning time and again to a pleasurable round object on a string of tiny hexagonal worry beads. Even when I forgot these words, I knew they were waiting close by, like a cat rubbing its back against your closed door. I'd even delay letting it in, knowing that as soon as I changed my mind, it would immediately rush in and jump on my lap—*You're the best thing that's happened to me this year.*

I had a vision of Clara wearing glasses still, in her men's pajamas and white socks, but nothing else. "So this is no longer *too soon, too sudden, too fast?*" she'd ask. "Fuck too soon, too sudden," I'd say, struggling with the urge to undo the drawstring of her jammies—drop the jammies, keep the socks, off with the glasses, and let me see you naked in the morning light, my north, my south, my *strudel gâteau,* Oskár and Brunschvicg ready to rollick, coiled up like reptiles flailing and agile. I wonder if the coffee would get cold. Split the muffins and bless the crumbs, the sticky buns, the icing on the cake, and stay in bed, reach out for the coffee until arousal sweeps over us again, and we'll call it *making strudel gâteau.*

In the shower this morning, hands off Guido.

"So did you make love to me last night?" she'd ask. "I most certainly did not," I'd say. Did not.

By nine I was walking out the door when the phone rang. I hoped I'd still answer with last night's tired, intimate, unguarded voice, perhaps I'd even try to affect it if it wouldn't come naturally. But it was only a deliveryman. The thrill with which I had rushed to answer told me how much I wanted it to be Clara, today like yesterday, like the day before, like every other day this week. I wondered if she'd sound as languid and hoarse as she did last night, heedless of everything that didn't bear on us—or would she be back to her blithe and sprightly self again, light and swift, alert and caustic, untamed rebuke all set to sting?

The delivery was taking longer than necessary. "He's already on his way," said the doorman when I called downstairs. I waited. By now it was past nine. I waited some more. Then I buzzed downstairs and told the doorman to see why the delivery was taking so long. I hung up. The phone rang again. "Yes!!!" I said. "Didn't you know I was going to call?" Obviously I must have sounded miffed and was sending the totally wrong signal. Her voice, as I suspected, was entirely sober. "Funny, I was just on my way to bring you muffins and coffee." But I knew I had picked something up in her voice. I couldn't quite tell what had tipped me off, but I knew that something didn't bode well. "That's so sweet, but I have to be all the way downtown. I was just about to walk out the door."

Why didn't I trust the drawn-out, doleful *all the way downtown* that wished to suggest that going downtown was an unwelcome and painful task that was surely going to ruin her entire morning?

Why had she called, then? To make contact, to keep last night alive, to reassure the two of us that nothing had changed? Or was it because I had taken too long to call and she'd gone into *high pandangst*? Or was hers a preemptive admission, truth as cover-up, which explained the peremptory haste and the diversionary blandspeak of her *all the way downtown*?

What made me furious was how I always let events and others dictate how my day was going to turn out. Passivity? Timidity? Or was it every man's diffidence, which invents honorable obstacles to avoid asking for fear of being turned down? I could have offered to go with her, but I didn't. And I could have told her I'd meet her immediately afterward, but I didn't. Clara, sensing I wasn't about to do either, may have suspected I wasn't so eager to see her. But that didn't make sense: Why would I offer to bring her breakfast if I wasn't eager to see her? But then, why was I making it so easy for her not to change her plans *downtown*? To hide my disappointment?

I knew I was letting the whole day—and Clara along with it—slide like sand between my fingers. Her uncompromising tone had snuffed out my desire to put up a fight or even attempt to.

"Where will you be around lunchtime?" I asked.

I was expecting something like *At a place where people eat.*

"Well, I'm having lunch with a friend."

I didn't like this at all. She had used the word *friend* to avoid using a name. I knew she knew I'd see through this. Was this, yet again, an instance of tit for tat? What made it worse—and what drew me like a moth to a flame—was that, even if she was trying to avoid being more specific about her *friend*, she knew I'd think she was doing it on purpose.

"What if I call as soon as we're done? How's that?"

But *How's that?* was not so neutral either. It could mean *Happy now?* Or it could mean: *See, I can be nice. Now, be a good boy and take this offer before I take it back.* She was, it seemed to me, willing to meet me halfway, but not more, even though both of us knew this wasn't halfway at all. It sounded like a final concession made to a temperamental child before one lost patience and resorted to warnings. *How's that?* could easily mean *Take that!*

I wanted to see her now, before ten in the morning. But she was saying she'd call me around three.

I already sensed that, at the earliest, we'd meet at the movie theater—if then.

What was I to do with myself all this time? Hope? Worry? Fight her? Sit staring blankly at my walls, at my carpet, at my windows, like one of those hollowed-out Hopper characters? Trundle up and down Broadway? Start calling friends I'd been too happy to neglect? Swim in my bathtub? Live with myself?

Wasn't this what I had been doing—living with myself—and hating every minute of it?

"Bummer!"

She heard it too. Not just the catch in my voice, but the extent of my distress and my hapless attempt to put a lilt on it.

"*Bümer?*" she said, making light of the word, which was always her way of deflecting tension.

Meanwhile, the two cases of wine arrived. I signed for them and tried to put more authority in my voice. But there was no hiding the whimper, even in front of the deliveryman.

"I was just about to come over . . ." I let the thought trail. There was no point. She had already conceded with the promise of a call. No need to push.

"Where will you be?" she asked.

"Sitting in the dark by my *télyfön*."

We laughed. But I already knew that at no time today would I enter a building where I'd risk losing the phone signal.

•

It was 9:30. At 9:30 on our third day together we were already past Hastings. Now it felt so very far away. Even the scones, the coffee, the obscene gesture that had totally disarmed me felt far away. I wanted Clara today. Clara so as not to be without Clara. Clara to screen me from things that may have nothing to do with Clara but that found in her a stand-in for life's inflections. Her image would be before my eyes all day now. To walk about the city and project her image on every store, every building, everything. Run into people and wish you were with her instead. Meet a friend and want to talk of nothing else. Share the elevator with neighbors and wish to unburden every sorrow if only they asked, *How are you today?*

We'd agreed to call each other by mid-afternoon. I couldn't prevent myself from saying it: Don't make me wait forever.

I won't.

Firmly, but summarily spoken, and with attitude—meaning, *Let it go, hon.* By the very tone in her promise, I inferred not only that she probably wasn't going to call me but that she'd made up her mind precisely because of my way of asking. Whiny and mopey. I might as well have said: If you don't call me, I'll kill myself.

"That'll be good," I said, trying to muster a decisive, chummy-business air myself.

"That'll be very *güd*," she echoed back, instantly poking holes in my bogus firmness.

We hung up.

I immediately wanted to call her back. What would be so terrible about calling someone right back and speaking frankly about the things

eating you—the dashed hopes, the worries stoked, wishes left hanging
and then nipped before you'd even had time to nurse them and coddle
them and get to know them better? Crush and rip, how easily it came to
her. Nip and rip. This would have been my morning with her, our morning. Had we spent the night together, she'd never have pulled that *friend
all the way downtown*. Had I spent the night, we might be sleeping still,
sleeping after *strudel gâteau*, sleeping then *strudel gâteau* again. Eventually,
I'd sneak out to buy muffins and scones and go back to lovemaking on
our bed of crumbs, our bed of cum, breath of my bread on her bed in her
mouth, languid, tender, and raucous her voice, as it was last night after so
many cigarettes, the Clara who'd say I was the best thing that happened
this year, the Clara who seemed about to break terrible news to me but
ended up telling me she spoke my name in the dark—and I believed her,
and still did—the Clara who called me *idiot* in French and meant it, in
German, in Russian, in English.

This was definitely going to be the ugliest day of the year. I had hated
this year—now I had every reason to want to put it behind me, put her
behind me, forget her, forget the party, Straus Park, Leo and strudel and
the ice cackling away on the frozen Hudson to the rhythm of the Bach-
Siloti prelude. Forget. And if I couldn't forget, then learn to hate. Suddenly I wanted to find a way not just to hate but to hurt her. Or rather, not
so much to hurt her as to watch her suffer. She wants to play rough? I'll
show her rough. I'll not answer my phone. I'll go to the movies with someone else. And then head out to the same bar afterward. That's what I'll do.
But I thought we had a date. Fat chance! Just you barging in on people when
you want to and spilling your venom all over their lives, trashing and
sweeping everything they hold for dear life, and in your wake, when you're
over and done with them, nothing but stains and salt on a rug, a glass trin-
ket from a factory workers' den called Edy's, and the taste of your mouth
on their breath, taste of your mouth in my mouth, the bread of your
mouth, the food of your mouth, the crumbs from your mouth that I'd
pick up one by one, just leave them at my door, bloodstained and wine-
stained and heaped with salt and dollops of bile, and I'll watch over them
and bury my seed in them. I wanted you to call me, to want me, to be
patient and kind to me. Not this *friend downtown* malarkey.

But what was I thinking! What if I had offered what she'd offered me
last night and waited for a call that never came this morning? What if
she's doing what I had been doing myself from the very start? What could

possibly have made her beg me not to keep her waiting last night at the bar while I went to the bathroom if I hadn't already signaled that I was Mr. Reluctance Amphifibbing personified?

•

This, I could tell, was not going to be a good day. I'd have to put myself on hold, find a quiet spot somewhere, and, like an animal about to hibernate, stop breathing, hold still, make no plans, just wait for her call.

By eleven, I couldn't stand it. I tidied up the place a bit, if only to start working. But working at home was not what I wanted, so I put everything aside, decided to pay some bills, tried to answer some e-mails. But I couldn't focus on anything. I picked up my wallet and keys, put my coat on, and headed out.

Life without Clara had officially started. Going down in the elevator where I'd heard her laugh so loudly, I repeated to myself: Life without Clara has officially started.

I knew that there was no reason to despair, that we might be back to the movies this very evening, but I also suspected that something had cracked and that I had better start rehearsing the loss now.

It occurred to me that rehearsing loss to dull the loss might bring about the very loss I was hoping to avert.

What crazy ideas you have, Printz.

The thought amused me. Just trying to think the worst-case scenario would most likely bring it on; the anger I felt each time I thought of losing her would, if she suspected it in my voice or on my face, turn her against me.

I walked down Central Park West and then decided to cross over to the East Side and head to the Met. I liked walking on the bridle path, liked the chalk white city on winter mornings that could take a miserable day and white out the sun long before sunset. I even liked the frozen, whey-hued ground that made me focus on my steps as I crunched my way across the park, step by step, like an invalid learning to walk again, her image before me all the time, and the sound of my footsteps going crick, crack, crack, crick, crack, crack, how I had loved that day. We'd enjoy this too if we were together, she forever nipping every moment of effusion by adding a livelier form of effusion herself. She and I just crunching along together, step by step, each trying to be the first to break the icicles along the way.

You'll never forgive me for last night, will you?

I never held last night against you. But maybe you're right.

Don't keep saying that.

I could feel it coming—this whitening of the landscape gradually closing in around me and spreading out like stage fog, wrapping the entire city in the oppressive color of eggshell and blanched almond verging on the dirty gray-white of industrial cataracts humming away in the distance. The oppressive whiteness of the day swimming before my eyes.

I was going to be alone all day. Who knows, tomorrow as well. And the worst was, there was no one I wanted to be with to stave off the loneliness. I could have called people. But I didn't want them. I could go to the movies early today, but movies, especially after the past four nights, would drive the point home even more fiercely now, as though even movies, from being my staunch allies, had gone over to her side now. Why were people so easily available to her? Why did someone forged in the same smithy as I need to gather so many people around her? The answer scared me: because she's not you, not your twin. Simple. Or is it that she can be of your ilk and everyone else's as well? The woman she is with them is totally unknown to you, and what she'll share with them or want from them has names she's never even told you.

No doubt about it. I'll be alone all day and learn to look things squarely in the face. It may not have much to do with her. It had to do with wanting, and waiting, and hoping, and never knowing why or what I wanted. And this creature made of flesh and blood and a will so strong it could bend a steel rod simply by staring it down, was she another metaphor, an alibi, a stand-in for the things that never worked out, for what draws close but never yields? I was drowning, not swimming to Bellagio. I was on the outskirts of things, and being on the outskirts of things was how I lived life, while she . . . well, while she'd simply flipped on me. Yes, that was the cheap, petty, sordid word for it: she'd flipped on me. From extreme this to extreme that. Tit for tat.

And the worst part of it was that there were no explanations.

When I reached the East Side, I watched the traffic lights turn red, one after the other—pip, pip, pip—their blotchy red halos suddenly reaching all the way down into the Sixties, casting a premature evening spell, which seemed to wipe off this entire big mistake of a day to restore a semblance of peace by sundown.

But when I watched the lights suddenly turn green again and the day prove far younger than I'd hoped, I saw that I was hours away from her promised mid-afternoon call, five long grudging hours, with the weight of five long winter afternoons before I'd leave the Met, watching the tourists wander through corridors abutting each to each, leading to an overwhelming question—Are you losing your mind, Printz?

I looked at the green lights dotting Fifth Avenue. They seemed so cheerful, like office receptionists blinking their false eyelashes while uttering tame, perfunctory, upbeat greetings to clients who've lost everything, a poinsettia at one end of their desks and bonsai evergreens at the other, festive and mirthless, like all season's greetings, like today, like Christmas itself, like Christmas parties, with and without Claras or a bowl of punch sitting right in the middle of them. If you didn't bring your own warmth, these lights had none to give. They just glittered like party sparklers across the city, bringing neither joy, nor love, nor light, nor certitude, nor peace, nor help for pain. All these words, words, words coming to haunt me, not rescuing, just waving—why was I losing my mind?

Could I really be losing my mind if I knew I was losing my mind? Tell me, Clara.

Ask the pumice stone.

Tell me why.

It's quantum stuff, dear, for the answer is both yes, you could be, and no, you couldn't, but not the two at the same time.

But if I know that the answer is yes and no, but not the two at the same time, am I still losing my mind?

Hieronimo doesn't know, Hieronimo won't tell.

I knew what I was doing. Cobbling fragments together the way my father, once he began losing his memory under the spell of morphine and more morphine yet, would quote long stretches from Goethe and Racine to show he remembered each in the original. I was reaching out to the poets like a cripple lurching for a cane.

The Met, when I arrived, was mobbed with tourists. Everyone was milling about me like flat, two-dimensional cardboard figurines capable of producing stentorian sounds when speaking French, German, Dutch, Japanese, and Italian, their children especially. People fretted their way about the great hall like souls awaiting transmigration in this great Grand Central of God's kingdom. They're all craving to be New Yorkers this time around, I thought, suddenly struck by the notion that I would give anything to be a native of their own sunless, pallid cities, Monte-video, St. Petersburg, Bellagio, how distant they all seemed this morning. Wipe this life clean and start all over again, less shipwrecked, less want-ing, less damaged.

Are you damaged? Am I not what you like?

Really, lady!

Suddenly, all these aimless, jittery foreign souls threading their way about me seemed to strap on billboards like sandwich men, displaying large playing-card portraits on their fronts and backs, some parading as kings, others as queens, and still others as jacks. The handsome jack of hearts and the queen of spades. The Gorgon and the Joker. You Gorgon, me Joker. There are places on this planet where they stone women like you. Then the man slits his own throat or hurls himself off a bluff.

I had never hated myself so much as I did now. I'd brought this on myself, hadn't I? Me with my quixotic *too soon, too sudden, too fast* shit, and she with her cheap, petty, sordid flips. My shit and her flip. Flip for shit. Tit for tat. Flit for ship. Ship that slipped, that got away. A whole life summed up by bip, bip, bip, and crick, crick, crack.

I was losing my mind, and the more I grew aware of it, the worse it became. I tried letting my thoughts drift to other subjects and settle on anything that might strike a cheerful note—one good thought, my king-dom for one good thought—but everything my mind landed on seemed to start out quietly enough, only to rouse satanic images, three good thoughts morphed into three blind mice. Three queens of diamonds walked by me, twittering away in a strange tongue, followed by a king of spades and two jacks with tiny electric gadgets sulking each to each. King stopped me and, pointing to timid number 2 wife, asked for directions to the bathroom. I must have turned away in shell shock. You're a Shukoff, I said. You rude, mister. Me very sorry, most very, very sorry indeed, I said. How I missed her, how I loved her, how I wanted to laugh with her—all I want is to laugh with you, Clara, hold you, make love to you, laugh with you, and if we do nothing else in life but spend each day sans friends, sans children, sans work, and speak of Vaughan and Handel and *strudel gâteau* and a lifetime of nonsense words studding our love like medals on the tattered uniforms of White Russian generals turned pan-handlers after they've had everything taken away from them by the revolution, it would still be the right life for me. I wonder what she'd say when I told her. I'd have to tell her, had to tell her, for this fat doting husband/father, who'd asked directions to the *vaterklosèt*, was more important to me now than anything in this entire museum, for all I wanted was to take out my cell phone and tell her of my brush with the king of spades and his number 2 wife keeling with pipi trouble.

Suddenly I felt the need to stop and hold on to something and make sure the world around me wasn't reeling. Must leave the museum. I rushed out into the cold and saw the steps of the Met before me spill like the Spanish Steps all the way down onto Fifth Avenue, turning white-gray before me like the cold waters of Venice flooding the embankments and reaching down to the pretzel vendors, whose diminutive trucks seemed bolted to an ever-receding sidewalk. I directed my path down to one of the vendors. Heading toward him gave me a direction. When I finally reached his stand, I saw him spread mustard on one of those large salted pretzels. The sight turned my stomach, and I felt something surge in me, something like nausea, but not nausea, more like seasickness after a forgotten nightmare. The sweat was collecting on my face, despite the cold. I grabbed a pole around which a rider had chained his bicycle. I could hear my heart racing. And what didn't help was the antiphonal whine of a bus bickering with its inability to kneel for an old lady with a cane, as if heart and bus were busy arguing like the piano and violin in the *Kreutzer Sonata*, talking back each to each, tit for tat, pip for pip, shit for flip, all loose ends tied together into a crusty warm pretzel with bilious mustard dolloped on top, the whole pretzel resting on my nose like a pair of binoculars, my eyes are your eyes to my eyes, your tongue and my tongue is one tongue, and your teeth on my lips, your teeth, your teeth, what beautiful God-given teeth you have, you have, you have.

I was—there was no question—losing it, yet obviously faking composure quite well. No one was staring at me, no one even noticed me, so I wasn't about to embarrass myself. I finally understood why people who have heart attacks in public suffer on many counts: for the pain, for the shame, for the pure fear of falling to pieces in full view of every tourist and every messenger and hot-dog vendor. Just don't let me soil myself. If I have to die of a broken heart, let me go gently and vanish at dusk through narrow streets and put an end to this bungled life that started on the wrong foot. Was I dying?

No sooner had the question crossed my mind than I decided to rush myself to Mount Sinai. I hopped into a cab and told the driver to take me to the emergency room. I knew the drill well from taking my father there several times. Simply tell the guard that you're having chest pains and they roll out the red carpet and let you bypass all the stops. Indeed, they immediately put me on a bed. Next to me with his mother was a ten-year-old boy who was bleeding from the leg while a nurse was patiently removing shards of glass with a pair of surgical tweezers, speaking softly, telling him that there were a couple more, and a couple more pieces after that, but that he was such a brave boy, not one tear, not one, she kept saying with her comforting Jamaican lilt as she dabbed the wound ever so softly with a piece of gauze held delicately in between her thumb and her index finger.

The resident intern was wearing Crocs.

I explained that my heart was racing.

I had nausea too.

A strange film was clouding over my eyes. As if fog were closing in. Was closing in. *Were, was*, I couldn't decide which.

"Any disorientation?" he asked.

Big-time, I answered, thinking back to the stairway spilling down from the Met over into the lagoon on the way to the Lido. Ever been to the Lido, Doc?

He ordered a regular cardiogram.

I had expected an echocardiogram, maybe an angiogram. I was dying, wasn't I?

Ten minutes later: "Everything checks out fine. You're a very healthy man."

"I thought I was having a heart attack."

"You were having a panic attack."

I looked at him.

"Maybe you've got too much on your mind?"

"Not especially."

"Family issues?"

I was single.

Love troubles—heartbreak?

I suppose.

"Tell me about it."

I was about to tell him when I realized that *Tell me about it* meant *Say no more, we've all been there.*

If all this was as common as he let on, why hadn't I experienced this before?

Because you've never loved anyone, Printz.

What had I been doing these past eight-and-twenty years, then?

Barely been alive, Printz, barely been to the rose garden. Waiting for me, that's what. You came to life when we stepped onto the balcony on that first night and stood watching the beam together, you and I, Printz, and you watched my suede shoe kick the cigarette butt down to floors measureless to man, you and I leaning together on the parapet like two notes on the same staff, both of one mind, as you stared at my breast in my very crimson blouse.

Where had I been all this time?

Where were you? You were waiting. Except you grew to love the waiting more than the love you waited for.

You see, Doctor, I was just pretending to be like others who find love if they look hard enough for it. But I wasn't like them. I was just pretending. I'm like her. It's love I want, not others.

"Take this," he said, producing a Xanax in his palm like a magician bringing his hand to your ear to retrieve a coin. He watched me swallow it with the help of a tiny plastic cup of water, then tapped the front of my shoulder a few times and let his palm rest there in a sympathetic gesture of fellowship and male solidarity: *We're all in this together, bro.* The last time someone had touched me on the shoulder was less than twelve hours ago. "You'll be all right. Just rest awhile." He grabbed a stool and sat next to me to take my pulse again. Just having someone sit next to me like this was comforting.

He reminded me of Officer Rahoon. Officer Rahoon, whom I'd totally forgotten, but who stood over me now as policemen do when they gather around your stretcher in the ER, filling regulation forms and papers, their walkie-talkies squawking away loudly, as they seek to comfort you while confabulating about this or that hockey player last night with the Filipino head nurse. His apparition now made me think of a me who had stopped being me; Rahoon was the last person to see me before I'd molted that old self on the night after the party. Perhaps I'd gone back to Straus Park that night and sat there the way snakes seek out a hidden, scraggly rock against which to squeeze and rub their old skin off. Perhaps this was why I liked to return there every night, and had wanted to come back there last night as well, because there was a part of me that either didn't want to let go of its old slough or hadn't shed it completely, and coming back felt safer than going forward. Two steps forward, three steps back. Story of my life too, Clara. This was where I would heal, not here in a hospital. Suddenly I was dying to go back and sit in the park. Just sit and find myself, just sit and learn why I kept coming back to Clara's world.

Perhaps I was right not to sleep with her last night: had she pulled any of this after making love to me, I'd have slit my throat with one of her father's kitchen knives, killed myself first, then her.

Or maybe I was no different than she was. She had simply beaten me to it. I remembered that moment when, alone in the bathroom at the bar last night, I'd planned to slip away after making love to her. This is about tonight, I had kept telling myself, but make no promises about tomorrow. We were each other's mirror image. Is this why I wanted her so badly?

"Maybe talking to someone might help," said the intern.

I had never "talked" to someone before, I said.

"I'm surprised," he said.

Why was he surprised? Because I was a visibly self-tormented, insecure, prone-to-self-hatred, depressive type you'd never think of leaving alone before an open window on the eleventh floor?

"No, it's just that everyone has a setback at one point or another."

And my point was now, right? A setback. Was this the polite way of naming what had happened to me? A setback. I see eternity one day, and the next we're talking setbacks?

All I could think of asking was how long they were planning on keeping me there.

Till my heartbeat was back to normal.

Here was a prescription for more of these. And: No caffeine. No drinking. Lay off cigarettes too.

Six days with the world's most beautiful woman and I was a wreck headed for the loony bin.

Suddenly I heard my phone ring.

"It's the *télyfön*," I said.

"I'm going to need to ask you not to use your cell here."

I could just imagine Clara responding to such contemptible blandspeak: Are you needing to ask me now, or are you going to need to ask me in some fabricated moment in an undefined, politely ambiguous future?

"I have to take this call," I told the doctor. "It's from"—and I whispered the word—"*the heartbreak*."

"Well, make it very brief, and don't get all wired up again."

"I *am* all wired up," I said, pointing to the wires of the cardiogram still suctioned to my body.

"I'm free," she said. As always she cut to the chase, then greeted you. I looked about me and couldn't help snickering: But I'm not.

Oh?

I'm actually tied up. Then, realizing the joke had gone far enough— "I've got wires stuck in every part of my body."

"What are you talking about?"

She was yelling, and I was hoping that junior-internist here might get a sense of the madwoman I'd been up against these past few days.

"I'm in a hospital."

A grapeshot of questions. She was coming over.

No need to. I can take care of myself. They're letting me go.

Where was she?

On *Printz* Street—added emphasis—about to hail a cab headed uptown. Was using my nickname a good sign, or was she just making nice to cover up being downtown still?

I put a finger on the mouthpiece of my cell phone. "How long before I can walk?" I asked.

The young resident made an almost disappointed smirk. Time to remove these wires, put my clothes on, fill out the paperwork.

"Can you meet me downstairs in my building?"

"I can do that."

I can do that. What on earth did *I can do that* mean? Did she have to speak Amphibabble too? Didn't everyone?

Was she coming because she was eager to, wanted to, or was hers a lukewarm acquiescence bordering on indifference?

Finally, there it was: *Don't keep me waiting long.*

•

"What were you doing in the hospital?" she asked.

She was sitting on a sofa in the lobby of my building. She had

removed her shawl and her coat, so she had to have been waiting for a
while. When she stood up, she looked absolutely stunning. Slender, dark
colors everywhere, her hazel-eyed beauty simply forbidding. Diamond
stud sitting on her sternum. Last time I'd seen it was ages ago. All of it
reminded me that whatever bridges we'd crossed last night had been
completely blown up this morning. The *corvus* had tumbled off the ship.

"I'm just staying for a few minutes. I wanted to make sure you're okay."

Did she want to come upstairs?

"Yes, but only for a few minutes."

I felt weak and sapped. I had no stomach for emotional haggling and
tussling. I was just relieved to see her in the very same place where we'd
picnicked twenty-four hours before. But she was chilly, wasn't sitting.
The meter was obviously running.

"So, are you going to tell me what happened?" she asked once we
were in the elevator.

From the way she framed the question, I could tell she'd already
guessed the answer. There was no point hiding the truth.

"Call it recurrent shell shock from my years in the trenches."

"In the what?"

"In the bog, in the quag, the trenches."

She nodded. But she seemed to have forgotten. Or perhaps she
hadn't. "It was a *panique* attack," I finally said, hoping she'd pick up the
rhyme with *garlique*. She shook her head.

She took her time getting out of the elevator, and once again was
brusquely shoved out by the door. "This is not the time." She turned to
the elevator, then kicked it in the equivalent of its shin. "Fucking heart.
Fucking, fucking heart."

We burst out laughing.

I opened the door. Thank God I had tidied up the place this morning.
Someone next door was cooking what appeared to be a late-afternoon
soup. How I wished we'd had breakfast together this morning.

I turned on the lights. The day had aged so fast.

She dropped her coat on one of the chairs, yet another sign that she
wasn't staying long. "I'll make tea."

Had they given me something?

Yes, they'd given me something.

"I disappear a few hours and you end up in the ER. Nice."

I looked at her. I didn't have to say anything.

"You're blaming me, aren't you?"

"No, not blaming. But the tone this morning was so different from last night's, it sent me into a tailspin."

"So you *are* blaming me."

"It's not a question of blaming. It's more like I don't recognize me, and I don't recognize you."

"That's right."

"*That's right* what?"

"We change. We change our minds."

"That fast?"

"Maybe."

"What happened to yesterday?"

"You're one to ask." She paused for a second. "Besides, I can't be tied to yesterday."

She walked over to where she must have stowed away the chocolate cookies, found the box exactly where she'd left it yesterday, and freely took two out. It thrilled me that she was behaving as if she were at home. At other times, though, I'd seen her take out a dish and stack four to six of these cookies, arranged, as I suddenly remembered from our very first night, in a Noah's ark formation.

Neither of us had made a gesture to boil water. She'd obviously given up on tea and had headed directly for the cookies. *Bad sex tea. Very, very bad sex tea*, I remembered.

"Look, I don't want us to fight."

Obviously I must have raised my voice when asking about *yesterday*.

"What makes you think I want to?"

"Well, you're obviously upset."

"Any idea why I might be?"

"Why don't you tell me, since you're about to anyway."

From the tone of her voice I could tell she'd been through this exact conversation endless times before. She dreaded its coming and could probably spot all of its signposts, its shortcuts, cross streets, tangents, and escape routes long before I could.

"I'm sure you already know what I have to say."

"I think I do. But go ahead," she added, with an implied *If it makes you feel any better*.

"Maybe there's no point."

"Maybe not"—meaning, *Suit yourself.*

"Let's just say I'm sorry you changed so fast."

She stared at her cookie like a child being chastised, or like someone trying to gain time, collect her thoughts, and come up with the right answer. Or just sitting out a cloud. How I wished that she'd tell me I was completely off the mark, that she hadn't changed at all since last night, that I should stop putting words in her mouth and making her say things she hadn't meant to say at all.

"Maybe that's my hell."

"What's your hell?"

"Always letting people down."

"Do you blame them?"

"No. I can't say I do. I set them up for it, then I let them down."

She made it sound that setting people up for disappointment was far worse than the disappointment that rushed them to the hospital.

I stared at her. "Just tell me one thing."

"What?"

Her *What* had come too quickly, as if it were concealing a timorous *What now* behind a seemingly confident, open-faced *Ask-anything-you-don't-scare-me-of-course-I'll-answer.*

"Was it because we didn't make love last night?"

"That would make me cruel and spiteful. It had nothing to do with last night."

"Then it's worse than I thought."

"Maybe we just got carried away. Or maybe we ended up wanting the same thing—but for entirely different reasons."

"Your reason was not my reason."

"I don't think it was." Then, to soften her words but to show that softening them was not going to change her mind: "Maybe it wasn't."

"And you'd warned me against that."

"I did."

"And I listened."

"You did."

"Until you told me that I shouldn't have."

"Until I told you that you shouldn't have."

"We're a mess, aren't we?"

"A big mess."

I was standing in front of her, and suddenly put both hands on her face, rubbing this face with its lips and hazel eyes that meant more to me than sunlight, speech, and anything inside or outside this room. I kissed her, knowing, with a certainty I had never encountered before, that she would kiss me as passionately and as desperately as I longed to kiss her, and that she would do this because the escape hatches between us were wide open and tomorrow was no longer in our vocabulary. It would be aimless, desultory lovemaking, safe and shiftless—with, once again, my usual blend of goodwill and tact, not the stuff of last night.

She kissed my neck as she had last night. I loved the way her hips moved with mine, the way we held each other tight, not letting the air creep between us. We were, it took a second to notice, almost dancing. Or was it lovemaking and I didn't know it?

I unbuttoned her shirt and let my hand travel under it. For the first time ever, my hand touched the breast I'd been dreaming of for days. She didn't resist at all, but she wasn't participating. I let her be. Moments, just moments later, she was already buttoning her shirt.

"Please don't," I asked. I want to see you naked, want to think of you when you're gone, want never, ever to forget that you stood naked in this room by the failing light of the day rubbing yourself against me, with your breath that smells of bread and of old Vienna and of the bakery by your house where last night you and I, just you and I—

"I really have to go."

I'd known this from the very start. She had looked dressed up downstairs. Not just dressed up for the long lunch she seemed happy to have cut short when she called me at the hospital, but dressed for something that was due to occur yet and about which she hadn't said a word.

And then I saw it. She had kissed me no less savagely than she'd kissed Inky or Beryl at the party. She probably didn't know how to kiss otherwise—which was why so many got hooked and tangled. They took for large bills what for her was loose change. She probably made love no differently. What was a mere gesture—consent, as she called it—for others was the full monty, the once-in-a-lifetime you get to tell your grandchildren about when they're old enough to ask about the woman who called you by the name of a ship.

I wondered if there was or might soon be a third party who was going to be given minute-by-minute dispatches of this fellow called Printz, who came after another called Inky was spurned, kissed, sent packing. Pretty soon I'd be leaving messages on her answering machine, or calling her at the movies, while she'd ask whomever it was she was with to look at the caller ID and mutter a muffled curse on being told my full name. *It's Printz,* she'd say.

I wanted to be cruel to her. Say something that would scar her for years, or at the very least stick on her like a stain or a bruise that was sure to ruin her whole evening.

Clara, I feel this is the last time I'm going to see you.

Clara, the moment you walk out my door it will be as though we'd never met.

Clara, I don't want this to tailspin—I want to save it—help me save it before my ego or yours gets the better of it.

Clara, do you read me?

"Don't go now," I said.

"You don't want me to go?"

"I don't want you to go."

"You don't get it, do you?" Was she about to tell me? "Listen, last night was last night. As you said: Too soon, too sudden, too fast. It ends there."

"I don't want it to end. This is not just about last night. It's what we both know is bigger than either of us—it's about our life, I don't know how else to say it. You are my life."

"You are my life," she repeated—clearly not the sort of thing one said in Clara's world. It went with not singing in the shower, not rhapsodizing over sunsets, what else?

I hated her.

"Do you enjoy making me sound stupid? Maybe I am stupid."

"Maybe I am stupid," she mimicked. "Two home runs in a row, Printz. Now it's my turn—and I don't know if you're going to like it."

"With or without tea," I interrupted, reaching for humor, however lamely.

"Teatime is long past. Here is what I have to say, and live with it as you please."

"Shoot." A touch of fading irony in my voice, but I was buckling up for the worst.

"The truth is this. And I'm not the only one who says it. The soothsayer woman said it too. I care for you. Call it what you will—love, if it pleases you. You, however, just want to get me out of your system, and if mistaking this for love helps you, you'll call it love. I want you in my system, not out. I know what I want from you and I know what I have to give for it. You haven't got the foggiest idea what you want and certainly not what you're ready to offer. You haven't thought that far, because your mind isn't really interested—your ego, yes, and your body, maybe, but the rest of you, not a clue. All you've been giving me so far is the hurt, sorry puppy face and the same unasked question in your gaze each time there's a pause between us. You think it's love. It's not. What I have is real and it's not going away. That's what I have to say. Now can I go?"

She had so persuaded me that I started to believe her. She loved me, I did not love her. She knew what she wanted, I had no idea. Made perfect sense.

"Just stay, will you? Don't go yet."

"No, I can't. I promised I'd meet someone."

"Someone? Is this a friend of the friend who lives *all the way downtown*?" I was trying to show I was mimicking her.

"No, this is another friend."

"Do you *care for him* too?"

She gave me a withering glance. "You want war, don't you?"

"That's not what I want at all."

"What do you want, then?"

She was right. I had no idea. But there was something I definitely did want and it had to do with her, or it was through her that I would find it. Or it was her I wanted and all my doubts were just my last-ditch way of avoiding seeing this simple truth. That I wanted her. That I was destined to lose her. That I had shot my wad and didn't have a single card left to play.

"I want you to give me another chance."

"People don't change, you certainly won't. Besides, what does *another chance* mean? Is this something you picked up at the movies?"

"You're always tweaking and putting me down."

"That's because you've been giving me palaver. When you're good and ready, I want this," she said, suddenly putting her right hand on my crotch and grabbing everything I had there in her palm, not letting go, all the while doing something that felt like a squeeze. "I want you—not the puppy face, not the snide antics, nor your evasive asides. I want you in the moment, here and now. For this, I already told you, I'll go the distance and do anything you want, anything, anything. When we're good and ready." She stopped squeezing me without letting go yet. "But don't ruin it. You ruin it with your silly games and your cold feet and your other nonsense, and you'll never live this down—this much I can promise you." With that, she put her hand inside my trousers and reached for my cock. "You want my breasts? I want this."

"Now can I go?" she asked, as if I were holding her back with my cock.

I nodded.

"Are we going to the movies this evening?"

I hated my voice.

"Yes, we are." Why? I asked, not knowing why I'd asked her why.

"I thought I just told you why."

"And what are you doing now?" I couldn't help myself.

"Now I'm going to meet someone who's been kinder to me than I deserve."

·

I had already purchased our tickets and was waiting outside the movie theater, drinking my large cup of coffee to keep warm. I was doing penance, and she was late. Something had already warned me she'd be late. I was trying not to let it bother me. I knew that five more minutes of this would make me more anxious, that anxiety might upset me, that I'd try hiding being upset, but that it would all leak in so many oblique and treacherous ways that were sure to draw her fire and finally erupt in all-out war. I tried keeping my anxiety in check. Please don't stand me up, Clara, just don't stand me up. But I also knew that it wasn't the fear of being stood up that had caused the surge in anxiety. It was the image of her doing to this other friend what she'd done to me, her hand squeezing and caressing his cock, making the same speech. No, not the same speech. She'd make love to him, totally and completely, then hop in a cab headed uptown and show up at the movie theater, all wired and frisky, *didn't want to miss the credits, have been thinking of you all afternoon, not upset, are you?* Who knew what she'd been doing on the afternoon of our first movie.

But if I was sincerely worried about her *someone*, it was also to avoid thinking how she'd touched me, or at least not use up the thrill of that moment by thinking too much on it. I wanted to dip into it, take furtive nips, and then run to safety, like a bird nibbling tiny tidbits. I was a leave-some-for-later type, she the here-and-now, guzzle-all-you-can-in-the-moment. No woman had ever put her hand there without first knowing that she could. Even my caresses last night, for all their boldness when we leaned against the wall of the bakery at three in the morning, had none of her nerve. I wondered if hers was a merely symbolic groping for a man's balls, which explains why she rubbed my crotch somewhat before letting go of it, as if to make light of the package, or whether she had pressed me with the heel of her palm to tease me, to feel me, to turn me on, to show what she was capable of?

In between the worrying and the fading memory of how her hand had held me hovered hazy reminders of what had happened earlier outside the Met, things I didn't want to think about, and could still manage to banish, but that were still there, like an enemy waiting for the gates to open, but equally capable of breaking them down or of digging under them if he wished. This morning I'd almost buckled on the ground—the tourists, the stands, the children, the crowd milling everywhere, the sandwich men dressed as playing-card kings and queens, everyone sucking the air till I seemed to be floating on helium. I'd never forget this day. It had started bursting with desire, my hands off Signor Guido, and look at me now, sipping coffee, which I wasn't even supposed to drink, humbled, crushed, vulnerable, prone to new setbacks as soon as the Xanax wore off. I did blame her.

Why had I allowed this to happen? Because I had hoped, because I had trusted? Because I'd failed to find something to hate in her? Because everything, just everything was beautiful and promised to take me to that one place where I felt I belonged but had never seen, and that my life would be one big nothing without it?

"You didn't think I'd come," she said, after stepping out of a taxi in front of the theater.

"Well, maybe you wavered a bit. Did you want me to worry?"

"Stop."

She took the second coffee from my hand, no doubt in her mind that it was hers.

I also produced a roll of Mentos, which made her ecstatic. Or perhaps she was making up for not thanking me for the coffee by throwing profuse thanks for the candy.

"Want one?" she asked, tearing open the package. The first one was red. She always loved the red, hated the yellow. "I want the red," I said. But she had already put it in her mouth with a teasing you're-not-getting-this-one-unless-you-come-and-get-it-if-you-dare smile. I would have kissed her in the mouth, found the candy, stolen it with my tongue, and, after playing with it awhile, given it back to her. Suddenly, with our imagined kiss racing through me and the thought of her fingers passionately combing my hair, something arrested me: they may not have made love this afternoon, but they got very close, almost too close.

Meanwhile, not a word about where she'd been or what she'd done. Her silence on the matter confirmed my worst doubts. I stewed in them all through both of Rohmer's films, poisoning both films.

By the time we were out at midnight, it was impossible not to sulk. "What's eating you?" she asked. My "Nothing" was not even trying to be dramatic or visibly cryptic; it was a glum "Nothing," and I didn't care to hide it.

"You didn't like the films?"

"I liked them."

"You don't feel well?"

"I'm fine."

"It's me."

What lay ahead was a field of nettles that I wasn't eager to cross barefoot.

"Did I say something wrong?" she asked. "Let's have it. Let's just put it out there."

It took me a few moments to find the courage.

"I just wish you hadn't left this afternoon. I felt terrible."

"I had to see someone."

I tried to put on a placid, indifferent face, but I couldn't resist.

"Do I get to ask who?"

"Whom? Sure, ask away."

"Who, then?"

"You don't know him, but he's a very dear friend. We talked about you. About us."

I was trying to find my bearings, but didn't know how.

"Everything confuses me. I've never been this confused. Nor have I ever told anyone I was so confused. Ever."

This was the most honest thing about me that I'd ever managed to say to her. This way of speaking was new to me, and I wasn't sure I liked it.

How was I going to let down my guard with her tonight and ever attempt to recapture last night's kisses with this plague standing between us?

·

When we arrived at the bar, things couldn't be worse. A man wearing a dark blue suit, a white shirt, though without a necktie, was sitting at the table next to what had become ours, and no sooner had he seen Clara than he stood up and embraced her. No introductions, of course, until he turned to me and introduced himself. On his table were what looked like loose galleys of a book of black-and-white photographs.

He was nursing an oversized martini with a bunch of olives skewered on a long toothpick that he hadn't touched. There followed an awkward moment, during which Clara and I were trying to decide our seating arrangement. It only made sense that she should sit next to him on the banquette, which spanned from his table to ours, but this precluded my sitting next to her, as had become our habit. She would be in between us, but the men would be sitting too far apart. So I did the obvious: I sat across from her, facing the two of them. She hesitated for a moment, which I took as a positive sign, but then she opted to sit so close to him that we found ourselves occupying his table. I was furious with her for not insisting that I sit next to her. Yet Clara's hesitation had pleased me, as had the waitress's histrionic enthusiasm: *Here they are!* The man, whose name was Victor, didn't seem to pick up on Clara's momentary hesitation or on the waitress's clamorous greeting.

I wondered what he knew about Clara and me. Were we just friends? More than friends? What were we anyway? And what were they? He explained he had decided to come here for a drink after spending the evening with his assistant. He wanted to go through the pictures one last time before turning them in in the morning. Somehow he wasn't pleased. He'd just come back from two shows, one in Berlin—grand, just grand!—the other in Paris—*sensationnel!*—and London and Tokyo in three weeks—could you ask for more? What was the subject? I asked, trying to make conversation. *Manhattan Noir*, which, given his French accent, he pronounced *Manattàn Noir*. Clara threw me a quick squint. There was mirth and collusion in it. We knew we were putting this on hold for parody and demolition later on.

Victor, dapper blue suit and starched white shirt, French cuffs, couldn't be happier with the project. Next year's Christmas coffee-table sensation, he explained, trying to make light of the project. But he was clearly pleased with himself. Even the gleaming white shirt and wide-open *sans cravate louque* was going to be the subject of ridicule once we were alone together, to say nothing of his name in bold letters on the cover: Victor François Chiller. The initials made me want to laugh.

Talk of *Manhattan Noir* kept us animated and laughing way past midnight. Everyone had a theory about *Manhattan Noir*. We took turns: The *noir* city in each of us, even if we'd never seen a film noir before. The *noir* city we love to catch glimpses of, because it takes us back to another Manhattan that may never have existed, but exists by virtue of films and their afterimage. The *noir* city we sometimes long to live in. The *noir* city that disappears the moment you go out to find it. The *noir* city that is more in us than it is out there in the real city, I threw in. "Well, let's not get carried away," he said.

She corrected his pronunciation. Not *Manattàn* but *Manhattan*. Not *aunting hower of ze nait* but *haunting hour of the night*. He thought the joke and his English pronunciation very funny and, with confident hilarity, placed an arm around Clara's shoulder, pulling her toward him each time he laughed out loud, which forced her to rest her head on his shoulder. Perhaps, sensing his arm around her, she had automatically leaned toward him as a way of being pardoned for joking at his expense. Or was it: press the touch button and she's instantly yours?

His arm stayed there awhile. He caught me staring at it. I looked away and turned my eyes to her, only to sense that she too had caught me staring and, like him, had instinctively looked the other way. Neither of them moved; she didn't lift her head away from his shoulder, and he didn't remove his arm. It was as though both were independently frozen in that position, either because it was too late to undo the gesture or because they wanted to show there was nothing awkward or improper in it and that—come to think of it—they could do as they pleased, seeing they had absolutely nothing to hide or be ashamed of, and would stop if and when they were good and ready.

Were they, was she doing this to spite me—was she egging him on? Or was she too weak to stop him, or was this her message to me? You have no rights, no claims, and if I want to lean on his shoulder or touch his hand or feel his balls, well, I'll do so in your face—live with it.

Was theirs perhaps the threadbare familiarity that lingers among ex-lovers?

Or was it a murky friendship between man and woman, the way ours was no better than a murky friendship between man and woman?

Was I perhaps misconstruing everything? Or had I not even scratched the surface? My doubts, like proofs of the Pythagorean theorem, suddenly outnumbered the stars.

Or, with the Xanax wearing off, was it this morning's anxiety speaking again, making me spin these thoughts, all the while urging me to keep a straight face before them—in case I was making it all up?

Which was worse: making it all up and not enjoying anything, or watching them together and not knowing anything?

Tossing and turning. Not tossing, but turning . . .

Clara, I've disappointed you, haven't I?

Oh, Hieronimo, Hieronimo, what have they done to your mind? Your thoughts are all scrambled, and the sedge is withered by the lake. I could feel it coming on again.

I excused myself to go to the bathroom. I knew the bathroom would break my heart. I splashed some water on my face. I liked the cold water in the stinky bathroom. Dabbed my face again. Wet my nape, wet my wrists, the area behind the ears. I remembered the pressure of the steel nut against my head and how it had dented the skin on my forehead. Poor, poor scalawag. And my trying to cool things down a bit, thrilled to the marrow of my boner, me with my how-do-I-leave-graciously-after-we-go-at-it-tonight? Last night she'd lowered the collar of my turtleneck and kissed me there. Hands groping everywhere, all the while I'm reining in Sir Lochinvar, charger and steed, till we kissed by the blessed bakery of blessed memory. Happy, happy, happy hour. Tonight, her heart's with another man. Turncoat. Clever trick, that, hesitating before taking a seat next to his. Ah, you think that would fool Printz Oskàr? Why wasn't this last night, why couldn't it be last night, turn back the clock, undo the bad dream, unmake every mistake, put time on splints, work things back to the point where I'd taken the wrong turn and found myself standing in the snow in Straus Park after we'd kissed and heard her say, "We met here this morning, here we are again." Ach, Sir Tristram, you bald-pated simpering sop, I thought you were all glittering with the noblest of carriage, but you're only a Guido. I thought you great in all things, you're but a puny. Bear down, old fool, and sink hereunder.

When I came out, she didn't see me approach. They were talking.

This was a party and I wasn't invited.

They were about to order a second round. I decided not to. She was surprised. Didn't I want fries with ketchup?

Was this her way of asking me not to go yet?

The question spoke so many good things.

It's been a rather long day, I said. And I think I may be coming down with something. Bad, bad day.

He didn't ask why. His reticence and the haste with which he wanted to return to what they were discussing told me she might have told him about my incident at Mount Sinai and he didn't even want to pretend he wasn't aware of it.

Nice work, Clara.

"Plus I really shouldn't drink," I added, remembering the young doctor's recommendation.

"Stay a bit. You don't have to drink." It sounded very off-the-cuff, almost like a polite afterthought, but I knew that, with Clara, casual did not mean perfunctory. She was speaking in code. The informality was aimed at him, not me. She might have been pleading with me to stay, I, instead, chose to take her nonchalant tone to the letter. I was operating in bad faith, until I realized that the casual accent of her request might have been intended for me as well: she wanted me to stay, because it would look better if I did, but it made no difference—one way or another.

What I wanted all along became instantly clear to me as soon as I stood up to leave. I had expected her to change her mind and not order anything once she saw me stand and put my coat on. She'd leave with me, and I'd walk her home, as was our habit. The bakery. Straus Park. This time I'd ask to come upstairs even if she didn't.

"I hope you feel better," she said. She was pretending this was all about not feeling well and about catching up on sleep. I looked at her to mean, So you're really not coming? "I think I'll stay awhile and have another drink," she said.

I shook his hand, and Clara and I kissed goodbye on both cheeks.

I'm never having anything to do with her again. Never seeing her again. Never, never, never.

This had been one of the worst days of my life. The worst, actually. It would take a few days, maybe another week, then I'd put the whole thing behind me. Or was I underestimating the damage? Give it a year, until next Christmas Eve—the soul holds its own anniversaries and all that . . .

Instead of walking downtown, I walked up to Straus Park. No more, no more, no more, I thought. This is the last time I'm coming here. I remembered the candlelit statue filled with votive tapers standing upright, and the crystallized twigs, and the bleeding for love, and the walk to and from the cathedral as she drifted away from her friends and brought me to this quiet spot and, just as we were getting very, very close, said she wanted a strong, ice-burning shot of vodka. She'll pass by, and each time she'll think of me, and be with me, and one day, with her husband, when they stare out of her living-room window at the snow falling over the Hudson, she'll break down and say, Sad is his voice that calls me, and she'll turn old and wizened and nodding toward life's close and be filled with gall and remembrance, telling the first beggar she'll find in Straus Park, He loved me once in the days when I was fair.

This cruel and spectral city. *Manattàn Noir*. All of it was *noir*. The snow was just a screen, a lie—for it too was *noir*. Snow hurts because it deceives you. With gleaming asphalt you know you're dealing with dark, hard stuff and beaten-down slate underneath and shards of glinting glass mixed in. Snow is like pith and like molten tar, except it's soft on the outside, like velvet and bread, and the good things that yield as soon as you just touch them. But underneath, it's black, blunt, and bituminous, and that's how everything felt tonight. Black, blunt, and bituminous.

I stood around a moment, hoping she'd have second thoughts and come after me. But no one was coming this way. The area around Straus Park was deserted. Everyone was gone. The stranded Magi with their heads ablaze were gone, Phildonka Madamdasit was gone too, Rahoon and the beggar woman had probably come and gone. Just our shadows now, or just mine. Leopardi, the poet, was right. Life is bitterness and boredom, and the world is filth.

SEVENTH NIGHT

I hoped she'd ask one day, when none of this mattered, *Why did you leave
that night?* Because I was angry. Because I grew to hate myself. Because I
didn't know what to do. I didn't want to sit quietly and go on struggling
with him, with you. I was losing you, and sitting in a bar watching the
loss unfold before me unleashed more bitterness yet, because you seemed
determined to speed up its course. I felt ridiculous, weak, ineffectual. I
hated you, and I hated you for making me hate myself. I was pissed.
Pissed that you never once let me catch my breath on those nights when
all I did, it seemed, was watch the torrent of missed opportunities race
past us. I blamed you for inhibiting impulses that had nothing wrong
with them, then for holding these very same inhibitions against me. I
blamed myself for thinking it was your fault. It was mine, always mine.

All I saw that night was the lightness with which you turned a new
leaf and were letting yourself off ever so easily—*see, one hand, one hand*—
while fate in the form of a jack-in-the-box waved a broomstick over my
head. *Yes, we could have gone somewhere with this, but see, we all change.*
You made me find solace in self-pity. I could never forgive this.

I'd thought of waiting for you inside the park. I was even tempted to
send you a text message and say something either funny or obscene about
Monsieur VFC, or so cruel that it would burn all bridges between us if I
hadn't already burned them at the bar. But you'd pick up your phone
and, on the pretext of not wearing glasses, hand it to VFC, ask him who
the caller was, then grab it from his hand and shove it back into your
coat pocket. *Printz!*

I stood in a pool of white light trying to feel enchanted and cleansed
as I'd felt on my first night here. But it didn't work. I recited more verses
by Leopardi to myself, squeezing out some comfort, knowing that if no

solace came, then beauty might come in its place, and that beauty on this most sullen *noir* night in December would be good enough. But nothing came. Then I saw a yellow cab. I hailed it, got in, and was welcomed by the comforting warmth of old upholstery, and the vague acrid smell of curry and cumin. I was in a *noir*, black-and-white world, and I wasn't being let out of it.

No sooner in the cab, though, than I asked the driver to take me to Riverside and 112th Street. He'd have to go all the way down to 104th Street, he said, then turn around and head uptown. Did I mind? No, I didn't mind. All I wanted was to return to the spot where I'd stepped off the bus and gotten lost on the night of the snowstorm. The blizzard had lasted all through the party and hadn't quite cleared when she walked outside with me hours later. Now I was going back to where things seemed safe no matter how clueless my steps that night. Just me and two silly bottles walking up the stairs by the statue of Samuel J. Tilden.

As the cab passed by her building, I looked up at her window to see if she might be home already. But the car came too close, and it was impossible to look up.

I got off right at the spot where I'd seen the St. Bernard. Or had I imagined the dog while thinking of medieval Weihnachten towns that turn dark and gray and then empty faster than the last grocer can pull down his roller shutters in the winters of pandangst? Who walks alone in the dead of night in Saint-Rémy but madmen and seers and those longing for *otherpeoples*?

Longing for others. What a concept!

I walked east on 112th Street, aiming for Broadway, but enjoying the suspense, because I knew where I was headed but didn't quite want to admit it yet. This, by the way, is what I'd do in two days if I decided to go to Hans's New Year's party: walk up toward the cathedral, turn right on Broadway, walk down another six blocks, and finally turn right on 106th. Is this what I was planning to do tonight as well? Or was all this a roundabout ploy to pass by her building or, better yet, run into her as she's heading home on her way back from the bar?

What are you doing?

I was taking a walk in the snow. Or just venting.

Venting?

As in learning to live with myself, now that you're no longer in my life.

No longer in your life?

From the look of things—

From the look of things you're the one who walked out, not me.

Yes, but from the look of things . . .

From the look of things you should take a hike. If I were to run into her on her way home, I'd more than likely run into the two of them together. Even if he wasn't going upstairs with her, he'd still have to walk her home. Would she give him her arm when they walked together and burrow under his armpit?

When, as I knew would happen, I approached 106th Street, I began to walk slowly. I didn't want them to see me. But I didn't want to see them either. Had they had enough time to order another round before leaving the bar? Then I realized why I was hiding—because I *was* hiding, wasn't I?—I was ashamed of skulking like this, of hanging around her house, of spying, on them, on her. Stalker. *Stalk-er!*

If I had to bump into her at this late hour, all I'd want is for her to be alone.

What's wrong?

Couldn't sleep. Didn't want to be alone. That's what's wrong.

What do you want from me? Spoken with impatience, pity, and exhaustion.

I don't know what I want. I want you. I want you to want me as desperately as I want you.

Why had I let her walk away from me this afternoon? What was I thinking? A woman walks into your house, is clearly telling you she cares, grabs you by the gonads, and you just stand there, jittery Finnegan running for cover while panic-stricken Shem and Shaun race fast behind, clamoring up the Pelvic Highway.

But if she wasn't alone and if I had to bump into the two of them, I'd utter a mirthful "Couldn't sleep" and shrug my shoulders, adding, "I was on my way to the bar, hoping you hadn't left." I could just picture the two of them standing together on the sidewalk in front of me, disbelieving glances thrown back and forth, all three of us looking so uneasy. Good night, Clara. Good night, *Manattàn*. And I'd scurry home, knowing that the first thing I'd want to do was call her and say, *Manattàn noir, c'est moi.*

On the corner of 106th Street and Broadway I decided to walk one block south, turn on 105th, and come back to 106th by way of Riverside.

I wanted—or so I told myself—to take a last, farewell look at her building, especially if I wasn't going to the party in two days. Could be years the next time I come around here, years and years.

But I knew this was just a ruse to take another peek.

The road down 105th couldn't have been quieter along the row of white town houses that seemed to slumber in an otherworldly, snowbound era of fireplaces and gas jets and hidden stables. No one had shoveled the snow, and it looked as pristine and wholesome as Rockwell's towns on snowbound nights.

By contrast, her large building, when it came into view on the corner of 106th Street, bore a minatory scowl on its forefront, as though its Gothic windows and friezes knew of my whereabouts in the snow and, like two distrustful Dobermans, were lying still, almost feigning sleep, vigilant and set to pounce as soon as I took another step. Then I spotted Boris's light and his side entrance door. I could never tell where exactly he sat, but no sooner would we near the door every evening than he'd always be there to let her in. If I wasn't careful, he'd spot me. I looked up and to my complete surprise noticed that the lights in her living room were all on. How shameful, I thought, spying.

So she must have gotten home while I was walking slowly down Broadway. This either meant that they had had a hasty round of drinks or had decided against it and simply left the bar soon after me. Or she may never have turned off her lights before leaving this morning. Was she the type to leave her lights on all day? I didn't think so. Chances were, she'd just gotten home and had turned on the lights in the living room. Maybe watching TV. Unless, of course, she was not alone.

I crossed the street at 106th and Riverside and headed north, trying to catch a glimpse of the other rooms immediately upstairs. These were lit up as well, though I couldn't tell if their light was being referred from the living room. I was not even sure that one of the side windows belonged to her apartment. She had forgotten to show me around after offering to. I had probably tried not to sound too curious, or too eager, and had finally come out sounding indifferent, which perhaps was why she didn't insist. I remembered wanting to see her bed but not wanting to show I did. Did she make her bed every day or did she leave it undone?

On the corner of 107th I had to make a decision: either walk back down Riverside or walk over to Broadway, and then loop around 105th once again. In the snow, it might take me ten minutes.

There was something so peaceful about walking. It would allow me to think about things, speak to her in my mind, find reasons to see how all this might work itself out one day, even if I knew that such walks seldom bring answers, that no one resolves anything, much less sees through the fog we burrow in, that all walking does is keep our legs and eyes busy the better to keep our mind from thinking anything. The most I'd be capable of right now would be to think about thinking, which meant sinking deeper into myself, which meant blunting everything else, including my thoughts, which meant spinning something everyone else would call daydreams. Perhaps all this wasn't necessarily headed downhill—even thinking in this quiet, aimless manner was itself, like amnesia and apha-sia, a form of healing when the body comes to the mind's rescue and ever so gently numbs it, wiping bad thoughts one by one as I'd seen the nurse do with the child who was bleeding from the leg, blotting his cuts with soft, delicate, occasional light dabs with a folded piece of gauze, while with deft tweezers she picked out shard after tiny shard of shattered glass, dropping each one in a plastic trough, trying not to make a sound so as not to scare the boy. All my mind wanted now was to fantasize, because images were like feathers on a bruise, while thoughts flowed like iodine on open sores. She and I together when we'd make up. She and I together on New Year's Day with those friends she said she wanted me to meet. On the last evening of the Rohmer festival, she and I together.

Now I was just walking. Walking to bid farewell. Walking to spy on her. Walking to be one with all the stonework that had watched her grow and knew all about her comings and goings as a child, as a student, as Clara. Walking to drag out my presence in Clara's world and not to go back home and be alone with my thoughts that aren't even thoughts any longer but leering gargoyles sprung from a monstrous netherworld I never knew existed in me until I'd seen them milling about me dressed as sand-wich men. Walking, let's face it, in the hope I'd find a portal back into her life. Walking as prayer, pleading, and penance. Walking to refuse the end of love, to refuse the obvious by picking at it, step by step, shard after shard, taking in the truth of it in tiny doses, as one takes poison so as not to die from it.

In years to come, when I'll pass by her building again, I'll stop and look upstairs. I don't know why I'll look upstairs or what I'll be looking for each time. But I know I'll look upstairs, because this purposeless looking upstairs in this kind of dazed and balmy mood I'm in right now is itself remembrance and soul gathering, an instance of grace. I'll stand there awhile and remember so many things: the night of the party, the night I thought I'd done the right thing by saying goodbye without lingering too long outside her lobby, the night I first felt my nights were numbered here. The night I knew, just knew, she'd change her mind the moment I said, Yes, I'll come upstairs with you, the evening I looked out her window and wished my life might start all over again, in her living room, because everything about my life seemed to converge on this one room, with Clara, the barge, our strange lingo, and Earl Grey tea, as we sat and spoke of why this piece by Beethoven was really me, while part of me began to think I'd made the whole thing up to make conversation, to stir things up a bit, because I really had no idea why the quartet by Beethoven was me, any more than I knew why Rohmer's stories were me, or why I wanted to be here on so many winter afternoons with Clara, trying to understand why the best in life sometimes takes two steps forward and three steps back.

I looked up and knew. It was all there: fear, wanting, sorrow, shame, bitterness, ache, and exhaustion.

Now, as I spied the very end of her block from Broadway with its one lit window that must have been the maid's room overlooking Straus Park, it struck me that though we'd never really had anything here, still maybe we'd also lost everything here, as though something from being so piously wished for had managed to become the memory of something lost without having existed at all, a wish with a past that never had a present. We'd been lovers here. Once. When? Couldn't tell. Perhaps always and never.

•

I walked down 105th Street once again—placid, serene, white-pillared lane. The town houses stared at me with frowning suspicion.

Why are you here again?

I am here because I don't know why I'm here.

Her lights were still on. But too bright. What on earth could she have been doing? Should I look for a human, two human shadows flitting

behind the drapes? Would she come near the window when her cell
phone rings? Just tell me I'm not spying at the wrong window.

Could she be the type who sleeps with all the lights on? What if she
left the lights on because she likes to come back home and find the
whole place lit up, the way I do sometimes, to forget I live alone? Or was
she moving from room to room, which was why the place was all aglow?
Or were the lights on everywhere because she hated the dark when she
was alone and this was her way of showing she was alone and hated it?

Suddenly someone turned off the lights in her apartment. She's gone
to bed. A frightful thought raced through my mind: *They've* gone to bed.

But on 106th Street, I noticed that her kitchen light was still on.
Who goes to bed with a lover and leaves the kitchen light on?

No one.

Unless it's in the heat of passion.

What was she up to?

Cognac? Hot toddy? A little snack? How easy can human contact be,
how easy had it always been? Why was it so unusually difficult with
Clara?

The kitchen light still puzzled me.

What can a kitchen light possibly mean? How many times do I turn
mine on and off before going to bed?

And then it hit me: I'll never ever know why that light was on so
late, nor ever see that kitchen from the inside again. Suddenly the
kitchen light stood like a distant beacon that was far crueler than the
storm itself.

Boris!

He stepped out into the cold to finish his cigarette, stood there awhile
gazing at nothing, then flicked the butt halfway across the street. I made
certain he didn't see me.

The moment he stepped back into the lobby, I crossed the street and
found myself headed toward 107th Street.

I could not stay on the sidewalk too long. She might look out of her
kitchen and catch my eyes glued to her windows. For all I knew, she
might have been looking out of her window and staring straight at me.
Or perhaps the two of them were. So I walked by in a rush. But having
reached the end of her block too soon, I realized that there was nowhere
to go, and rather than go the long way around to Broadway and back, I

started walking back on Riverside, slowly, then once back to 105th, went up again to 107th, back and forth, again and again, always affecting a busy air, not realizing that there wasn't a reason in the world why anyone should walk by eight times on Riverside Drive and look so busy at such an ungodly hour of the night.

My passacaglia, I'd tell her one day, not Leo's prelude, not your sarabande or your Folías, not Beethoven's Adagio. Just my passacaglia, my passing along here, and losing my mind.

Perhaps I should call, I thought. Not to talk. But to remind her I wasn't out of her life quite yet. I'd let it ring once, then hang up. But I knew myself: having called her and found it wasn't so difficult, I'd be tempted to repeat the call. It was the sort of thing Inky might do. Take forever to call the first time, call a second time twenty minutes later, then every five minutes, then all the time. If she wanted to speak to me, if she was alone, she'd call back. If she didn't call back, well, either she'd turned off the phone or she wasn't going to play this game. In the end, she'd ask him to pick up the phone and tell whoever had called that she was in Chicago. *Say I'm in Chicago.*

Had I encouraged them to sleep together?

Suddenly the lights in the living room are on again.

She is unable to sleep. She is fuming. She is upset.

I should call, shouldn't I?

What if she knows I am downstairs? She is the sort who would intuit just that. She knows I am downstairs this very moment.

Or worse yet, what if she simply wants me to spin these thoughts in my head, including the worst one of all: that she isn't even thinking of me?

Then the lights go out.

Only a pale, bluish light near her window. Was it a night-light? Was Clara really the type to use night-lights? Or was it a dusky, weakened incandescent light from another room, or light reflected from a nearby street sign? A candle? God forbid, no, not a candle, not a lava lamp. Clara Brunschvicg would never own a lava lamp!

Ah, to make love to Clara Brunschvicg by the light of a lava lamp.

Noir, noir thoughts.

●

I did not call that night. The next morning I was awakened by a light pattering on my windowpane, the sound of rainfall, timid and tentative, without the hysteria or conviction of a downpour, like rain on an August afternoon that might stop any moment and restore things to how they'd been minutes earlier. It felt like afternoon. I wouldn't have minded if I'd woken up six months later. Let time, not me, deal with this.

I'd had a fitful night, perhaps with weird dreams flaring through a wasteland called sleep, though I couldn't remember a single dream, save for their collective pall, which lingered in my sleep like smoking stacks on a parched landscape after a great fire. At some point toward dawn I felt the same rapid throbbing in my chest that had made me go to the hospital the day before. But I must have fallen back to sleep. If I have to die, let it be in my sleep.

. By morning, I knew exactly what it was. It didn't surprise me; what surprised me was its ferocity, its single-minded persistence in every part of my body. No ambiguity, no doubt, no cloud could be summoned to give it a kinder name. This was not a whim. It was a commandment that must have started somewhere in mid-sleep, slogged its way out of one nightmare into the next, and finally worked itself out into this morning's light. I wanted her and I wanted nothing else in the world. I wanted her without her clothes, with her thighs wrapped around me, her gaze in mine, her smile, my every inch inside her. "Perse me, perse me, Printz, perse me one more time, and another, and another still," she'd said in my sleep in a language that seemed English but might just as easily have been Farsi or French or Russian. This is all I wanted, and not having it was like watching life drained from my body and, in its place, a false serum injected straight into my neck. It wasn't going to kill me, and I wasn't going to die, and things would go on as before, and I'd definitely recover, but not having her was like laughing and drinking while watching every single person I grew up with being taken to the gallows and hanged, until my turn came, and I'd still be laughing.

My own body was pounding at my door, pushing the door open with the dogged truculence of a crime about to be committed in which I was both felon and victim—open up, open up, or I'll ram the door down— *Perse me, perse me, Printz, perse me one more time,* she'd said, to which I finally replied, I'll perse you with everything I have, just make me make trouble, make me do something, make me hurt you, as I want you to hurt me, Clara, and hurt me hard, because this staying put like two boats tied to a dock is like waiting decades on death row, make me yield to you as I know I must and have been craving to ever since I kissed you and you snubbed me with a *No* that I want you to take back with the very lips I kissed that night, take back the curse and spit it from your mouth and I will take what you cast out because it was mine before it was yours.

Part of me did not want to admit any of this, or yield to the impulse, because yielding now would be like letting the enemy dictate terms I'd regret signing no sooner than the ink had dried. This was not like our second night, when shutting my eyes and thinking she was in bed with me had seemed so easy and so natural that I didn't even bother hiding it from her the next day. Where had that openness gone, why couldn't I speak to her like this any longer, why with so much in common did my body feel so gridlocked and bottlenecked? The more I knew her, the more fettered my impulses; the more reclusive my body, the more muddled my speech. Could it be that the older I was, the more callow I got? Now that I knew how little there was to fear from others, I was turning shy; candor was more difficult the more fluent my speech. In the alchemy of desire, the more we know, the less we fear, but the less we fear, the less we dare.

Now, in bed and with the words she'd spoken in my dream still ringing in my ears, I felt as though something had broken the sluices, mocked my inhibitions, and flooded every improvised sandbag I'd put between us. So what if I surrender to her, so what if she knows? I'll tell her first thing in the morning.

I decided to call her. Better yet: send her a picture of Sir Lochinvar, bonnet and plume. Top of the morning, greetings and salutations, from prow to aft, starboard and portside, all aboard, beware of our *corvus*, this is the captain speaking . . .

Call and pick up where we'd left off two nights ago.

I ache for you.

Do people still ache for people?

Not really.

Then speak differently.

I know you'll want to hang up on me, and you have every reason to, and I know you'll think I'm drunk or that I've lost my mind, but just speak to me, stay on the phone with me, say you know, say you know exactly, because you're going through it yourself, for if you know, then I know how you'll take the raspy, churlish snigger in your soul and unbraid it till it loosens into strands of passion, prayer, and thanksgiving.

I put a pillow between my thighs, said the word *Clara*, thought of her legs wrapped around my back, and then knew, when there was no turning back, that I was signing over my life to her, that I was handing her all my keys for her teeth, her eyes, her shoulder, her teeth, her eyes, her shoulder, her teeth, her eyes, her shoulder—after this I would never be able to say it was nothing, or that morning had made me do it.

Later, I went out in the rain, bought three papers, had breakfast at my crowded Greek deli, then headed for a walk to Columbia, maybe farther. I like rainy days, especially light rainy days that are just barely gray but whose overcast sky does not hang oppressively over the city. Such days make me feel cheerful, perhaps because they are darker than I and therefore make me seem happy by contrast. This was a good day for a walk. I knew there was no point in checking my e-mail or even expecting a call from her. She wouldn't call because she knew I wouldn't have called either, and I didn't call because I knew she wouldn't. But I knew she had thought of calling, because I myself had thought of it. She'd want me to make the gesture first, if only to hold it against me, which is why I wouldn't call, which is also why she wouldn't call either. It was this twined and tortured shadow-thinking that both paralyzed us and drew us closer. *Aren't we so very, very clever.*

Clara, you are the portrait of my life—we think the same, we laugh the same, we are the same.

No, we're nothing similar. It's just love makes you say this.

By the time I approached Straus Park, I knew I had absolutely no interest in going any farther uptown, that this whole expedition to Columbia or past Columbia was a ruse to step back into Clara's world.

In Straus Park the snow had already started to melt. I stood where I had stood on the day she'd come to meet me. The tenor of our relationship was so different on that day, or on the day before that: the quick dash to the restaurant in the cold, Svetonio, the visit to her home, our Lydian tea, that sacrosanct moment when in the kitchen she put two mugs on the counter and, with a resigned, uneasy air that sprang from the depths of reticence, had said, "I have no cookies. I have nothing to offer."

I went back to 105th Street to go over last night's footsteps. I didn't know why I was doing it, just as I didn't know why I trundled down the same area so many times last night. But last night everything seemed

shrouded in a spectral fog behind which I took cover, the better not to
see the void looming before me. Last night I knew I was a shattered
being. Today, I didn't feel shattered at all. Things must be getting better,
I thought, I must be healing and already getting over the hardest part.
How fickle the human heart. I was almost about to take myself to task for
being so frivolous when I suddenly caught sight of her window. I was
jolted by an overwhelming sense of panic. It told me that the wound I
thought was already healing hadn't even been thoroughly inflicted yet,
which was why it didn't hurt so much. The knife wasn't all the way in
yet, things hadn't started getting worse.

Through her window I caught sight of the very large plant I'd seen in
her living room a few days before. I hadn't really noticed it at the time.
Now I remembered we'd been discussing Rohmer and Beethoven, and
she was sitting right under its leaves and I'd been staring at it all the
time.

I decided to walk downtown. I hadn't crossed the street when an
impulse made me pass by the bakery and stop once I noticed that the
windows were all fogged up inside. I could use a croissant, I thought.
There was a long line, there always was by mid-morning, especially during the holidays.

This was the spot of two nights ago. To stir the memory of our kiss, I
came even closer to the glass and, so as not to arouse suspicion inside the
bakery, pretended to be straining my eyes to make out whether the line
was long inside, almost pressing my nose flat against the glass. Clara was
with me again. Our mysterious hip movements were as alive to me now
as they were then. Nothing had changed. It amazed me to think that this
bakery not only remembered the night better than I could but, in the tra-
dition of all great bakeries on holidays, it remembered it for me and was
offering me the choicest slice, the one with the king's charm. One could
keep this charm for life. Clara would become like one of those diseases
that can definitely be overcome but that leave their mark on your skin
and, sometimes, disfigure you completely, and you'll call it a blessing all
the same because it opened the way to God.

If I should ever wish to see her in the weeks to come, the easiest way
would be to come here instead of walking around her building. Or I
could do both, the way people go to a cemetery to visit one tombstone
and, since they're there already, might as well put flowers on someone
else's too.

I opened the door and walked into the bakery and, when my turn came, on the spur of the moment decided to buy one of their large fruit tarts. Then, on second thought, added four pastries as well.

"I could have sworn it was you," said a man's voice. I turned around. It was a friend I hadn't seen in months. He was having breakfast with his girlfriend, seated at a tiny round table. "I saw you peeking in from outside, and for a moment I thought you were about to flatten your whole face at me."

He introduced me to Lauren. We shook hands. What was I up to these days? Nothing, I replied. I was headed for a late lunch with some friends on Ninety-fifth Street—hence the cakes.

The idea of visiting my friends had occurred to me only after I'd purchased the cakes.

We were almost a week past Christmas and I had yet to find toys for their children, I added. How old were my friends' children? asked the girlfriend, clearly interested in children. Two and four, I answered. "There are children's shops a few blocks down." Was she a schoolteacher? She shook her head.

I looked at her. What a lovely person. *There are children's shops a few blocks down.* A whole lifetime of kindness, sweetness, and goodwill in these eight words. We joked about buying gifts for children we hardly knew at all. She had no handbag; just a coat, which she was wearing buttoned down, both hands digging deep in her coat pockets—tense and uncomfortable, she'd finished her coffee long ago, it seemed. They had the look of a couple who'd had some words.

"We were headed that way, anyway," she said, "We'll walk down with you." They'd help me pick out toys. Did I mind? Not at all.

How sweet of her simply to volunteer with a complete stranger. Then I realized why this wasn't what I wanted at all and why I'd floated the plan of visiting friends on Ninety-fifth Street. I had bought the cakes in the hope of finding the courage to call Clara before announcing I was coming up with a tart and four pastries.

If I don't ditch these two now or tell them I've changed my mind, I may never drop in on Clara this morning, may never see Clara again, and—who knows—life may take a completely different turn, just because of a pair of toys and a stupid fib concocted with a fruit tart in my hand! Like those tiny, arbitrary accidents that determine the birth of a great piece of music or the destiny of a character in a film—a small nothing, a

meaningless fib, and your life spins out of orbit and takes a totally unexpected turn.

So here I am with a cake and four pastries going to a place I had no
intention of visiting and about to buy gifts I couldn't care less about.

In the toy shop, all three of us seemed to disband for a while. He was
interested in bicycles, while she simply ambled about looking at the cribs
and baby furniture, her hands still digging into her coat pockets. I found
myself right next to her.

"I think you should buy a fire engine," she said, pointing at one under
a glass counter.

How come I hadn't seen it? It was staring right at me.

"Because you don't see, maybe?"

"*Because I don't see, maybe.* Story of my life, isn't it?"

"I wouldn't know, would I?" she said.

The huge fire engine was made of plastic with rounded corners and
no sharp edges, which gave the truck a friendly but unintentionally car-
toonish character that was not likely to please a boy of four.

"Does the ladder move?" she asked the owner.

"It also has a rotating functionality, see, madam?" he said, with a
thick Indian accent, showing how the entire ladder assembly could be
rotated 360 degrees.

"But the same model also comes with a nonrotating functionality.
Fewer parts, breaks less easily." He turned his attention to a woman in
her fifties and her pregnant daughter. They were wearing identical wigs.
They wanted to buy furniture but did not want it delivered before the
birth of the baby. "We're a bit superstitious," said the mother, speaking
for the daughter. "I understand," he replied with the deferential empathy
of someone who'd lived his entire life with superstitions far creepier than
this.

Minutes later he was back. "So, which do you want, with rotating
functionality or without rotating functionality?"

By now, Clara would have been tempted to mimic his Indian accent,
and together we would have been on the floor and added one or two new
words to our clandestine lingo. Want to see a rotating functionality? I'll
show you a rotating functionality if that's the last thing I do.

With Lauren I wasn't sure it was good form. I fiddled with the rotating ladder.

"Which functionality do you think they'd like?" I said, turning to her and trying as discreetly as I could to coax laughter out of her.

She smiled.

"You were the four-year-old boy once, not me."

"I think I never grew beyond four."

"I wouldn't know, would I?" Obviously this was her way of acknowledging without really responding to another hasty attempt at bridging the distance between us. Then, probably suspecting she might have snubbed me without meaning to, she added, "You're not in bad company. Most men seldom grow beyond four."

We stood before the fish tank. I noticed she was staring at a fluttering flat Aleutian fish streaked with very loud blues; it looked like an imitation iris about to blossom. She saw me staring at her, looked away, and gently began tapping her fingernails on the glass pane just in front of the fish. The fish didn't flinch but kept staring at her. She smiled at it, gazed at it more intensely, and then back at me.

"He's not taking his eyes off you," I said.

"Now, there's something unusual," she replied almost distractedly, with a roguish melancholy smile that could have said more about the man she was living with than about all the fish in the Pacific.

I looked at her and couldn't resist. "I wouldn't know, would I?"

She shrugged her shoulders and, taking my tit for tat like a good sport, continued the flirtation with the fish, which suddenly got flustered.

"Oh no, he's gone," she said, feigning a crushed face. Then she looked at me, as if for confirmation that something unusually sad had indeed happened and that she hadn't just imagined it. Her fingers were still touching the glass pane. She was lost in thought.

If she were Clara, my heart would have gone out to her and I would have kissed her, because there was something incredibly moving in her sorrow. "Can I call you sometime?" I asked.

"Sure," she replied, her face still glued to the fish tank. I wasn't sure she understood.

"I mean: can I call you?"

"Sure," she repeated with the exact same casual air that continued to find fish far more important and that seemed to say, *I heard you the first time.*

Her number couldn't have been easier to remember. The whole thing had happened in less than ten seconds.

"Anything else you care to look at?"

I shook my head and decided to buy two of the rotating models. The owner of the store asked his son to gift wrap the boxes. "Wrap them separately, Nikil, not together, not together, I said." I was ready to burst out laughing and was trying to control the quivering on my lips. She must have thought I was smiling broadly for the joy such gifts would bring the two boys.

"Put yourself in the place of the boys when you walk in with these huge packages," she said.

I tried to and was only able to think back to my childhood. A stranger walks into my parents' living room with a wrapped box a few days after Christmas. I'm not sure the box is for me, so I contain my excitement, and to master it rush to my bedroom. Meanwhile, the stranger mistakes my quick exit for indifference or, worse yet, for arrogance. I wanted him to coax me out of my bedroom, while he wanted to see excitement and gratitude. When I am no longer able to contain myself and ask someone if the box is for me, they tell me "Probably," but that the guest has already left and taken the gift with him.

"Maybe this is why we like Christmas so much. It brings out the child in us," I finally said.

"Which is a good thing?" she asked.

"Which is a very good thing."

I liked her very much.

"I can't wait to call you," I said.

She gave an absentminded shrug, as if to say, *You men, all the same!* There wasn't the least touch of guile in her, unless absentmindedness itself was its most rarefied form. She might have been saying, *You mean to call, but you won't.* "Call me this afternoon. I'm not doing anything."

When my friend joined us, he seemed surprised by the speed with which we'd managed to find and purchase two toys. He put his arm around her shoulders. She simply dug her hands into her coat pockets again and seemed preoccupied by the patterns on the floor. What a complicated woman, I thought. Then I corrected myself: perhaps not complicated at all; perhaps she was the more candid person of the three. Perhaps Clara was too. It was just I who needed them complicated, if only because finding guile in them was my way of making them like me, of assuming they spoke my language and that I could speak theirs.

There'd been a moment at the wrapping desk when we were both resting our hands against the counter. By accident, our hands had touched. She did not remove hers, and I didn't remove mine. You'd think we were both totally engrossed by the fire trucks.

We separated a block later. I watched her reach for his hand and find it before springing through the slush to make it across the street before the light changed.

Yet she'd cheat on him in a minute, I thought, thinking back to Clara, who, for all her kisses at the party, was busy telling friends and strangers how easily she'd ditched Inky. I was sure she did the same with me: weep with me while listening to the Handel, have me over for tea, want me to spend the night with her, then double-cross me *all the way downtown* first thing the next morning.

I was hardly better myself.

On Ninety-fifth Street I had a moment of unbearable hesitation. Should I bother going at all? Had I even been invited? I couldn't remember, but assumed I was always welcome there. I'd have lunch with them, even if they had already started without me. I'd drop the toys with the boys. We'd have cake. Then by four o'clock I'd call Lauren. It had been my intention earlier this week to bring Clara along and introduce her to Rachel and her friends and open up my life to her, bit by bit. Now, I'd call Lauren by three- -to put Clara out of my mind.

Before ringing at their brownstone, I could already hear the hubbub of voices chatting loudly within. I even heard my own ring, and the effect it had on the noise in the house. At first silence, then the patter of feet, and the sudden burst of greetings. A stranger bearing gifts It did remind me of my childhood.

We've so much food. And all this booze.

Rachel came out of the kitchen and kissed me. Her sister said she would fill a plate with a bit of everything. An Indian couple had brought a stew that was to die for, and there was still lots left.

I called this house the Hermitage, because there was something good and wholesome about it, though it was never clear who lived there, who didn't, who was sleeping over and who just passing through. Always plenty of food, always new friends, children, and as always a bevy of pets, laughter, good fellowship, and conversation. What a relief to stop by this sanctuary and see everyone again, as if I were just dropping in on a sick

ANDRÉ ACIMAN

friend, or just needed to pick something up or borrow a book, reconnect, touch base.

Sometimes I pass here by cab without stopping. Just look in through the large dining-room window to make sure everything is all right. Someone is always bringing in something from the kitchen, and around the dining table there are always people, good friends. Once, while passing by, I even caught sight of two bottles of white wine which they'd left outside the window to keep chilled. I'd taught them this trick, which my father had taught me. When the bottles were stolen once, Rachel decided the refrigerator was good enough.

As usual, I made my way straight into the kitchen. It felt safer there, and gave me time to settle in and get used to faces I hadn't seen in a while. I found a huge uncut French cucumber and right away put it in my trousers. "They put people in jail for sporting such huge ones," said Rachel. "And this while it's resting," I said, which brought a guffaw from all those in the kitchen. Someone suddenly burst in: "They're fighting again." "They should get a divorce," said Rachel, "they're jerks." "Who's the jerk?" asks her sister. "I am," said the man who was just quarreling with his wife and who thrust his way into the kitchen to get a glass of water, "I'm the jerk, I am. *I. Am. The. Jerk.* See?" he said, ramming his head against the wall. "The biggest jerk on earth."

The wife, who couldn't resist, followed him into the kitchen. "At least no one's hiding it from you."

"What?" he asked.

"That you're a jerk!"

"You people are so boring," broke in Rachel's ex-husband, who was already preparing dinner for everyone tonight. "Can we at least pretend we're all still friends? Tomorrow is New Year's, for Christ's sake."

Rachel in the kitchen was busy cutting the fruit tart I had brought. She turned to me once the kitchen was cleared of people. "And I want you to be nice to the Forshams," she said. There was reproof in her voice. "But I am nice." "Yes, but I know you'll say something nasty, even without meaning to; you'll imitate them, or make fun of their boy, I know you'll do something." Clara would have encouraged me to do nothing short of that. The Forshams always dropped in on Sundays. I called them the Connubials, or the United Front of Wedlock Appeal. She played bad cop, he played supercop. She was never wrong and he was just perfect.

"And what's with the disappearing act?" Rachel asked as she continued putting things on a large salver. Julia walked in. "Ask him." "Ask
him what?" "Ask him where he's been all week and why he doesn't
answer his phone."

I decided to tell Rachel about Lauren so as not to say anything about
Clara. Halfway through my story, though, she told me to follow her into
the living room, which was when she told me to start the story all over
again. "Tell everyone? Including those I don't know?" "Including, and
especially, those you don't know." This, I knew, was my punishment for
not promising to be nice to the Forshams. It was also the price for my
disappearing act, she said. I loved being put in the pillory.

They listened to the story about the toy store, laughed when I imitated *rotating functionality.*

"Just like that—because of the way she tapped the fish tank?" someone asked.

She tapped with two fingers, the index and the middle finger, in
succession. I wanted to kiss her.

Rachel was serving the wedges of tart. She had asked me to bring in
two large espresso pots. In the middle of the room stood a very large glass
plate on which lay an uncut hollowed circle of wobbly Jell-O for the
children. It jiggled each time someone took a step in the room.

"What fish tank?" asked the Forsham wife.

"The girl he met."

"What girl he met in what fish tank?" asked the husband.

"So when were you planning to call?" someone interrupted.

"Around three."

"Want us to spot you?"

"No, thank you."

"Can we listen in, then? We promise, we won't make a sound."

I loved the teasing.

Julia brought me a plate with all kinds of leftovers. Gita, the Indian
lady, insisted I have a second helping of biryani. She was wearing a sari
over blue jeans. Her husband was busy explaining the scales on the piano
to their five-year-old son. I took a seat on a low stool, put the square
plate on my lap, and, resting my back against the large television set,
began eating. Someone brought me a glass of red wine. Here's a napkin,
said Rachel, hurling a folded cloth napkin at me. I loved this.

•

One of the guests began to discuss the Rohmer festival that was playing down the block. Tonight was to be the last night. I made a point of not saying anything, because I knew that once I mentioned Rohmer, I'd have to spill out everything about my evenings with Clara. At first they wouldn't suspect anything, but before long they'd sniff out a rat and start plying me with questions, and my evasive measure would only give me away. Which is why they kept prodding. And which was exactly what happened once Julia seemed to remember that I loved Rohmer, didn't I? I did, I said, continuing to stare at my food. Had I been to see any of the movies this week? Yes. Which ones had I seen? Before I could answer with *All of them*, the Forsham husband said he'd once seen a Rohmer film but still couldn't understand what all the fuss was about. He doesn't appeal to everyone, said Julia, who suddenly recalled seeing a Rohmer film with me a few years earlier. I tried to change the subject. The Forsham woman thought there was something sick and twisted in wanting to touch a minor's knee. Her husband couldn't agree more: "He likes the knee more than he likes the woman it belongs to. Fetishistic!" "My point exactly," echoed his wife, "fetishistic." Julia brushed the comment aside and told the Forshams' son to keep his fingers off the Jell-O unless he was going to eat it, in which case he had to ask for it. In the kitchen she had described him to me as the most repellent child in the world. "Why didn't you tell me?" she asked, turning to me, after giving the boy a second menacing stare. "We could have gone together." "I went at the last minute," I said. Was I going tonight? I didn't think so, I replied, surprised at the total lack of hesitation with which I found myself lying to a woman who was one of my best friends. "Maybe you can bring Lauren along."

The thought did not displease me. It freed me from thinking I had to go with Clara only. If Clara did happen to go tonight, well, she'd find me with Lauren, and if not with Lauren, then with friends, and frankly, I'd rather be with good friends than with a prickly Clara out to remind me how little she needed me, with all the friends and all the men in her life, and all her comings and goings uptown and downtown that made me feel like a puny, far-flung planet demoted from satellite to testy asteroid. God knows what she'd been telling her friends about me. Or was she like me:

not saying a word about us to anyone for fear of seeing the dying wick of friendship snuffed by the merest breath of gossip? Say nothing, smile, and move on. Say nothing because you're aching to tell the world but fear no one could possibly understand, but if they did understand, then there'd be nothing special to understand in the first place, would there? Say nothing because you don't want to see where hope trails off and loses luster and, like a lumpy bolide tailspinning to earth, finally thumps down on the desolate, dark folds of the Siberian tundra. Say nothing, because the two of us were perfectly ready to say there was indeed nothing.

And yet Clara would be crushed on seeing me with Lauren in a place where we both knew we'd meet if all other plans failed. This was sacred.

Or would Clara burst out laughing, and so loudly that I'd better think twice before going to the movies with Lauren.

And then it hit me. Clara could easily show up at the movies with someone else. The thought sent me into an instant frenzy, and I could see myself free-falling into a pit of anger and despair. What would I say if I saw her with another man? Leaning on his shoulder once they sat down. Or standing together at the entrance, drinking coffee, trying to decide where to sit, chatting up Phildonka about *Amerikon wezer*. After the movies, if it's still raining, they'll wait outside the main entrance to the theater.

Where would I be, then?

To forestall this new wave of anxiety, I came up with a brilliant compromise: I would be willing to give up Lauren altogether on condition that Clara not show up with another man.

The idea had come to me the moment I imagined Clara putting herself in my place and guessing that I'd probably want to go to the movies with another woman tonight. She must have figured, however, that I'd renounce taking someone if she too agreed not to go with another person. I could just see her sorting this knot out, smiling abstractly at my smile once she saw how, in this as well, our thoughts ran on the same lane. This kind of thinking aroused me. Thinking she was thinking what I was thinking, and enjoying it, as I was enjoying it, reminded me of our hug by the bakery past three in the morning. I wanted to be with her now, both of us partly naked in one of the bedrooms upstairs in Rachel's house, tripping over the fire trucks as we finally locked one of the bedroom doors, Perse me, perse me hard, harder, harder still.

Maybe I wasn't going to call Lauren after all.

"Why not?"

Someone else intervened: "Just give me this Lauren's number, and I'll call her."

"And tell her what?"

"Tell her for starters that she's always welcome to come here. There's always a plate, a spoon, a knife, and a fork here for new friends."

How I loved the sounds of these words: *A plate, a spoon, a knife, and a fork.* Where would I be without them?

There was a time when I too was a stranger here. Rachel might have told Julia the same exact words about me: *Tell him there'll always be a plate, a spoon, a knife, and a fork here for him.*

Clara was right: others were important, and sometimes they're all that stands between us and the ditch. Why wouldn't such an idea have occurred to me—that others were important—why did I have to fish it out from under a sheet of ice in an ice-fishing hut? *A plate, a spoon, a knife, and a fork.*

Would that they had said this about Clara now.

"You're not saying anything, and I don't like it," said Rachel, breaking the silence around me with another one of her prods.

"I'm eating," I replied, trying to suggest that if I was quiet it was also my way of avoiding saying anything unkind to the Forshams.

"You're so weird today. You're hiding something, I know it," she said, continuing to speak to me.

"And?"

"I think we should toss him in a blanket."

"Someone get a blanket."

Rachel's four-year-old boy, whose loyalty I thought I'd purchased with a fire truck, was the first to race upstairs. He returned with his five-by-three-foot blanky.

Someone insisted they find a real blanket.

"Okay, I'll tell everything," I said.

Which was when I realized that the one thing I wanted most right then was to talk to everyone, the Forshams included, about Clara—tell the world about this woman who with three words six days ago had jiggled my universe and turned it to Jell-O.

Rachel's ex replenished my wine.

I took a sip and for a moment was quiet, because I didn't know how to begin. "There is someone," I said. "Or, at least, there was. I don't think there is any longer."

"A phantom woman. I love it. And?"

"We met on Christmas Eve."

"Yes, and?"

"And nothing. We went out a few times. Nothing happened. Now it's over."

Silence.

Rachel's ex: Did you steal the jewels?

Mrs. Forsham: What a terrible question.

Me: I did not steal her jewels. But she offered to let me see them.

The ex: And?

Me: I took a rain check.

A man named David: He's lost his mind.

The ex again: Do you even like her?

My answer caught me by complete surprise. "Immensely," I said.

Julia: So what's wrong with her?

Me: She's flighty, arrogant, prickly, caustic, mean, dangerous, maybe perfect.

The ex: I see a very long winter. Go to the cave, open sesame, plunder the jewels, handle the thieves.

A moment of silence.

Rachel: You're not going to call Lauren?

Me: I'm not going to call Lauren.

Rachel: Not nice.

•

Later that afternoon we decided to walk the dogs. I walked next to Rachel on our way to the park and told her about my evenings with Clara after the movies, the hours at the bar, the dancing by the jukebox, the walk back through Straus Park, the nights when I was sure all was lost, the heartthrob when I was proven wrong, the night when life put everything on the table, then took everything back and put the cards away.

We were walking into the park, as we always did when we went out as a group, and were headed to the tennis courts and beyond that toward the tennis house, which, by early twilight that day, seemed already sunk in darkness, its two puny lamps scarcely lighting the way across the bridge leading over to the icy reservoir. All I need is for the ice to start cracking and I'll want to run away, be elsewhere. But we were already elsewhere, lost in a winterborne forest, away from the tall buildings off Ninety-third and Central Park West, cast in Corot's winterscapes, where twilight had blurred the colors to pallid earth tones right in the very heart of Manhattan. Another country, another century, our two dogs scampering around on the grounds of a small provincial French town. This part of Manhattan had never seen me with Clara and should not have reminded me of her. But because it reminded me of places she and I had invoked on the terrace that night, my mind was immediately drawn to her. It would be nice to *go to France* from here. Walk down Ninety-fifth, buy something quick to eat along the way, and be there in plenty of time. I wanted her to be with us now. This wasn't elsewhere at all. The set was right, but the play and the players all wrong.

"All I did was not sleep with her," I explained.

"Because?"

"Because for once I didn't want to rush it. Maybe I wanted this to be different. I didn't want ordinary. Maybe I wanted the romance to last longer."

Rachel listened.

"What comes after courtship?" I asked.

"Who ever knows. Besides, you're asking the wrong person."

I must have stared with a baffled look.

"We're back together again," she said. "We were friends, got married, got divorced, became friends again—now he wants to get married."

"And you?"

"I'm not against it."

Dangling the leash of her freed dogs, Rachel then crossed her arms and with her boot gave a gentle kick to a clump of clay. "It might actually be a good idea." Rachel was not given to enthusiasm. This could have been a clamorous endorsement. Then, looking away, and just as I was about to put my two cents in, "What do you think our phantom woman is doing right now?"

"I don't know. She could be with friends. Maybe another man. Who knows? One thing she is not doing is sitting waiting for my call."

"Were you supposed to call?"

"No. We make a point of never calling. We'd just meet on impulse, kept it light and improvised."

"What will you do?"

"I don't know that there's anything I *can* do."

"But you must do something."

I did not answer. I felt like shrugging my shoulders, but I knew she'd see through this too.

"It's hard to tell what we had. At first I thought she wanted nothing, then that she wanted friendship of a sort, then that she might have wanted much more but wasn't really sure, now we're strangers."

"And I take it you know exactly what you want."

There was irony in her voice.

"I think I do."

"You think you do. Put it this way: she's probably not sure why *you've* been seeing her either. I think she's very interested, the way you are. She wants friendship, she wants love, she wants everything, and nothing. No different from you. Nothing either of you does is wrong, even if you do nothing. But you should never have said no to her. Find a way to fix it before it's too late."

My smirk meant: And how do you propose I do that?

"Look. Perhaps she may not want to end it yet. Or she may want to end it before it sours. Either way, though, you can't not call her."

By then her two dogs had reappeared. The other guests were approaching us, Mr. Forsham had lit a pipe. "The phantom lady," she repeated. "I like that."

Then on second thought: "Do me a favor. Go over to that tree where no one can hear you, take out your cell phone, and make the call."

"And say what?"

"Say something!"

"Chances are she won't pick up."

"Why?"

"Because that's what I'd do if she called."

"Just call." Impatience sealed her words.

She was tousling her collies.

Perhaps Clara had said nothing about me to anyone. Or perhaps she'd spent a good portion of the afternoon as I had, speaking to her friends about someone who was opaque, difficult, fractious, and transparent. Perhaps she'd taken a walk along the marina by the boat basin, where I pictured her with Pablo and Pavel today, discussing me with the same dismayed shrug I had shown Rachel after she'd asked me if I liked Clara and I said *immensely*, hoping Rachel might think I was probably exaggerating, which would allow me to think I was. Perhaps Clara too was being told that this thing between us was most likely leading nowhere, but that we were headed there with such locked steps that there was no telling where any of it was going. I saw myself taking a few steps on the hardened, cold earth and walking away from Rachel toward the very tree she had pointed out. Here, against my better judgment, I'd force myself to make the phone call as soon as I knew I was no longer within earshot of anyone. I just wanted to call, I'd say. A lapse of a few seconds. Agonizing silence. You just wanted to call? she'd repeat. Well, now you've called.

There'd be many voices in the background. Probably she'd be at a late lunch on the marina. Did I think she'd stay home knitting?

Where are you? How are you?

How am I? Is that what you're asking? How do you think I am?

We'd have a hard time hearing each other. Or we'd pretend not to hear each other. Either way, the breakups on the line would help defuse the tension between us and give a flustered sprightliness to our words. She'd be in the boathouse. Where was *I*? In the park. It'd be just like us, I'd say, one in Riverside Park, the other in Central Park. It might thaw the chill. I'm so bored. Are you bored too, Clara? I'd ask. *Terribly.* Was either of us honest, or were we simply exaggerating to show we wished to be together instead? Would I want to come? Did she want me to come? Only if I wanted. Give me an address. She did not know the exact address, but it was on the marina off Seventy-ninth Street. I'd have to call her once I got there, and someone would come out and open the gate to the houseboats.

•

"Did you at least leave a message?" Rachel asked when I told her I wasn't able to reach Clara.

"Yes," I said.

"So, if she doesn't call back, we'll know."

"I suppose so." I must have sounded too vague.

"Did you really leave a message?"

I looked at her.

"No, I didn't."

"You're really something. Let's go home. I've found this extra-scented tea from Sri Lanka. And we've got so many cakes."

By then it had grown dark.

When Rachel unlocked the door, we were struck by the smell of beef stewed in wine sauce. Her ex-no-longer-her-ex was sitting in total darkness watching the History Channel, drinking bourbon. He thought we had arrived too soon. Bag the tea, we'll have drinks instead, someone said. There was a rush to one of the closets by the bookcase, glasses were produced, bottles, mini-snacks, including my favorite, pistachios roasted in hot spices. Someone put on a CD, even the Forshams were pleasant to be with. I began to look forward to this evening. From a limping afternoon-evening that was headed into a deep abyss filled with the darkest scree below, this was turning into a night that could last into the wee hours and remain as pleasant and warm as if Clara had promised to show up and might any moment ring the doorbell. It would have been so good if Clara came. I suddenly thought of 7:10. Seven-ten was less than two hours away now. There was still time to decide. What if I did call?

No, I wasn't going to call—never ask the question again.

But after downing a glass of Scotch, I couldn't remember why I'd been putting off calling her or why I'd even hesitated. I went into the empty pantry and took out my cell phone. I had the best intentions, I thought. I was simply going to ask her to join us for dinner. Light and simple.

She picked up exactly as I'd imagined: "Speak!"

I told her I was with friends and that I'd love her to join us for drinks. I didn't say anything about dinner, figuring it might scare her off.

"I can't."

It still caught me by surprise. I threw in my one and only trump card. "I'm so bored. I'm bored out of my mind. I'm dying to see you. Say yes."

"I'm sorry you're bored. But I can't. I'm busy."

No apologies, no explanation, not even feigned regret in her voice. Hard, glacial, petrous.

"Bummer," I said—my way of coaxing a smile to her voice. But she didn't respond. Her voice seemed drained of its warmth and humor.

Everything came off deadpan, the silence of a cobra that had just bitten
and is watching to make sure its victim has collapsed.

She didn't bring up 7:10. I didn't either.

The conversation couldn't have lasted for more than half a minute. It
left me stunned—which was exactly why I'd been avoiding calling her.
Stunned was worse than hurt, worse than snubbed, told off, insulted, or
just simply ignored. Stunned was like being totally paralyzed, good for
nothing else afterward, scrapped, zombified, eviscerated. I turned off the
telephone completely. I didn't want to hope, didn't want to think there'd
be anything good to expect from this phone. There were never going to
be other calls. Serves me right, serves me right.

When I returned to the living room by way of the dining room, I saw
that the large country table had already been set, with its usual selection
of ill-assorted dishes and glasses. And then I remembered. I'd wanted to
tell them to add a place setting for an extra guest. Then I'd gone to make
my phone call. Is this *the* guest? Rachel would have asked. Yes, the guest.
I had told no one her name. So where shall we seat *the* guest, across from
you perhaps? I loved Rachel's irony. This table, though, would never see
Clara. Clara would never see Rachel.

●

That night after dinner and our second dog walk later in the park, I
did walk up Broadway. On 106th I dawdled about awhile, then strolled
around her block once and, for good measure, a second time. Her lights
were out, both the first and second time. Obviously she wasn't home,
might not come back, or had gone to bed already. Then I walked to
Straus Park and stood there, remembering the candles I'd imagined on
the statue a week ago, remembering Officer Rahoon and *Manattàn noir*
and Leopardi's short poem about life being all bitterness and boredom.
Busy, she'd said. What an ugly word. Lethal, flat-footed, snooty, dismissive *busy*.

The rats have all gone under, I thought. There was something good
and soothing about standing here and feeling one with the specter of
things, something wholesome in watching life from the bank of the dead,
siding with the dead against the living, like standing by the river and
hearing, not the Bach, but the hard, glacial, petrous cracking underneath
the prelude—hard, glacial, petrous, like her, like me. Outside of time we

were so good together, as the dead are good together. Outside of time. In the real world, the meter was always running.

For a while I thought of the man who had pledged to sit outside his beloved's window for one thousand and one nights, but on the one thousand and first deliberately did not show up. It was his way of spiting her, of spiting himself, as if spite, in the end, and love, its bedfellow, were coiled together like two vipers that bite the hand that feeds them, one with venom, the other with its antidote—the order makes no difference, but the biting must happen twice and hurts both times. I thought of how everything I'd done with Clara, from the very first night to the last, was governed by spite and pride, and, in between, lots of fear and admonition, while the one word that should have mattered most was the one condemned to remain silent, till it too became hard, glacial, and petrous. I had never said the word, had I? To the snow, to the night, to the statue in the park, to my pillow, I had. And I'll say it now, not because I've lost you, Clara, but I've lost you because I loved you, because I saw eternity with you, because love and loss are surefire partners too.

EIGHTH NIGHT

Phildonka Madamdasit, say hello."

The voice mail, when I finally turned on my cell that night, told me what I'd known about Clara from the very start but could never bring myself to accept: that everything I thought about her was always going to be wrong, but that knowing I was wrong was wrong as well. She belonged to another species. Or maybe I did. Or both of us did—which explains why we saw eye to eye on very small matters and timeless ones—but couldn't seem to connect when it came to middling day-to-day life. There were two Claras: the one who ribbed me and could show up Just when I couldn't have wanted her more, and the other Clara, the one whose next comment you couldn't foresee but stood in awe of, because the couple of words she might say flipped and sparkled around you like a newly minted coin that was a plea for love or another one of her barbs that start with a smile but could just as easily land you on a stretcher in the ER?

"Phildonka Madamdasit, say hello," began her message, with traces of suppressed mischief in her voice, as though people were laughing in the background and she was cupping the receiver to prevent me from hearing them. I knew by now that this was her way of underscoring the humor of the moment and, by so doing, communicating a semblance of mirth and sprightliness. "He kept glowering at me until I said whatyoustaringatbustah. The poor fellow got so flustered that he spilled the popcorn on me. You should have seen him apologize, the bulging whites of his eyes wincing contrition as he kept gawking at me." A moment of silence. "And yes. In case you were wondering and hadn't figured it out, this is my subtle way of saying that I, Clara, did manage to *go to France* on the last night of the Eric Rohmer festival, while *you*, Printz—well, there's no telling where you went and what you did after you called. Phildonka sends his greetings." Attempted humor once again. "Needless to say, I'm very *très* hurt. And the funny thing"—I could hear her smoking, so she must have been calling from home—"the funny thing is that I did call you no more than half an hour after we spoke to tell you that I would have come for drinks. So, yes, I am sorry. But you should cringe with guilt and mortification."

This was followed by yet another message. "By the way, I called you a million times—but Mister, here, had to turn off his phone again." When I looked at the screen more carefully, it showed that she had indeed called a million times.

There was a third message: "Just to say I know you were upset last night. I'm sorry. I'm going to bed. So don't call. Or call if you want. Whatever."

The jab and the caress. Never one without the other. Venom and antidote.

Yet another voice mail was waiting as I got out of my elevator. It had come an hour later.

"So you're really not going to call. Great!"

It made me smile.

"This feels worse than heroin addiction."

A few seconds later, she hung up. Then she hung up again. Finally, another voice mail.

"What I meant was, don't call. Come to think of it, don't call at all." Then silence. Just enough ambiguity in the air for me to suspect something vague but nothing to panic about—until it hit me that she could have meant *Never call again.* "You're just pitiful," she added. It had come from nowhere.

Then, as always, the line went dead. I could tell she'd hung up the phone. This was the last word I had from her. My entire being, our entire week together summed up in one word: *pitiful.* Suddenly I went numb again.

Pitiful dropped on me like an ancient curse that once uttered cannot be undone, lived down, or forgotten. It hunts you down, finds its mark, and brands you for life. You'll go down to Hades with the wound still bleeding. *Pitiful.*

I am pitiful. This is what I am: pitiful. She's right. One look at me and you'd instantly tell: pitiful. He hides it well, but sooner or later, out it comes, and once you've spotted it, you'll see it everywhere, on his face, his smile, his shoes, the way he bites his fingernails—*pitiful*.

As always, hers was the last word.

I tried to find holes in her assessment of me as I unlocked my door and saw my pitiful household with its pitiful perpetual bedroom light on, which was meant to let me think someone was already there, waiting for me, and would at any moment jump out of bed on bare feet and greet me with *Where have you been all this time?* Pitiful because I needed this fantasy to make coming home easier. Pitiful because the person I wished might appear in my pajama shirt and no bottoms was the very person who had just completely brushed me off. Pitiful because she had seen right through all my little shenanigans, my deferrals, demurrals, my struggle to fill each silence when silence became unbearable, because during those moments of silence I felt like a poker player whose bluff is about to be called but who must keep raising the stakes to keep covering up his bluffs, until he forgets whether he is bluffing or what he is really bluffing about and ultimately knows he must and is expected, sooner or later, to fold. Pitiful because, even in tonight's voice mails, I had let her ride me through an entire spectrum of posts, from feigned mirth, to hurt avowal, to dignified defeat, and when I could have sworn I had the matter still in hand, she'd finally turned on me, light and swift, venom and scorn. It had barely touched me at first, like a tiny immaterial pinprick far narrower than the point of a needle, but it had pierced my skin and didn't stop digging and kept growing wider and wider till it became thicker and more viciously serrated than the tooth of a giant white shark. A nothing at first—a giggle on the phone, the illusion of rakish fellowship, and then the slash of a stiletto right across my face.

She *Folía*. Me *Pitiful*.

I went over to the CD player and put on the Handel. How I loved this piece. The ice cracking, Clara's tears, the impromptu kiss when we lingered in the living room that afternoon in the country.

You wished me not to call you; well, I'm calling now.

You woke me up.

I woke you up. You kept me up. We're even.

What do you want from me? She couldn't have sounded more exasperated.

What did I want from her? What I wanted from her was her. Naked. In my bed. Or better yet, I wanted to hear my buzzer ring, watch her come out of the elevator with her shawl still wrapped around her face, the way she'd worn it when we kissed by the bakery, cursing at the elevator door when it slammed shut behind her to remind her it wasn't scared of her. *Damn your fucking elevator door. And damn your fucking cell phone too.* The courage to come up to my apartment at two in the morning. She had it. Did I have the courage to call her now? Yes? No?

Pitiful.

I had an impulse to prove myself wrong, but then thought better of it.

After my shower, I put on my bathrobe and immediately grabbed the phone. So what if it was past two in the morning? Either way, it's already lost.

I liked calling while still wet. It gave a totally impulsive and informal air to the call, as though it were the most ordinary thing in the world; I could focus on my toes, my ears, or her voice, the whole thing relaxed and candid.

"I can't sleep," I said as soon as she picked up.

"Who's sleeping?" she retorted, clearing her throat, as if to mean *Who ever goes to sleep these days?* It seemed to clear the slightest inflection of hostility from her voice. But there was sleep in her voice. Hoarse, raw, listless, like the smell of a woman's breath when you wake up at night and her head is on your pillow. Was she embarrassed to be caught sleeping past two in the morning?

"Besides, I knew it was going to be you."

Why not Inky? I was on the verge of asking, when I realized that her answer might be *Because he is right here with me.*

So I didn't ask.

I could have asked why she knew I'd be calling so late. Instead, I told her I had just come out of the shower and was about to go to bed. "I wanted to call because I didn't want to leave things where we'd left them last night."

She made an amused semi-grunt. She was agreeing things couldn't be worse. So there was no chance I'd imagined it.

"Can you talk?" I asked.

There was silence at the other end of the line. Had she, perhaps, fallen back to sleep?

"You mean am I alone?"

Such razor-sharp clarity, even in mid-sleep.

"Yes."

All I had meant to ask her was whether she was up to talking. As always, she'd read the real meaning behind my question.

"What did you want to talk about?" Her equivalent of *This is your quarter; speak.* She was giving me an exceptional but necessarily brief audience. So many seconds, but not an instant more. Always with the meter running.

"I was going to say—" But I didn't know what I was going to say and couldn't think that fast. "I just wish we were a week ago. I wish we were still at the party and had never left and were trapped there forever."

"The things you come up with, Printz." This was sleep talking. "You mean, as in that Buñuel movie—"

Was sleep making her unusually conciliatory?

"Trapped forever, snowbound forever, as in Maud's house." And then I said it. "I wish this was two nights ago."

"And last night."

My heart started thumping as soon as she corrected me. In the dark living room I stood facing the night and the dark sea of Central Park. "I'm staring out the window. I'm staring at the salt on the carpet. And I wish you were with me now."

"You want me to be with you now?"

Why did she sound so surprised?

"I want you to be with me now . . . and always. There," I added, as if, using a pair of pliers on my gums, I had managed to pull out an impacted tooth.

"And you want me because?"

I should have known that the triumph in my avowal wouldn't last. Something sharp and unkind in the rise of her question came like two fingertips snuffing the candlelit amity I'd just found in her voice. Irony, which I loved and found comfort in and which had drawn us together from the very start and made us think we were two lost souls adrift in a shallow, flat-footed world, was not a friend. It cut the incipient warmth between us like a pointed spur wounding the belly of a loyal and beloved pony.

"I don't know why. There are so many answers. Because I've never known anyone like you or been this way with anyone, never this close, or this exposed. Never like this, because every time I turn over my cards and show you my hand—I don't know why I'm telling you this, because chances are you'll never forgive me—but just telling you who I am and how I feel as I'm doing right now makes me hard." I knew I'd been deferring the word, as though trying to test my sentence before finally deciding to speak it.

"Hard?"

I sensed I had caught her totally off guard. Was she really going to ask me not to be obscene?

"Printz." She sounded heartbroken. Or profoundly disappointed. Or was this still her sleep speaking, or had she read right through me and seen the cost, the yearning, and ache behind this word—taken sex, which was the easy admission, to the heartbreak of sex, which was the impossible and far more difficult one? Or was this just her way of mulling over a tamer version of *You're more pitiful than ever now*, her preamble to a long reprimand meant to cut off my balls and slice them into julienne strips.

"Why, *Printz?*" I said, imitating the strain in her voice, not sure yet whether this was my way of taking back and playing down my admission or of making her feel silly for taking it at face value. Or was I trying to get her to say something she wasn't saying, hadn't quite said, might never say, or that she'd just vaguely glossed over a second ago and needed to clarify so that the two of us might seize its full meaning?

"Why? Partly because this is hurting you, and I don't want you being hurt like this."

"And partly?" Come what may, by now I was ready for anything.

"And partly"—she was obviously hesitating, as though she was about to raise the ante and break new, dangerous, painful terrain between us, taking those julienne strips we'd been exchanging and mincing them down into sheer slithers—"because I don't want you calling me tomorrow morning and saying, Clara, I made love to you last night."

I was devastated. I felt hurt, exposed, embittered, embarrassed, like a crawfish whose shell has been slit with a lancet and removed but whose bared, gnarled body is being held out for everyone to see before being thrown back naked into the water to be laughed at and shamed by its peers.

"You didn't have to make fun of me, nor did you have to hurt me that way." This was the first time I told her I was hurt. "As you said, I may be pitiful indeed, and this is clearly my big, over-the-top, mushy-gushy, sulky-pouty thing limping on its last leg—"

There was a moment of silence, not because she was dutifully hearing me out or humoring my little tantrum, but as though she couldn't wait to break in.

"Did I make it go away?"

In a second she had won me all over again.

"Most certainly did."

I could hear her smile.

"Why are you smiling?"

"Why are you?" Then after a moment, out of the blue, as if she'd seen a connection that I hadn't: "What are you wearing now?" she asked.

"Was wearing bathrobe, now in bed."

My heart, which was already pounding, was going like mad. I hated this, but I also loved it, as though part of me were staring at a river from a very tall bridge, knowing that I was securely fastened to a bungee cord and that fear, more than jumping, was the thriller. Still, the silence was unbearable, and I found myself saying the first thing that came to mind so as not to say what I wished to say.

"You remember, the striped blue-and-white bathrobe hanging on the back of the bathroom door?"

It took me forever to utter this one bland, halting, breathless, complicated sentence.

"Yes, I remember. Old, thick terry cloth—it smelled good."

Same one, I was going to add.

It smelled good, she had said.

What made her smell it?

"No reason. Curious."

"Do you do this often?"

"I grew up with dogs."

An intentionally makeshift excuse. She must have sensed I was groping for a quick comeback.

"If I knew you better, I'd go down forbidden grounds."

"You know me more than anyone I've known in my life," I said. "There's nothing you're thinking that I haven't already thought of."

"You should be ashamed of yourself, then."

"You and I enjoy the same shame."

"Maybe."

"Clara, I can be at your front door in less than ten minutes."

"Not tonight. I like it like this. Maybe it's my turn to say—what was it?—*too soon, too sudden.*"

It thrilled me to know she remembered.

"Besides, I'm supermedicated and zombified and fading," she added.

"I can take rejection."

"It's not rejection."

Had anything ever gone better between us? Was this Clara speaking or was it the medicine? Her breath was on my face again. I wanted the wet of her lips on my face.

"Why didn't you come for drinks?" I asked.

"Because you gave me the silliest reason to."

"Why didn't you say so, then?"

"Because I was angry."

"Why were you angry?"

"Because you're always so slippery, always avoiding things."

"You're the one who can never be pinned down."

"I don't turn off my phone."

"Why didn't you give me a hint, then?"

"Because we've run out of hints, because I'm tired of double-talk."

"What double-talk?"

"Printz, you're doing it now."

She was right.

Long silence.

"Clara?"

"Yes."

"Tell me something nice."

"Tell you something nice." She paused. "I wish you'd been there when I called out your name in the theater."

She was breaking my heart, and I couldn't even begin to say why.

"Were you going to come for drinks tonight?"

"I had hoped to, Mister-I'll-turn-off-my-phone-to-show-her-who's-who."

This time she took my breath away.

Without warning, tears began welling in my eyes. What on earth was coming over me? This had never happened to me, and certainly not on the phone, naked.

"Sometimes I'm terrified you'll know me long before I know you."

"I'm no different. It scares me too."

Silence.

"Why are you letting me do this?" I asked.

"Because tomorrow when I see you I don't want us to be like today."

"What if you're different again tomorrow?"

"Then you'll know I don't mean it."

"But haven't we been through this already?"

"Yes. And you should have known it then too. Are you thinking of me now?"

"I am. I am," I repeated.

"Good."

•

The sky was overcast once more the next day, the last day of the year, giving the morning light that luminous, bleached quality we'd been having all week long and which skimmed the surface of the city like the inside fleece of a white shearling coat draped munificently around the sun. It made you long for more snow and for wintergreen and wool-lined gloves and the delicate scent of waxed gift paper lingering all during Christmas week. I couldn't have been happier. I got out of bed, put on old clothes, and headed off to my Greek diner around the corner, hoping it might be full, or empty, it didn't matter which, because in the mood I was in, drafty, stuffy, grungy or not, all were good and welcome. When I opened the door and was greeted in Greek by the usual hostess cradling a giant menu in her arms, everything felt lithe and buoyant, as if a weight had finally been lifted and I was allowed to love the world again. I liked being like this. I liked being alone like this. I liked winter. I'd been yearning to do this for a whole week. Breakfast without cares. I'd have buttered Belgian waffles first, orange juice, then a second cup of coffee; then I'd get back home, shower, change—or was there any point in changing before heading uptown to her lobby, where we'd arranged to meet before going to shop for extras for tonight's party?

But I also knew there was another reason why I was happy. As if something had been finally cleared between us. A few hours before that, the year was hurtling to a dark and ugly finish. Now, merely a phone call later, life seemed to have been restored to me and things seemed so promising that, once again, I found myself refusing to look over to the brighter side for fear I'd dispel its magic or be proven wrong. How long before she and I found yet another way to bring back the darkness that had shrouded me all day yesterday and then sat on me till two this morning? How long before despair again? Lauren in the bakery, laughter in the kitchen, the walk with the dogs, sundown in the park, and dinner, during which I kept thinking, A plate, a spoon, a knife, why isn't Clara with us tonight?—all of it so very dark.

But even these enforced reminders of yesterday's gloom were little else than a smoke screen I was putting up between me and the crowning moment I meant to revisit ever since going to bed last night. I'd been saving this for later, putting it off each time I seemed about to give in to the thrill of opening the surprise package I was taking my time unwrapping.

Now, with my head resting on the steamed windowpane as I watched people and children trundle along the narrow strip of shoveled snow on the sidewalk, I let my mind drift awhile. "Why did you let me do this, Clara?" I'd asked. All she'd offered was an evasive "Me?" I'd fumbled for words and could tell I was blushing, yet I'd struggled not to lie to her or cover up or deflect the truth or do anything but stay in the moment. Weren't these her words, *in the moment*? All I had thought of saying was How do we end this conversation? Or: How do we never end this conversation? But I'd spoken neither sentence.

"Printz?" she'd finally said.

"What?" I blurted out to mean, What more do you want from me?

"In case you're wondering." There was another moment of silence: "I didn't mind."

"Clara," I said, "don't go yet."

"I'm not going. On second thought, aren't you supposed to turn over and fall asleep?"

It had made both of us laugh.

In the end, what made me happier was not just how close we'd suddenly grown to each other but that I'd heeded the impulse to call her. Another second and the year would have ended abysmally. Bravo, Printz, I wanted to say, as if what thrilled me now was less the woman on the phone than kudos for finding the courage to call her.

But just as I was thinking of her, the conversation between us began to pulverize, like an underground mummy exposed to air. By tomorrow, will this be nothing or will this be the best we've ever had? Tonight's party seemed hours away, and Lord knows, a nothing could undo everything. Undo what, I thought, undo what? I kept asking, as if resolved to see that nothing had changed for the better since last night, and that perhaps it was time to stop banking on a moment of heat caught in midsleep. Will she even remember, I thought, or would I be back to *pitiful*?

Or was I simply trying to scare myself?

While eating a waffle, which I drenched in real syrup, I remembered how the conversation had taken a different turn. I'd meant to ask why she had called me pitiful. Instead, I'd stopped myself and asked why she hadn't come to dinner. This one question led to the next and to the next after that, not because we were saying anything special to each other, but because question and answer, however to the point, allowed us to speak in rhythms and near-whispers that bound us closer and followed a course that had less to do with our words than with the tenor of our words, of our voices. Anything we said last night, any course taken, however arbitrary, would have taken us there and nowhere else, unavoidably.

"Why didn't you come for dinner?"

"Because you said you were bored, and it sounded so false."

"Why didn't you say so, then?"

"Because you'd take it the wrong way, and we'd have argued."

"Why didn't you help me save the evening, then?"

"Because there was so much double-talk, and I knew you were punishing me."

"What double-talk?"

"This double-talk, Printz. The kind that stands in the way of so many things."

"What things?"

"You know exactly what things."

"Why not give me a sign?"

"A sign? Meeting you on a freezing cold night, going upstate the next day, spending every minute with you—you needed a sign?"

"Do you have any idea what hearing you say all this does to me?"

There'd been a silence between us. And I knew what it was. Not lack of words, but lack of ways to avoid saying the words both of us knew needed to be said.

"What you want I want," she'd finally said.

"Do you know me so well?"

"I know what you think, how you think, I even know what you're thinking this very instant."

I could have said any number of things to throw her off course. But I didn't.

"You're not saying anything, and you're not denying anything, which tells me I'm right in exactly the way you want. Admit it."

"I admit it," I said. I felt as naked as a newborn, thrilled with life, thrilled with my living body, thrilled by my nakedness, which I'd have given over to her in a second.

"If I wasn't so zombified right now, I'd ask you to come with your coat and your bathrobe and your snowshoes, and not a thing more. Because I want you all the way—and you, Misteramphibalenceman, can take this any way you want—from my mouth to your mouth."

Nothing she had said to me before had stirred me as much. It was as if she had spoken directly to my heart and through the airwaves reached for my cock.

The silence settling between us said everything.

I didn't want to say good night yet.

"Are you thinking of me?" she'd asked.

"I am."

And then the words that pierced me to the quick: "You can if you want to."

•

While waiting for my third cup of coffee, I did what I'd been watching so many people with pocket calendars do. It was my way of hoping, without admitting it, now that the Rohmer festival was over, that there'd be the Alain Resnais festival, followed by the Fellini, and the Beethoven Quartet series—weeks on weeks of evening rituals till we tired of them and decided, Tonight, let's hang out.

She called me while I was having breakfast. "Change of heart?" she asked, which told me she was in a good mood. None whatsoever, I replied. Someone was giving her a ride to pick up some stuff for Hans's tonight. Did I mind if we postponed meeting?

"Had we arranged to meet?" I asked. Why did I say something so stupid?

"Yes, we had. You forgot already?" she said almost reproachfully, as if unaware that I was only pretending, which was why she laughed. They *really* needed her help this morning, she said, we'd meet at the party. Pause. I wasn't going to end up in the ER, was I? No, I wasn't, Clara.

Around eleven in the morning I decided to call my friend Olaf. I found him in his office. He had just returned from the Islands. Horrible vacation. Why? Why? Because she's a cunt. He wasn't planning on staying at the office much longer, but didn't feel like heading home. I could come over and we'd walk back uptown together, like the two pricks we are, he added. "What was so wrong?" I asked when we finally met. "We just don't get along," he said, using the knuckles of both fists to mimic the cogs of two gears that fail to mesh. Let's face it, she's a cunt and I'm a dick.

But I wasn't paying attention. I knew exactly what I was trying to do. Leave his neighborhood, go elsewhere in the city, run into Clara.

Has it been a good year? I asked. Too soon to tell, he replied with his usual sarcasm.

Did he want to have lunch? Just had something—not hungry. We decided to have coffee instead. I was surprised to find him at work, I said. Only Jews celebrate Christmas. Jews and Dominicans. He was in one of his moods again.

On our way uptown we decided to stop at MoMA, where we'd hoped to sit down for coffee and exchange the latest in our lives, but the lobby was mobbed with tourists, and everywhere you looked teemed with human bodies. The fucking human race, he began. They don't go to a single museum in Europe, but they come here and all they do is drag themselves through art they can't begin to fathom, then rush to buy fake watches in Chinatown. Olaf and his rants. There was a time when you could sidestep life in the city and take time out with a friend here. Now look at this—the Mongolian horde. We threaded our way through the lobby and decided to head out to the closest Starbucks. But even the nearest one was mobbed. We ended upstairs at a place on Sixtieth Street—still too loud, too crowded, rich teenagers on Christmas break. We got up and tried a row of places around the low Sixties, till we gave up and ended up taking the Sixty-seventh Street crosstown bus. I knew why I was finding something wrong with each place. She was giving me the slip each time, or I kept missing her by a few seconds at every turn.

What was his reason for wanting to go elsewhere every time we stopped somewhere? There was only one explanation: he was looking for someone too, wasn't he? "You've met someone?" I finally asked him. He didn't stop, but kept walking, looking straight ahead of him. "How did you know?" "I can just tell. Who is she?" Without meaning to, Olaf managed to remind me that he was perhaps my best friend because of the way he answered my question: "You can tell because you too have met someone and are simply projecting. But you happen to be right. We're both love-starved."

Eventually, we found a Starbucks in the low Seventies and located a small table in a corner by the window. I borrowed an extra chair from a table nearby while he stood in line and ordered two coffees. I could hear him arguing with the barista. "Medium, I said, not *tall*, not *grande*, medium—and it's not *next guest* but next customer. I'm a customer, not a guest, get it?" I was tempted to ask him to pick up a couple of muffins or scones, but then thought I was setting things up too much, and besides, if indeed we were to run into her, I didn't want her to suspect that I was trying to replay our breakfast in the car. Then a counterinstinct told me that being caught replaying our breakfast might indeed propitiate running into her. The stars sometimes worked that way. Wasn't this how I'd arranged to run into Clara at the movie theater the first time? Since we were close enough to some of the stores where she'd most likely have gone with someone to buy food for the party, chances were we'd run into each other in this very place. Stuff of dreams and Rohmer films. But then I realized that thinking such double thoughts was a way of snooping into the affairs of fate and was precisely what might backfire and prevent us from meeting. I was just about to negotiate a way out of this double bind when there she was, walking past Starbucks with her friend Orla.

I dashed out of the coffee shop with just my shirt on and, from across the street, called out the name of one and then the other. What was I doing here? What were *they* doing here? Hugs, kisses, laughter. They were each carrying bags of food. I didn't have to persuade them to come in and join us for coffee. I am so happy, so happy to see you, I said to Clara once I'd introduced Orla to Olaf. That palm on my face, as it lingered on my face, and kept touching parts of my face, spoke all the tenderness I'd lived so many, many days and nights without. They still had tons of things to buy, she said. She ran down some of their unfinished errands.

They couldn't stay too long. Are you happy? I couldn't help myself from asking when Olaf and Orla were busy talking. Are you happy? she echoed, her way of saying that, yes, she was—or was she parodying what I'd just said, which, in the end, might just have been her way of saying, *Yes, I am happy.* But we scarcely have ten minutes. Just sit down, take your coats off, I'll get coffee. I had the strange feeling that I was fighting to keep her with me, struggling against strange odds that were determined to draw her into my life, only to pull her away, and I didn't know whether these odds were in her will, or in the universe of unfinished grocery errands, or just simply in my head. Part of me couldn't believe in the sheer luck of running into someone simply because I'd wished it. This could be taken away in a second. Play it light, keep it simple, lie low, you already told her you were happy.

A man almost my age who was sitting alone at the table next to ours had raised his head from his laptop and was staring at us. The women mantled in legend and swank, the errands, the party, the nicknames tossed left and right, those who'd been asked to buy this and that and who were probably busy running similar errands farther downtown, the light hysteria of bumping into each other on the eve of the New Year, the complicated coffee one ordered and the small black with two sugars-and-something-sweet-if-you-can—Oh, Clara, Clara, will I ever forget this day?—I looked at him and put myself in his place, trying to imagine what he thought of our lives: Were we ridiculous or were we indeed mantled in splendor and dreams? Women, party, New Year's; suddenly our lives, my life, acquired an incandescent aura I wouldn't have noticed but for his gaze.

I liked our little corner at Starbucks. I'd imagined something similar happening exactly a week ago on the afternoon of the day we'd met at the movies. Now, seven days later, it was being given to me. How punctual the soul, as if secret alignments between our flimsiest wishes and an obliging if sometimes fractious deity were constantly organizing things for us. There'd be awkwardness at the moment of parting, but I didn't want to think about that right now; I knew Clara would figure out a way and choose the least difficult path when it came to resuming her errands. Perhaps it was better we didn't have a moment to ourselves right now—too soon, too much to say, perhaps a hampered and oblique glance was all we needed to know we'd be back to where we'd left off last night on the phone. Once again I tried to stave off disturbing thoughts. Olaf was speaking to both women. I went back to get more sugar for Clara. I loved this.

When I got back, I saw that Clara was wearing the same sweater she'd worn at Edy's. I wanted to rub my face against it, smell it, snuggle into it. Little lamb, who made you, Clara? Even now, I'd give anything to touch her face, push her hair back with the palm of my hand. I liked the way she spoke to Olaf or, rather, listened to him and nodded away, somewhat gravely, as his metallic voice rang in our little corner. I already knew that not a minute after seeing me tonight she'd make fun of his name and mimic his voice. Olaf goodenough, Olaf bellylaugh, Olaf, chuff chuff, had enough, and we'd laugh and laugh at Olaf's name and draw closer because of it, though he was my best friend and she clearly seemed to like him. I caught her eyes once as she listened to him. I know, they said. We're planning a character assassination, I responded with a glance, I just know you know I know. *I know this too*, she seemed to say. Oh, Clara, Clara.

I should have noticed her earlier. Someone was standing outside and literally staring at us—at me. The boy had stuck his face right against the glass window. When I stared back at him, it hit me that the little boy must surely be with his mother, and that his mother was staring in too. Rachel.

Once again I dashed out of Starbucks. She had just left the house and was going to buy a few things for tonight's dinner. The sisters were doing their usual last-minute thing. I led her in, managed to grab two chairs from two tables nearby, and widened the circle at our table— introductions, introductions, my offering to get coffee, taking the little boy to the counter to have him pick something, his ice-cold hand in mine, perfunctory jokes with those on line, until it was my turn to order and give out my name to the cashier. Rachel, who was used to being at the center and always the one to make introductions, must have felt uneasy; she was among strangers. To compensate, I let the others infer that I'd known her long before meeting any of them. Perhaps I wanted her to feel that no one would dream of challenging her seniority or attempt to unseat her. But perhaps I also wanted to keep Clara mystified and on her toes. *Who on earth are these people you're with?* said Rachel's inquisitive gaze, not without a hint of irony aimed at them, or at me for knowing them. I shrugged my shoulders to mean: People, just people. Clara had stopped speaking to Olaf and was eyeing Rachel, as though searching for an opportunity to break the silence between them, or, as I instantly sensed while watching her size up Rachel's ash green winter coat that I'd seen her wear for years on cold days, to find one good reason to dislike her. Two New Year's parties, and I was invited to both and, before setting eyes on Rachel today, had never thought I'd have to decide between them. This could get very awkward, I kept thinking, hoping neither would bring up the subject of the evening's festivities, though I'd already resolved to go to one party and then the other, except that if I went too early to one and left, any idiot would figure I was on my way to another. For a few years now, it was always at Rachel's house that I'd watched the countdown on December 31. Was I already betraying her, casting her off?

Suddenly the barista called out "Oscar!" very loudly. Right away I stood up to pick up Rachel's coffee. I was trying not to be too obvious about my nickname, but without looking, I already knew that Rachel was startled. Clara had scored a point and was at this very moment gloating over her victory, which she'd be dying to communicate with something like a wink in my direction. I also knew that, owing to her victory, Clara might stop looking for reasons to dislike Rachel and no longer wear her bored, slightly absent, glazed look that made you feel like a toad among giants.

I began to wonder whether I had given that nickname to the cashier to keep Rachel equally mystified—side with Clara after siding with Rachel, make Rachel think she'd lost me, if only to remind her there'd always been a side of me she never knew or ever cared to ask about and for which she was now paying the price for ignoring all the years I'd known her. Rachel, who may still not have suspected it was my nickname she'd heard, was in no mood now to make friendly overtures to Clara, nor would she be inclined to respond had Clara attempted any. Besides, there was nothing the two seemed willing to speak about, and my jump-starting a conversation to break their chill seemed futile. Had they decided to pick on me as a way of drawing closer to each other, I'd have been willing to play along. Watching Clara make fun of me for this, or for that, and hearing Rachel confirm the criticism and add something like "Don't you especially hate it when he . . ." to which Clara would easily agree, and just as eagerly add yet another zinger of her own—anything would have been worth the price if only they'd become friends, and in being friends close a circle around the three of us, like three toddlers winding a twisted belt round them. What I feared was that, to spite me for threatening to leave her out, Rachel might start dropping hints either about Lauren or about a phantom woman who had drawn everyone's attention yesterday afternoon.

A woman with a loud voice had seated herself beside us and was speaking to her baby in a stroller while chatting with her husband on her cell phone. "Now, isn't it funny how Mommy forgot to put sugar in her coffee? Isn't that *fuhnnn-nnny?*" Then, turning to her husband on the phone: "Tell him to ram it up his ass, that's what your brother should do." Clara, who had no patience with loud cell-phone conversations when they weren't her own, couldn't help herself: "Wouldn't that hurt?" she asked aloud, turning to the woman on the phone.

"Pardon me?" said the startled wife-mother-sister-in-law, looking indignant at the intrusion.

"I meant, wouldn't it hurt ramming something up your brother-in-law's ass? Or would it be *fuhnnn-nnny?*"

"I can't believe these people," went on the woman, continuing her cell-phone conversation with her husband. "Rude, rude, rude. Listening in on our conversation, don't they have anything better to do with their lives?"

"Oh no, we do plenty. We ram things up our asses all the time," added Rachel. "And we'd love to tell you how we do it."

"Yuck!" She rolled her eyes. "I'm trying to speak to my husband, would you mind?"

"If you lowered your voice, we'd never know what you and hubby do to your asses—so would *you* mind?"

"Get a life." Then, turning to her baby with a righteous maternal gaze, "Mommy will take your coat off and it'll be all better."

Olaf couldn't help himself: *"Mamy weell mek it ohhhhll betuh!"*

Everyone among us burst out laughing, including those seated behind us and the young man staring at us from the nearby table. For a moment I noticed that maybe the reason why I liked both women and couldn't understand why they hadn't instantly taken to each other was that I'd always known they shared this one sprightly, roguish thing in common: the ability to draw ever so close to meanness without being cruel.

Or was I once again mistaken about Clara? Was she perhaps just cruel, and nothing less? Or did I like running into her presumed cruelty only to have an instance of kindness brighten up her face like compassion on the features of a stern inquisitor?

I noticed at some point, when the two had begun to speak, that Rachel was trying ever so subtly to draw my attention. When she caught my glance, she shook her head once, twice, very fast, as though to signal a question: *Who is she? Where did you fish her out from?* I hastily looked away, not wanting to engage in secret messaging, but then realized that she was asking an altogether different question: *Is this the one you were bellyaching about all day yesterday?* I was about to answer her signal, with a No, this is someone else, because I did not want Rachel, who knew me so well, to know that yesterday's phantom woman was indeed sitting across from her. I did not want her to know more about us than I did, though, at this point, her guess was as good as anyone's. I forced myself to think about last night's phone conversation—our fleeting, blissful, shameful secret when her voice had touched my ear with its furry breath and then lingered on my side of the bed when she said, *You can if you want to.* Now, as I looked at her, I kept thinking that perhaps there was no reason to bank on anything whatsoever—nothing had happened or, if it had, it hovered in mid-sleep awhile and then vanished in the wee hours of the night without a trace—weren't we both pretending it was a dream neither was sure the other hadn't dreamed? A growing sense of alarm seized me as soon as I realized that this thing I'd been incubating all week without telling anyone was no better than a bubble that the slightest quizzical glance could puncture. Had I lost Clara again? Was I losing her right now by wasting my ration of time with her at Starbucks? Or was I always already losing her—because, in the end, I was in a state of perpetual furlough, hence on borrowed time, in hock?

Perhaps I didn't want Rachel to know how much like strangers Clara and I were. Which is why I avoided answering her silent prods.

Perhaps I wanted to scare myself.

I had had no time to reply, when Clara raised her eyes and intercepted Rachel's inquisitive glance, and immediately turned to me, catching the blank, noncommittal look on my face, which, despite my efforts not to respond, still betrayed there'd been clandestine communication between us.

"Wait a minute. What's all this?" she asked.

"What?" I replied.

"This." She imitated Rachel's motions of the head. "What are you two talking about?"

"Nothing." I liked being found out and enjoyed the naughty evasion that was really no evasion at all.

"Look at these two," said Clara, turning to Olaf. "They're sending each other secret signals."

"I think we've been caught," said Rachel. I could tell Rachel was going to give me away. Let her.

There was no point in pretending. "Do you want to know?" I asked Clara.

"Of course I want to know." And seeing I was about to spill the beans: "Wait," she said, "will it make me happy or unhappy?"

Rachel and I exchanged glances.

"You two!" said Clara.

"Okay, it's about yesterday. Rachel was basically trying to figure out if you were the one I'd invited for drinks last night."

"He did call—but with him one never knows," Clara added, turning to Rachel for support. "Did he tell you how the idiot—me, that is— ended up going to the movies all by herself, hoping to run into genius here?"

"He did say something about going and not going, but then going and not going. We all told him he had to go."

"Did he say why he wouldn't go?"

"He looked upset." Then, turning to me: "Is it okay for me to say you looked upset?"

Yes, it was okay for her to tell the world I was upset. And no, how could I possibly mind? Would she have the good tact not to mention Lauren, though?

"What happened at the movie theater?"

"Aside from the fact I was alone in the dark with every sexual pervert ready to pounce on an innocent single girl—nothing. Even the usher hit on me."

"So, did you punish him?"

"Who? The usher? Or Oskár?"

"Oscar," said Rachel, without the accent mark.

Rachel smirked as she spoke my nickname for the first time, trying to hide her hesitation. She was tasting a strange dish she didn't want any-one to know she'd never heard of before and wasn't quite going to swal-low until making sure it agreed with her. "Oskár," she said, as though she'd just discovered an amusing new mask on my face, a new me she was still reluctant to admit into her world and whom everyone in her house was sure to talk about later, certainly behind my back. It made me feel that this new identity, which Clara had cemented the day we'd driven up to Hudson, was no more me than a new pair of shoes I'd been parading in all week in the hope that everyone might think they'd long been inte-grated into my wardrobe, but whose price tag, as far as Rachel was con-cerned, was still showing and was not to be removed until those who knew me better had decided that they matched the real me. "So you for-gave him?"

"I did try to make him pay for it, but I always fail at making men pay."

This was certainly not the Clara I knew. Was she attempting some sort of us-against-them solidarity with Rachel, or was this her oblique way of undercutting Rachel's attempt to tease me for my new name?

"Actually," she continued, "we made up. He had the wisdom to call last night."

I knew what Rachel was thinking. We must have slept together last night.

It occurred to me that Clara knew exactly what had crossed Rachel's mind, and so as not to disabuse her, she reminded Orla that they really had to finish their shopping, got up, put on her coat, and, just as she was saying goodbye to everyone, leaned down and gave me a moist, hard kiss, tongue all the way in my mouth. *"Bis bald."*

If anything could have made physical contact between us mean so lit-tle, this was it. Had we reached perfunctory touching already? Or was this her way of reminding me that, after last night, there were no more holds barred? Or was this intended for Rachel and not me? Or was this a replay of Inky's kiss?

•

A short while later, Rachel started putting mittens on her son and insisted on wrapping a scarf around the child's neck. The boy struggled; eventually she relented.

"Will we see you tonight, Oskár?"

"Probably," I said, ignoring the lambent rise in her voice as she spoke my nickname.

She knew she'd irritated me. She also knew I wasn't speaking the truth.

"Well, try. Bring her along too."

As she put her gloves on, she couldn't help herself: "She is stunning."

My shrug-in-silence was meant to pass for unassuming agreement.

"Don't do that!"

"Do what?" I asked.

"This." She mimicked the postured indifference on my face. "She didn't take her eyes off you."

"Her eyes off me?"

"You're the most exasperating person I know. Olaf, you explain it to him. Sometimes I think you purposely avoid seeing things. As if you're scared you'd have to get undressed with the people you really care for and God forbid they should see your pipi."

As soon as Rachel left, Olaf couldn't contain himself.

"Cunts, all of them."

"She may have a point."

Olaf shrugged his shoulders as though to mean, *Yes, she may, still a cunt.*

His wife had asked him to order a case of Champagne for tonight, but he had completely forgotten, and now he worried they wouldn't deliver it on time. Then, with his typical expansive bear hug, he embraced me, uttering his usual salutation, which was "Strength and honor" followed by "Stay hard."

"She's the one you were going to tell me about?"

"Yes," I said.

"Figures."

"And yours?" I asked.

"Don't ask. You don't want to know."

•

If I called Clara now, I could offer to join them while they were shopping. I could just see all three of us inside a packed Fairway. Laughter. Laughter. *Eggs*—I saw her saying—*We'll need eggs for tomorrow morning.*

I was soaring.

Just hope you don't pay dearly for this.

When I got home early that afternoon, I decided to take a nap. Was it my way of restarting a day that had gone well so far and having it all over again? Or was it the lure of clean pressed sheets that beckoned— crisp, taut, and lightly starched, as I like them? Or was it the rapture of the afternoon sun slumbering like a cat on my bed, where I knew I'd doze off listening to music?

I had promised to call her in a few hours and wanted nothing more now than to coddle the vaguest thoughts of her and take these thoughts to bed with me, the way we take a wish we suspect may never be granted but whose contour, once we've shut our eyes, we begin to unpeel, layer after layer, leaf after leaf, as though hope were an artichoke whose heart lies so deeply buried that we could afford to take our time, mince our steps, step back, sidestep, take forever.

If we weren't fated to be lovers, or friends, or casual whatevers, well, I'd sleep that off too. In the mood I was in, I too didn't give a damn about getting hurt, just as I didn't care if she got hurt. Just get in bed, curl up, think of her with me, our bodies cuddling and canoodling like the two spooning halves of Venice, the space between us we'll call the Grand Canal and the footbridge my Rialto. My *corvus*. My Guido. My Lochinvar. My Finnegan. My Fortinbras.

Why didn't you come for dinner?

Because I picked up resentment in your voice.

Why didn't you say something, then?

Because I knew you were angry and there'd be more double-talk.

What double-talk?

This double-talk.

Can I tell you something, then?

Don't you think I know already, don't you think I know?

Oh, Clara, Clara, Clara.

•

It was already past five when I woke up. There were three missed calls on my answering machine, two hang-ups and one from Clara. Had I slept so soundly that I hadn't heard the phone ring and missed her voice once my machine picked up? When I listened to her message, she seemed inexplicably irked and fatigued: "You could at least pick up!" I checked my cell. But no one had called. "I've been calling everywhere. I can't believe I spent all this time tracking such a pitiful, pitiful man." I could feel the numbness and rising nausea in my chest. Was I as vulnerable as all that? All this well-being suddenly zapped because of a phone message?

I thought we'd made up last night, and at Starbucks today she couldn't have looked happier to see me, her palm not leaving my face as soon as I rushed out to greet her in the cold. Now this? As the five o'clock darkness kept closing in on the day, it finally struck me that this was the worst possible way to welcome New Year's. Was it a preview of the coming year, or a finish to a terrible one? Or, in Olaf's words, was it still too soon to tell?

Then I realized. These were last night's phone messages, not today's. Could anyone have sounded so enraged? No wonder she sounded so curt when I called her from Rachel's!

I shaved, took a long shower, and, for good luck, decided to do exactly what I'd done last week: drop in on my mother again, wear the same black shoes, same dark clothes, same belt even; then dashed off, caught the first cab on the side street, and straight off to Mother's building, thinking to myself what I'd caught myself thinking of last week as well: Hope she's well, or well enough, hope I don't have to stay long, hope she won't bring him up again, remember to buy two bottles afterward exactly as I'd done last week, then hop on the M5, it'll give me time to look out the windows and stare at the snow and the ice floes and at the scant traffic on Riverside Drive and think of nothing, perhaps think of my father, or simply forget to think of him, which is what happened last week on the bus when I promised to think of him and had simply allowed my thoughts to drift.

Mother was all the way at the back of the apartment, in her bedroom, so that, after opening the front door, I had to walk down the long, dark corridor, turning on the lights along the way as I walked past closed doors—she kept the old bedrooms and bathrooms closed, she said, because it gets cold by nightfall. Perhaps she had stopped enjoying the illusion there were others in the house and had shut the door on them. Her old mother-in-law, her husband, my brother, my sister, me.

I found her next to the old Singer, hemming a skirt. "Hardly anyone comes anymore," she said, meaning *You don't come often enough.* She didn't know whether to give away the skirt or mend it. Mending it made more sense. If it didn't work, she'd simply throw it away. In any event, it kept her busy, she said. I've grown smaller.

I promised to think of her too on the bus. But, with one thing and another, I knew I might totally forget. I'd be thinking of Clara. The last time I was here I hadn't met Clara yet, didn't even know, couldn't possibly guess what lay in store for me that night. Fancy that! I had come, dawdled awhile making small talk, then left, bought Champagne, gotten on the M5 bus, done so many meaningless small things, and all of them belonged to a life where Clara didn't even exist yet. What was life like before Clara? Now I wondered about the old days, which weren't so very old, when we'd celebrate New Year's with a wine tasting by covering the labels on the bottles and managing to fool even the connoisseurs among his guests. I remembered the crowd of friends back then as people milled about the living room, the food and desserts heaped in pyramids upon the tables, and Mother's baked prunes wrapped in bacon, as we all waited to see which wine was voted best, and the laughter, and the noise, and Mother rushing back and forth, making sure the vote was in before the chimes of midnight, followed by my father's usual apology for using last year's little speech in rhyming couplets. I know he would have liked Clara.

Outside, on the terrace, where he chilled the white wines, he'd asked me to help before uncorking the bottles. We stood still in the cold weather with just our shirts on, staring at this black-and-white Manhattan night, making out echoes of the merrymaking from the neighbors' crowded rooms across the tower, two years ago today, *Theirs is the real party, ours is make-believe.* He'd taken me aside and said, with veiled distemper in his voice, Why don't you just marry her, which meant, *Why don't you just marry anyone and bring us children before we're gone—twins for the price of one, so it'll be faster.* Then, changing the subject, he'd stare through the glass door into our crowded living room: "Just look at your mother, catering to everyone but me, Xanthippe the shrew, if ever there was one."

I was wrapping numbered red paper napkins around each bottle of wine to hide the label, applying Scotch tape tightly around the napkin while he held a finger to it to hold it in place, as he automatically did when helping me tie a difficult package, his way of apologizing for the improvised homily about children and twins and the chronic distemper in his voice.

I remember how Livia had come out onto the terrace to smoke just as he was finishing his little talk. She too would help me wrap the starched napkins around each set of silverware while our Brazilian cook was putting the finishing touches to her yearly *bombino*, the music filtering in through the glass window. I placed both hands on Livia's hips, spun her gently around, and proceeded to dance a few steps with her on the freezing terrace, then back into the living room, my rakish whim passing for tacit reassurance intended for my father, meaning, See, Dad, I'm working on it, knowing the whole thing was a fib, because I knew he knew she knew we wouldn't last a month, a season, ten days. "What were you two speaking about?" she'd asked.

"Nothing," absentmindedly.

"About me, wasn't it?" She knew he was growing to like her. It was just like her to put two and two together, minus my dissembled *nothing*, and come out with Dad's pep talk about kids.

Not even ten days, I kept thinking. My father must have caught that look on my face as I watched her go back inside and turn to the other guests in the room. "Funny how they cater to everyone but us—as if they've always known we'd never love them a single bit."

·

"So where to tonight?" my mother asks.

"Party."

"Just one?"

"Just one." Obviously I'd abandoned the idea of going to Rachel's tonight.

"Going with someone?"

"With, without. Unclear."

"Unclear to you or unclear to her?"

"That too is unclear."

Mother snickers. Some things never change. Did I need anything? No. Had just come to wish her a Happy New Year. Well, if I had nothing better to do later tonight, maybe I could drop by again—always a sap when it comes to Champagne on New Year's. There's a cold bottle in the fridge, one never knows. Maybe, I say, meaning, Yes, but don't bother waiting up for me. "At least try," she throws in, a last appeal. I say nothing.

"Just be an angel, could you replace one of these bulbs for me?"

No wonder it feels like a mausoleum in her house. I dig out a spare bulb in the pantry, stand on a chair, remove the dead one, and twist in a new bulb. "Finally," she exclaims; now she can see me, she adds. I am about to put on my coat.

One more thing, she almost apologizes. That coffeemaker I'd bought her for Christmas, would I mind terribly going over how it works?

I know what she wants. She doesn't want me to leave, at least not just yet. Oh, stay another minute, will you! So I take out two capsules of espresso, fill the water tank, plug in the machine, push the red button, and wait until the green light stops blinking. She wants to try it herself this time. We go through the motions once again.

Two minutes later we are sitting at the breakfast table, drinking two foaming cups of decaf cappuccino.

He would have loved this, she adds, stirring listlessly.

I hate it when she starts in about him—"I know, I know," she apologizes, and right away lights a cigarette. But then she remembers and makes a silent motion to put it out. No, don't stop, I say, it doesn't bother me. Just because I'm trying to quit smoking doesn't mean I'm obliged to hate cigarettes. The same, I suddenly realize, might be said of people, of so many things. Just because you can't have them doesn't mean . . .

My mother must have read my mind or been on the same wavelength herself. "Ever hear from that Livia woman?" We've made the same connection, yet neither wishes to disclose the train of thought that led from cigarettes to Livia. "She used to smoke a lot," she adds, as though to cover up her tracks, "didn't she?" All the time, but no, I hadn't heard from her at all. Just like you to blow up bridges behind you. Sometimes, she says, we never want to see people again for fear we still care. Or that they still do. Sometimes we turn from our past and look away in shame. But few of us let go. We find others. What's hard is having to start all over again with the little that's left each time.

She catches her breath, puffs, then looks away. She's trying to ask me something.

"Is this new person better than Livia?"

"Better, worse, too soon—or too late to tell. Who knows."

"You're a funny one."

She stubs out her cigarette halfway. She looks at me and then past me.

"I met someone."

She met someone.

"You met someone?"

"Well, that's not quite accurate. He'd heard about Dad and decided to call one day."

"And?"

"He'd lost his wife a few years back."

I must look either dumbstruck or totally vacant.

"So?"

"We were together once."

"You were together once."

I find it hard to think of her with anyone but the man I'd seen her with all my life.

"I don't understand."

"There's nothing to understand. I used to know him long before your father. He went away West for a year, maybe more, he said. Then I met your father."

She makes it sound so heartless, so savage almost.

"How did he take it?"

"Not well. He found someone out West and got married even before I did. Of course, I never forgave him. Never forgave him each time your father and I bickered, and we bickered all the time at first. Never forgave him when the ice I walked on cracked under me to remind me that Dad was just a man who'd been put there to tide me over."

"And?"

"And nothing. We had a few dinners. He's with his daughters tonight. But he said he might show up. Though with him, you never know."

Now I understood the bottle of Champagne.

What did he want from her?

"Who is he?" I finally asked her.

"Listen to you. *Who is he?*" She smiles expansively, mimicking my tone. "Soon you'll be asking what he earns or how he plans to support me."

"I'm sorry. It's just that I worry."

"For me? Are you sure it's worry you feel?"

I shrug my shoulders.

"If it's any consolation, your father knew. He knew from the very start. Now, thirty years later, this man calls. We're widowers, he says. That we certainly are, I say. It took a lot of courage."

"What are you telling me?"

"What am I telling you? It's not as if you didn't know things were a shambles here. I'm telling you that all the years I was his wife, part of me was elsewhere. All the years I stayed home and did homework with the children and took his mother to the doctor and was the partner's wife at so many tedious banquets, and the years I helped with his wine parties, and the summers we all traveled together, and the nights I slept by him at the hospital after they'd scraped him clean of everything he had, poor man—all this time my heart was elsewhere."

"Now you tell me?"

"Now I tell you."

My mother stands up and fills a bowl with pistachios, obviously they're meant for me. She brings another bowl for the shells.

"What is it that you two had that was so special?" I finally ask.

"We had the real thing. Or the closest to it—maybe even better."

"And what's that?"

She takes a moment, then smiles.

"Laughter. That's what we had."

"Laughter?" I ask, totally baffled.

"Who'd have known. But it was laughter. Right now we're feeding off old jokes. In a few months we'll find them stale. But put us in a room together and we start laughing."

She stands up to put our cups and saucers in the sink. All that stands between us now is the bowl of pistachios and the bowl with shells.

The years she stood by him at the annual party and helped order the food for guests she couldn't have given a damn about, and the years she beamed when he delivered his annual speech in rhyming couplets before the chime of twelve, the years and years of it without laughter.

"Do you miss him?" I ask.

"Why are you asking me like that? Of course I miss him."

I look at her. She averts her eyes. I must have offended her. "Now look at you, you've managed to clean out this entire bowl in less than five minutes."

She takes the emptied bowl and the one containing the shells. I thought she was going to empty the bowl and leave the other on the counter. Instead, she replenishes one with pistachios.

Left alone in the dining room, I stand up, open the glass door, and step onto the balcony. A mound of snow makes the passage difficult. It makes me want to summon old times for a second, see what it was like back then when we had guests and chilled the wine out here. Were those better days because he was still alive, or were they better because they belonged to the past? I want to think that Livia is with me now, or that he is right outside with me here in the cold, baring his soul about the grandchildren he wants, all the while looking past the windows into the living room, spotting his bickering wife catering to everyone but him, and beyond our windows to the neighbors' party in the other tower. He had always known about her, though God knows if he'd ever cared or been able to put his finger on the demon that snuffed out his life but kept him alive so many decades later. And I'm thinking of the other Livias in my life as well, Alice and Jean, each trying to help with the wine tasting as best she could, laying out the bottles on the balcony after they'd helped me wrap the mystery labels around each one, while some of the guests kept guessing, the blind test always getting out of hand, which happened every year, the crowd agreeing that bottle no. 4 was as good as no. 7, but that no. 11 was the best, the usual suspects always disagreeing with everyone else, Father refereeing, some people no longer really caring, because the test was always a success, would always be a success, was just another way of putting a good spin on the certainty that part of us always dies in December, which is why it was the only holiday he celebrated each year, because the part that didn't die by year-end was as thrilled with the extended grace period as he was that something like love had not entirely run out of his life, though where he went scrounging for it and where he found it, if find it he did, no one knew or wished to know; the black snows of yesteryear, I didn't miss them a bit.

If I were a better son, I'd do what the father of that dying princess promised he'd do for his daughter each year. I'd bring out his old bones so that he might feel the winter sun again and shiver at the thought of good mulled wines and thick, warm butternut soups sprinkled with diced chestnuts, bring out his body to savor the elegy of moonlit snow as he dreams of an old Weihnachten world that went under and of a love that addled before its time. It didn't addle, it never happened, he used to say, and for all he knew, the other woman never knew she was the light of his one short, unfinished life—a love most chaste, a love most chaste, *Your mother never knew either, and no point telling her now.*

Mother asks me not to dump the glass bulb down the chute. I lie and say I'd never dream of such a thing. How empty the apartment looks with all the doors shut now: *How doth the city sit solitary, that was full of people! How is she become as a widow.* I must bring Clara here.

One day, I'll come to clean the place out, picking up the shards of her life, of his life, worse yet, of my own life here. God knows what I'll find, what I'm not prepared to find. His alarm clock, his address book, his pipe tools. A large ashtray bearing his yellowed meerschaum pipes with their engraved turbaned Turks scowling like two bookends who can't stand each other's sight. His vintage Pelikan pen and Caran d'Ache silver pencil lying, like camp inmates in the same bunk bed, head facing toe, like a dessert fork and spoon, his lacquered lighter, and, first among them, waiting cross-armed, running out of patience, his horn-rimmed specs, probably folded ever so warily, yet abandoned without false pretenses at the last minute when he said, *Okay, let's go face that witch doctor now.* I can just see the resigned admonition in his gesture when he placed his glasses right smack in the middle of his emptied, clean glass desktop, meaning, *Now watch the fort and be good to others,* which reminds me how he'd take out a twenty-dollar bill and tuck it under an ashtray before leaving a hotel bedroom, meaning, *You've been good to me, now be good to the next fellow.* He was good to things, good to people. Listened, always listened. Somewhere, I am sure, Mother has stowed away his wine tools.

I remember the care with which he laid them out one by one on the sideboard in the dining room, cleaning and polishing his huge collection of antique corkscrews and foil cutters, Mother saying in front of everyone he reminded her of a mohel laying out his tools for a bris. *Last time I laid out my tool, tell me, where, in which land that was*—Someone immediately interrupts and cracks a joke about Abélard's tools and Abélard's love. *It was Héloïse did the deed, I know wherefrom I speak,* my father says, *Héloïse and wedlock.* Laughter, laughter, and all the while we're laughing together, there she is two-timing him, while sorrow addles his heart for someone he'd met decades elsewhere, a love most chaste. These were the words with which he marked time in that private little ledger where we measure what we lose, where we fail, how we age, why we get so little of what we long for, and whether it's still wise to hold out for something as we sort the life we're given to live, and the life not lived, and the life half lived, and the life we wish we'd learn to live while we still have time, and the life we want to rewrite if only we could, and the life we know remains unwritten and may never be written at all, and the life we hope others may live far better and more wisely than we have, which is what I know my father had wished for me.

"Who is this man?" I ask my mother.

"You've met him before."

"What's his name?"

"If you want to know, come before midnight."

She smiles, but she still won't tell me. There is nothing to say.

"Are you going to be all right?" I ask.

"I'll be fine." Lambent and resilient Mother. I've seldom seen her like this.

"You've never told me any of this."

"No, I've never told you."

A long silence, during which my mother makes a face at a bad pistachio.

"She must be a knockout."

"How do you know?"

"I just know. You've been killing time here, haven't you? You should leave."

She was right. I was killing time.

I wish her a Happy New Year, just in case we don't see each other tonight.

Yes, yes, she says, but she knows there's hardly a chance I'll show up. At least I hope you won't. We hug. "I've never seen you like this," she says.

"Like this, how?"

"I don't know. Different. Good. Maybe even happy."

On our way to the door, she turns off the light in the dining room, then in the kitchen. She'll head back into her bedroom the moment she closes the door behind me, like Ulysses' mother slinking back among the shades. This is what I've come to, she seemed to say.

I heave a sigh of relief when I finally shut the door behind me.

As usual, I reach into my pocket and hand the doorman his annual tip. The second doorman, who doesn't know me, receives something as well, just in case Mother forgot to tip them.

•

The gust of wind that greets me as soon as the doorman opens the front door could not brace me more or stir greater joy. It shakes off the stuffy and oppressive torpor weighing on me ever since I entered Mother's home.

I've always loved the lights of the city in the winter, the view of the midtown buildings towering over the skyline, the hail of brightness erupting like a galactic storm over Manhattan, while the sweep of weaker lights elbowing the old residential buildings on Central Park West speak of quiet, contented lives and quiet, contented New Year's parties. I love watching the surfeit of lights blanket the city, something unseen and unrivaled since the night Pharos beaconed antiquity and mariners came out to watch, saying, *There is nothing can rival this in the world.*

If I were a good son, I'd have met Clara ages ago and brought her here. If I were a good son, I'd have picked Clara up earlier today and said, I want you to meet my mother, because I wish he'd been alive, he would have loved you. With her, for an instant, I'd walk into his study and disturb the restless sleep of his things: his Pelikan, his Caran d'Ache, his scowling Turks, his glasses, and she'd rouse them back to life, the way she'd shaken the slumber of my kitchen, my rug, my bathrobe and made me find love in my things, my life.

I'd bring her in, as in the old days, and, before introducing her to the guests, simply take her onto the balcony and ask her to help me cover the wine labels. What are we doing? she asks. We're hiding the names of the wines. "I know!" she replies. "I meant, *What are we doing?*" I know exactly what she's asking, even if for a while I'm pretending not to, because I find it no less difficult to tell her why I wanted to bring her to my parents' home than it was to ask her to stop the car and take a quick walk with me to my father's grave, because there are so many things I find so difficult to ask, Clara, because in asking the small and simpler things I reveal more than when I ask for the big ones. And if he's not there to meet you any longer, well, let's drop in anyway tonight, before you and I get naked together, and we'll uncork Mom's Champagne, and if staunch Don Juan happens to be there tonight, we'll be a merry foursome as we toast the New Year and then rush back to 106th Street, leaving la

Veuve Clicquot and good Dom Pérignon to sort out the good from the bad in their lives. In the cab, I hope you're not zombified, I'll say. *I am so not zombified*, you'll say.

I am so not zombified. It sounded just like Clara.

Say it again, Clara, I am so not zombified.

I am so not zombified. Happy?

I am, I am.

The wine store where I've been hoping to buy a few rare bottles for tonight's party turns out to be mobbed; the line horseshoes the length of the counter. I should have gone in with Olaf. He was right to panic this afternoon.

Skip the bottles, then. Flowers? I'll send flowers tomorrow. Actually I should have sent flowers last week. Skip the flowers as well.

All I want is to ride the M5 bus as I'd done last week during the snowstorm, scarcely able to see anything outside, and yet grateful for the snow, which seemed to expire in exhausted, pallid puffs no sooner than it brushed against our widows. From time to time, through the lighted Riverside Park, I'd catch a glimpse of ice floes bearing down the Hudson like stranded elks quietly working their way downstream. Crick, crack, crack. Tonight I won't even go to Clara's apartment but will head straight to Hans and Gretchen's. I'll get off at 112th Street, as though by mistake again, try to lose my bearings as I did that night when I walked up the hill by the statue of Samuel J. Tilden and, for a second once again, think myself in France because of a St. Bernard, or because the city seems so strangely medieval tonight, or because a confluence of dream making and premonition has made me feel I'd stepped into a film of my own projection where snow falls so peacefully that everything it touches feels at once spellbound and imperishable. I'll arrive at the party, be greeted by Gretchen, who never budges from the entrance door, hand my coat to the coat check, make sure I keep the stub this time, dawdle about in the living room by the piano before ordering a drink, stand by the Christmas tree exactly where I stood a week ago, and who knows, perhaps we'll play at being total strangers, because she likes this as much as I do, and while she's about to reach out to shake my hand, I'll interrupt and say, Aren't you Printz's friend, to which she'll say, *And you must be the voice from last night's télyfön?* I am, I am. And we'll sit by the same window, and she'll bring me something to eat, and together we'll roam from room to room in this large apartment and drink something light like punch, though we hate punch, and we'd head downstairs, as we did last time, through the crowded staircase, open the door leading out onto the terrace, and stand there together, watching the New Jersey shoreline, trying to catch the same beam circling over Manhattan and think of Bellagio, Byzantium, St. Petersburg, and remember we saw eternity that night.

I see the evening unfold before me as all wishes do when we know they're about to be granted: the walk from the balcony to the kitchen, then upstairs to the greenhouse, Pavel and Pablo, the three Graeaes, and Muffy Mitford herself with two daughters no one can stand as my mind drifts past the mound by Samuel J. Tilden's statue, past last week's blizzard, past Rohmer or the small slate-roofed town of Saint-Rémy, which had risen before me on the borders of the Hudson to suggest a floating city invented for Clara and me.

I want to step up onto the balcony with her again and watch her stub out her cigarette in the snow, watch her foot kick it all the way down to the cars lining up in double-parked formation, watch the snow close in around us like luminous white hands, timeless and spellbound. And there would be so many temptations along the way. Rollo would surely parley for Inky again: *For the love of God, woman!* And who knows, Inky himself might show up to plead, lean, dashing figure that he cuts, as he'd lead her away to a corner unknown to most guests, and all I'd do then is stand and wonder whether I should intervene or simply stand and wonder, trying to make out if the thing between them has dissolved into friendship, or hasn't dissolved at all, or whether she couldn't care less if he hurled himself off the terrace, friendship or no friendship; friendship there's never any after love, scorched love, burn all bridges and the docks along with them. We'd stand together among the others, and suddenly Clara would ask me to give her a couple of minutes and, joining Orla and Beryl in the middle of the room, would, without warning, start to sing an aria from *Der Rosenkavalier*, while I'm trying to look the other way, because I know myself, and one more second of this singing and I'll burst out crying, and if I do start crying, well, let it happen, she'll come up to me and let the same hand that had held me so savagely the other day rest on my face and say, *This song's for you, Printz, this my overdue Christmas present for the man who may just love me less than I love him.* And I know myself and know I won't be able to resist, but will rush her into the crowded coatroom and, pressing her against a row of perfumed mink coats, ask her point-blank: Do you want to have children with me even though I've no idea where my life is headed, yes or no? *Yes*. Do you think we'll be happy together? *Yes*. At what point does this fantasy end? *Don't know, never did know . . . Have I answered all your questions?* Yes. *Are you sure?* I think so. She'd ask me for another minute, and I'd say Fine, and watch her run off elsewhere in the house, and then I'd wait and wait and wait some more, until it would finally dawn on me, as it had last week, that she'd simply disappeared. Inky. Of course! I should have known.

Which is when I'd make up my mind to leave, leave if only not to show how smitten and desperate I was, or how much I wished the evening had taken another turn. I'd ask for my coat, put it on, and quietly step out, then walk briskly to Straus Park, hastening my pace, in case she'd spotted me leaving and was rushing to stop me. Once in the park, though, I'd slump down and sit there, as I'd done all week long, hoping that Clara had indeed followed me to ask me why I'd left so soon. Is that what I'd want, for her to follow me and ask why I'd left so soon? Just me, I'd say, just me doing my usual letting-go-of-what-I-want-most, because the things I crave are so rarely given that I seldom believe it when they are, won't dare touch, and, without knowing, turn them down. Like turning off your phone? Like turning off my phone. Like saying *Too soon, too sudden, too fast* when I've been shouting Now, goddamnit, like saying *Maybe* when I'm shouting I'll go all the way, like not going to the movies when you knew, just knew, you fucking asshole, there was no way I wouldn't have gone last night? Yes, I would say, like not showing up, knowing you'd never forgive me. So? So, nothing. I come here every night to think I've lost you, because every night feels it could be my last, and all I do here, without even knowing I'm doing it, is pray the day never comes when I won't have been without you. I'd take this park a thousand nights in the cold and on whatever terms you please rather than never not see you again.

Double negatives, future anterior, past conditionals—what's all this, Printz? Nothing, this is nothing. Just counterfactual stuff from my counterfactual life.

In Straus Park all I'd want to remember is my first night here or the second, or the third, or the night when I came back and stood dazed here after our kiss and could feel everything rise in my chest each time I looked over to the bakery and remembered how I'd pushed her body against the glass panel and kissed her, our hips pressed together, heeding an impulse I thought I'd been following all my life when, in fact, I'd been rehearsing it just for Clara, as everything was rehearsal, and deferral. Do you want us to stay together, or is this one of those bland, mushy-gushy friendships that spilled over into passion one evening when we'd both had too much to drink, tell me again, you sweet, bitter stoneheart, tell me again, did you wish that time stopped for you as well? Am I making sense to you? Am I what you want? Yes. Before you change your mind? I've never changed my mind, but if this is how you see me, then I've changed my mind—it's you who can't and won't make up yours.

I'd stand there and think of the Magi with their heads ablaze who might show up tonight, their shuffling feet already sinking underground, saying, You shouldn't be here, why have you left, why are you here? I'm here to think whether I should go back or stay here instead. And? And I don't know. You feel with a forked heart, and your heart is a muted organ. In five years, as in Rohmer's film, you'll bump into her in a beach town in Europe, and she'll be with children, or you'll be with children, and you'll watch and stare and draw the tally of all your might-have-beens. You haven't changed, she'll say. Neither have you. Still Printz? I guess. And you, Clara? The same. Still lying low? Still lying low. You remember, then? I remember everything. And so do I. Well? Well.

By the time I'm my father's age with distemper in my soul and one chaste love to look back on, standing on a terrace thinking of wine tastings and of stubbed-out cigarettes free-falling to the ground and of parties across our tower that are always the real parties, will I have learned to live all this down, or would it turn into imperishable dream making all of it—from the day it stopped when it started, to the day it started when it stopped on nothing more than a baker's wall one hundred yards from here, one hundred years from now, a hundred years ago. From a small park in Berlin to Straus Park in New York. The gas jets of a century ago and the unborn stonecutter a century from now, centuries apart. Immeasurable.

So what should I do now? Stand and wait? Stand and wonder? What do I do?

And it would be one of the lampposts in the park that would break the silence.

Did you expect guidance? An answer? An apology?

Go back, the voice would say; if I could go back, if only I could go back.

I'd know that voice among millions.

And from Straus Park I'd walk back to the corner of 106th and River-side and watch the people upstairs leaning their backs against the windows as I'd seen them do a week ago, when it was cold outside and their candlelit faces beamed with laughter and premonition, all holding glasses in their hands; some, I could guess, leaning on the piano where the singer with the throaty voice made everyone sing carols. And I'd even say hello to Boris, who would know me by now, and I'd watch him stick his arm inside the elevator and press the penthouse button as he'd done last week, and no sooner would I be let into the apartment than there'd be a chorus of hellos. Well, what do you know, he's back, Orla would say, I'll run and tell Clara. No, I will, says Pablo, she's upset with you, and standing her up last night didn't help. We're all headed to the Cathedral of St. John, want to come with us? And before I can answer, a Champagne flute is handed to me. I recognize the wrist, your wrist, your wrist, your sweet, blessed, God-given I-worship-your-wrist. "Ist ein Traum, this is a dream," she says, "and the New Year's just begun."